MW01144153

KEEPER'S CHILD

CHILD

Leslie Davis

EDGE SCIENCE FICTION AND FANTASY PUBLISHING
AN IMPRINT OF HADES PUBLICATIONS, INC.
CALGARY

Keeper's Child
copyright © 2007 by Leslie Davis

Edge Science Fiction and Fantasy Publishing
An Imprint of Hades Publications Inc.
P.O. Box 1714, Calgary, Alberta, T2P 2L7, Canada

Editing by Richard Janzen
Interior design by Brian Hades
Cover Illustration by Jeff Doten

EDGE Science Fiction and Fantasy Publishing and Hades Publications, Inc.
acknowledges the ongoing support of the Canada Council for the Arts and the
Alberta Foundation for the Arts for our publishing programme.

Library and Archives Canada Cataloguing in Publication

Davis, Leslie, 1972-
    Keeper's child / Leslie Davis.

ISBN-13: 978-1-894063-01-2
ISBN-10: 1-894063-01-5

    I. Title.

PS3604.A954K44 2007   813'.6   C2007-904449-2

FIRST EDITION
(q-20070917)
Printed in Canada
www.edgewebsite.com

Timeline

2008: The cruiser Sacramento goes down off the coast of the southwest, dumping genetic material into the seas. George Bruster's grandmother, Elisa, is one of the 631 migrants hired to clean up the mess.

2028: George Bruster is born. Not long after, the seas begin to show signs of lingering contamination.

2046: Bruster develops his 'Fixit' bacteria.

2048: Bruster's Syndrome is diagnosed.

2053: The government confines the diseased and their relatives to quarantined camps. Frightened, those citizens that have the means begin to leave the continent.

2058: Houses for the *Desgastas* are subsidized.

2068: Jesse Grange, age 15, leaves one such House and journeys to *Carpenteria*.

2082: Jesse develops his Mark.

2088: Jesse returns to Harold's shore. There he discovers that his brother has only one ward left, Robin.

1

Jesse searched his brother's face as he stepped from the sea, hoping for some sign of welcome. From boyhood Harold had loved the sea, delighting in the gifts it disgorged onto the sand. Jesse remembered running together on a warmer beach in a softer time, two boys collecting the treasures waves had given up overnight. Now Harold's mouth was set and hard, his eyes bitter. This delinquent brother the ocean had spit back onto his shore was apparently one gift he did not want to take into his House.

Harold stood motionless on the shadowed porch of the old House, waiting. Determined, Jesse took measured steps across the sand. The wind off the beach scraped across his wet skin and plucked at his scalp. It blew icy cold, and by the time he stood under the eaves of the House goose bumps puckered his skin.

"Why did you come?" Harold asked. As if in reaction, Jesse's teeth began to chatter. He resisted the impulse to rub at his freezing arms.

"Andy called—" Jesse began, but Harold wouldn't let him finish.

"Are you alone?" He glanced at the boat anchored beyond the waves. Jesse nodded. Scowling at his brother's nakedness, Harold shook his head and waved a hand.

"Then come inside and put some clothes on." Harold turned his back to the sea and pulled open the screen door. Damp had corroded the latticed metal. Thin flakes of rust loosened beneath Harold's hand. More flakes shivered and fell when Jesse brushed the screen with his shoulder.

A girl hovered in the shadows just beyond the door. Jesse was a slight man, smaller than most cityborn half his age,

but the child who watched him from the darkness was tiny.
The crown of her head barely reached Jesse's ribs.

The disease breeds them smaller and smaller, Jesse thought.
He had seen many sickened, stunted children. This girl was
different. She lingered just inside the screen door, regarding
him with a lively curiosity. Jesse saw that she was like many
of the healthy cityborn children, slow to grow and quick to
learn.

"Hello," he tried. The girl watched him with bright blue
eyes. She didn't seem startled by his lack of clothes. She
would have seen nakedness before, Jesse knew. She probably wondered instead who he was and why he ruffled the
usually placid Keeper.

When he smiled at her she didn't smile back, and when
he offered his hand she didn't take it, so he shrugged and
walked past her into the depths of the House. The old building was much quieter than he remembered, and much
darker. Despite the daylight, candles burned in sconces on
the faded walls. Jesse remembered their smell. As a boy he
had helped his brother make the tapers. He remembered
dipping the wicks and the soft beeswax burning his fingers.
Before the candles there had been electricity, and no doubt
the House was still wired. Once electric lamps had burned,
keeping back the long nights, and there had been hope.
Now the walls stank of mold.

Harold had vanished into the gloom of the House, so
Jesse found his way on his own through the dim hallways
and into the kitchen. The room hadn't changed. The plank
tables and wooden benches that had seated so many friends
and lovers were still painted blue, and still worn smooth
with use. He opened one of the whitewashed cupboard
doors and then another. Each shelf stood empty. When Jesse
tried the kitchen faucet the pipes squealed, dry and unforgiving.

A pale light filtered through dusty kitchen windows,
reminding Jesse that winter was coming. Cold and wet, he
sat down on one of the benches and waited. He didn't see
any sign of either Harold or the girl.

Eventually his brother returned, carrying a faded towel
and followed by the child. She held a shiny green robe,

clutching it to her chest as if for warmth, wrapping her hands in the fabric. The towel was a yellow terry cloth. Jesse used it quickly and then accepted the robe from the girl. The fabric felt like silk to his fingers. The robe smelled sweet and looked as though it had never been worn. When the garment slid perfectly around his small shoulders Jesse decided that it had been made for a woman. Manufactured in the city, he knew. Silk of such quality wouldn't be found outside Carpenteria. He wondered which of Harold's wards had left the pretty robe behind.

He belted the garment carefully and then sat back down. Harold looked as if he was fuming, but Jesse understood his brother's moods. So he sat quietly, using the time to gather what information he could.

The girl wore Robin Dupree's *tronera* around her throat. The medallion hung on a ribbon instead of Dupree's old gold chain, but Jesse recognized the tangle of copper and silver. As a child Jesse had watched Dupree make the thing, had watched the man craft that perfect badge of faith. Jesse remembered Dupree's face, drawn in pain and flushed with joy. As a boy, Jesse had found the legend of the *tronera* romantic and had longed for a medallion of his own. But that had been over a decade ago, and now this girl wore the badge, which certainly meant that Robin Dupree was dead.

As if reading his mind, the girl reached up and touched the burnished *tronera*. She stared defiantly. Jesse looked right back. At her movement Harold sighed and stirred.

"Robin," he said, gazing at his brother. "Go and check the nets. Bring us back some dinner."

The girl's mouth tightened. Jesse thought for a moment that she would argue. Then she turned on her heels and dashed from the room. In the distance the screen door banged and for a second the air in the room moved.

"Robin?" Jesse ran a hand over his cropped head. "You named her after Dupree?"

"I gave her Robin's name when I gave her Robin's *tronera*. It seemed the best way."

"Yes," Jesse said, "you would think so. Doesn't the girl get a life of her own?"

Harold's face set. He had aged, Jesse saw. Fine lines now wrinkled his face, while time and cold had weathered the soft skin. His long hair had grizzled and there were threads of silver showing at the crown. The changes were not unexpected, but they still startled Jesse.

"He must have died recently, then," Jesse said.

"A year before the villagers brought the girl along the sand to this House. She was a babe, and abandoned. And *desgastas*. One of the village doctors had enough courage to leave her on my porch." Harold ran fingers over his chin, eyes vague. "She was so tiny, and at first I despaired. But she lived, and she grew. I gave her Dupree's name because it felt right. The old ways are the best. And I think he would have been honored."

"I know it," Jesse said. He shook his head. "I always thought he wouldn't last for more than another year. He seemed so weak."

"He was a good man," Harold frowned. "One of the first from Carpenteria to shun the laboratories and the drugs to put on a *tronera*. He knew how to live a peaceful life, and he believed in Miguel's tenets. You were just a boy, you couldn't have understood."

Jesse shifted on his bench. The argument was an old one and he no longer felt like battling over old disagreements. Instead he bunched green silk between his fingers, waiting.

"Why did you come?" Harold asked when the silence became too heavy.

"Andy called me. Apparently she'd managed to keep a phone in working order. I always said she was your smarter half."

"Andy's gone," Harold said. He turned toward the kitchen window. Through the glass clouds raced in the sky.

"Yes."

"And Kris." Harold studied the ocean. Jesse wondered when he had given his wife's lover to the waves.

"Dead," Jesse said, "like all the others."

"There will be more from the village."

"No. I'm sorry, Harold, but it's almost over."

His brother sent him a sharp look. Jesse kept his face expressionless, revealing nothing.

"There will be more," Harold insisted. He ran a finger over the smudged window, tracing patterns on the glass. "There was Robin."

"How long ago? Ten years... twelve?"

"Thirteen," Harold admitted. "Just over thirteen."

"You used to get five a year. Things have changed. The city has changed everything. The last of the villages are dying."

"What did Andy want?" Harold switched subjects abruptly. "Why did you come?"

"She said Kris was gone and that she was dying. And she said you would be next."

The finger on the glass stilled. "She knew."

Briefly, Jesse felt anger. He squelched it. "Of course she knew. She knew you better than you thought, brother. She loved you more than you wanted." He took a breath, summoning resolve. "How long? How much more time do you have?"

"A few months. A week." Harold shrugged. "I've lived longer than most. Freer than most."

Jesse hunched forward. He looked down at the sand on his toes and tried to swallow back the grief that clogged his throat.

"Andy didn't want you to take me to your city."

"I don't know." Jesse admitted. "Maybe. Yes, I think maybe she did."

"If that's why you've come, then you've made a mistake. Andy hated the idea of your Mark. She hated Carpenteria. She knew our work was out here. She remembered the old ways. She remembered the past."

"Yes," Jesse said.

"I won't go. I won't leave the House."

"I know." Jesse shifted on the hard bench. "You were always stubborn."

Harold turned from the window, eyes bitter. "So why did you come?"

"To keep you company. To give you to the sea when you're ready. And to shut down this House when you're gone."

Harold's lips flattened in rage. "I don't give up so easily."

"I know. I remember."

"What about your work? No doubt the city will fall apart without you there."

"No doubt." Jesse smiled grimly. "But I can work from here. There's a transmitter on the boat. And Andy's phone must still be here, if I need it. I'll keep in touch. I could use a vacation."

"A vacation." Harold echoed, still bitter. "It will be a long one. I'm not so ill yet."

Jesse looked up at his brother. "I'm here to help."

Harold's face, gray in the gloom of the kitchen, sagged in disgust and disbelief and, finally, resignation.

"Sleep in Kris's room. There are clothes in his closet. They'll be better suited for the cold than anything you brought from Carpenteria."

Jesse supposed Harold meant Kris's room as a punishment. He did not bother to object. Harold glanced out through the glass one last time and left the room. The House groaned, battered by the weather.

Jesse rose and walked to the window. The robe swished around his ankles. Outside, waves foamed in the dusk. Harold's ward ran along the shore away from the House. Jesse watched her as she ran, noting the net that flapped over her shoulder and marveling at the froth of pale hair tangled in the net with the fish. The girl had good breeding. She should never have ended up on the shore. Her fine bones and light hair spoke of wealth and genetic privilege, and those of such privilege had fled the continent many years before. How had such a child come to run along Harold's sand?

Frowning, Jesse traced the smears his brother had left on the window and wondered why Andy hadn't bothered to mention her husband's latest ward.

The next morning Jesse sat down to a breakfast of bread and cold fish. The fish tasted sharp and metallic but the bread cleared the sour taste from his mouth. The sun stained the sand and the day had already begun, but Harold didn't emerge from his attic bedroom. The girl sat at the other end of the kitchen table and peered across at Jesse as he ate. She picked at her own piece of fish with delicate fingers, considering his face.

"You'll need to get your boat out." She sounded sullen, but Jesse heard the beauty beneath her sulky tenor. The possibility charmed his soul. He wanted her to warm to him.

"The water will eat it away," Robin said, "the bottom of your boat. The ocean's bad and if you leave anything in it too long, the water eats it."

"*Desgastas*," Jesse murmured.

Robin straightened at the word. She leaned across the table, breakfast forgotten. "I know the way," she said. "I know the safest way to bring your boat in."

Jesse hesitated for a moment, and then nodded in agreement. He didn't know what to think of Harold's ward, but if she had knowledge of current and reef and rock, then he would use it. The boat didn't belong to him and the girl was right about the sea. Better to beach the craft as soon as possible and avoid costly damage.

"There's a block out behind the House where Kris used to keep his old canoe when he wasn't using it," the girl continued. "Before it sprung a leak and we sank it."

At Jesse's snort she went defensive. "We tried to fix it, but it kept leaking. Kris didn't want to waste it, so we sank it. To make a reef. We sink a lot of junk just off the shore. The fish like to breed in places like that. We get our best catch out where we sunk the canoe."

"Is the block big enough for a full-sized craft?"

"Sure." Robin shrugged.

"All right then," Jesse said. He pushed his plate to the center of the table and climbed to his feet. "Shall we do it now?"

Robin jumped up. "I'll go get my suit. There's an extra up in Kris's closet."

Jesse shook his head. "I don't need one. Go ahead and I'll meet you on the beach."

Beyond the eaves of the House the sand was cold and wet. Jesse crouched in the shadow of the porch and watched the waves. Mist sat on the water. The ocean cooled overnight but began to warm as the sun rose. During the day the bacteria in the water absorbed heat, sucking at the sunlight until the waves steamed. The perpetual clouds did little to stop the damage. In the afternoons, Jesse knew, fish would be overcome by the heat and wash ashore. That had interested him, years ago, when he was a child. He had once tried to revive three of the fish by dumping them into a bucket of cold water. When he could not save them he had washed the mutant bodies and left them in the kitchen for Andy. She had been young, then, barely into her twenties. She had loved to cook and Jesse had longed to impress her.

The screen door rattled and Robin ran down the steps, dressed in an old diver's suit. Someone had cut the rubber down to fit her size. There were tears along the knees and thighs but Jesse guessed that the suit still afforded some protection.

Trying not to think of stinging fish or sharp rocks, Jesse crossed the sand. Pausing before the shallows, he stripped off the jeans and sweater he had found in Kris's closet. Beyond the breakers the boat danced in the ocean.

"Why don't you wear a *tronera*?" Robin asked suddenly.

Jesse turned his head and found her studying his bare chest. The question surprised him. He knew she had seen the absence the day before, but he had assumed she would be too shy to ask.

Robin watched him, waiting, and Jesse rubbed his chin. "I wasn't born *desgastas*."

The girl's eyes narrowed. Jesse could see that she hadn't decided yet what to think of him. He hoped she wouldn't make any hasty decisions. It would be unpleasant living in an empty building with two unfriendly faces to keep him company.

"But you lived here?" Robin pressed. So Harold had explained one thing at least.

"Yes, when I was a boy." Jesse stepped gingerly into the sea. The water was not yet hot, but it made his skin ache and itch. The swim would be unpleasant.

The girl splashed up beside him. "Aren't you afraid?"

"Of what?" he asked.

"Of us."

He frowned down into her pale face and wondered at her question. He found her ignorance jarring, and yet somehow refreshing.

"No," he reached out and touched his palm to her hair. "I'm not afraid of you."

He took three running steps through the shallows and jackknifed smoothly into the water. The ocean pulled at his skin, thick as oil, and the smell made his stomach turn. The swim from boat to shore had been after sunset, and the water had been cooler. Now it steamed about Jesse. He imagined his skin cooking to a savory pink and for a moment he floundered. Then the girl flew past, stroking easily at the edge of his vision. She swam with the strength of one used to the water. When she glanced back Jesse saw by her grin that she enjoyed his discomfort. He set his teeth and swam after her, determined to take the lead.

Just beyond the waves the water swarmed with fish. The bigger creatures were blind and harmless, cursed with thickened gills and listless tails. Their ancestors had survived the warming of the ocean, if only barely. Jesse suspected that their lives were not very pleasant. The smaller fish could be trouble. Paper thin, they were quick and poisonous, their fins razor sharp. Jesse hated the small monsters. They destroyed nets and lines and occasionally suits. Worst of all, they tended to be impervious to the heat, thriving while their bigger cousins found death on the shore.

Robin waved her hands in the water, scaring the fish and clearing a path through the schools. Jesse thrashed his feet and the fish scattered, only to turn around and pace him. They watched him with yellow eyes and wrinkled feelers. Jesse glared back until he had to rise for air.

A large school of the creatures surrounded the boat. Jesse kicked at the water in irritation as he hauled himself up and over the stern. Alerted by the splashes, the fish swam closer to the surface, lurking just out of reach. Robin ignored the schools and eeled over the side of the boat, rubbery as the suit she wore.

"Fish grow nastier every year." Squeezing water from her hair, she settled in the bottom of the boat. "They're just barely polite now. Pretty soon I'll have to start carrying a knife."

"They taste worse than I remember," Jesse said, remembering breakfast.

"That's why the people from the village don't fish here. We don't have much choice."

"Can't you buy something fresh from the grocer?"

Robin slanted blue eyes in Jesse's direction. "They don't sell to the House anymore. And they don't sell to anyone wearing a *tronera*."

Jesse had forgotten. "I'll go this afternoon. Harold could use some fresh fruit and maybe some real eggs."

The girl flushed. "We have eggs from the gulls. We've always depended on the seagulls. They're good enough for us."

Jesse met her glare calmly. "You could use some milk in your system. And I could use some clothes that fit. I'll go this afternoon."

"They won't sell to you," Robin muttered. Jesse sensed another sulk coming on. He considered her temper, and then decided to ignore it.

"Couldn't hurt to try," he said cheerfully.

"They'll see you come from the House. They'll think you're *desgastas*."

"I have a city Mark," he said, unfazed. He displayed his left hand, palm to the sky, and showed the girl the pattern of color beneath the first joint of his thumb. "This says I'm clean. They will sell to me."

Robin hunkered in the boat and said nothing. Jesse edged past her, checking the craft with his eyes and hands. His equipment was still safely locked in a hatch behind the steering panel, and the boat appeared to be in good shape. He had borrowed the craft for an indefinite period, but he planned to return it in one piece. He flicked a switch and the engine hummed to life. At the push of a button the anchor dragged from the water, pulling up brown seaweed and mud.

Robin moved to his side, petulance forgotten. She peered under his elbow and watched the panel in amazement.

Amused by her curiosity, Jesse hid a smile and sent the boat forward.

"Kris just used a rudder," she said, awed. "A rudder and an outboard motor."

"Kris was a better sailor than I," he said, turning the boat slowly to shore. "I need all the mechanics I can get."

"You knew Kris?" He felt her eyes on his back.

"I knew him before he put on his *tronera*. And for a little while after."

"Did you know him well?" She bent over the side of the boat, eyes fixed on the rushing water.

"I lived with him when I was a boy."

"He was Andy's lover," Robin said. Jesse turned from the panel, but the girl dipped her hands in the sea and refused to look around.

"Harold didn't like it much," she continued. "It hurt him."

Jesse glanced away. He studied the ocean as it washed by, watching for rocks and the color of shallow danger. Once, Robin indicated a change of direction with a nudge and a motion. Her casual touch contrasted sharply with the reserved expression on her face. The shore grew on the horizon. The House grew up from the dunes and loomed. A figure paced in the mist, waiting.

"If you knew them so well," Robin asked, "why didn't you come before they died?"

"Harold didn't want me here." The boat bounced off a wave. Jesse rocked on his feet. The girl stayed steady, firm in her need to know.

"Does he want you here now?"

Jesse watched his brother wade out through the breakers to meet the boat. He hesitated, trying to find something to reassure the girl. But there was nothing, and at last he shrugged and shook his head. Robin stared at his face for a moment. Jesse fidgeted, uncomfortable, until at last she moved away. She knelt in the bottom of the boat and answered Harold's wave. Out of the corner of his eye, Jesse could see that her face was drawn and thoughtful. But when Harold splashed up alongside the boat, she smiled and laughed and scrambled eagerly into the sea.

Jesse kept his promise and by sunset he had fresh food for his brother's table. Harold ate the eggs and apples without comment. Robin would not touch even the milk. She picked silently at the fish Harold had grilled for dinner, gazing at Jesse from across the blue table. He had bartered away city treasures for the food, trading away tabloids and poker cards for a meal. Battered paperbacks and trendy glass jewelry won warm dungarees and a pair of rubber boots for himself, plus a sweater for Harold and a worn pair of jeans for the girl. Robin wore the jeans, but only because Harold had asked her to.

Jesse could tell from her frosted stare that she didn't like the way he wore Kris's rugby shirt over a villager's discarded pair of denim trousers. Already he thought that she had absorbed too much of Harold's pride.

"Move your equipment up to your room," Harold told Jesse. Candles set around the kitchen flickered in a draft, reflecting off silverware. Harold picked up a knife and began to peal an apple with gentle skill. "It won't be safe outside."

"Why not?" Robin asked, startled out of her thoughts.

Harold coiled the apple skin on his plate and diced the fruit. "They'll have seen in the village that Jesse has come from Carpenteria. By now they'll be curious."

"They won't come down here," Robin argued. "They never have before."

Jesse thought of the period just after Harold had taken over the House. Then government officials shipped food and antibiotics to the small crowd living on the shore. They had still been delivering vats of fresh water and crates of experimental medicine when Jesse had left to live in the city. Now he looked at the pitcher of milk on the table and wondered how he would manage to keep it fresh without a working refrigerator.

"Move the equipment inside," Harold repeated. "You don't want the salt to rot the wires."

Jesse looked at the apple core in Harold's hands. Years ago salt and damp might have damaged city circuitry, but no longer. He only nodded and took a bite of cold fish.

Harold had salted it with ground sea grass and the spice almost masked the sour taste of poisoned flesh.

"There's a drugstore in the village," Jesse said. "I'm sure they still sell Benox. And even vitamins."

Harold finished the apple. He set down his knife.

"Andy had a store of Benox," he said. "There are a few left. I take one when I need one. City painkillers have never done much good."

"You should have one every day. It might help you to rest."

Harold moved irritably on his bench. "There are things we need more. The fruit, the warm clothes."

Jesse laughed "I stockpiled enough junk to buy out the village grocer. A few books for a bottle of Benox—"

"City drugs. I don't need them," Harold said.

Jesse was immediately furious. "You may be willing to take the risk. But what about Robin? When it starts on the child, do you expect her to follow in your stoic footsteps? Do you really need another disciple? Haven't enough people suffered for your cause?"

Robin paused in her eating, a forkful of fish dangling in the air below her chin. She watched Harold with sudden interest, and part of Jesse noted the hunger burning in her wide eyes.

Harold pushed himself to his feet. Jesse reached across the table, and grabbed his brother's wrist, pushing for a miracle. "I can take care of her, Harold. I can take care of *you*. Why won't you listen?"

The Keeper gazed at Jesse. "Have you saved one *desgastas* with your technology? Can you name me one person who was born with this disease that you have saved? Born *desgastas*, die *desgastas*. You know the way of it."

Jesse ground his teeth together. Harold shook free of his grip and stalked from the room, stiff and impossible. Heart pounding, Jesse let his brother go.

"Andy didn't die of it," Robin said. Jesse started. He had briefly forgotten the girl.

"What do you mean?"

"I saw her face." The girl ran a finger along the edge of her plate. "It was unblemished. So were her hands."

"How did she die?" Jesse bent forward, intent.

The candlelight deepened Robin's scowl. "She had an envelope of powdered redfish. She used it to kill the rats in the winter, when they come into the kitchen for warmth. She kept it in her room so nobody would accidentally get into it."

Jesse thought of the small poisonous fish that had swarmed about him beyond the waves. "She swallowed the powder?"

The girl nodded. "I checked her room after Harold buried her. The envelope was empty."

Jesse shut his eyes. Robin's voice began to shake. "I wanted to know how she died. It wasn't like Kris. She wasn't sick."

"Harold buried Andy? He didn't give her to the sea?"

Robin made a noise and Jesse opened his eyes. He thought of Andy, who had loved Kris with all her heart, but who had loved Harold even more than life itself. And he thought of Harold, who had never before denied tradition and consigned a body so carelessly to the earth. And he thought of Robin, who had seen Kris eaten by the painful disease that would eventually consume her own flesh.

Jesse stood up, pulling the dead man's shirt closer about his shoulders. "Finish the milk or it will go bad and be wasted."

Robin's mouth set, but she lifted the pitcher and poured a glass. "Where are you going?"

"To get my equipment out of the boat before the tide gets too high," he said, and left the girl to the candles.

A violet moon reflected on the steaming water and the beach chilled Jesse's feet even through the bartered boots. He crossed behind the House and studied his borrowed boat. The craft rested carefully on the solid blocks, off the packed sand and away from the crawling creatures of the shore. Moonlight shone on the dull fiberglass hull and inside the canopy he could hear the transmitter buzzing the eternal language of the satellites.

Jesse squatted in the sand beside the boat and turned his back on the House. He looked out past gray dunes and brown grass A smudged trail snaked over the dunes and into the distance. He followed the path with his eyes until it disappeared into the darkness. The air felt heavy. Beneath the wind he could hear the sleepy mutter of gulls. Jesse considered the trail again and thought of the village. The settlement had been smaller than he'd remembered, and dirtier. Many of the shops had appeared empty. Some of the buildings had obviously been left to rot. The church with its loud brass bell sagged. Jesse guessed the bell itself had not been used for almost a century.

The people had been friendly enough until they discovered he lived at the House. Then they had closed up, rushing transactions and watching him with suspicion. He was relieved that no one had known him. They might have recognized him in white. His face above a pristine lab coat was familiar, iconic. Even a small village with no terminal hookup would have access to old newspapers and school books. He was glad that he hadn't needed to show his ID, glad the Mark was enough. He enjoyed the new anonymity.

Before Jesse had left for school the world had still been struggling to maintain some normalcy, and the village behind the House had still been growing. Contractors had streamed in from over the mountains. Some had drawn up plans for a resort. The hospital had gone up quickly, and the church, and houses with screened-in porches and real fireplaces. Men in orange hard hats had even started to put up a mall, and the village had been given a name and placed on maps. He couldn't recall the name, now.

He wasn't sure about the name, but he could remember the tourists who came to feel the hot waters. Instead they saw the House and went away. At first the waters were an attraction. Then they had thickened. George Bruster's wonderful bacteria turned into a preposterous mistake. And the great gray House that loomed over the beach was enough to squash dreams of riches. Men came from the metros to bargain with Harold. But it was against the new laws to evict *desgastas* from their havens, and Harold refused to budge. He stuck to tradition. He would not take a new home with better facilities, he wouldn't take money. He stayed in his House, and eventually the businessmen gave up and went away and the beach was again deserted.

Jesse had been fourteen when the last heartbroken con-
tractor had walked away from the House, chased away by
Harold's temper. He remembered watching the man
stumble away through the sand to the village, and he remembered thinking that Harold had made the wrong decision. For the very first time he doubted his older brother.
Jesse tried to bury his unease but doubt remained. The next
winter Jesse left the ocean and moved behind the walls of
Carpenteria.

By then the last of the metros had dried up. Any remaining holdouts who could still afford to leave the continent
had fled. Those few rebellious souls who were too poor to
run to the Europes, and too stubborn to move into the city,
found themselves eking out existence in dirty villages, sharing a poisoned land with the *desgastas* in their Houses.

In the village they had given Jesse everything he needed,
but only because he had come prepared. Treasures from the
pulp culture of his city would buy food and clothing that
money often would not. Here, wealth was no longer measured in city terms. The people wouldn't leave their village.
They lived and died on the same plot of land, in the same
house, and had little interest in city currency.

Jesse knew that these villages were also dying out. The
life was too hard. More and more people finally understood
that hope lived only in the city, where life was still easy.

Footsteps crunched in the wet sand. Jesse looked up and
away from his thoughts. Robin came around the corner of
the House and into the moonlight, swinging a bucket. She
went barefoot, and she walked very lightly. Jesse remembered the scorpions that roamed the dunes at night and was
glad of his boots.

"It's getting cold," the girl said. "You should come in
soon."

"What are you doing out?"

Robin lifted the bucket as evidence. "Collecting water for
the dishes. Ocean water scalds them cleaner than fresh."

There were Houses that were not near the sea, Jesse
knew. Houses erected on land where water was precious
and not used for cleaning, Houses where filth was an every

day part of life, where germs blossomed. Jesse had seen such places. He knew that in some ways, his brother was lucky.

Reading his expression, the girl shrugged. "Good for bathing, too, in the winter. In the summertime it's usually too hot and we have to heat the fresh."

"Why don't you just collect the salt water and let it cool?"

"Ruins the buckets," Robin said. "They crack."

The water had never gotten hot enough to warp plastic so quickly when Jesse had lived on the shore. He stared up at the moon and wondered at the mistakes of his generation.

Robin hunkered down in the sand. She rested her bucket on one thigh. "The ocean doesn't get so hot near the city?"

Jesse shook his head. "We're far enough north, for now. Someday, maybe soon, the poison will reach our seas and the bacteria will follow. Then the waves will begin to heat."

"Do people know?" Robin wondered.

"Some," Jesse said.

"It doesn't really matter," Robin said. "Nobody comes to the ocean anymore."

Jesse knew there was a generation of city children who had never seen the sea and who probably never would. "No," he agreed. "It doesn't really matter."

"What's it like there? In the city?"

"Ask Harold."

"He said that nobody there wears a *tronera*."

"Some do," Jesse said. "Not many. There aren't very many *desgastas* in Carpenteria."

Robin didn't even blink. "Are you going to take me there?"

Jesse studied the girl but could not find any expression on her face. "Probably. You can't stay here alone."

"I could." She was stubborn, and strong.

"Would you want to?"

She scooped up a handful of sand and shook it through her fingers. The grains fell at her feet. Jesse wondered if they were falling on Andy's unmarked grave.

"Where did your father bury Andy?"

"I don't know," Robin said. "He never told me. I looked. I thought I would be able to tell. But I couldn't. I couldn't find her."

Jesse shook his head at the moon and tried to recall Andy's fast laughter and quick temper.

"I think," Robin said after a moment, "I think maybe Harold was angry at her."

"Why?"

"I don't know. But why else would he let her die? He waited for her to die and then broke down the door. Why else would he wait?"

"Harold knew Andy was dying?"

"Yes," Robin said.

A cloud passed over the moon and Jesse shivered. Rubbing his arms, he ducked away from the boat and stood up. The transmitter in the craft, alerted by his movement, began to chatter again.

"Why doesn't it stop?" asked Robin.

"It will when we've gone inside. Come on, it's cold."

"You can't turn it off?"

"I can't turn it off."

"Why not?" the girl asked. She jumped to her feet and hastily knocked sand from the bucket.

"It doesn't have an off/on switch. Come now, I'll help you with the dishes."

"I have to get the water."

"All right." Jesse followed Robin around the House. "But hurry up."

Robin took several steps toward the rumbling ocean and then stopped and turned. "Harold said you brought machines from the city?"

Jesse leaned against the House and nodded.

"What kind?"

"Computers and lab equipment."

"Will you show me?"

"Ask Harold."

Silence settled. The wind blew Robin's hair about her face, obscuring her eyes. Cold stung Jesse's bare skull.

Abruptly he decided that he would let his hair grow out until he returned to Carpenteria. Or perhaps he would find a hat in the village.

Robin danced for a moment in place, and then ran to the ocean and filled her bucket. Jesse waited patiently in the cold, watching as the waves foamed about her small figure. She ran back up the shore, a half-grown child full of energy, and when she reached his side she smiled.

"I will, you know," she said.

"What?"

"Ask Harold. If I can see your machines. If you can teach me."

"Teach you?" Jesse arched his brows in surprise.

"What you do with your machines. And what it's like in your city."

Jesse decided that his equipment could wait one more night. He turned and followed the girl up the porch steps. Her enthusiasm gave him hope, and the sudden rush of delight in his gut made him laugh.

"What's so funny?" Robin asked, pushing past the screen door.

"Nothing." Jesse smiled. "Let's get these dishes done so I can go to bed. Wash or dry?"

Robin looked over her shoulder. "I'll wash. Your hands are too soft. Mine have already been callused."

She was quite serious. Jesse, closing the front door on the night air, felt his amusement blown away by the wind.

2

Afternoon sun broke through thick clouds as Jesse followed Harold across the dunes. The sand stayed dry to the east of the House where it rolled gently away from the sea. The dunes sucked at Jesse's feet, pulling at his ankles. Jesse remembered the high grasses that spotted the dunes, but he had forgotten the time and effort it took to harvest the weeds. The blades cut his hands as he tugged up their stalks and many of the plants left their roots behind in the earth.

"The grass itself is important," Harold said as he handed Jesse a bag fashioned from the denim of old jeans. "The roots are life."

The vitamin C in the white roots kept the *desgastas* from scurvy. Jesse knew it well enough, but he let his brother explain the importance of the grass again anyway. Sometimes it was easier to keep silent.

Harold moved quickly over the sand, uprooting the grass with one hand, swinging his own bag with the other. Jesse wandered behind, fascinated by his brother's grace. Harold had always been cerebral. Even locked away in a building by the sea the man had managed to avoid manual labor.

Apparently things had changed. Jesse knew that Harold had refashioned his life for Robin. His brother's newfound priorities amused him, but he was saddened as well. Harold should have grown up in one of the expensive white towers that lined the city streets and lived out his life as a professor in the high-tech college, or perhaps as a retailer in a fancy shop on a busy street. Instead Harold found himself farming a greedy land for survival.

Farther south along the dunes the ruins of an old Interstate highway split the sky. Jesse could just make make out spars of broken pylons beyond Harold's bent head. The concrete edifice towered over the shore and then crumbled into the sea. When they first moved into the House the highway had still been intact. It had skimmed along the shore, west and then north. Cars had zipped across the span, tourists from the mountain states or corporate workers using the length of road to scuttle from one metro to another. Just before Jesse left for school the highway had gone silent. In a matter of years the span was closed. People no longer traveled the country.

When he was ten, Jesse had chipped his initials in the concrete, marking one of the old pillars. Now, as he drew closer, he could see that most of the columns had completely fallen. Erosion shortened the highway, and much of the overpass had been shaken away by shifting earth. Jesse looked up to the east and followed the remaining curve as far as his eyes could see.

Harold sat down to rest. He settled into the sand and leaned against a jagged chunk of concrete. Jesse studied his brother, and then bent at the waist, to pluck a handful of the sparse grass.

"I remember when they promised us they were going to reopen that eyesore," he said.

Harold glanced up at the highway. Its shadow fell across his brow.

"Robin climbed it once," he said. "She was gone all day and when she finally came home she brought back an old tire."

Jesse dropped onto a piece of pillar and dangled his denim bag between his ankles. "A tire?"

Harold smiled. "She found it along the road, and didn't know what it was. The thing was shriveled with age, harder than plastic. Kris tied it to a beam in the kitchen and Robin swung on it for weeks. Made an awful noise."

"She'd never seen a tire." Jesse marveled.

"Are you surprised? Do they still drive in the city?"

"No. But it makes me feel old."

Harold laughed. Jesse pulled up another stalk of grass and sucked gently on the root. It tasted sweet and sticky. His stomach growled.

"How did she manage to get up there?" he asked.

Harold shrugged again. "I couldn't do it. She's small, she's light. She's also crazy and stubborn. Much like her mother was."

"Her mother?"

Harold's face twitched but Jesse couldn't read it. The shadows from the highway had stretched across his brother's face and closed about his throat.

"Andy thought of herself as the girl's mother," Harold explained.

"Do you want to tell me what happened?"

Harold set his face toward the ocean, seeking the sun. "I guess the girl has told you most of it already."

Juice from the grass dribbled along Jesse's chin. He wiped it away with a careful hand.

"Some of it Robin told me," he said. "And some of it I guessed. But I'd rather hear it from you."

"Andy couldn't live without him," Harold said. "So she swallowed poison."

Jesse sat quietly, listening to the sigh of the ocean and waiting for Harold to say something more. He had learned the value of silence in the city college, and the value of thought. He had been hasty as a boy, but now he knew how to sit still and be patient. In the end he could outwait even his brother.

"We argued," Harold told the old highway. "The night Kris died, Andy and I fought. She went mad. And she couldn't forgive me enough to stay."

"You didn't give her to the sea. Even Robin wondered about that."

"She took poison. She gave up her life and broke with her faith."

Harold looked at Jesse. "I loved her. And she left me, at last. And for good."

Jesse sucked the last of his roots dry and wiped a sticky hand across one knee. He tried to imagine Andy without her husband. She, also, had loved his brother very much.

"What did you fight about? Not about Kris?"

Harold's face contorted into a mask of cynicism. For just a moment he looked healthy again, and the older boy who had continually beaten his brother at checkers, foot races and poker looked out of his eyes. Briefly, Harold was once more the neighborhood genius who should have won a scholarship to the city college, the bright young man who felt nothing but contempt for those of lesser wisdom. Then he seemed to remember that it was his little brother who had won the prized degree, his little brother who was one of the richest men in the city. He shrank, and then he smiled and finally, he laughed.

"Tell me," he said, "tell me about your city. About your home. Is it the huge mansion you used to dream about?"

Jesse hesitated. He stroked the sand with one idle foot. Then he told his brother about the joys of the booming city and about the house he had engineered near the city gates. Harold continued to laugh and Jesse was glad that his brother had forgotten for a moment the fear and decay and the ruined highway that cast a final dark shadow over both of them.

In the evening Jesse went into the village for water and fresh poultry. Robin argued that the fish in the nets were plentiful and that there was enough sea grass to make a healthy sauce. Jesse listened to her with interest but the girl's discontent didn't change his mind. In the city he ate chicken three times a week and he did not intend to do without eggs.

The wind blew through his sweater as he descended the path into the village. The empty bucket knocked at his thigh. The old hospital at the edge of the town reflected the dull light of the setting sun, and for the first time Jesse noticed that many of the mirrored glass windows were broken or missing. An abandoned metal generator rusted in the dirt not far from the front of the building. He stopped to study the jumble of metal. Rust had decayed the shell of the machine. From all appearances the building beyond sat forgotten.

A woman and a young boy hurried past, heading for the cluster of houses at the center of town. The woman hunched her shoulders, weary. She ignored Jesse, but the child turned a dirty face in his direction. The woman spoke a sharp word and the boy grabbed at her hand. In a moment they were gone.

Jesse walked up the grass-choked driveway and crouched in the gravel next to the generator. The rust had eaten large holes through the metal, but inside the shell he could see a tangle of wire. The thin threads of plastic looked free of rot. Jesse made a mental note to come back for them later. In a town where electricity was no longer a certainty, no one would bother to repair the old machine or miss a handful of wire.

As he stood up he caught sight of his form reflected in a cracked window. Amused by the stranger staring back from the glass, Jesse hesitated in the shade of the hospital. His hair had started to grow out. It covered his skull in small dark spikes and patches of fluff, and curled in ringlets about his ears. Kris's sweater and the worn dungarees enveloped his body, changing the famous silhouette into something sexless and bulky. For a moment he could not tell if the reflection lurking in the mirror was male or female, young or old. Then he tired of the game and turned from the empty hospital. Shifting the bucket in his fist he made his way to the center of the village.

There were very few people moving through the narrow streets. Those who were out paid Jesse little attention. The sun had dropped behind the decrepit homes and it began to get dark. Jesse hurried on.

Traditionally the well was guarded day and night by the older men of the village. They took the duty in shifts, sitting and smoking, watching the world with lined, brown faces. Jesse found their tenacity amusing. An old law forced the village to share the well with the House, but now federal decrees meant little. The villagers kept the well open because of simple fear. They were frightened of the *desgastas*, afraid of what might happen if they kept the dying from the well. As a boy Jesse had learned early on to recognize fear and superstition, and he saw the same old dread on brown, watching faces as he carried his empty bucket down the dusty street.

He approached the well slowly, taking time to look into dark windows. Just before he reached the well Jesse changed his mind. He turned down the side street and into the grocer's shop. Past the front window the shop looked cool and refreshingly clean. Jesse ducked through the door. The man behind the counter had white hair and yellow skin and took the time to smile at Jesse before turning back to his customers.

There were two customers already in the store. Together they argued with the grocer over the price of produce. The grocer nodded and bowed to each complaint but did not change his price. Vegetables were scarce in the fall, he explained, and a man needed to make a living. His daughter wanted to go to the city for school.

The two women only fussed more violently, but in the end they bought the vegetables. There had never been any doubt, Jesse guessed, just as he suspected that the grocer was selling the food at a price he knew the women could afford.

Jesse waited quietly in the corner of the shop until the vegetables were wrapped away in cloth sacks. The women hurried out into the street, turning away pink cheeks as they passed Jesse. He wondered if they were ashamed of their pride.

"What can I do for you?" the grocer asked. "More milk? We're out of eggs, but Jen should be bringing some in late tomorrow afternoon."

"Chicken," Jesse said, approaching the counter. The bucket clattered as he set it on the wooden floor. "Do you have a whole bird?" Jesse asked.

The grocer nodded. "Two left. Do you need so much?"

"Yes. Do you want currency?"

The parchment face froze. The grocer sized Jesse up. "Most people prefer to barter. Currency is rare these days. Real currency."

"Real currency," Jesse said. He pulled a gold coin from the pocket of his dungarees. "City currency. *Pesos*."

The grocer picked up the coin, chicken forgotten. "I haven't seen city currency for at least two years."

Confused, Jesse became immediately apologetic. "I thought those women paid in currency. So your daughter could go to school."

"They did," the grocer said. "Federal currency. People say they'll still take it in the city. Not worth much else these days. But the Misses Johnson still have a box left. And their chickens aren't laying, so they don't have much to trade."

Jesse shrugged. The sun had set and he was hungry. "City *pesos* will do, then?"

"I don't have the change—"

"Keep the whole thing. Set up an account. I'll be coming back."

The grocer pocketed the coin. Jesse saw that the man's fingers were shaking.

"I'll just get your chicken."

The grocer hurried into a room at the back of the shop and Jesse turned his head in lazy curiosity. A young woman slipped through the front door and stopped to brush the dust of the street off her jeans. She was large and lean, her thin face a twin to the grocer's. She shucked off a pair of muddy canvas shoes and set them outside the door. Then she turned to Jesse.

"Is Father helping you?"

"He's in the back," Jesse said. He stared down at her feet. The socks she wore were full of holes but beneath the torn fabric her bare toes were clean and delicate. She cleared her throat and he twitched, embarrassed.

"Getting me two birds," Jesse explained.

The woman laughed and moved forward until she stood over him. She was very tall, Jesse thought again, and not much younger than himself. She looked him over thoroughly before she stepped back behind her father's counter.

"If I don't take my muddy shoes off, he has a fit. Says the dirt will scare the customers."

"Smart man. Are you the daughter who wants to go off to school?"

She blushed. "Father's been spouting that line for five years. It'll be another thirty gone before we raise the money."

"Don't give up," Jesse said and held out his hand. "I'm Jesse."

"Isabella Barnes." She clasped his palm in a firm grip and then took her hand back. "Where are you from?"

"I'm living on the shore," Jesse said. "In my brother's House."

"Everybody's talking about you. Coming in to speak with Father. They want to know your story. We don't get much gossip around here."

"People aren't afraid then?"

She met Jesse's hard gaze and flushed slightly. "Some are. But you don't wear the *tronera*."

"I'm not *desgastas*."

Isabella opened her mouth to say more, but her father bustled back into the room. He carried a bulging cloth bag and he grinned at Jesse.

"I noticed you forgot a bag," grocer Barnes said. He nudged his daughter's arm in greeting. "So I hope you'll take this one."

"I have one back at the House—," Jesse began, but Isabella cut him off.

"It's better for the chicken," the woman said. "It won't dry out as quickly if it's in a bag."

"Take ours," her father insisted. "Bring it back next time you need something."

"All right." Jesse lifted the bundle away from the grocer. The chicken was heavy and the handles of the bag were frayed with use.

"Jesse's from the city," the grocer told his daughter.

Isabella glanced up in surprise. Jesse swung the cloth bag over his shoulder and picked up the water bucket. He had said nothing to the old man about either his home or his past. So the grocer had wits. Or maybe he had recognized Jesse's Mark.

"Are you?" his daughter asked.

"Yes," Jesse said. The bag rubbed painfully against his left arm.

The grocer passed Isabella the coin and she looked at it stupidly.

"City *pesos*," the man said. "We'll put it with our savings."

"But this is too much," the woman protested, looking at Jesse's bundle. "I'm sure it's much too much."

"I've opened an account," Jesse said. He turned to go. "I'll be back soon. Maybe in time for some eggs."

He could feel Isabella's eyes resting on the back of his neck as he pulled open the door. He wondered what she was thinking, and he considered turning back to ask. But it was late and it was dark outside, and suddenly he wanted nothing more to do with the villagers.

Stepping out into the cold street, Jesse paused to shoulder the chicken. Then he went resolutely to the well for water.

As soon as he got the chance, Jesse moved his machines from the boat to a battered table in Kris's room. He carried the plastic consoles carefully, lifting them across the sand and into the house. Robin trailed him up the steps, her eyes bright with curiosity. Jesse thought about sending her to check the fishing nets for supper, but it had been several cold days since he had last seen a smile on her young face. He enjoyed the change.

Harold spent most afternoons in his room. He made appearances only for dinner and for a few hours with his ward, but Jesse was not terribly worried. Harold looked healthy, if tired and thin. Jesse suspected his brother merely needed some time to himself.

Robin seemed uncertain about how to spend her days. She huddled for hours on the steps below Harold's room. When she wasn't crouched in the shadows, she followed Jesse about the House. It occurred to him that the girl had seen more than her share of death and that she was probably afraid to be left alone in the old building, so he accepted her presence without comment.

As Robin watched, Jesse arranged the computer equipment across Kris's table and began testing Andy's old phone. The phone was a satellite model. It would work without a land line, but the battery was beginning to decay and Jesse had trouble making a charge stick. He wondered how Andy had managed to keep the phone working without electricity to feed the battery. When he asked Robin, the girl only shrugged.

"I didn't know she had it. I'd never seen it before Harold found it for you. Does it really work?"

"Only barely," Jesse said. He plugged the phone into a jack on one of his consoles. Robin eyed him carefully and then moved to sit on Kris's hard bed.

The dead man's room was austere. Jesse couldn't feel comfortable in it. The walls were dirty and naked. A small watercolor hung on the wall just to the right of the door. Jesse thought the mush of color was meant to be a seascape. The wooden cot had been painted to match the scuffed blue benches in the kitchen. When Jesse couldn't sleep he imagined Kris pacing the room, wandering to the painting and then across the room to a small window that overlooked the sea.

On cold nights Jesse would dream of Kris, but he could never decipher his words or understand his expressions. In the dreams the dead man looked older than Jesse remembered. Sometimes Kris's face was devoured by the sickness that had killed him.

Robin shifted on the bed and Jesse glanced up under his elbow. The girl crawled to the center of the bed and sat cross-legged, a book propped on her knees. The volume appeared well thumbed, the pages yellow and blotched. Robin opened it on her lap and ran her fingers across one page.

"What are you reading?" Jesse asked.

Robin watched him fiddle with the phone a moment longer before she blinked. "My lesson." She glanced self-consciously at the volume. "It's Harold's. I have to learn one every week."

"He wrote it?" Jesse was astounded. He paused in his work, the forgotten phone dangling in his hand.

Robin shook her head. "Sam Brier did, before she died. I think Harold asked her to. He wanted a history of the *desgastas*, and Sam knew most of the stories."

Jesse stifled distaste. "Which lessons are you learning?"

"About Father Lopes and the first eaten ones. About how his son Miguel found the first *tronera*. All the stories of the first *desgastas*."

Jesse eased his hip against the table and studied the child. "What are you reading now?"

Robin pursed her lips and ruffled the pages of the book. "I'm supposed to reread the part about Miguel. Harold wants me to recite it to him tonight."

Jesse lifted his brows. The girl shrugged defensively. "He wants me to memorize them all. He thinks people will forget."

"People will," Jesse said. When Robin's eyes flashed, he lifted a hand. "Harold is probably right. Stories of any kind should be remembered. And Miguel was an interesting man. Tell me the legend."

"Don't you know it?"

"Tell me anyway, for practice. We'll see if you can get it right." He began to pry the back of Andy's phone apart, but he kept one eye on Robin. "How does it begin?"

Robin shut the book. "I know it without looking at the pages."

"All right," Jesse said. "Then tell me about Miguel."

"He was born in a camp near the border," Robin said. "Back then everybody who had the disease lived in a camp. Because they weren't really sure how the people got sick. Miguel probably got it from his mother, because she was *desgastas* too. She died three years after he was born, so Miguel's father, Grego Lopes, took care of Miguel and his sisters."

"Was Grego Lopes *desgastas* also?"

"No," Robin said, disgusted at his attempt. "You ask questions like Harold does. I know the story so shut up and listen."

"Okay. Go on."

"Father Lopes lived in the camp because he loved his family and wanted to be with them. But also because the govs made all the families of the sick live in the camps. Even if they weren't *desgastas*, because the govs were afraid."

"But the families were afraid, too." Robin stared out Kris's window. "And a lot of them didn't want to live in the camp, or be near their families. Some of them tried to escape and were killed. Some of them even killed their sick relatives. And outside, all over the states, people were even more afraid. They were afraid they'd be taken to a camp by mistake, or that they'd come in contact with a *desgastas* who hadn't yet been taken. And the land was changing. There were riots and more people were killed. Because nobody really knew where the disease came from, or what was happening to our world, or how to stop it."

"What about Miguel?" Jesse prompted. He had heard the story many times before and didn't enjoy it.

"Miguel was the youngest of Father Lopes's sons," Robin said. "Father Lopes started a camp church. He wanted people to believe in mercy, in a higher power. And even though he was afraid, he gave his people hope. Miguel helped his father build the first church in one of the new camps. They made it out of cardboard and bricks. When they were putting up the last wall Miguel dropped one of the bricks and it broke open. There was a stone buried in the brick, and Miguel freed it. The stone was brown and gold and looked like the eye of a cat. Miguel said that the stone was a sign, and he bore a hole through its center, strung it on a lace from his boot, and wore it around his neck. It was the first *tronera*. He believed that it was a window to the dead, that he could hear the wisdom of his ancestors through the stone. They say it saved his life, twice."

"It kept him alive long enough to fight the Regatta Act," Jesse said.

"The Regatta Act?" Robin asked, face blank.

"Honiara Regatta was the daughter of a migrant worker. She went to the capitol to abolish the camps. Eventually the govs agreed to tear the camps down, but only if each free *desgastas* agreed to wear an ear tag. The sick were allowed to regain society. Many people thought the tags were demeaning. By the time Miguel made his pilgrimage to the capitol, the government was disintegrating. People were already running away across the ocean. They didn't want to listen, and Miguel was sick, very sick.

"But Miguel fought until they gave in. They revoked the ear tags as one of the last acts of the old government. Miguel died soon after."

"And before he died, his *tronera* spoke to him," Robin said, touching her own silver and copper medallion. "He wrote down everything he heard through the stone, and we remember his warnings."

"That's the legend," Jesse said. He wound a small strand of corroded wire around his thumb and thought of Harold asleep down the hall.

"You don't believe?" Robin asked. "Harold does."

"There are many things my brother believes that I don't," Jesse said. "I believe Miguel thought he heard voices through the stone. I understand his fear that the new technologies he saw developing would cause more damage than the sinking of the *Sacramento* ever did. He didn't understand that the new sciences were developed to shore up the damage."

"He believed that the voices in his head were the voices of the dead, the voices of his ancestors. But I believe that the stone he called his *tronera* was just a stone, not a window. And that his warnings have caused the *desgastas* more pain and trouble than they deserve."

Robin chewed her lip in silence, considering, but didn't speak. After a moment Jesse turned back to his work. The phone was a mess and he became absorbed in the puzzle of repairing it. When he finally surfaced and looked back under his elbow, Robin had disappeared. Her book remained, abandoned in the center of the bed.

When he felt it was time for supper, Jesse went out to gather the nets. Harold still hid alone behind a closed door. Robin had locked herself in her room. The water burned at his fingers as he pulled the nets to shore. The fish caught in the filaments were already near death.

He laid each net out on the sand and began carefully plucking fish from the tangle. It was easier to work inside near the kitchen sink, but Jesse found the quiet House lonely and depressing. He shed his rubber boots and squished his toes in the sand while he worked. The icy grit made his blood race.

Jesse had picked two of the three nets clean when he heard a soft rustle. He straightened and craned his neck, peering into the vanishing light. Someone picked their way slowly down the dunes, someone too tall to be Robin and too thin to be Harold. Jesse thought he knew who the unexpected visitor was. He sat down in the sand beside his pile of fish and waited.

Isabella Barnes crossed the beach steadily. When she reached Jesse's side she stopped and looked down at him. Her long nose wrinkled and Jesse wondered whether it was the smell of fish or the stink of man that offended.

"Does your father know you're here?" he asked.

Isabella pulled a small cardboard box from the pocket of her coat. "Eggs. Three of them. Jen brought some in this morning and he saved them for you."

"And told you to trot over to the House and drop them off?" Jesse shook his head.

"I do what I want," the woman said. "Father knows that. And the eggs might have spoiled if you didn't come back to the village before the week was out."

"Thank you, then," Jesse said from the sand. He reached up and took the cardboard box.

"Be careful." Isabella warned. "They break easily."

Jesse cocked an eyebrow and Isabella laughed.

"I've never been here before," she admitted. "Those fish look bad, you should throw them to the birds."

"I'm going to eat them. They don't taste quite as bad as they look. And they're cheap."

The woman flinched. "We don't really bother to wonder—"

"How the people down here survive. I know," Jesse said. "Don't feel too bad. They dislike you almost as much as you dislike them."

Anger colored her cheeks. "I don't dislike them. I just don't know them."

"And you're afraid," Jesse said. "So why did you come down here? Would you have knocked at the door if I wasn't out here gathering supper? Would you have been brave enough to climb onto the porch?"

"Probably not," she allowed. "But does it matter now?"

"No," Jesse said.

"I came down because I wanted to talk to you. Father wanted me to talk to you, but he thought I'd wait until you came for more groceries."

"I'm here." Jesse smiled in the dusk. "Talk away."

"I want to ask you a favor," Isabella said. "I want you to tell me about the city."

"Why?" Jesse asked. "Read the magazines I gave your father."

"*You* don't like me," the woman accused.

"I don't know you. And I don't know your father. But you've both lived more than two decades in that village and never once set foot on the shore."

"I'm here now."

"Because you want something for yourself," Jesse pointed out.

"I know who you are," Isabella said. "I saw your picture in those tabloids. I read the article about your lab. You can tell me everything I need to know about the college in Carpenteria."

"I can," Jesse agreed. "But why would I want to?"

The woman scuffed a large foot in the sand. "You grew up here, and you got a chance. You've made your place in the world. Don't I deserve the same chance you got? Don't you owe it to this place?"

"I'm already paying my debt," Jesse said, biting back anger.

"By harvesting fish?" The woman laughed bitterly. "Even in the village we know that the House is almost empty. Have you come to watch them die? What good will that do anyone?"

"What good will you do?" Jesse countered.

"Give me a chance. You don't even know me. Give me the same chance you got."

"I did it all myself," Jesse said. Isabella shot him a look that was almost hatred and crossed her hands over her chest.

Jesse sighed. He sat on the cold sand, breathing in the reek of dead fish and listening to the growl of the ocean. The sun had dropped behind the clouds. He could barely see Isabella in the darkness, but he could hear her angry breathing.

"I won't go to the village to teach you," he said at last.

"All right."

"You'll have to come down here."

"Fine."

"Into the House," Jesse continued. "I don't want to sit out in the cold if I don't have to."

"All right." The woman's voice trembled. Jesse could sense her sudden fear.

"In the city," Jesse said, "uninfected people share apartments with *desgastas*. The few *desgastas* who have chosen to enter my world are given respect. Cityborn and a handful of Marked *desgastas* share the same jobs and restaurants and air and water. No one knows the diseased but by the color of the Mark on their thumbs, or by the medallions around their necks, if they still chose to wear the *tronera*."

"I said all right," Isabella said, angry again.

Jesse rose to his feet and began loading the fish into his bag. Isabella watched him until the bag was full. When he turned to throw the nets back into the sea, she brushed her hands across her thighs and then started across the sand.

"Come again in two days," Jesse said to her back. "After supper. And bring some fresh meat and some milk. Put it on my tab."

The woman stumbled up the dunes without saying a word, but Jesse knew that she had heard and understood. He tossed the last net in the water, anchoring it to the shore with practiced hands, and slung the bag of fish over his shoulder. The night grew pitch dark as he crossed the sand. When he reached the porch, Robin stood in the cold waiting for him. She held the screen door open and he brushed past her, out of the night and into the warmth of the House.

3

Jesse served the eggs for breakfast. Robin ate one without enthusiasm. The girl sat at the breakfast table, poking silently at the yoke. Jesse watched her while he sucked his own egg from a bowl. Robin looked unusually tired. Her frosty eyes were glazed and she continually cracked the knuckles on her right hand. Jesse wondered what he could do to ease her. He had trouble understanding the young, and had little experience at soothing a child's quicksilver emotions.

"Eat your breakfast before it gets cold," he said. He tried to sound as though he knew how to nurture, but the words felt stiff as soon as they passed his lips.

"It's cold already," Robin said. She slouched over her plate.

"Eggs are expensive," Jesse replied. "Finish at least the one. I won't ask you to eat another."

This time she looked up and glared. "You're saving the last one for Harold. I won't have to eat it either way."

"Eat your egg," Jesse growled.

The girl poked at the mass of white and yellow mush, then slowly began to eat. Jesse waited until she had swallowed three forkfuls, and then he lifted his gaze to the window. Beyond the glass, shrunken seaweed littered the sand and a cluster of gulls were feasting on dead fish. Once the sun chased away some of the cold he would have to make the trek up to the hospital generator. He had managed to fix the phone, but the wiring in the battery charger was beyond repair.

"Is Harold going to come down today?" Robin asked.

Jesse pulled his attention from the electrical cord. "Don't worry. If he doesn't, I'll bring him his egg."

"Did you take him dinner last night?"

"No. Last night I figured he could take care of himself. Today I've decided he's being stubborn."

"Do you think he's ill?" The girl popped a knuckle.

"No. I think he's tired and confused and probably sulking a bit. You know he doesn't like me here."

"Confused about what?" Robin wanted to know.

"I think," Jesse said carefully, "that maybe he's worrying about the same things you are."

Robin lowered her eyes and kicked at the leg of the table. "I didn't hear any sound in his room last night or this morning. It's like when Andy died."

Jesse slid off the bench and dumped his bowl into the sink.

"You need to go outside," he decided. "You've been cooped up for the last few days. Go get some air."

"I want to be around if he needs me."

"Tell you what," Jesse said, "I'll look in on Harold and you can run an errand for me."

"What errand?" she asked, distracted.

"I want you to get something from the old hospital for me."

"There's nobody in the hospital anymore," Robin said, the remains of her breakfast forgotten.

"Then you won't have any trouble getting what I need. Do you know what a generator is?"

The contempt showed plainly on her face. "Sure."

"Good," Jesse said, undaunted. "I want you to take your fishing knife and cut some wires out of the generator for me. The one in front of the building."

"It's all rusty. It doesn't work anymore."

"But there are some good wires left inside." Jesse pulled Robin's plate across the table and dropped it into the sink. "I want you to get all the red wires you can see. Cut them at the very ends, so you can get as much of the wire as possible."

"It won't shock me?"

Jesse shook his head. "I checked. No electricity flowing through it at all."

Robin considered. "You're going to use the wires on your machines?"

"I'm going to see if I can fix a few things."

"Will you show me?"

"If you can sit still long enough to watch," Jesse teased.

Again the contempt showed, but the emotion was quickly overshadowed by curiosity. "Okay," Robin said, "I'll go."

"Go now before everybody in the village is up and about. I'll take breakfast to Harold."

"Tell him to come down soon," the girl said hopefully.

"All right."

She left the room as she always did, in a controlled dash. Jesse waited until he heard the screen door bang, and then he began to fry Harold's egg.

Harold sat at ease in a block of cold sunlight, basking in the white glare and flipping through one of Jesse's old magazines. Jesse kicked the bedroom door shut and set the plate on the floor in front of Harold's ragged armchair.

"How'd you get a hold of that?" Jesse asked. He jerked an elbow at the faded magazine.

The bedroom window ran with tiny cracks, and when Harold looked up, the dark lines were reflected on his cheeks.

"Robin stole it from your room after you arrived. She didn't think you'd notice."

"I didn't. I only brought the things to barter. I never read them."

"Even though your face graces every other advertisement?"

"I need all the *pesos* I can get."

Harold's eyes glinted. "You have more money than most people. Don't you ever get enough?"

"I decided I deserve it," Jesse said. "And the money from the endorsements helps to pay the bills. Why don't you stop complaining and eat your breakfast."

Harold set the magazine on the floor in his block of light and transferred the plate to his knees. He waved vaguely in Jesse's direction and then began to eat.

Jesse took the gesture as an invitation and sat down cross-legged on the floor. Harold's room was even emptier than Kris's. The faded blue armchair was the only real furniture. Harold slept on a flat futon mattress he kept rolled up in a corner of the room. A chipped china bowl and a wedge of candle occupied the very center of the floor. Several mildewed books were piled randomly around Harold's chair. Jesse knew the room was always kept spotlessly clean. Most of the time it was also empty of life.

"Did Robin read the magazine?"

Harold swallowed some egg. "I took it from her. I didn't want her to know about your checkered past."

Jesse laughed. "It may be too late. Someone in the village found out."

"Who?"

"Isabella Barnes, the grocer's daughter. She brought us the eggs."

"Brought us? You mean she came down to the shore?" Harold stared at his brother.

Jesse shrugged. "She wants to go to the city. She thinks I can help her."

"Brave girl," Harold said.

"Or spoiled." Jesse studied the light that stretched across Harold's hands and up his arms. It seemed drawn to Harold's *tronera*. "I told her I wouldn't teach her anything unless she came here, inside the House."

"And will she come?" Harold asked.

"I think so."

"Maybe it's a good idea." Harold scraped more egg from his plate. "Robin could use some company."

"She could," Jesse agreed. "So why don't you stop hiding and come down?"

"Is that what you think I'm doing?"

"You're not sick. Maybe you're tired. But I think you're hiding."

Harold nudged the magazine with his foot. "I've been reading. And thinking."

"Hiding," Jesse insisted. "For over two days."

Harold placed his empty plate on the floor and folded his hands in his lap. "Tell me more about the city. Is life really so better there?"

"Most people think so," Jesse said. He hesitated, and then admitted, "You wouldn't like it."

"Because I'm old fashioned?" Harold smiled. As Jesse watched, seams of black shadow bisected his brow and the white light gathered at his breast. Harold seemed unaware. He brushed once at the *tronera*.

"Because you believe wholeheartedly in Miguel's teachings. You'd imagine poison lurked everywhere, you'd see disaster in every corner. Your mind is convinced you're safer out here. I don't think you'd ever teach it otherwise."

"But you say there are *desgastas* in your city," Harold mocked. "You say Robin would be comfortable behind your walls. And I'm to believe you?"

Jesse rubbed a hand over his eyes. Harold shifted in his chair. The Keeper looked at his brother and sighed.

"You're hiding something," he said. "What?"

Jesse propped his chin on his hands and lowered his eyes.

"Are you still Marking them?" Harold asked.

"The choice is theirs."

"The choice." Harold was disgusted. "Your miracle is really no different than the govs' ear tags, is it?"

"The *desgastas* who decide to live in the city are Marked," Jesse said, "but not discriminated against. There are not very many who choose the microbe; it goes against their beliefs. But I think those who have chosen the city eventually find some happiness." He eyed Harold. "At least they get fed regularly. And they get medical treatment when they need it."

"Medical treatment!" Harold spat. "Painkillers to dull their minds and make them forget their history. *Desgastas* should die remembering."

"I'm sorry. But this is the way it has to be. Why do you even bother to bring it up?"

"To make you think," Harold snapped. "I cannot believe my little brother has fallen so low. Have you forgotten your family?"

"How can you say that?" Jesse jumped to his feet. "You know how hard I've worked to save the *desgastas*."

"And yet the disease still kills us."

"*Desgastas* in the city now live almost as long as the uninfected," Jesse argued.

"And they live full lives," Harold sneered, "if regret doesn't drive them to madness first."

Jesse paced once across the room and then back again. He frowned down at the glossy magazine and studied the greasy yolk smeared across Harold's plate.

"There are articles in that magazine," Harold said. "They suggest that the president's laboratories have come up with a cure. A vaccine, one that will reverse the disease. Is this true?"

Jesse passed his hand over his skull. His hair had grown in quickly. He felt more tufts than solitary spikes.

"But these articles claim that the President won't give out this vaccine," Harold said. "They would prefer the *desgastas* dead and the problem forgotten. I ask you again, is this true?"

Jesse walked to the window and laid his palms against the broken glass. He wondered if Robin had managed to pull the red wires from the generator's guts.

"Maybe," Harold said, "you've sold away your loyalty as well. Do you want us dead, Jesse? Dead and forgotten?"

Outside the window the clouds were beginning to burn off and the sickly sun tried to heat the sand. Jesse turned from the window and collected Harold's plate from the floor. Snagging the magazine, he stuck it under his left arm.

"Why do these *desgastas* give in?" Harold asked. "What happened to their faith?"

"I told you," Jesse said. "They live nearly normal lives. Maybe they're tired of self-imposed exile. Maybe they're tired of living in the cold, without food to eat. Maybe they're tired of pain."

"That same food should be crated up and delivered to our door. The govs have forgotten us, Jesse. Why don't you make them remember?"

"Do you really have to ask?" Jesse clamped his fingers around the edge of the plate. "Look around you! Look at the dying village. Nobody lives outside the city anymore. Look at your empty House. The president finds your choice simple, Keeper. Come to the city and live in comfort. Or hide from our technology and die in the mud. The govs have better things to worry about. Your struggle has been going on too long. Nobody cares anymore, Harold. Nobody cares."

Bathed in the cold sunshine, Harold looked up at Jesse and squinted into the surrounding gloom. Jesse turned around. Balancing the plate on one hand, he pulled open the bedroom door and stepped into the hallway. He paused to glance back at his brother.

"Stop reading the tabloids if they upset you," he suggested. "They're just trash anyway. And stop hiding. Come out of your hole. Robin is worried and she deserves your attention."

Harold stared back. His eyes burned in his face. Despite the pounding in his heart, Jesse lingered. He couldn't understand the passion on his brother's face. Jesse saw the sunlight gathered around Harold's *tronera* and the bright flare of light made him somehow uneasy. So he backed away from the sight, forced it from his head and shut the door. He waited until his eyes adjusted to the gloom, then he padded down the stairs to clean the dishes.

Jesse introduced Isabella Barnes to Carpenteria in Kris's room. He stole an old wicker chair from the porch and set it before the plastic computer console. Isabella perched on the edge of the chair, stiff and unresponsive, but she watched carefully as he showed her how to use the machine and access the city newsnet.

"It's like a newspaper," he explained, "but it's updated constantly. We run it through the old satellites. It's much cheaper than a bundle of black and white paper."

The grocer's daughter experimented with the matte touch pad, learning how to scroll from one article to another. Jesse piled magazines on the floor at her feet.

"Look at the text," he said. "Ignore the pictures. They're trash."

Isabella looked up from the console's neon screen and blinked. "But it's culture."

"It's trash," he said again. "Leave it alone."

While Isabella worked the console, Jesse sat on the floor and read Sam Brier's book. Isabella Barnes knew how to study, and Jesse knew how to be still, and nothing moved in the dim room until late afternoon. From his post on the floor Jesse heard Robin's footsteps in the hall. When she stepped through the door she disturbed the room with the smell of the sea.

Isabella kept her eyes on the screen, but the tap of her fingers on the touch pad grew sharp and stiff. Robin strode across the room and climbed onto the bed. She eased forward until the colors of the screen reflected in her eyes. Jesse hoped fascination would keep her quiet. Leaning across the bed, she brushed snowy hair behind one ear and frowned at the terminal.

"You were going to show me," she accused. "You said if I brought the wire you'd show me how it worked."

Isabella's fingers on the pad became staccato. Jesse rolled his eyes at Robin until her frown cracked.

"I showed you how I patched the phone. I taught you how to clip and solder the wires."

"Where will that get me?" Robin asked. "I want to learn what she's learning."

"You don't need to learn anything more than you already know," Jesse said. He bent over the heavy book in his lap.

"You're going to take me to the city when Harold dies," Robin said. Jesse didn't answer. "Aren't you?"

"I thought you wanted to stay here."

"You promised me you'd show me how to use your machines." Robin sounded angry. Or was it jealousy Jesse heard?

Jesse was annoyed. "And I told you to ask Harold."

"I did. Last night. He said he didn't care."

"Typical," Jesse said. Robin's eyes glittered blue.

Isabella stopped pecking at the touch pad and silence fell. The walls of the House hushed the sea. Jesse couldn't hear past the blood throbbing in his ears.

"You're reading *my book*," Robin said at last.

The grocer's daughter swiveled in her seat. "Can you read?" she asked.

"Don't be stupid." Robin glared. "I said he was reading *my* book, didn't I?"

"Robin," Jesse warned.

The girl made a face and slid off the bed. "She should have thought before she asked. Harold always says so. I can read," she said to Isabella. "Who are you?"

Jesse watched Isabella as Robin stepped up behind the wicker chair. If the woman felt any fear, she managed to hide it well.

"I live in the village," Isabella said. "My father owns the grocery shop."

"I saw you once before," Robin admitted, "a few days ago. You came before dinner, with the eggs. What do you want with us?"

Isabella glanced at Jesse and tried a smile. "I'm going to the city. Jesse's teaching me about it."

"When?"

"What?"

"When," Robin asked, "are you going to the city?"

"When we have enough money to pay for the housing."

"Soon?" Robin persisted.

"No," Isabella said. "No, probably not for a long time."

"Then why are you coming here now?"

"It's smart to be prepared."

"You're right," Robin allowed. "I'm going to the city too. But soon."

Isabella gave Jesse another quick look. "Really?" she asked Robin.

The girl examined the village woman and there was no mercy on her pixie face. "Very soon," she said. "When Harold's dead."

"All right, Robin." Jesse rose to his feet. "You're too young to be digging up trouble. Go downstairs."

"Why doesn't she stay?" Isabella suggested, trying to defuse Robin's anger. "She can watch. I don't mind."

"You're not afraid?" Robin asked. "You're not afraid to be here while I'm around?"

"Maybe you can teach me not to be."

Jesse saw the scorn in Robin's eyes and hoped that Isabella Barnes did not.

"All right," Robin said. She thrust out her hand.

Isabella took it without any obvious hesitation, and then she handed Robin a pile of magazines.

"Read the text, and don't look at the pictures because they're trash," she said, laughing in Jesse's direction. He waved away her teasing and picked up Robin's book from the floor.

Robin accepted the magazines without comment and scrambled back onto the bed. She looked smug, but her triumph made Jesse's stomach burn. He dropped the book on the end of Kris's bed and went to the window, wishing he could see past the fog to the dunes and the forgotten promise of the freeway.

Harold no longer spent the days locked up in his room, but he was quiet and slow to rouse from prolonged silences. Sometimes the older man was absent from the house for hours, wandering the beach or working on the dunes. Once or twice he took Jesse's boat on the water. He would run the craft past the horizon, and Robin moped on the front porch until he was safely back in sight. When he was not out, he slept in a chair on the porch.

Jesse took over Harold's responsibilities. He tried to keep the present running smoothly, while at the same time he struggled to find the time to teach Isabella and prepare Robin for an uncertain future. Robin learned quickly and silently. The grocer's daughter asked the questions. While Isabella excelled on the computer, Robin seemed content to flip through magazines and stare at the glitzy pictures for hours.

"Where do the women get all the clothes?" she wondered once over a cold supper. "Do they get paid to stand there like that?"

"They get to keep the clothes. Some of them get paid quite a lot of money. Fashion is big in the city."

"Can anyone do it?"

"Anyone with the right flare."

Her fork clattered, and then she asked the nightly question. "Is Isabella coming tomorrow?"

Jesse knew Robin didn't like Isabella. He thought it was something more than the prejudice. He suspected the emotion was simple jealousy, or a streak of resentment in Robin's childish personality. Harold's ward didn't want to share her world with a villager. The girl sulked in Isabella's presence. Jesse knew her funks were copied directly from Harold. He still wasn't exactly sure how to handle Robin. He found it easiest to ignore her bitter looks and snide remarks. He always felt sorry for Isabella.

As Jesse's sessions with Isabella became more detailed, Robin began to withdraw. Jesse often forgot her presence completely. He would remember her in the evenings, when shadows swallowed Kris's room and Isabella began to gather her things. Then he would find Robin curled in the last patch of light, studying the same glossy pages. She had dismissed the pictures and now devoured the text, curious about the city's most prominent people.

When Isabella was gone and the House was quiet, Robin would ask her questions as Jesse served out cold fish. Jesse tried to be patient but he found her interests shallow and irritating.

"Maybe you're the wrong sort of teacher for Robin to have," Harold suggested when Jesse complained. "Isabella is expressing interest in the sciences, so of course you're going to prefer her questions to Robin's. You've never had a soft spot for people."

Eventually, Robin stopped asking questions. She ate dinner in silence. Breakfast was lonely. On the rare occasions when Harold ate, Robin's excitement became painful to watch. More often, Harold was absent and Robin sour and withdrawn.

Sometime into the third week of schooling, Robin stopped coming to Kris's room entirely. Jesse took Isabella's lessons to the beach. He led her across the dunes, allowing her the freedom to explore her ideas. He found the anger in Harold's House tiring, and something in the scent of salt and sand caused the knot in his chest to ease. Isabella laughed and teased, and commented often on the beauty of the water. Jesse enjoyed the woman's enthusiasm. He grew pleased when she spoke seriously about her dreams of a future in the city. He found he looked forward to the daily walks.

"The girl misses you," Isabella said one afternoon. The wind off the waves snarled her hair and wrapped her skirts around her legs. Jesse took a minute to admire her smile.

"Robin misses Harold," he said. "If anyone's to blame for her temper, it's my brother."

"Maybe." Isabella picked a blade of grass and stuck it between her lips. "But it's you she glares at. I think she's angry that you haven't noticed she's ignoring you."

"She's childish. I've stopped trying to understand her."

"She doesn't look like village stock." Isabella chewed absently on her stalk. "She looks like the tourists that used to come from Carpenteria when I was a child. Her color's so pale."

"European. High class."

"We used to pretend the tourists were aliens. They always brought lots of *pesos*. We used to imagine that they lived in houses made of gold and silver."

"You weren't far from the truth."

"And you're now the king of them all," Isabella teased.

Jesse snorted. Isabella spit her grass onto the sand before stopping to watch the dark waves.

"You know," she said, brushing her hair from her face, "some people, in the village, say that Robin is Harold's child."

"That's not possible."

"Why? Because she doesn't look like him? Because he had a wife who never bore him a child? The old women say that Harold's wife was a monster."

"I'm supposed to be surprised?"

Isabella winced. "We're not all that bad."

Jesse continued to walk along the shore. The damp air clung to his skin and made his boots slick and shiny. He closed his eyes against the wind.

"Harold's wife wanted a child very badly," he said at last. "But Harold wouldn't give her one. And so she started sleeping with another man."

"Kris?"

"Yes. But she never conceived."

"Harold knew she was Kris's lover?" Isabella wondered.

"Yes. Harold loved his wife very much. So you see, he would never refuse to give his wife a child and then go and get one on another woman. More than anything, my brother is afraid that he might father a *desgastas* child."

"I think," Isabella said, "that more than anything your brother is afraid to die."

Jesse scowled. "It's late. I have to get supper."

"All right." She tripped after him, dragging her skirts in the sand.

Jesse walked quickly, and if Isabella said anything more, her words were whipped away by the wind, unwelcome and unheard.

Jesse and Harold ate dinner alone that night. Robin did not come in from the beach. Her dinner sat untouched. Harold ate slowly and it was Jesse's turn to be silent and withdrawn.

"Will the woman be ready for the city when she goes?" Harold asked.

Jesse glanced up at his brother and briefly hated the placid face. "She's more than ready now. All she needs is the money."

"Are you going to give it to her?"

Jesse frowned. "Why would I do that?"

Harold chewed his fish. His closed his eyes in concentration and Jesse noticed the black that bruised his lids.

"You've been spending a lot of time with her. You have the means, you think she's ready, why not?"

"I don't just give *pesos* away."

"Obviously not." Harold took another bite of dinner. Jesse saw with surprise that his brother was trying not to laugh.

"Why should you care what happens to Isabella Barnes?"

"Robin doesn't like her."

"So?" Jesse set his fork on the scuffed tabletop. "Robin doesn't like anyone these days."

"It's not easy on her."

"And it's not easy on me. She's stubborn and she's immature."

Harold smiled. "I think you should take the Barnes girl with you."

"Why?"

"She might be able to help Robin adjust."

"Harold," Jesse began carefully, "I'm beginning to wonder if maybe we should go now. So *you* can help Robin adjust."

Harold shook his head. "I intend to die here."

"I'll bring you back. We can get Robin settled. Enroll her in the college. She can make friends. Maybe then it won't be so hard on her."

"No."

"You're not being fair," Jesse protested. "The girl is unhappy. She needs help. She needs more than I have to give her."

Harold stood up and shoved his empty plate onto the kitchen counter.

Jesse followed. "You're right. I don't care much for people. I have my own life. And Robin is hard."

"Robin has to be hard. We all do."

"Harold!" Jesse lifted a hand to stop his brother. Harold froze him with a look.

"I don't have time to deal with your insecurities," Harold said. His voice was flat and his eyes were black. "It's time for you to grow up."

The screen door banged in the front of the House and Harold left the room. Jesse listened to his brother welcome Robin. Their voices echoed down the hallway, low and sober. Jesse bent over the sink and stared down into the drain. He realized with a start just how much he missed Isabella's bright smile and friendly laughter.

Jesse searched the grocer's daughter out, for what would be one of his last lessons, late the next evening. She walked with him on the sand. Together they watched the rain as it drifted near over the ocean and painted the horizon purple.

"Show me your Mark," she asked, as if prompted by the boil of color in the distance.

He stopped in his tracks, buffeted by wind, and held out his left hand. She bent over his offering, studying the swirl of color beneath the pad of his thumb. She reached out and then hesitated. Jesse nodded his permission.

She stroked her thumb across the Mark, rubbing her flesh against his own.

"It's not ridged," she said, incredulous.

He shook his head. "It's beneath the skin. A tattoo, if you want. The Mark itself isn't important. What it signifies is."

"That you've been injected with the Fixit microbe. Isn't that what they called it?" Her eyes twinkled.

"They did," he said. "Years ago. When they still called me the greatest thing since George Bruster."

"And they still do." Isabella dropped his hand and sought his eyes. "Bruster cleaned the land, you've cleaned the body."

Jesse's lips twisted. The rain came closer across the water. He could feel the damp on his face.

"Do you know Bruster's story?" he asked.

"Some of it. George Bruster—"

He put a hand on her wrist, stopping the words. "Let me tell it. Not the way the city magazines write it up. I knew George, I'd like to think I learned from his mistakes."

Isabella shrugged and smiled. She crouched on the sand, out of the wind, and after a moment Jesse joined her.

"George Bruster was only forty when I came to the city. But his life had soured, he had already given up on the *desgastas*, and maybe even on the land. He took me under his wing. I was a boy of fifteen, but he said he saw the adult I would become." Jesse snorted. He framed his face with a quick sketch of his finger. "This man is very different from the man he imagined."

"More successful."

Jesse felt his brows twitch. "More *pesos* to my name, surely. But that is because people worry more about their bodies than the land they walk. And maybe also because by the time I developed my Mark, George's mistakes had been found out.

"George wasn't born when the cruiser *Sacramento* went down off the southern continent. His grandmother was one of the six hundred and thirty-one migrants hired to clean up the mess."

"The first *desgastas*."

"Technically. Although those six hundred and thirty-one people didn't show any signs of the disease. Neither did their children. Their children's children were the first to bring up blisters. The disease waited a long time, hibernating over two generations before it bared its claws. By that time, people had begun to hope disaster had been averted. The govs believed the genetic material freed when the *Sacramento* went down had all been recaptured."

"But then the oceans started to go bad. And the plants and animals inland began to get sick and die."

"Exactly," Jesse said. "About the same time the grandchildren of those struggling migrants began to show signs of disease, the ocean and the land began to sicken as well. Same material, same poison. The govs were wrong. The mess hadn't been cleaned up. We had been fooled by normalcy.

"George Bruster's three young sisters were diagnosed with what he later labeled Bruster's Syndrome. All three were dead by the time George turned thirty. And so he made it his life's work to undo the damage we had done to our continent. He worked desperately to save the *desgastas*, and to re-engineer the land and the seas.

"He managed to sterilize the land, in spots. And the poison was slow to spread. Those people who hadn't already fled the continent, those people who hadn't the means, the poor and the sick, the families of migrants, still believed they could settle safely in the north. The seas were harder. His bacteria, once introduced, did as he promised. It ate up the genetic material still contaminating the oceans, and it saved the food chain."

"Or so we thought."

Isabella stared out past the waves, forehead wrinkled. "It didn't?"

"Bruster's bacteria did its job," Jesse said. "But not quickly enough. The poison continued to spread. Up the coast, along the currents. The bacteria chases after, warming the seas as it goes. George didn't know how his miracle would affect the food chain he had tried to save. He didn't know the oceans would warm and the fish mutate. His miracle is changing our seas. And who can tell how much good it's actually doing. George Bruster moved too hastily."

"He tried to do too many things at once," Isabella said. "The mess was too extensive."

"It was, and it is. He couldn't cure the *desgastas*. The oceans are warming up and down the coast. As for the land?" He picked up a handful of sand and let it scatter to the wind.

"Are you saying the city isn't safe?"

"My Mark has made it so," Jesse answered. "But sometimes, I wonder. What if I have moved as hastily as my mentor? Who am I to say that my microbe cleansed the last of the residue from each cityborn? Who am I to say that I have saved our bodies from the *Sacramento's* curse? The little diseases, the little mutations, yes. But the *desgastas*? For the descendants of those six hundred and thirty-one souls who had to swim amongst the poison, and their descendants, the exposure was too great. The taint continues, from one generation to the next."

He looked into Isabella's face and saw immediately that she did not understand. To the grocer's daughter, George Bruster was a wizard. His city glowed in her mind as a haven. And Jesse Grange, nearly thirty-five himself and still unable to save a single *desgastas* from their fate, was a hero.

4

Jesse noticed the first sore two days later. The lesion grew slowly on Harold's left hand, purpling the cleft between thumb and forefinger. Harold wouldn't speak of it and Jesse kept quiet. Robin closed herself in her room and refused to eat. As a ward of the House, the girl would know exactly what the ulcer meant. Jesse knew that his brother would have taught the child very early on the nursing skills she would need to live as a *desgastas*. But Robin kept as far from Harold as possible. She showed no interest at all in her Keeper's care. Jesse decided her reticence was fear and tried his best to ignore her sulks.

Harold took to sitting motionless on the front porch, watching the waves and soaking up the cold sunlight. Jesse left his brother every afternoon and walked into the village for clean water, fresh fruit, and Benox. Harold wouldn't swallow the painkillers. Isabella often met him over her father's counter, eager to share laughter and condolences. Jesse no longer had time to teach her. When he was trying to coax Harold into bed or patiently forcing food down Robin's throat he missed the woman's long face with painful intensity.

A week passed before Harold's second eruption blossomed to the surface. The new sore grew bigger than the first. The ulcer broke the skin just below Harold's right ear and devoured the flesh from lobe to shoulder blade. Harold sat on the porch as usual, studying the rain clouds that gathered over the horizon. Jesse swept the porch. When Robin saw the stain on Harold's throat she pulled on her rubber diving suit and swam out to sea.

Harold watched the child run out over the sand and dive into the foam, but it was Jesse who set aside his work an

hour later and walked onto the shore to wait for her return. He sat on his haunches and inhaled the scent of rain.
When the storm broke, Isabella Barnes came with the rain
over the dunes and onto the gray sand.

The grocer's daughter carried a heavy denim bag. She
set it down on the beach before wrapping her skirt about
her feet and crouching at Jesse's side.

"Hoping for lightening?" she asked, smiling at the
black clouds and then at Jesse's bunched jaw.

"Robin decided to go for a swim," Jesse explained.
"She's afraid of us all these days."

"Will she be okay?"

"She swims like a fish. But she's crazy enough to stay
out there all morning."

Isabella twitched in surprise, and he suddenly found a
laugh. "Don't worry," said Jesse "I'm sure she's too tired
to stay out there much longer and too temperamental to
let the sea take her. What have you brought?"

"Apples. Father picked a fresh lot yesterday." Isabella
wiped a splattering of rain from her nose and sat down on
the lumpy bag. Jesse saw that she was cold and he was
sorry, but didn't want to take her into Harold's House.

"How is he?" she asked, resting her pointed chin on
her knees.

"Quiet. Calm. Indifferent. Maybe afraid, but I can't
tell."

"How long will it take?"

"A while. A few weeks." Jesse thought of Robin swimming among the blind fish and shivered. "We'll be going
home soon."

"Are you glad?"

"To be going home? Yes, I think so. I know so."

"What will you do with Robin?"

"Enroll her in college. Feed her. I don't know how to
raise a child."

Isabella sat quietly. Jesse watched her run slender
hands over the lumps in her denim seat. He loved apples
and the smell of the tangy fruit made his mouth water.

"There is a doctor who lives in the village," Isabella
said. "A young doctor, the only doctor we have. His father

used to work in the hospital, before we closed it down. The old man died three years ago and Richard took over the practice."

"Richard?"

"Richard Front. He's a good man, but he likes to tell stories. He has one about Robin. His father delivered her."

Jesse shifted in the sand and frowned carefully at Isabella. "Have you been asking questions about things I don't want to know?"

She smiled. Jesse saw that her eyes were almost as dark as the troubled sea.

"I wanted to know. I like mysteries."

"And what did this doctor have to say?"

"You'll have to ask him yourself, if you decide you want to know," Isabella said, and then grinned. "I don't like to gossip."

"Tease," Jesse accused. He laughed in disbelief.

"Yes," Isabella admitted. Her smile vanished. "You should go and talk to Richard. Maybe these are things Robin needs to know."

"Are they important?"

"I don't know. Maybe." She lifted her head to the wind and the rain washed across her mouth.

Jesse watched her the grocer's daughter, and then the sky. He lifted a hand. "Look at the birds." He pointed. "They're afraid to land."

"Afraid of the rain?"

"Afraid of the wind. Gulls usually like to stay on the shore during a storm."

The white birds fell toward the land in a brilliant shower. Jesse and his companion watched them in delight. The silence lasted, turning into warm companionship in the sticky rain, until Robin floundered from the sea and stalked past them to Harold's House.

The rain fell in a steady torrent for five days. When it stopped Harold abandoned his chair on the porch and retreated to the privacy of his bedroom. Robin spent more time in the sea then on the land. Jesse stopped caring for the House. Sand gathered on the hardwood floors, and all but three of the household candles burned down to nothing. The fresh apples Isabella had carried from the village rotted on the kitchen table. Robin and Harold ate almost nothing, and Jesse's taste for the fruit had vanished.

He continued to harvest grasses from the dune and collect eggs from the gulls, but he no longer went to the grocer for milk or red meat. Robin wouldn't touch the village fare, Harold seemed to be living on air and sunlight, and the intermittent rain smothered Jesse's own appetite.

Jesse cut the green silk robe into soft strips and used the fabric as bandages. He wrapped Harold's limbs in a green cocoon and tried to keep the open sores from further infection. Harold had forgotten Sam Brier's volume on the porch and left it to the weather as though it no longer mattered if the carefully printed words might blur and run. Jesse left the book in the rain. He was tired of his brother's life and his brother's stories.

Robin carried Harold a meager dinner every evening. She stayed closed behind his door until dawn. Jesse listened alone to the rain, or walked along the shore, counting dead fish in the moonlight. Occasionally, when he picked at a solitary supper, he looked across the table at the bag of rotting apples and missed Isabella Barnes. Other nights he would sit in Kris's room, reading the news on his computer console and trying to remember the busy sounds of the city.

When Harold stopped eating altogether, Robin found Jesse walking in the rain and questioned him about Carpenteria.

"If we went now," she asked, "could you save him?"

"No."

"So you're just going to let him die?" Robin's cheeks were wet, but Jesse thought it was the rain and not sorrow. The desperate emotion on her face was something rougher than love, something closer to rage.

"His choice," Jesse said. "The choice of his whole House. You should know that."

"Isabella says you could own all of the city if you wanted. She says you're rich. She showed me your picture in a magazine."

Jesse listened to the thunder and tilted his head to the sky. In the sickly afternoon the clouds were more green than white. The storm growled as he considered Robin's words. He was surprised that Isabella had spoken to Robin. And also surprised that Robin had listened. But he had known, eventually, that Robin would learn the truth.

"You were uglier then, in the picture," Robin said. "Your hair was shorter. Almost bald."

Jesse stepped around the decaying corpse of an eyeless fish. "In the labs it's more hygienic to have less hair."

"So why are you so rich?"

"I developed a microbe. It cleanses the human body of many latent genetic mutations. It kills some disease, it fixes every little genetic mutation left over from the *Sacramento*. Except for Bruster's Syndrome." He knew the words by heart.

"Bruster's Syndrome?"

"George Bruster documented the first official case of your disease. His sisters were *desgastas*. His family was infected. By some chance, he was born free of it."

"Like your family. Like you."

"Like me."

Robin stopped and watched the rain splash on the sea. "Harold thinks you're lazy."

"He's right."

"He says you haven't done anything except sit on your butt and act officious since you made your first mountain of *pesos*."

"He's probably right about that, too."

"He says you've lost all your moral stamina."

Jesse looked sidelong at the girl. The rain had plastered her hair to her scalp.

"If you know so much about my life," he asked, "why are you asking stupid questions?"

"I wanted to hear what you'd say. Harold's usually right but sometimes he isn't. What about the tabloids? They say the scientists in the city have a new cure. Why can't you get it for Harold?"

"Those magazines are mostly trash. I told you so before."

"Harold says your president has a cure, but he won't use it. Because they want the *desgastas* to just up and die quickly."

Jesse shoved his fists into the pockets of his dungarees. He noticed for the first time the gentle sound the rain made as it fell across the ocean.

"If you're such a big hero," Robin said slowly, "and you have so much money and influence and time, why don't you make them fix us?"

Jesse dug the point of his booted toe into a tangle of beached seaweed. A rainbow of tiny gnats arched into the air.

"Is it because you don't care?" The girl sounded scornful. Jesse wanted to hate her.

"Harold wants me to be something I'm not," he said, trying to be patient. "Someone I'm not."

"Who?"

"You, probably. Someone just like you. But I grew up and went away instead."

"And now I'm going away," Robin said She rocked back and forth on her heels. "But only because Harold's dying and you're going to close up his House. So who will I be?"

"I don't know," Jesse said. "That's up to you."

"I don't think so," Robin said. And then, "Will I have to take the Mark?"

"*Desgastas* must be Marked before they can live in the city. Most of them choose not to."

"But this Mark turns black on *desgastas* flesh?"

"That's one of the things it does, yes."

"And you made it that way?"

"I had to. The president asked me to."

"I don't believe you," Robin said quickly. "I think you're lying. You're afraid, like all the rest. You want us gone. And because you can't kill us, you Mark us differently. Because you're afraid."

Jesse confronted the slender girl at his side. She was sinew and tension and, he thought, consumed by uncertainty. His own anger turned to disappointment and as he stood in the thunder he simply shrugged.

Robin raged at him a moment longer, silent in her fury. Struck dumb, Jesse suspected, by her fear. He waited as the muscles in her forearms bunched and rolled, watched as her hands trembled and her fingers curled. He thought she might hit him, but she only spat on the sand between his boots and whirled away into the storm.

Jesse watched her run through the rain, a two-dimensional slip of movement in the pale daylight. He feared that she was too much a creature of emotion, fueled by sorrow and shaped by the harsh environment of the House. Like Harold, she survived on faith and fed on death. Jesse was afraid the stark efficiency of the city would eventually snuff her out. As he wandered back along the shore, avoiding the uneven trail of footprints Robin had left behind, he felt smaller than usual. He struggled to remember that he was young, wealthy, and loved. Ease of one sort waited in the city for his return. But he had not seen Harold for many years, and he was not yet ready to let his brother go.

He did not mind the disease. It was the dying that repulsed him.

He skirted the waves and ran fingers through hair that had grown out into short, soft curls. He lowered his head against the rain and saw that he was treading on dead fish. He kicked a corpse away and it bounced into a pile of brown seaweed. When he passed again through the House he found that Robin had stolen two of the three remaining candles and locked herself in her room. She refused to answer his call, and after a brief twinge of loneliness, Jesse wandered back downstairs and disposed of Isabella's rotting apples.

Jesse lived his days on the beach. Robin stayed closed behind her bedroom door and Harold refused to die. Four more weeks into the deterioration and Harold's sores closed, leaving skin deformed by puckered scars. Winter storms rattled and wailed while Harold rose from his bed and went back to the porch to continue his vigil.

Jesse fumed. He could see that Harold was only days from death, and he didn't understand why his older brother did not attempt to salvage some dignity. He wanted Harold to give in quietly. He saw the pain in the hollowed eyes and knew that the disease was ravaging internal organs, working its way through the body. Jesse wasted away hours watching the man on the porch. He looked at the puffed pink tissue that nearly obscured the familiar face and hands, and imagined of the decay inside the damaged husk.

He wanted Harold to go back to bed. He wanted the rain to stop.

Jesse ate cold fish for breakfast and cold fish for lunch. He drank recycled rain water, ignoring its oily taste, and every night he broiled a broth of fish and grass for his brother. Robin ate nothing during the day, but Jesse knew she came down for food in the dark of the night. He heard her steps on the old stairs and sensed her rage as she passed his bedroom door. He wondered if she bathed and then decided that it didn't matter.

When Harold started to wheeze and choke, Jesse turned off his computer console and unhooked the phone. He piled the plastic equipment on Kris's bed, and took Isabella's wicker chair back down to the porch. He sat in the wind with his brother, watching the rippling sky and trying to ignore the dark blood that stained Harold's upper lip.

Sometime well into the last week of suffering Harold began to mutter and rave. The blood flowed more freely from his nose. His lungs seemed to stop and start. Jesse tried to convince his brother to stay in bed, but even in his witless state Harold wanted the sky and ocean. Mornings began when Jesse carried his brother past the screen door. The sound of the rain on the porch punctuated Harold's rambling delirium.

The night after Harold began to call for his dead wife, Jesse sat up after dark and waited for Robin. She came down the stairs in the heavy blackness. She was without a candle, and when she saw Jesse in the moonlight she gasped.

"He's not dead yet," she said, as if offended by Jesse's presence.

"He'll go soon," Jesse warned. "You should see him before he's unable to understand. You'll be sorry if you don't."

She was thinner than Jesse remembered, and angrier. Her hair and clothes looked clean, but her face was stained by sweat and sorrow, and her eyes were dark and swollen. Jesse thought she looked older. He worried that this last death was affecting her in a new way.

"Go see him," he urged. "Go see him tonight."

"He's not ready to die yet," she argued. "He'll last a while longer. I'll know when it's time to say good-bye. He's still got strength left, he's not gone yet."

"Go tonight," Jesse said. "Go now."

She stared at him with eyes that appeared heavy and indifferent, and then she drifted away through the House and into the night. Jesse listened to her steps as she crossed the porch. He wished that she had bothered to hear his warning.

The next morning was the dawn of Jesse's third month on the shore. As the sun rose behind the clouds Jesse carried his brother down the steps and into the kitchen. Harold muttered vaguely, looking for fresh air, but Jesse ignored his brother's sounds. He propped Harold gently on one of the scuffed blue benches and then stepped over to the plastic bucket that rested on the sink. Jesse had become accustomed to the clutter of dirty dishes that usually soaked in the bucket's green depths. He'd rinsed the bucket in the night, cleaning it with rain water and then filling it in the ocean. Cracks already marred the plastic surface. Clear water glistened just beneath the rim of the bucket. The water mirrored Jesse's round eyes perfectly. He was amazed to see sorrow in their depths.

Jesse lifted the plastic container and carried it to his brother. He set it at the older man's feet, and then the reflection in the water was Harold's. A smear of red ran into Harold's mouth. Jesse straightened up and carefully wiped the liquid away. Harold sat silent and still. Jesse wondered how much of his brother's mind was left, and whether he watched from the grips of madness. Then Harold coughed and mumbled Andy's name, and Jesse discovered he no longer cared.

He moved quickly, naturally, lifting Harold by the shoulders and plunging his brother's face and head into the bucket. The water was cold, but not unpleasantly so, and it soothed his hands as they locked about Harold's neck and held the Keeper under.

Harold struggled but Jesse thought it was only a body's natural convulsive grab for life. He watched the smooth water as it lapped over the side of the bucket and splattered on the kitchen floor. He waited until the body had stilled and the legs no longer shook, waited until water no longer rolled over the side of the bucket, and then he knew it was over.

He pulled Harold's gaping, wet face from the bucket and spread the body on the damp floor. Blood stained the ruined mouth and darkened Harold's chin. Jesse cleaned it all carefully away. He shut the staring eyes and reached down to finger Harold's *tronera*. As he touched the medallion he heard a sound in the hallway.

He froze. Robin stood by the kitchen table, her face blanched white and her eyes as clear as the water in the bucket. She had bitten through her lower lip and Jesse saw that her pale, bloodied face was too much like his dead brother's. She looked at Harold's limp body and up at Jesse and then she turned to run. Jesse caught her easily, capturing her wrist and holding it tight. She froze and for a moment she was his. Then she started scratching and kicking, twisting and clawing, wild. His hand slipped from her skinny wrist. He grabbed once more but missed and she was gone, away from the ghosts in the House, striving for the same fresh air Harold had loved.

Jesse watched her from the kitchen window, watched as she ran along the sand and over the dunes. He found it surprising that, of all places, she was escaping to the village. He wondered how she would be received there. He worried about her safety and then, suddenly, he noticed that it was no longer raining. The new sunlight fell across his face, warming his brow and causing his wet hands to shine. The glitter distracted him for a long moment and when he looked again at the dunes, Robin had disappeared.

Jesse gave Harold's body to the sea. The clouds gathered again but the remaining light was thick and orange where it fell over the sand and picked out the waves. Jesse dropped Harold's body on the sand and rolled it with his heel until his brother's closed eyes stared at the horizon. The waves lapped over the stiff feet, occasionally washing up past Harold's ankles. Jesse watched as the salt water wet his brother's trousers. He bent and unclasped Harold's *tronera*. He hesitated for a moment and then fastened Harold's necklace around his own throat. His hands shook and his fingers fumbled with the gold clasp, but once the thing was on it warmed comfortably against his skin. Jesse tucked it away beneath the collar of his sweater, hoping that it would be safe from curious eyes.

The sun flashed green as it fell behind the waves. Jesse waded into the ocean. His hands almost slipped as he grabbed Harold's ankles, but as Jesse struggled the water rose and after a moment his brother's body slid easily into the ocean. Still dragging Harold by the ankles, Jesse swam slowly out past the waves. By the time he reached still water the sky was dark and Harold's body had begun to smell of heat and death. Jesse released his hold, pushing the body under the surface. Harold bobbed up again almost immediately and the pink scars on the dead face seemed alive under a film of water. Jesse stood neck deep in the ocean, waiting until the body drifted into the current and away from the shore.

The fish would pick the body clean, Jesse knew, and in the morning there would be nothing left to wash up with the driftwood.

Jesse swam to shore and walked across the sand to his brother's House. His sodden sweater felt heavy across his shoulders and his thighs itched beneath the trousers. He climbed the porch steps, walked past Harold's empty chair and through the screen door into the shade. The House was silent. He stayed still for a long time, listening to the sound the seawater made as it ran down his body and dripped onto the floor. He could smell the dust and age of the building and he thought it felt empty, devoid even of his brother's spirit.

Outside the walls a bird screamed a high angry sound
of pain. Jesse waited for a second cry. When it didn't come
he padded upstairs to Kris's bedroom. He lingered in the
doorway and looked at the computer equipment piled on
the bed, and then walked down the hallway to Harold's
room. The quiet of the House was still with him. He let
himself enjoy the sound of loneliness as he stood in the
center of the room and shed his sodden clothes. Naked, he
sprawled across Harold's futon. He thought he would lie
awake and listen to the sound of the floor breathing, but
he fell asleep almost immediately.

In the morning Jesse made himself a breakfast of stale
fish and clear water and then sat on the porch and
watched the ocean. The clouds in the sky were dark and
thick with the heaviness of rain, but in the afternoon
patches of sky began to appear. Jesse sat in his brother's
chair and watched a group of sea birds fight over a piece
of rotten fish. When the gulls scattered again he found
that it was evening.

He was stiff, cold, and hungry. He'd just climbed from
his seat when two erect figures appeared over the top of
the dunes. Jesse recognized them easily, so he stayed
where he was and waited.

Isabella Barnes came first. The grocer's daughter
walked with assurance, holding her skirts up away from
the dunes, and her big feet left deep prints on the dunes.
Jesse found the set expression on her face amusing. Robin
walked more slowly, kicking up sand and almost obscuring Isabella's trail. Anger made her mouth hard and her
eyes were spots of blue light in black sockets.

Isabella strode across the shore, bypassing clumps of
seaweed, and stopped on the sand just beneath Jesse. She
frowned up at him through the slats of the porch railing
but when she opened her mouth her words were smothered by the growl of the waves. Robin stopped farther
away and stood sullenly. For the first time it occurred to
Jesse that the child might be afraid.

"Come up," he said at last. "It's warmer on the porch."

"Where's Harold?" Isabella asked, dropping her skirts. They fell over her feet and into the sand. Jesse was sorry to see the cloth dirtied.

"I gave him to the sea last night," he said.

"Then it's true," she said without emotion. "You killed him."

"He was dying," Jesse said.

"So you helped him on his way?"

Jesse leaned over the railing. He looked down into Isabella's plain face and saw that she was not afraid. She was not even angry. She was calm and detached, and maybe disgusted. She was the same, she had not changed. Jesse imagined she never would.

"He was tired of watching Harold die," Robin said. Her voice whispered beneath the wind, low and bitter. "He came here to help us and he got tired of it and wanted to leave. He wanted to go back to his city."

Jesse found himself wondering if the girl was right. But he did not want to think of Harold's choking breath, so instead he grinned at Isabella.

She gazed back gently.

"Robin stayed with us last night."

"Your father is a brave man."

"Robin didn't scare him much. Her message did." Isabella sighed. "You'll have to leave right away. The people in the village are frightened."

"Because I did what they wanted to do?"

Isabella closed her mouth. Robin stood like a stake in the sand. Jesse sat down in his chair and put his feet up on the rail.

"I'm leaving tomorrow morning," he said. "And I think you two should come with me."

Robin spat on the dunes. Jesse was reminded of their walk in the rain. He studied Harold's ward and found nothing in her pale face that could touch him. She was like Harold's House, he thought, cold and abandoned and filled with the Keeper's ideas.

"You will be happier in the city," he told Robin. "I promised Harold I'd give you enough money to enjoy the rest of your life. You can go to school, or you can set up a house

and run with the other rich children, or you can donate it all
to a church and live like a rabid monk."

Robin trembled and opened her mouth but Isabella
reached out and gripped the girl's shoulder.

"There's nothing left for you here," the grocer's daughter told the girl.

Robin jerked away and turned her back on the House.
Jesse waited for the girl to run again, but she stayed rooted
in place, watching Harold's wet grave. Jesse looked away
and smiled sadly at Isabella.

"I'll pay for your schooling, also. If you need the help.
More likely you'll earn a scholarship. But you can stay at
my home and learn to your heart's content."

"Why?" Isabella asked. Her voice was soft and sweet in
Jesse's ears.

"Because Robin needs someone to help her adjust. You're
ready for my city, but I don't think she ever will be." In the
corner of his eye Robin's back stiffened and clenched. "And
she won't be coming to me for help."

He added, "I owe Harold something."

"You killed him," Isabella said again. Jesse wondered
why. Her face was still calm, her eyes steady.

"It was easy," he said, and then Robin did run, up the
porch steps and into the House.

Isabella stood on the steps and watched the screen door
bounce on its hinges.

"Go get her," Jesse said. "I don't want her staying here
tonight. Tell her to pack what she wants to keep and then
take her back to the village with you. Keep her safe but
bring her back tomorrow after sunrise."

Isabella nodded and climbed onto the porch. Her skirts
left a trail of sand. As she edged past him, Jesse took a gulp
of air, hoping to taste the scent of fresh fruit he remembered
from her earlier visits. But the only perfume in the air was
the sweat and salt that was Robin. Jesse closed his eyes.

When he could no longer hear the rustle of Isabella's
skirts, Jesse pushed himself out of Harold's wicker chair
and left the porch. He walked barefoot on the shore and the
cold sand hurt his feet, but he continued to walk the length
of the water until he knew that Isabella had taken Robin

back over the dunes. Then he returned to the empty House and began to pack his own belongings.

Jesse didn't bother to close up his brother's House. He left the bedroom doors standing wide open and the screen door unlatched. The sand would creep through the cracks, Jesse knew, and the animals would crawl through the walls. The mold would eat the books and bed coverings and the old furniture would rot away quickly. He hoped the superstitious villagers would leave the House untouched.

Jesse gathered up his equipment and loaded it into the boat behind the house. He pulled the fishing nets from the sea and hung them on their nails inside the front hallway. Then he took the remaining tabloids and went over the dunes into the village.

He walked past the hospital and around the grocer's shop. Isabella would be packing the last of her things and Robin would be sulking among the piles of produce. No doubt grocer Barnes would be hovering about in shock.

Jesse stopped at the center of town and asked the old man who watched the well about the young village doctor. The man studied the stack of glossy media in Jesse's hands, and then said that Richard Front only practiced on the weekends unless there was an emergency.

Jesse made up an emergency and offered a magazine. Sufficiently mollified, the man gave Jesse directions to Front's house.

Jesse found the small shack easily. There were flowers growing below the front step and ferns thriving in a box beneath the home's one window. Jesse knocked on a door made of cheap cardboard. After a moment a woman answered. She cursed as she struggled with the stubborn door. When she grinned down at Jesse he saw the gap between her front teeth.

"Can I help you?" she asked. Her breath whistled through her teeth. Jesse suppressed a crazy urge to laugh.

"I'm looking for Richard Front."

"My husband," the woman said. "I'm Amy Front. Richard's around back."

"Around back?" Jesse asked, looking at the tiny homes that squeezed in on either side of the Front's one-room box.

"Just duck along the side of the house," Amy Front explained. "It'll open up behind."

"Thank you," Jesse said, carefully stepping around the flowers. He knew the doctor's wife watched him as he skirted the faded brown wall.

After a few steps Jesse cleared the houses and suddenly there was space all around. A wide field of black sand ran along the back of the little neighborhood. The sun bounced off the sand, forcing Jesse to squint to make out the figure that stood behind the Fronts' house.

Richard Front was a small man. He stood alone on the black sand and faced away from his home. An easel sat tilted in front of the doctor and a bright white canvas stretched across the buckling wood. As Jesse approached, the man drew a brush across the canvas in careful, meticulous strokes. The field of black sand had no color but the brush Richard used left a streak of brilliant blue across the canvas. Jesse wondered what the young doctor saw in his mind's eye.

Jesse's boots crunched on the sand and the doctor turned around. His eyes were yellow, his hair was long and black. A sparse beard sprouted from the tip of his chin.

"Hello."

"Hello," Jesse said. "Your wife said I would find you back here."

Richard Front nodded and lowered his brush. Blue paint dripped onto the black sand. Jesse thought the resulting pattern more beautiful than the lines on the canvas.

"I'm the Keeper's brother," Jesse said, "from the city."

"We've all heard of you." The doctor nodded. He looked at the magazines Jesse carried and then nodded again. "What can I do for you?"

"I need to know about Robin. The girl who lived in my brother's house. Isabella Barnes said you had a story to tell."

"And you came with a bribe?" Front laughed quietly.

Jesse shrugged and then set the magazines down on the sand. The doctor watched him and continued to smile. Jesse found the slight grin somehow unpleasant.

"Why do you want to know?" Front asked when Jesse had straightened.

"I'm taking Robin with me. She won't be back. Whatever there is to hear, she should know."

"Then why didn't you bring her?"

"Because I want to know what it is before I decide what she should be told," Jesse said.

"Do you have the right to make that decision?"

"No," Jesse said, unrepentant.

Front turned back to his canvas. While Jesse watched, the doctor ran a line of paint across the white surface.

"They say you murdered your brother," the doctor said without turning around.

"People like to gossip."

"Did you?"

"Yes," Jesse said after a moment.

"Why?"

Jesse kept quiet and eventually Front sighed. He set his wet brush down across the easel and then swiveled all the way around. He stood facing Jesse, his feet planted in the black sand, and sighed again.

"My wife thought maybe you killed him because you knew. Or because you suspected."

"Suspected what?" Jesse asked.

"Your Robin is a child of the city. Her mother was a blue-blooded lady."

"Are you sure?"

The doctor shrugged. "My father was."

"How did it happen?"

Front stroked his brush over canvas. "Rape. The lady was raped. By one of your Keeper's own. By a *desgastas*. Rape is a crime of the past, Dr. Grange. You and I both know that the *desgastas* couldn't afford to let it happen. Not when there was so much fear already. The Keepers were supposed to look after their wards. To prevent such crimes."

"But it still happens."

"It happened," Front agreed. "On this very shore. Probably not long after you left. This lady, she came with her husband to inspect the old highway. To see if it might be put back in working order."

"And one of Harold's *desgastas* attacked her?" Jesse shuddered. He couldn't imagine.

"Young man. Dark hair. Girlish eyes. Everybody knew. We waited for the Keeper to act."

"But he didn't." Jesse recognized the description. Only one of Harold's wards had been dark haired and pretty. Jesse remembered clearly how Kris had thrived in the House, making love to Harold's wife, teaching Robin how to be an adult.

Rape remained the greatest crime a *desgastas* could commit, a crime of insanity. A sin that, if uncovered, might bring fear and prejudice to a fever pitch once more. Yet Harold had let Kris go unpunished.

"Who was the woman?" Jesse looked at the hot black sand and wondered if Andy had known. He thought maybe she had, but only at the very end. He supposed that maybe the knowledge, the betrayal, was just enough to send her after an envelope of powdered redfish.

"Important bitch, I think," Front said, full of scorn. "Heavy with expensive perfume and silk and gold and always complaining about the food. Her husband wore one of those feathered turbans you used to see in the magazines. He talked of using the highway to complete his fortune."

"He was wealthy, then."

"She was. She carried a satellite phone and kept getting calls all day long. I remember that because I was a greedy child and I wanted the phone for myself. My father always said they were the type of people who should never have left the city." He laughed. "Father said she thought we stocked the ocean with fish every morning."

"When did they leave?"

Richard Front's laughter trailed away. "Day after the attack. Mad with grief, her husband was. But he wouldn't touch her. Wouldn't risk his own pretty self. They sent the child back, later. Not long after, we heard the mother died."

"You don't remember names?"

"I've forgotten his name. She wanted to be called Lady Sayers, but I think her first name was Mary."

"Mary Sayers," Jesse said.

"You knew her?"

"I knew of her."

"But not of her secret," the doctor nodded, smug.

"Her family is important. Very important. They said she died in a boating accident."

The doctor wagged his head. "Maybe. More likely she jumped out a window, somewhere. Or simply died of grief." His eyes turned suddenly opaque. "Do you know why your brother let it go?"

"No."

Richard Front thought the matter over. "Poor stupid woman," he said. "She should never have left the city." And then, "Is that why you killed the Keeper? Because he allowed such a thing to happen?"

"No," Jesse said, staring out across the expanse of black.

The young doctor smiled. "I didn't think so," he said, and turned back to his painting.

Isabella waited for Jesse in front of the House. Jesse didn't see Robin. He climbed down the dunes and walked across to the grocer's daughter. She jumped when he touched her on the shoulder.

"Where's Robin?"

"Putting our things in the boat," Isabella said. "I think she's scared."

"Robin's not scared," Jesse said. "She's angry. Did you pack everything you need?"

"I packed everything I own, which isn't much. How do we get the boat in the water?"

"We lift it," Jesse said, and took her hand. "Come on, Robin will help."

"Aren't you going to board up the House?" Isabella asked.

Jesse shook his head, and laughed at her confusion. Still smiling, he pulled her across the shore and around Harold's house. They found Robin slumped against the boat, scowling at the back of the old building. The girl wore one of Isabella's oversized skirts and looked so out of place that Jesse started to giggle again.

Both women frowned at him, but he couldn't manage to swallow his mirth.

"I wanted her to look presentable," Isabella said. "Besides, her own clothes smelled."

"They were old," Robin hissed. "And they only smelled like the ocean."

"Don't worry," Jesse said. "You smell about the same."

Robin ignored him. Jesse let go of Isabella's hand and leaned over the boat. Robin had pulled the cover free and stowed the baggage safely out of sight. He was glad that the girl still kept some sense in her resentful head.

"All right," he said. "Time to get her back into the water. Lift with your knees."

Robin looked disgusted, but she held the boat with more competence than Jesse had expected. Isabella tripped over the sand and stepped on her skirts but managed to hang on to her end of the burden. The craft was fairly light and Jesse knew that he and Robin could have handled the job alone, but it was heartening to see the older woman's naïve enthusiasm.

The boat slid into the ocean. Jesse helped Isabella step over the water and into the craft. He turned to Robin and held out his hand. She tossed her head.

"I'll help you swim it out."

"You'll get your skirts wet," Isabella said in alarm.

Robin made a face and pulled the huge dress over her head. Standing only in a thin linen shift, the girl tossed her clothes to Isabella and then dived into the water. Isabella flushed, but Jesse waved a hand.

"She's stubborn," he said.

"What will she do in the city?" she asked, worried.

"Chafe," Jesse said, and then shed his sweater and splashed into the water.

The boat floated easily under his hand, bobbing gently over the waves. Isabella sat in an awkward huddle in the stern. Robin swam across from Jesse. Once a wave crested and he heard the girl sputter and cough. He wondered if she had become immune to the heat of the water.

When they were past the swells, Jesse paused, treading water.

"All right, climb aboard."

Robin slithered over the side, startling Isabella, who quickly handed the girl her discarded clothes. Jesse followed more slowly and when Isabella passed him his sweater he left it off. The air was cold but he was sweating. Behind him the House crouched on the shore in the mist.

"Will it take long to get there?" Isabella asked.

"The rest of the day. We'll be inside the gates before nightfall."

"Will I get seasick?" the grocer's daughter asked. Robin laughed.

"Possibly," Jesse said. He walked to the front of the boat and started the engine. The machine hummed to life.

"I can't see the House," Robin said suddenly. "I can't see the shore."

Jesse looked around at the girl. "It's the mist," he said, surprised. She swam in the ocean every day and disappeared into the fog for hours. Had she forgotten?

"I can't see it at all," Robin said. Her face was white. Worried and silent, Isabella looked at Jesse.

"Come sit in the front," Jesse urged Robin. "You can help me steer."

Robin crouched in the boat and glared at him. Her hands fisted in the fabric of her shift and Jesse thought he saw her arms shake.

"Come on," he said gently. "You know the waters better than I do. Come help."

The girl moved slowly, but she found a seat behind the windshield. As soon as she settled she leaned forward, staring fixedly ahead at the water.

Jesse released the clutch. The boat lurched forward. He urged it ahead and soon they were racing over the sea, weaving through the steaming water and away from the cold shore. Isabella grabbed the side of the boat, and Robin bit her lip.

Jesse looked ahead and thought of his home in the city and tried not to remember his brother's body bobbing in the sea. In front of the boat the sky darkened. From the fog behind the boat Jesse could hear the screech of the seagulls. He touched the control panels, pushing the craft forward as quickly as possible, running away from the angry cries.

And in the belly of the boat Isabella began to laugh.

5

Robin watched Jesse's back as he brought the boat from the sea. He stood still as stone at the front of the strange craft, only his hands moving as they hovered over buttons and levers. Robin wondered how he managed to control the boat with just a twitch of his thumb, and how he could steer so easily through the fog that rolled along the water. But he seemed very much at ease even in the mists, his bare shoulders relaxed and his hands steady. Robin noticed the tilt of his chin and knew that he was eagerly awaiting the first glimpse of his home.

Isabella sneezed. The slight sound seemed overloud in the muffled silence of the fog. It echoed in the bottom of the boat and jolted Robin free of her thoughts. She tore her gaze from Jesse and glanced at Isabella instead. The woman seemed to be suffering in the cold. Isabella huddled in a bundle of damp skirts, her long hair frizzled by sea spray and her eyes reddened by the wind. As Robin watched, Isabella ran the back of her hand across her face, wiping nose and brow in one motion. She sneezed again, and snuffled, and Robin had to chew her tongue to keep silent. She wanted to say something nasty about the woman's appearance but she was afraid that any break in the silence would distract Jesse and send them all to the bottom of the deep sea.

So instead she forced her cramped legs straight and left her place at the back of the boat. The skin of the craft was smooth as glass, and slippery in the damp of the fog, but if Robin stepped carefully she was able to keep to her feet. She shuffled a few steps forward, past Isabella, until the boat rocked and she had to grab at the waist of Jesse's dungarees

for support. Here at the bow of the boat the cold had orga-
nized itself into a brisk wind that snatched at Robin's hair
and made her rock on her feet.

"Careful," Jesse warned. He didn't take his eyes from the
fog, but his lips curled into a smile. "Don't go overboard on
me now. We've almost made the shore."

Robin couldn't be bothered with a reply. Instead she took
her hand from Jesse and set it on the edge of the boat. Gripping the smooth lip carefully, she knelt alongside Jesse's
thigh, hoping to escape the claws of the wind. From her
new position she could see that the ocean had changed. The
water was no longer smooth. Breakers shook Jesse's craft
and flung a sheen of wet across Robin's cheeks. She licked
salt from her lips and squinted into the spray, hoping to
catch a glimpse of Jesse's shore.

For a long while nothing changed. And then, quite suddenly, the wind died and the breakers became curling
waves. The mist began to burn away and overhead Robin
imagined she caught a glimpse of pale sunlight.

"Hold tight," Jesse said, as the waves smacked the light
craft and sent it hurtling forward.

Robin heard Isabella yelp as the boat tipped. A foaming
wave, cold as ice, managed to find its way over the side of
the boat. Water slapped across the crown of Robin's head,
soaking her from forehead to knees. Struck blind and deaf
by the deluge of sea, Robin crouched against the lip of the
boat and coughed ocean from her lungs.

Then another wave caught the craft and rocked it from
front to back. Robin clutched the edge of the boat as they
rolled. She thought she could feel the wind and water rip-
ping a layer of skin from her cheeks. She clenched her teeth
and kept her eyes shut and silently cursed Harold for sending her away from her home.

They hit the land with a wail and a crack. Robin was
bounced forward against Jesse's knees, and Isabella slid
across the smooth hull until she fetched up against the back
of Robin's neck. Robin lay in the tangle and listened to Jesse
cursing. Then she sneezed, and her ears popped, and Jesse's
voice seemed to rise in volume.

She sat up slowly, clearing salt water from her lashes, and tried to find up from down. The very front of the boat seemed steady enough, although over her shoulder the stern bobbed and shook. Isabella lay in a crumpled heap, blinking stupidly. Robin peered down at the grocer's daughter, and for a crazy moment she thought Isabella resembled nothing more than a stunned gull, struck from air to sand by a particularly nasty gust of wind and left to flap around in helpless embarrassment. The sudden image made Robin snort.

The boat rocked again and Jesse bent over Robin's shoulder. He looked as sodden as Robin felt. His dark hair lay plastered across his skull and neck and his green eyes had become raw from too much salt.

"Everyone all right?" he asked, and extended a hand. Robin considered taking his delicate fingers but then ignored them. She climbed to her feet under her own power, turning away as Jesse helped Isabella up.

"Have we made it?" Isabella asked. Her voice sounded scratchy and hoarse. Robin wondered if she had lost all her enthusiasm so quickly.

"We have," Jesse said. "Look. Can you see the sun?"

Robin could feel the gentle warmth across her shoulders. The fog seemed to have disappeared completely. When she peered over the side of the boat she saw clear water and very white sand. This, then, was Jesse's shore.

Without waiting for permission, she scrambled out of the boat and splashed into the shallows. The water dragged at the skirts Isabella had wanted her to wear. The fabric tangled around her ankles. Rolling her eyes in disgust, she stripped the fabric over her head and tossed the skirts back into the craft. She wouldn't put them on again, not even if Jesse asked her to. She was happier in the loose shift, her limbs bare and free.

Jesse's sea brushed cool and soft against her ankles. Intrigued, she waded away from the beached craft and onto the shore. Close up, the sand was white as bone. She dipped her fingers into the beach, and found the sand warm and comfortable. Amazed, she settled into the soft heat, hoping the new sunlight would warm her skin, and waited for Jesse.

He seemed to be having trouble making the shore. As Robin sat and stared, Jesse helped Isabella over the side of the boat and then stood dumbstruck as she tripped on her sodden clothes and fell forward into the sea. Robin chewed her lip and tried not to smile. Jesse helped Isabella back to her feet and finally carried the woman over the shallows and onto the beach.

He set Isabella carefully at Robin's feet and tried to brush sand from his palms.

"I just need to unload my equipment," he said. "It'll take me one or two trips. Not much longer, now."

He lingered a minute. Robin wondered if he expected an offer of help. She didn't give him one. Eventually he turned and waded back to the boat.

"I don't see the city," Isabella said. She sounded tired and petulant. "I don't see anything but sand and seaweed."

Robin looked again at the incredible white sand and then turned her head to study the pile of seaweed that lay at the edge of the water. The weed looked healthy and rich. Curious, she hauled herself upright and kicked through the sand until she bent over a cluster of the plant.

The coils of seaweed were thick and plump, and more plentiful than any of the plant that had washed up on Harold's shore. She bent over one tentacle, running her fingers along the stem until she found a thick nodule. She pinched the round knot as she had seen Harold do, and it burst. Warm liquid ran between her fingers. The liquid was clear. On Harold's shore the nodules often spat oily black rot onto the sand. Here, the plants were apparently still thriving.

Robin rubbed her sticky fingers on her shift, and looked up and down the shore. Jesse still stood in the shallows, loading strapped black cases over his shoulders. The equipment weighted him down, bending his spine, but even from where she stood Robin could see that Jesse was smiling.

Robin walked a few paces along the beach before Isabella's cry brought her back around.

"What is it?" Reluctantly, Robin made her way back over the sand to Isabella.

"Look."

Robin followed Isabella's gaze, and drew in a breath. They were no longer alone on Jesse's shore. The sunlight brightened the sand and burnished the sea, and threw into stark relief the figure that limped across the beach. At first Robin wasn't sure what sort of creature paced along the sand. A shadow stretched behind it, broken by the light. The creature rattled as it walked. Robin thought she could hear the hiss of sand beneath its feet.

Then it turned slightly, and the bright light eased.

"A man," Isabella sighed. She climbed to her feet.

Robin sat on her heels in the sand and watched in amazement. A man, yes, but stooped and too crooked beneath the sun, both arms crossed behind him as he pulled a cart across the beach. His cart was low to the ground, crafted of rusted metal and gnarled wood. The wheels stuck often in the sand. Every three steps the man had to stop and heave until the cart pulled free.

Robin felt her mouth drop open. She shook herself and ground her teeth back together, but she couldn't stop staring.

"Grizwald," Jesse said. He waited at Isabella's side, loaded down by his equipment. Isabella took one of the heavy cases and, reluctantly, Robin climbed upright and accepted another. The strap bit into her bare shoulders when she straightened.

"What is a Grizwald?" Isabella asked, watching the man as he pulled his cart closer.

Jesse laughed. "His name," he explained. "Grizwald has been manning this stretch of beach for the last ten years. See the cart? That's his business. He waits on the shore for travelers, and then pulls their crafts to the city. For a fee." Jesse rummaged in his trousers, and Robin heard the clink of coins.

"He's *desgastas*," Robin said, as the man stepped closer and winter sunlight glittered off the *tronera* around his throat.

"Of course," Jesse said, and walked forward to meet the apparition.

Robin and Isabella followed. Grizwald was not an old man, as Robin had expected. He was young and beautiful beneath a layer of dirt and salt. His hair was golden and his eyes a wide blue, and his callused fingers long and slender. His clothes were brown and tattered, and his feet bare. Knotted shoulders bunched over the unwieldy cart.

"Lord," Grizwald said in a musical voice. He smiled.

Jesse laughed and clapped the *desgastas* on the shoulders. "This craft belongs to Jan Fitzgerald. She lives at the edge of the city. She'll be happy to get it back."

Grizwald nodded and smiled again as Jesse passed him a handful of coins. Robin wandered around the *desgastas* and along the edge of his cart. The man had padded the bottom of the vehicle with something that looked like new fabric. She wondered where he had found such a treasure. She noted the denim bag knotted around the back of the cart and seaweed tangled in the rusted wheels. She thought she saw the gleam of flesh among the stretch of plant and bent to look.

There were dead fish wrapped in the weed, knotted against the wheels. Recently dead, Robin thought as she brushed back the plant with the back of her hand, for the flesh had not yet begun to dry on fishy bones. She guessed that Grizwald had worked for another customer just before Jesse had grounded his craft. Maybe the cart wheels had picked up fish and seaweed from the shallows.

She grasped at one of the dead fish and pulled it free of the cart. The fish was cold and slippery in her hand, but when she brought it to her nose, it smelled fresh. She examined the scales carefully and saw nothing of mutation. The fish looked healthy, even fat. Apparently, the creatures near Jesse's shore didn't have to fight a steaming sea for survival. Apparently, they lived well.

Even so, Robin couldn't help her curiosity. She lifted the dead fish to her mouth and took a tiny nibble of cold flesh.

"What are you doing?" Jesse asked, startling her. She dropped the fish onto the sand and turned.

"They're fresh," she said, rolling the sweet flesh across her tongue. She ignored Isabella's look of disgust and swallowed. "The water here is still cool."

"For now," Jesse said. And then, "Are you ready?"

Robin hesitated. Without waiting to see if Robin followed, Jesse grasped Isabella's arm and helped her up the shore. The grocer's daughter slipped and stumbled but managed to keep her footing. Robin took a breath and hesitated, studying the footprints Jesse had left behind in the sand. Over her shoulder the *desgastas* was already backing his cart into the shallows for Jesse's borrowed boat.

Robin tracked slowly along Jesse and Isabella's trail, digging her toes into the beach, and enjoying the gritty warmth of the sand against her toes. She kept her eyes glued to the shore, somehow unwilling to meet the future Jesse had brought upon her. She savored the smell of salt in the air, the feel of salt on her skin, and the taste of it on her tongue. This was what she loved, what she knew. Somehow she understood Jesse's city would be free of salty air and pounding surf.

Ten yards above the waterline the sand trickled to a halt and Robin's toes stubbed against hot concrete. She rocked back in the sand and looked up at last. The beach was gone, replaced by a long stretch of rock whiter than the sand itself. Here spread a road wider than three men laid out nose to toe. Speckled with sand and broken by a web of cracks large and small, the road met the horizon and then wound on. Robin couldn't see its end.

"The main highway," Jesse explained, although Robin hadn't asked. He and Isabella stood where the road met the beach, waiting. "It used to be a marvel. It still is, although now it's breaking apart in many places."

They walked in silence away from the sea, bare soles against the burning road. Jesse and Isabella kept to the edge of the highway, as though it were cooler where concrete met sand, but Robin stepped along the center of the road. She enjoyed the feel of reflected sunlight beneath her feet. Life on Harold's shore had roughened her soles as it had callused her palms.

She noticed when the cracks in the road became potholes, and again when the potholes broke into tiny craters. Eventually even Isabella stopped to poke at one particularly rough piece of road. She looked questioningly at Jesse.

He only shrugged. "The highway is old."

"And barely serviceable," Isabella pointed out. Robin thought some of the woman's energy had returned beneath the warmth of the sun. "Why doesn't someone repair it?"

"Nothing outside the city is of much importance anymore," Jesse answered. Robin caught the twist of his mouth and wondered if he was embarrassed.

The sun dropped slowly from the sky as they walked, turning the heavens yellow, then orange, and at last disappearing in a haze of pale pink light. The horizon remained visible for a time after, but at last the old mist began to drift in, and a wind danced along the road. Robin shivered and Isabella's teeth began to click.

"If not for the fog we'd be able to see Carpenteria," Jesse said. He wrapped an arm around Isabella's waist and squeezed as though to reassure. She relaxed briefly against his side, and then wrinkled her nose.

"Garbage," Jesse said, before Isabella could ask. "The city dumps its garbage outside the gates."

Robin swallowed sour air and wondered what sort of city could ignore life beyond its gates so completely. The wind stank of more than garbage. She thought she could taste death beneath the rot of vegetation — death and disease. She shuddered, and peered ahead into the fog, afraid.

Then the mist shifted and broke and Carpenteria's great ivory walls rose into the sky. Robin knew the walls had been erected by man and machine, but as she stood on the broken highway and watched the evening light the city, she could almost imagine that they were organic. When she had first lived in Harold's House the sea had brought up tiny shells, pink and white and black, worn smooth by water. The city walls reminded Robin of those vivid shells. Neck craning, she studied the walls and imagined that some huge wriggling creature lived beyond the sweep of ivory.

When the evening wind blew again it brought a burst of billowing smoke and ash. Wheezing, Robin pulled her eyes from the city and followed the trail of gray to its center. She had to squint to make out the fires at the base of the wall. Flames smoldered in the haze. Even from a distance the smoke made Robin's eyes tear.

"They're burning garbage," Jesse murmured over Robin's shoulder. "They usually light the fires in the evening, when the wind blows away from the city. There are labor crews—"

Robin turned her head, distracted by a flutter of darkness just beyond the burning garbage, and immediately lost Jesse's words. There, just across the highway from the mounds of smoking refuse, the evening gathered into a forest of shadows. Fascinated, Robin edged forward, frowning in concentration, until the shadows became tents and the forest a broken village. She took three more strides and then stopped, inhaling smoke until her eyes began to run in streams.

On either side of the highway the land dropped away into a soup of mud. Standing on the very edge of the road, Robin could see trash mixed among the muck. Here fluttered a torn piece of denim, and there metal flashed. The mud stank of mold and soil, a thicker odor beneath the reek of garbage.

There were tents sprouting in the shelter of the city walls. Tents of ripped canvas and hovels constructed of wood and paper drooped in the mud. Robin saw one lean-to patched with sticks and more denim, and another of planks and string. The tiny village was closed against the wind and mud, every tent pulled shut and each hovels buffered by driftwood or cardboard. Robin couldn't see any real sign of life in the shuttered village, but when she moved forward and took a step from the road and onto the muddy ground she thought she could hear thready voices beneath the growl of the wind.

"Robin." Jesse grabbed her shoulder and yanked her back onto the highway.

"A *desgastas* camp," Robin said. She stood frozen beneath Jesse's hand. "Harold was right. But where are the people?"

"They keep a campfire hidden beyond the circle of tents." Jesse dug his fingers into her shoulder and pulled

her close against his side. "The women are no doubt finish-
ing supper and the men—"

"Are there," Isabella interrupted, voice hushed.

Robin turned and had to swallow the lump that rose in
her throat. A group of ten or fifteen men stood in a small
crowd before the city walls. Robin couldn't see their faces,
but she read weariness in the droop of their spines and in
the eerie silence they kept as they waited. She couldn't make
out the head of the line, couldn't understand why these
desgastas men stood in the middle of the road, whipped by
wind and smoke.

Jesse kept his hand on Robin. Shifting the equipment
that looped around his shoulders, he wrapped his other arm
around Isabella and pushed them on along the highway.

"The gates," he explained. "We'll have to stand in line
and wait our turn. They're usually busy at this time of day."

"Those *desgastas* are waiting to go in?"

Jesse stopped a few feet away from the last *desgastas*. He
held Robin and Isabella close, but didn't bother to lower his
voice when he spoke.

"These men are a labor crew. They are paid to clean the
city in the evenings. It's a form of business."

"Like Grizwald," Isabella murmured.

"The government pays them well," Jesse said. "They
make more money than Grizwald will see in a lifetime."

"Then why do they live outside the city walls?" Robin
demanded. "In the mud?"

The closest *desgastas* turned at the sound of her voice. His
face was sallow and the skin beneath his eyes drooped in
dark pouches. He wore a thin beard over his chin and a
wooden *tronera* around his neck. He appeared to consider
Robin, and then he moved away, pushing closer to the center of his fellows.

"He's afraid," Isabella said.

"No," Jesse shook his head, "he just recognizes my face.
These *desgastas* don't like me very much."

"Why?" Isabella wanted to know, but Jesse wouldn't
answer.

Robin knew.

Harold had spoken to her of his suspicions. She saw now that he was right. The *desgastas* who lived outside Carpenteria were those who refused to take Jesse's Mark, those who rejected the technology. Harold had guessed that there would be rebels, but he had spoken of only one or two. Now Robin realized that even the Keeper couldn't have guessed how many of his people would be left outside the city walls. Why had they not left Carpenteria? Why had they not returned to their Houses?

She looked to the group of *desgastas* men for answers, but Jesse wouldn't let her free. He kept his fingers embedded in her muscle, holding her at his side by strength of will. She thought she could break free but she knew that he would only chase her down. She wondered if he read her mind, or if he only expected her to bolt as they approached the city. Robin shifted, pushing her toes off the highway and into the cold mud. Jesse's fingers tightened and held her trapped.

Robin waited beneath Jesse's hand until the haze of evening disappeared and full dark fell across the highway. Lights came on across the city walls, small burning circles of red that tinted white to rose and made Carpenteria a jewel. More travelers gathered on the road. They arranged themselves in the line behind Isabella and Jesse and whispered softly in the night. Robin couldn't find their faces in the gloom. Their voices were strange, their words somehow slow, their vowels long and smooth. She picked up one or two phrases but for the most part they spoke too quietly to be understood.

Robin felt as though they waited forever there on the highway, wrapped in the smoke of burning garbage. The night grew cold and Isabella began to shiver convulsively. Robin watched the *desgastas* camp and listened to the murmurs of the people on the highway and for a long while nothing seemed to change.

At last the *desgastas* laborer in front of Jesse took a few steps and suddenly they stood at the front of the line. The red lights that had looked so pretty from a distance now cut like fire across Robin's face. She blinked rapidly, trying to see past the blaze, and after a moment her vision cleared.

The city gates shone beneath the glare of red spotlights. The gates themselves were made of the same ivory substance as the city walls. Someone — some artist, some engineer — had twisted the material to form an elaborate portcullis. The gates were beautiful, they burned red in the night, a sculpture of artificial flame. Robin wanted to reach out and stroke the shining surface.

The last *desgastas* shuffled towards the portcullis and a shadow tore away from the light to meet him. Robin brought her hand across her eyes, wiping away tears, trying to see. The second figure was a woman. A guard, Robin saw, a guard all done up in a clean white uniform. The woman's face was blank, her eyes impassive.

"She's lovely," Isabella whispered, but Robin didn't agree.

The guard wore her hair long so that it fell past her waist, gleaming in the light. Robin thought the drape from forehead to hip looked like flags of silk, and that *was* lovely. But the woman's chin was too soft, her cheekbones blurred by sagging flesh. The guard's eyelids hung at half mast and the corners of her mouth drooped. She looked as though she longed for sleep.

The guard lifted a hand as the *desgastas* approached. Robin stood on her toes, straining to see. The man's shoulders seemed to hunch as he approached the portcullis. Robin could see the reluctance on his face.

"Licensed *desgastas* are allowed into the city unMarked." Jesse shifted the load around his neck and held up his left hand. Just below the base of his thumb Robin picked out a small weave of color. Isabella grabbed Jesse's hand and held it firmly in the red light, and Robin looked for the second time at the smudge that was in truth only a simple pattern, carved into the flesh itself. Robin touched the scar with the tip of her finger. Jesse's skin felt very warm beneath her own.

"It allows me to pass into Carpenteria," Jesse said. "This little pattern contains my city identification, and the color means I'm still healthy. The Mark will turn black on *Desgastas* skin. Every cityborn wears the pattern, and carries my microbe. Because these *desgastas* are members of the labor crew, and unMarked," he gestured at the man as the *desgastas* slipped through the portcullis, "they carry medical cards instead. They won't take the Mark, but the president will hire a few such men to keep the city clean. They're checked for the most common of the infectious diseases, and the simple mutations. The card allows them limited access to certain areas in Carpenteria." He paused, and then glanced up, as though startled by a word. "Our turn. Ready?"

Robin wasn't. She slipped from Jesse's grasp and hung back. Isabella went first, urged by Jesse's nod. She laughed nervously as she stepped up to the portcullis. She spoke quickly to the guard, but Robin couldn't hear what she said. The guard nodded once, and took Isabella's arm, stretching it beneath the red lights and turning palm to sky.

The guard moved slightly, blocking Robin's view. There was a distinct popping sound. Then the grocer's daughter stepped past the portcullis and into the city. Isabella was through the gates.

Jesse followed easily. He held up his left palm and the guard ran a fist-sized black box over his skin. Robin thought she saw the Mark on his thumb turn luminescent. After a moment the portcullis clicked free of the walls, allowing Jesse entrance. He turned where he stood, looking at Robin.

"Ready?"

She nodded but didn't move. Jesse walked beyond the portcullis and disappeared. The crowd pressed against Robin's spine, pushing her forward until she stood before the guard. Robin blinked in the hazy red light. She felt dizzy and sick to her stomach, and she suddenly realized that she could no longer smell the sea.

"Robin?"

Jesse's voice called from somewhere past the glare of red. She squinted until she found him, just on the other side of the gates. He stood as though relaxed, one hip propped against the portcullis. Isabella lingered over his shoulder, eyes wide and eager. Robin scowled at her, hating the woman for her confidence.

"Passcard?"

"What?" Robin swung round, surprised.

"Your passcard?" The guard spoke again. She held out her hand and looking pointedly at the *tronera* around Robin's throat. The woman's voice was soft and measured. Frozen for the moment, Robin wondered if every cityborn spoke in slow motion.

"She's not labor crew, Lis," Jesse said through the gates. "She's with me. First time through. She'll be living in the city."

The guard shrugged and reached for Robin's arm. Robin jerked away. Cold wind gusted through the gates, ruffling the hem of her shift and making the people clustered on the highway grumble. Robin listened to their complaints and stared silently at Jesse.

"It doesn't hurt," the guard said, but Robin wouldn't give up her arm. Past Jesse, trapped in the glow of the city walls, Robin thought she could see the *desgastas* labor crew. What did they feel each night as they passed through the gates and remembered that they were faceless and un-wanted?

"Robin," Jesse said again, and this time he sounded an-noyed. The light colored his face and made his green eyes appear hard.

Silently, Robin held out her arm. The guard grasped Robin's wrist with competent fingers, turning the bone until flesh stretched. Robin swallowed a gasp. She shut her eyes, and then opened them again when she felt a spot of cold against the base of her thumb. The guard held an instru-ment of some sort, a smooth silver cylinder. The tool pressed against Robin's skin and popped. She felt a sharp stab of pain and then nothing.

The guard and the cylinder moved away. Robin was forced to stand alone under the lights. She couldn't see Jesse anymore. Her eyes were dazzled and her arm began to throb from fingers to elbow.

The guard returned and held up her black box. "Hold still. It's just a scanner.

Numbed by cold and shock, Robin held her arm motion-less and watched as the Mark beneath her thumb darkened. The box hissed and hummed agreeably.

"Done," the guard said. She gave Robin a sharp look. Robin stared back, dazed.

"Now walk through," the woman said impatiently and Robin did.

The first thing she noticed was the air. Gone was the stink of garbage, gone was the burn of smoke. Even the lights and the cold seemed muffled, sterile. For a moment she imagined she couldn't breath. She stopped and rubbed at her arm and tried to stay on her feet.

Jesse stepped from the shadows. He touched her cheek as though in sympathy, but when she found his face she saw his mouth was stern. For a brief moment he reminded her of Harold.

"It will hurt for a while," he said of her Mark. "But it's your key to the city."

"It's black," Robin said, looking at the pattern on her thumb.

"The colors of the Mark deepen when exposed to Bruster's," Jesse explained again. "You're one of the few Marked *desgastas* living within Carpenteria. That pattern on your skin allows you to pass inside the walls."

Robin chewed her lip and pinched at the bruise beneath her thumb. Jesse turned away and drew Isabella close. The grocer's daughter looked wild with excitement, her cheeks burning brighter than the lights.

"Where now?" Isabella asked, smiling down at Jesse.

"Come and see," Jesse said. "Come and see."

He took Isabella's elbow once again, and led her away from the portcullis, away from the flame of the walls. Still rubbing at her new Mark, Robin followed.

6

To Robin, Jesse's city seemed a giant explosion of sound and movement. The rush clutched at her almost as soon as she stepped through the portcullis and onto a clean white road. Inside Carpenteria, the highway continued, but inside the city the road became clean and unbroken. Standing on the glistening surface, watching Jesse steer Isabella, she could almost forget the pain in her pricked thumb.

She lost her fear of the unknown and even, in that brief moment beneath the red lights, forgave Harold's murder. Carpenteria was the hub of the coast and she knew that it was full of powerful people who did important things, but when she looked around she saw only the beauty and the strangeness and the frivolity.

And at first, her very blood was stirred.

That first evening, staring from the mouth of the gate, she hadn't seen past the brilliance to the real color. And once she wandered away from the city walls and the spotlights, into the night, everything looked white. Inside Carpenteria, the lights were softer. They sat atop simple poles and provided a colorless glow. Beneath their gentle radiance the streets were white and very clean.

As Jesse pulled them deeper into his city, buildings rose from the pavement and pierced the sky. They were all sharp towers or curling high rises. Again, she was reminded of bits of shell. She couldn't see any windows. In the night the walls were multicolored, lit by soft pastels or deeper blues, greens, and purples. Standing beneath the towers, stunned by the city air, Robin thought the buildings were wonderful.

It wasn't until daylight that she found they were white and sterile and truly colorless. Once the sun rose, even the sky appeared bleached, as though washed out by heat and chemicals. Jesse's city belonged to the night and its beauty was fragile.

Eventually Robin found that anything not white grew green. Trees and ferns sprouted everywhere. Every leaf looked immensely healthy, and each frond grew the same pale green. The plants were glossy and cool and inviting. Robin imagined that they had been painstakingly developed and then arranged aesthetically. They were alive, but they were not natural. She wondered if they had been grown in Jesse's lab.

When the sun was in the sky, every white was the same white, and each green was identical.

The people, Robin soon learned, did their best to forget their city's sterility. Clothes were bright and garish, people were young and wild and hilarious. Parties were frequent, opulent, and dangerous. Nothing was too shocking, nothing was too expensive. Children were born rich, and in every young eye Robin imagined she saw a patchwork reflection of green and white. They grew up in apartments with no windows and schools with no playgrounds, and when they were old enough to step away into the night they still saw the encircling city wall that closed out a dying world.

For many nights after Robin first stepped through the city gates, she watched these people from the top of Jesse's house. There, high above the jeweled city, she felt safe. The roof lay flat and was surrounded by a low wall. Jesse had cultivated a garden there, beneath the sky, and the green plants thrived in the space. The air stank of herbs and flowers, but Robin loved the height. After sunset the streets below burned bright and in the multicolored light she could watch the cityborn play their games. She spent hours leaning against the white curb that blocked off the roof. From that lofty perch she wondered where the old went to die and whether there were any poor or sick in Jesse's city.

When she grew brave enough to leave Jesse's home, she wandered the streets during the day. Under the sun the city seemed sleepy and safe. Most of the cityborn spent their daylight hours indoors, away from the glare of white pavement. The unending haze was so strong that Robin often

lost her shadow on the sidewalk and didn't find it again
until the sun began to set.

Shops lined the streets. The storefronts were squat and
mostly glass. The only real windows Robin ever found
were in the front of such shops. She loved the glass. She
would press her hands against the smooth surface and
peer through the windows until her breath fogged a circle.
She found treasures this way. She discovered shops that
sold tiny castles of glass, and amazing creations of silk,
and spices of varying scents. Often she longed to touch an
item, but for days on end she never left the streets, never
stepped inside a store.

That is, until she found Atlass's café. Perhaps she had
been searching for the restaurant since she learned of its
proprietor, or perhaps chance led her to the tiny building.
She lingered for a moment on the front stoop, cautious and
suddenly shy. The door was fashioned of carved ivory and
blue stained glass. As she wavered on the sidewalk, she
noted the spotlights buried at the foot of the building and
learned by their color that, in the night, Atlass preferred to
tint his shop green.

At last she took a breath and stepped through the pretty
little door. Immediately Robin inhaled warmth and the bitter smell of coffee. The drink was a luxury she had never
seen on Harold's shore, but she had already learned to enjoy it in Jesse's home. She liked the sudden rush that
buzzed in her head when she took a sip of the sharp drink.
Often she carried one with her onto the roof and sipped the
warm liquid as she watched the night pass.

Atlass's cafe was done up in blues and greens. The floor
beneath Robin's feet looked like white hardwood. The bar
on the opposite wall seemed to be carved of ivory shell.
Round tables crouched across the floor in little groups. The
tables were draped in blue and green silks, while the chairs
squatting around the tables were made of ivory spindles
and blue cushions.

Nearly every table was full to capacity. Eager cityborn
crowded the bar. Robin ducked to the back of the shop,
searching for space, and found a lonely table. She settled in

one of the low chairs. The silk tablecloth felt smooth beneath her fingertips. Someone had set a small red rose in a blue vase at the center of the table. At the foot of the vase Robin found a folded menu. She didn't understand most of the offerings, but it hardly mattered. She sat at her table and rolled the menu between her fingers and searched the crowd for Jesse's lover.

Robin had been in Carpenteria, living in Jesse's home, for two weeks and three days and she had managed to avoid Atlass completely. Maybe it was coincidence, maybe it was because Robin spent her days in her room or on the city streets, and her nights on Jesse's roof. Maybe it was because, as Isabella suspected, she was shy and unwilling to meet a new face. Robin didn't really know care to chase the answer herself. She was too busy trying to untangle the knots in her heart to be polite to a new face. She hadn't found the time or the energy to puzzle out Jesse's beloved.

But now here she sat, finally curious, and she couldn't find Atlass in his busy shop.

In the end he sought her out, approached her table, and bent over her chair. He was a tall man, an ugly man. His arms were too long and his ears too large. But his short crop of hair was pleasantly curly and his dark skin very hand-some. Robin recognized Atlass by his nose. He had broken it once, a long time ago, or so Isabella had reported, and now the man's beak was crooked and blunt.

Robin looked past the crooked nose and saw his charming smile. Embarrassed, she hunched in her chair and picked at the crumpled menu.

"Lady? What can I get you?" He sounded cheerful and likely amused.

"I'm not cityborn," Robin said after a moment of sharp unease. "I'm *desgastas*." She turned her left hand and showed him the blackened Mark on her skin.

Atlass's brown eyes were quick and friendly. He glanced at the Mark, and then at her *tronera*, and then nodded. He held a wrinkled bar rag on his left forearm, and he touched it lightly as he bowed.

"I know who you are, Lady. What can I get you to drink? Or eat? It's a hot day. How about a nice, cold frosted?"

He was so very proper. His voice had the low drawl of the cityborn and he wore their foolish silk trousers and a billowing blouse, but Robin felt an unbidden tug of affection. His face appealed in its ugly way, and his grin suggested secret mirth.

"A frosted," Robin said. She found herself grinning back.

"Good choice." Atlass chuckled and waved a finger, signaling to someone at the bar. He slid into the empty chair at Robin's table. He dwarfed the delicate furniture, and his bony knees brushed the tablecloth.

"I've been wondering when you'd finally let me see you," he said, propping his elbows on the table and his chin on his hands. The bar rag slid down his forearm and gathered at his elbow. "I've tried to linger over breakfast, but you never show. And I'm out most evenings."

"I've been busy," Robin said.

"Do you like our fine city?"

"I haven't decided yet." Robin ran her thumb in an oval on the tablecloth. "It's very warm."

"No breeze," Atlass agreed. He nodded quickly as though delighted. "The walls block the air from the ocean. Although winter is coming. But for now you're dressed too warmly." He cocked a thumb at her old sweater and worn denims. "Why do you think everyone goes about in silks? It's not because of their wearability, let me tell you."

Robin made a face. "They're ugly."

"Only because you're not used to them."

"They're so baggy. Like wearing a tent."

"Just *try* a pair," the big man urged.

He seemed ready to launch into an impassioned defense but was interrupted by a waitress. The cityborn woman had a face painted with a garish orange dye, and her hair was knotted and looped above her shoulders. She winked at Atlass as she set Robin's mug on the table.

"This is Maria," Atlass said, jerking an elbow at the woman. "Her uncle sells some of the best silk sets around. His shop is called Sevor's. It's on the main drag. Some of the most wonderful fabric around. Isn't that right, Maria?"

The woman stretched her arms, showing off her own brilliant trousers and tunic. "Lovely prices, too," she said with a smile.

"Are they comfortable?" Robin asked.

"Very," Atlass promised, and cityborn Maria agreed.

Still doubtful, Robin pulled her mug across the table and sucked at her frosted. The liquid was ice cold, at once bitter and sweet. The drink tasted of heaven. She shut her eyes in appreciation.

"Like it?" Atlass asked.

Robin licked her lips and the big man laughed.

"I always give good advice," he said, as though admitting a secret failing. "I'm right about the silks, too. Come with me, tonight, after sunset. I'll buy you a set that'll make Jesse green with envy. A little thing like you, with your hair and eyes, you'll look a cityborn Lady in no time."

Robin wasn't so sure. But the frosted was sweet on her tongue and Atlass's smile was persuasive. Even the painted cityborn waitress seemed friendly. So she took another swallow of the wonderful drink, and then tilted her head in agreement, and Atlass crowed in delight, making such a racket that his cityborn customers began to laugh.

Jesse's home was a marvel. The mansion rose into the sky at the very edge of the city, all planes and angles and one or two slight curves before the roof. A series of rough steps led from the street to the front door, and most of the surrounding land was green park. The nearest neighbor was up the street and around a verdant corner. The building stood far enough from the center of Carpenteria to allow Jesse his longed-for privacy, but just close enough to the center of things that Robin could enjoy the sights and sounds of the cityborn from the roof.

The house had been built around a cavernous foyer. Just inside the front door, Jesse had layered the hall in veined marble. The foyer seemed empty, Robin's feet always echoed in the huge room, but Jesse loved the space. Halfway along the marble hall a door emptied left into Jesse's private study, and halfway again another hid the huge kitchen Atlass adored.

There were three levels above the foyer, most of them empty and unused. Again, too much space, and often Robin wondered why Jesse needed to flounder in so much emptiness. Jesse and Atlass lived in the suites on the first floor, Isabella had made her home on the second level, and so Robin had found herself relegated to the third. The suites were sumptuously appointed and she wanted to learn to love them, but the echoes made her nervous, and the lack of color became depressing. The carpets were ivory, the walls the color of sand, and even the huge bed seemed to blend into the colorless room.

There were no real windows. Holographic screens adorned each wall. The screens could be turned off and on, hidden or revealed, and set to view any part of the city. When they were on, they looked like glass. They relayed sound as if there were only a single pane between Robin and the real world.

Sometimes, when the windows were on, Robin could hear the false panes humming. The sound was slight but she knew it was there. And if she forgot and accidentally leaned against one of the false windows, the screen would quiver and vibrate, stinging her skin.

In the deep of the night she would sprawl on the huge bed, alone in the massive room, and miss Harold's House. The Keeper would never have approved of his brother's voluptuous surroundings. Harold would have been angered by the ready luxury. He wouldn't have agreed to wear the cityborn silks, as Robin had. He wouldn't have eaten in the restaurants or browsed in the city streets.

Robin knew exactly what Harold would have thought of his brother's city. She tried to ignore the guilt. Most of the time, sitting in Atlass's shop or pressing her face against the front window of a pretty store, she could forget the medallion that hung around her throat, or the black pattern at the base of her thumb. But at night, in the massive bed, the *tronera* lay heavy against her breast, and sometimes she imagined the Mark still stung her flesh.

Alone in the darkness she missed the broken windows in Harold's house, missed the fresh salt air that eased through the cracks of the building and stroked the skin. Often, when she finally fell asleep, she dreamed of Harold's shore.

Isabella adjusted to Carpenteria very quickly. She wore cityborn silks every day, and the vibrant colors seemed to brighten her long face. She spent most of her time at the city college. Robin herself soon learned the loathe the university. There were no windows of any kind at in the low building, not even the ever-present grids. The perfectly rectangular rooms were full of perfectly square white cubicles. Each cubicle housed exactly one chair and exactly one terminal screen.

The terminals were as flat as the college. They hung black against white walls. Robin had become comfortable enough with Jesse's machines, but the college learning tools were different. The machines responded to voice only, and the lessons they taught seemed pointless to Robin.

Isabella became friendly with the other students, but Robin had no patience for the young cityborn. Like their elders, the students were soft and lazy. They wore baggy silks and dyed their knotted hair to match the night city. The women lined their eyes with brilliant kohl and the men wore studs in their ears.

These cityborn children were rich and bored. Robin soon became their pet project. The students asked endless questions about Harold's shore and the Keeper's House. Robin answered the questions when she had to, and kept silent when she could, but Isabella supplied her own version of the truth, and soon the students were the champions of the *desgastas*. They spoke of easing the diseased camped outside the city gates, and of supplying food and medicine. Robin watched the students closely, but never saw any real sign that the impassioned promises were anything more than idle fantasies.

Soon enough Robin stopped going to the college entirely. When she could, she avoided Isabella as well.

Hazy days waned and cooler nights followed, and Robin grew lonely. Jesse spent most of his time in his labs, while

Atlass lived his free time at his shop. When the two men were home, Jesse lurked in his study, and Atlass in his kitchen. Often they retreated together to the first floor suites. Robin felt forgotten, and she tried to stay away from Jesse's empty home. She missed the sea terribly but couldn't yet find the courage to pass outside of the city.

So she wandered streets and alleyways. She tromped through jungles that were the city parks and eventually found her way to the very edge of Carpenteria. Close to the city walls, buildings became scarce and greenery grew more plentiful. In one of the parks she came across a man-made lake. There, for a while, she found happiness.

The park was one of the oldest in the city. The trees grew almost as tall as the city high rises. Grass sprouted as past Robin's knees and at the base of every tree, deep green hedges boxed out the city. Berries grew on the hedges, bright red buttons that broke easily from their stems. Robin ate a handful and found the fruit salty.

The lake cut into the exact center of the park, but Robin found she could ignore the unnatural symmetry. The water was cold and clear, fed by a winding stream. At one bend of the lake, near the mouth of the stream, a tiny silver plaque warmed in the sun. Someone had cut words into the silver. Robin traced the indentations with her thumb, reading out the dedication. She didn't recognize any of the names. She supposed that the plaque was almost as old as the city itself.

She spent her afternoons in the park, swimming in the lake until the cold water numbed her flesh, and then dozing beneath the pale sun until sunset. Once or twice she stayed an entire night on the grassy shore. More often than not she left before dark. Carpenteria's streets were crowded after supper and Robin had begun to hate the crush of people.

One afternoon she fell asleep beneath the indigo sky and woke late. The sun had already set and the air was beginning to grow cold. Robin dressed quickly, pulling silks over her pale skin and twisting her hair into a rough braid. She grabbed one handful of hedge berries and then pushed through the grass and ducked from the park.

On the edges of the city the streets were still clear, but Robin could already hear raised cityborn voices on the wind. She scuffed her bare feet against the street and munched on her berries, reluctant to find Carpenteria's center. The pavement warmed the bottoms of her feet, and the berry juice tasted tangy against her tongue, and if she kept her eyes slitted just so, she could almost pretend she walked alone in the world.

Striding with her head down and her ears closed against the violence of Jesse's city, she nearly tripped over the *desgastas* labor crew. The men stood in a clump at the edge of one of the smaller parks. The *Desgastas* waited quietly, and Robin fell into their midst before she realized they blocked her path.

She stumbled over an ankle, fell against a thigh, and at last dropped to the pavement, releasing berries as she fell. The little red fruit bounced over the street and left stains on the pristine pavement. Robin lay still and watched the berries roll. Her breath rattled in her throat. For a moment she feared she had broken a rib.

Then hands reached down and hauled her upright.

"Still in one piece?"

Robin had become used to the drawl of the cityborn and the *desgastas's* sharp syllables made her blink. The clipped speech was familiar. It belonged to her family, it belonged to Harold's shore. It was the speech of the *desgastas*, and the *desgastas* were her people.

She looked up into concerned eyes and felt her cheeks flush. She crossed her fists over her breast and tried to glare.

"You should watch where you're walking." The *desgastas* who spoke was a compact man. His short hair was gray at the temples, and Robin thought he was old, older even than Harold had been. Sun had roughened his face and carved lines around his mouth. His eyes were tired and impatient.

"You should watch where you stand," Robin shot back, embarrassed by the pounding of her heart. "Do you always laze around, blocking the streets? Shouldn't you be working?"

His mouth twisted. "My apologies, Lady. We are just waiting for the park to clear so we might—"

"Anderson. Look! She's *desgastas*." A smaller man interrupted.

"What?" The labor crew clustered around in excitement. The man called Anderson crouched down, trying to meet Robin's eyes. She turned her chin away, scowling, but his fingers caught her *tronera*.

"*Desgastas!*" he echoed. "What are you doing inside the city?"

"She's not of our camp," a third man whispered. Robin decided she'd had enough. She tried to push through the crowd, but Anderson's hand was still clasped around her medallion. He tightened his grip and held her tethered.

"What are you doing inside the city? Are you Marked?" he asked again.

"I live here," Robin began. She tugged on his arm, trying to loosen his grasp.

At her words the group started to rumble. More hands snaked about, anchoring her to the pavement. She struggled, but the *desgastas* were immovable.

"No white-haired, blue-eyed *desgastas* child lives in Carpenteria," Anderson thundered. "I know the faces of those who have given up the tradition and given in to temptation. What are you doing here?"

"I live here," Robin said again. She twisted in his grasp. When he still wouldn't release her *tronera*, she lashed out, and managed to land a solid bare foot on his thigh.

He released her medallion and Robin rolled free. Her knees scraped against the pavement, and the silk of her trousers tore. She scuttled on her hands and knees, and then climbed unsteadily to her feet.

The labor crew stood in a loose circle, watching her with shadowed eyes. She thought they would have reached for her again, but Anderson stopped them with a word.

"Let her go," he ordered, and the *desgastas* drew back.

Robin brushed stinging knuckles against her trousers and left spots of blood. Air whistled from her lungs and rage scalded her brow.

"*Desgastas* don't belong in the city," Anderson said from the gloom of the trees.

Robin wiped her hands over her trousers again, and turned to go. She could feel the eyes of the labor crew across her back. The blood raced in her veins but she forced herself to walk slowly, and to keep a steady pace. Anderson held the crew still with the force of his emotion, but Robin felt vulnerable alone on the street. Her knees throbbed and she stumbled. The chain of her *tronera* felt icy around her neck. When she looked back the *desgastas* were barely visible, slim lines of darkness against the lights in the park, but she imagined she could still feel the weight of their gaze.

7

A day after Robin tangled with the *desgastas* crew, the bleached sun disappeared behind clouds and Robin saw her first city rainstorm. Water splashed over the parched buildings, threatening to drown the ferns. Robin stood on the street outside Jesse's house, watching. She remembered the heavy rain that had battered Harold's gray House. She let the storm wash over her face and ruin the silken trousers she had picked from her closet. The wet silk clung to her thighs and plastered her arms. She missed the sweaters and denim of the shore. Although she was not cold she felt naked.

The people on the streets used parasols to keep the water off. The circles of fabric were orange and purple and occasionally a demure blue. A few were fringed with garish feathers. Robin watched a man and a woman arguing over something as they hurried through the rain. Faces seemed to sag and pout in the wet, and dye on skin and hair began to run. Robin saw then that the cityborn preferred the sunshine.

At last Robin stepped away from Jesse's home and hurried through the rain. She had a vague thought of stopping in at Atlass's cafe, but she wasn't in the mood for good cheer, and she found herself tired of his foolish stories. She turned away from the center of the city and toward her park, wondering idly what a swim in a man-made lake beneath a stormy sky would feel like, but eventually her feet ground to a halt.

The restless horizon brought with it memories of Harold's shore. She recalled running on his beach, braced by the rain and whipped by winter winds. If she closed her eyes she could almost hear the splash of raindrops against the steaming sea, almost feel the scrape of wind across her skin. The fish were always wild during winter storms. Robin remembered the sight of their horrible bodies rocking against the whitecaps.

When Robin opened her eyes again, her feet were taking her in a new direction, away from her private lake, away from the solitude she had imagined she wanted. The street turned slick with rain. Water soaked through her flimsy silk shoes. The cityborn hurrying past went barefoot. They hopped fastidiously over puddles, grasping their slippers tightly in one hand. Each person seemed shocked and personally insulted by the drippings that fell over their parasols. They cursed the puddles and made Robin laugh.

Eventually Robin removed her own ruined shoes and tossed them into one of the many trash bins lining the streets. Feet cold and naked against the wet pavement, she wandered along several city blocks until she reached Atlass's store front. There she paused and glanced through the windows. Most of the tables were crammed with sodden cityborn. Customers sipped at hot liquid, inhaling the sweet fumes and waiting impatiently for the storm to ease. Robin lingered for a moment, searching each bored face, but she didn't find Atlass's distinctive features. If the ugly man lurked anywhere in the crowd, she couldn't see him.

She waited a minute longer and then walked on. As she moved outwards away from Carpenteria's center the green again overtook the white. People preferred to live and work away from the enclosing walls. The edges of city were lush with vegetation. The plants grew wild, and were trimmed once a month, but otherwise left alone. Robin thought of the rain across the silver face of her lake and almost turned back.

But instead she passed through the green and approached the gap in the wall.

The gates were deserted during the daytime. Very few people left the city under the hazy afternoon sky, and the *desgastas* labor crews only passed through in the evening. Two guards stood at the portcullis. Their eyes were glazed and their lips slack. They straightened when Robin approached. The one closest to Robin held out a limp hand.

Robin extended her fingers. The guard wrapped bony fingers around her wrist. He glanced at her Mark without interest, and then ran it beneath his little box. He bent his head over the box, waiting for something Robin did not understand. As she waited, she realized that the guard was not much older than herself. Glittery makeup encircled his brow and eyes, but his hair fell in a clean, shaggy mass to his collar.

The guard looked up and dropped Robin's hand. Her thumb felt suddenly greasy. She rubbed it against her side as the gate swung open. In the daytime, the portcullis was soundless and heavy, free of color. Atlass swore the mechanism never broke down, and that in emergencies it could be opened or closed very quickly. Now, ages seemed to pass before the portcullis clicked open. Robin waited, watching a trail of rain drops run over the ivory bars.

Before she could step through, the second guard suddenly looked in her direction and waved a hand at her feet.

"You shouldn't go out without shoes," he warned. "It's not clean out there. You might step on something dangerous."

"I'll be careful," Robin said, surprised by his concern.

The man was thin. She could see his cheekbones clearly. He looked worried. "Maybe you'd better go home and get some shoes first. There's all sorts of rotten trash out there in the dirt."

Robin felt impatience nag. "Shoes won't make much of a difference. Fabric soles won't protect me from anything. I'll be careful where I step."

The guard shrugged and waved her through. Robin looked up at him as she passed by. His face was streaked with wet and his eyes were bloodshot. She was surprised to see he wore a *tronera* around his neck. The medallion looked like it had been fashioned from a small piece of stone. The man wore the tiny pendant outside his shirt. He met Robin's gaze for a moment and then turned to say something to his companion.

Outside the city walls the broken highway ran in a straight line into the distance. Immediately the smoke of burning garbage blurred Robin's eyes. She took only a few steps out across the white surface before her bare toes lost the pavement and squished into mud.

The *desgastas* were still camped right alongside the wall. Through the rain Robin could see their ragged tents and sagging hovels. Smoke rose from somewhere within the forest of tattered cloth, and she could hear high-pitched voices. Children, she thought, and wondered if they loved the rain as much as she did.

She stepped off the edge of the road. Bits of paper and scraps of fabric mixed in the mud. Beneath the scent of garbage she could smell again the rich perfume of the soil. Jesse had not seemed to see the trash in the dirt. Robin trod carefully, taking tiny steps and inspecting the mush for signs of metal, plastic, or bone. As a child she had learned to walk gingerly on Harold's shore. After a storm one had to avoid dead fish and sharp driftwood and occasionally spots of warm tar or pieces of broken glass. The mud felt different than the wet sand. The muck ran deep and Robin feared rusted metal hidden in the dirty stew.

Even though she walked slowly, the makeshift town seemed to spring up immediately. She could smell the smoke and the shrill cries became words. They were not the voices of children but of women, and their laughter echoed from beyond the first line of tents. Robin moved slowly beyond the wall of fabric until she breached the camp. There she found the *desgastas*.

A group of skinny women sat around a large fire, cooking and laughing. They looked up when Robin approached, smudged faces unreadable.

Robin stood in the muck and stared back. Mud had splattered up around her ankles, and her feet were caked. The skin itched and her toes were numb.

One of the women laughed. "Did you lose your pretty parasol, child?"

Robin frowned. The woman looked young and her smile was bitter. Straight dark hair hung in lank strands about her face. Grease dirtied her blunt chin, and dry skin chapped the corner of her mouth.

"I'm not cityborn," Robin said. "And I'm not afraid of the rain."

The women chuckled. They were all brown and worn and hard. They were *desgastas*, Robin reminded herself. They were her people. Pots of thin stew cooked on their campfire, and the scent of old meat reminded Robin of summer picnics on Harold's beach.

"What do you want with us?" another woman asked. She looked little older than twenty, but already the disease ate at her neck.

Robin hesitated as she searched for the correct words. Didn't they see past her silks to the *tronera* around her throat? She wanted to say, *I belong here.* But the words wouldn't find their way past the taste of longing in her mouth.

She hesitated, mud squishing around her toes, and remembered the *desgastas* crew.

"I'm looking for Anderson," she said.

"All the rich girlies want Anderson," someone snorted. "We can't keep them away." There was more mirth, and a spatter of snide remarks.

Robin crossed her arms. She stood in the muck, waiting, until eventually the women noticed her again. The girl with the straight hair seemed embarrassed. She rose from the fire and nodded in Robin's direction.

"Anderson's tending to his boy," she said. "Who are you?"

"Robin. Which tent is his?"

"Molly," the girl introduced herself. And then, "Where are your shoes, little Robin?"

"There aren't any shoes in the city," Robin said. "Just pretty fabric that melts in the rain."

The women screeched again. Their laughter was shrill and Robin heard no real humor beneath the shrieks. Molly stepped closer, and then stopped abruptly. She had seen Robin's *tronera*. The medallion burned red in the firelight and Molly took a breath.

"Come sit down by the fire," she said after a moment. "I have some boots you might borrow."

"I just want to see Anderson."

"I'll tell him you're here," Molly said. "Does he know you?"

Robin considered.

"Not really," she said. "We met yesterday."

"All right. Sit down. I'll bring him back."

The girl ran off in a swirl of patchwork skirts. Robin slogged through the mud to the fire. The *desgastas* perched on logs and rocks. A few sat on jagged pieces of the broken road. All of the women wore heavy skirts and bulky sweaters. Most of the faces were tight in the cold.

Robin sank onto a jagged piece of concrete and tried to scrape the mud off her feet.

"Step on anything sharp?" her neighbor asked. Robin shook her head.

"People don't usually come out in the daytime," a woman spoke across the fire. "People don't usually come out at all, unless they're dumping the trash."

Robin didn't answer.

"You're *desgastas*," her neighbor ventured after another silence. "But you wear city clothes?" The woman made it a definite question.

Without looking up from her muddy ankles, Robin extended her thumb.

"Marked," an older woman said from across the fire. "You should be ashamed."

"Hush," a girl scolded, but Robin looked up and across the cook pots.

"There are *desgastas* in the city," she said. "There was a man tending the gates just now. He wore the *tronera* around his neck."

"A few break with tradition," a woman replied. "They are to be pitied."

"More than a few," a young woman with some flesh on her cheeks argued. "Every day they turn to the city. Ten are Marked and live within the walls now, to our thirty-five."

"Plus the labor crews."

Robin's closest neighbor wrinkled her nose. "Anderson's men do what they have to to keep us fed."

The man's name brought silence. Robin noticed a few guilty glances from across the campfire. She ignored them, and concentrated on the sparks dancing around the cook pots.

"Shouldn't you be in school?" the woman to Robin's left asked. Robin supposed she was trying to be friendly. The woman had a kind face. Something in the curve of her mouth reminded Robin of Andy.

"I don't go much anymore," Robin said.

"My daughter hates it, too," the *desgastas* smiled. "Her father sends her to the city college, but she'd rather be out having fun."

"She can go to school in the city?"

"She lives in the city. With her father. We decided it would be better. We wanted to give her a chance."

"Greta's husband and daughter are two of the Marked," a woman growled, and was immediately quieted.

"What about you?" Robin wondered, looking at the soft mouth and avoiding the dark eyes.

"I believe in the old ways," the woman said. She touched the badge at her throat. "But it's getting harder every day."

Robin scraped mud from her kneecap with her finger-nails, and thought of Harold's decision to send his last ward into a world so opposite from his own. The fire burned low, but it was warm, and the raindrops sizzled on the coals. The storm was easing up, but the afternoon sky remained dark and cold.

"I know what you're thinking," the *desgastas* said to Robin's silence. "But I'm not ashamed of my husband. Nor of my daughter. Things are changing."

Robin looked into the fire and imagined she glimpsed Harold. "What's your daughter's name?"

"Anna. She was born out here in the mud ten long years ago, and she's still untouched by the disease. She's happier in the city, and I don't regret the decision to let her go."

"Carpenteria won't protect her," someone muttered. The women around the campfire shifted uneasily in their seats.

"People say they're working on a cure in the city," Greta ventured. "Is this true?"

"I don't know," Robin said, and then looked up when a shadow blocked the warmth of the fire.

"Anderson can't leave his son," Molly said. "Will you come and see?"

Robin bounced up quickly. She could feel Greta watching her. The older woman considered the mud on Robin's ankles and the ruined silk around her shoulders. She shook her head and her eyes were sympathetic.

"Remind Molly to find you those boots," she said. "You don't want to ruin your feet."

Behind Robin the women chuckled. She stiffened her shoulders and tried to swallow her pride, but as she walked away from the fire she looked at Molly striding ahead through the tents and flushed. The woman swung through the mud and Robin had to trot to keep up. Muck splattered on her thighs and on her arms. The thought of returning home to Jesse in such a state made her stomach roll.

Molly paused. She waited until Robin reached her side and then stepped on through the slop.

"Where are you from?" the girl asked as she walked. "Have you traveled far?"

"I lived by the sea." Robin peered into the mud, trying to step cautiously and match Molly's speed at the same time. "South of here. I lived in a House, until the Keeper died. I was the last of his wards."

"So you came to the city?" Molly sounded doubtful.

Robin slogged silently on, unwilling to answer. Molly shrugged. "I've read of the Houses, but never met a ward. What was it like?"

"Not so different from your muddy tents, but we didn't have burning garbage blowing constantly across our faces. Why don't you move the camp?"

Molly's face twitched. Robin wondered how the other girl could be so astonished. Was it so hard to imagine breaking camp and moving on? Were the *desgastas* here as unwilling to face change as Harold had been?

Molly stopped. Robin realized they had left the campfire behind. She could no longer smell dinner.

"There," Molly said, picking out one of the tents with a tilt of her chin. "Knock before you enter. Anderson doesn't like to be surprised. I'll see if I can find you some boots."

She turned away, slipping slightly in the mud, and left Robin standing alone among the squat tents. Anderson's tent rose a full handspan above the group. Worn fabric embraced a door fashioned of rain-slicked wood, and the ropes that anchored canvas to the ground looked new and strong.

Robin edged closer until at once she could hear sounds through the fabric wall. She recognized the pained muttering of delirium, and her heart began to thump. She took a breath, inhaled decay, and knew what she would find in Anderson's tent. For the first time since she had followed Jesse into his city she felt real fear.

She took another breath of stormy air, and then lifted her fist to pound on the wooden door. She thought she heard a muffled reply, so she pushed back the heavy plank and ducked out of the rain.

Inside the tent it was warm, but the heat was that produced by sweating bodies living together in a tiny space. Robin fought the urge to stop breathing and instead swallowed several huge gulps of the foul air. She held still, waiting for her eyes to adjust to the dim light. The rain was muffled but she could hear the shrill voices of the *desgastas* women through the thin canvas wall.

"Don't stand there in the doorway," Anderson said. "You're blocking traffic."

So he remembered her. Robin squinted, trying to make out the *desgastas*. From outside the tent had appeared roomy, but as her eyes forced away the darkness she could see that it was cramped and awkward. Cardboard and straw covered the floor. The mix prickled under her bare feet. She took two careful steps away from the flap of the tent and as she did she saw Anderson.

He slouched in a corner against the opposite wall, head bent as he mixed the steaming contents of a cracked bowl with one thick finger. To his left a sagging mattress spread across the straw. A boy lay curled on the cot. The child had Anderson's blunt features. He mumbled and shook in his sleep. His small hands were rotted and scarred by disease, and Robin could make out welts across his brow.

The boy was younger than Robin. Harold had trained Robin in *desgastas* healing lore. The Keeper had repeated story after story of the diseased and dying until Robin could recite symptoms and progressions in her sleep, but never had Harold spoken of blistered children. Anderson's son was much too young to be showing any signs of the disease. Robin knew this from Harold's lessons, but even more importantly, she could feel the wrongness in her gut.

Shocked, she looked up at Anderson. The man met her gaze for the briefest of moments, and then concentrated again on his bowl.

"What are you doing here?" His tone was polite, but the set of his spine was not.

Robin shifted in the mud. She wasn't sure she had an answer. Then the boy on the mattress shifted and moaned, and Robin forgot her fear. She crossed the tent in three quick steps and knelt on the prickly ground at the boy's side. His brow felt cool, but he cried out at the touch of her hand. Robin soothed him automatically, much as she had soothed Kris, much as she had watched Harold soothe so many before.

"Don't disturb him." Anderson crouched at her side, expression fierce.

"What's his name?"

"Jason," the *desgastas* spoke grudgingly. Robin understood then that the boy was the center of Anderson's world.

"He's your son?" she asked as she ran competent fingers down the boys arms, feeling for the pulse that bumped in his neck.

"Of course," Anderson growled.

"His mother?" Robin asked.

"Dead," Anderson said without emotion. "And his two sisters."

"He's very young to be dying."

"He's not dying," Anderson protested.

Robin looked in disbelief at the *desgastas*. One quick glance at the man's face and she knew he didn't want to see the truth. Denial was not a luxury to be had on Harold's shore, but here she saw that the emotion still had roots.

"He's dying," she said, unable to soften the blow. "Look." She ran her hands under the boy's grimy shirt, lifting the fabric away. "He's scarred already. The surface sores have healed over. It's eating away at his insides. Look at his eyes. See how the whites are turning black? And look at his joints. Deposits have already grown under the skin."

"I know Bruster's," Anderson snapped. "I know the signs."

"He has a day," Robin continued mercilessly. "Two at the most."

"He's my son," Anderson cried out. "He's my last."

"And you'll give him to the sea," Robin replied coolly.

The boy shifted again on his cot. Anderson brushed Robin away. He crouched at the boy's side and began patiently spooning a bit of stew into Jason's mouth. Most of the liquid trickled uselessly across the boy's chin. Robin had to bite her tongue. Feeding the child was a waste. Anderson would do better to eat the stew himself.

"We don't give our dead to the sea," Anderson said after a moment of silence. He wiped stew from Jason's chin and then lifted another spoonful. "Here, so far from the ocean, we burn them."

"Like the garbage," Robin said, astounded.

Anderson's hand trembled, and he nearly dropped the chipped spoon. He set the bowl down and stared at Robin.

"You're barely older than my son."

"He's too young to be eaten," Robin agreed.

"And yet you speak as a cynic," Anderson continued as though he hadn't heard. His eyes shuttered, and then he sighed and met Robin's puzzled gaze. "More and more *desgastas* children are dying of Bruster's. My first daughter blistered when she was ten, and my second when she was only six. The disease is changing."

Robin shook her head. The man's claims were unlikely. She thought grief had turned his head.

"Look at my son," Anderson demanded. He reached up, clutched Robin's chin between his fingers, and twisted her neck until she looked down at the shaking child. "How long to you think he's been on this cot?"

Reluctantly, Robin considered the state of the boy's scarring.

"A month," she said, "maybe six weeks."

"Three days," Anderson corrected. He released her chin in a savage motion. "My son's first blister appeared three days ago."

"That's impossible!"

"Impossible but true." Anderson picked up his spoon and poked at the remaining stew. "Bruster's is changing. And only the *desgastas* in this camp can see it."

"Impossible," Robin said again, rubbing the imprint of his fingers from her chin.

"What's your name, child?"

"Robin."

Anderson nodded at the stew. "And you said you give your dead to the sea. So you must be from a House on the shore. I didn't know there were any left."

"I think my Keeper held one of the last."

"Probably. As I said, things are changing. So, pretty Robin, what are you doing in my camp, in my tent? Did you come only to watch my boy die?"

"I came to help," Robin said, and realized as she spoke that the words were true.

"Help? How?" Anderson challenged. "What can you do that we haven't already tried?"

"I don't belong in the city."

Anderson looked up across his bowl. His eyes were implacable. "You wear the city Mark on your thumb. The microbe is in your body. You don't belong here, either."

Robin's heart trembled. She reached up to touch her *tronera*, but Anderson shook his head.

"It isn't enough," he said. "You've made your choice."

"It was made for me," Robin protested, angry

"It isn't enough," Anderson said again. He leaned over his son, dismissing Robin completely.

She lingered for a moment longer, searching for an argument, but the only words she could dredge up were bitter. Tears gathered in the corners of her eyes and she found the moisture humiliating. She wiped the tears away and rose to her feet, leaving father and son alone in their tent.

Molly waited outside in the rainy afternoon. She didn't appear to see the expression on Robin's face. She held up a pair of black rubber boots and smiled.

"You should put them on now," she said. "You can clean the mud from your feet later."

"I don't need—"

Molly shook her head. "Take them. They're extra. And everybody knows city shoes are useless."

So Robin accepted the gift. She pulled the boots over her feet with some grace, and was surprised to see they fit.

"Thank you," Robin said.

"Is there anything else you need? Supper?"

"No," Robin said. She turned to go.

The girl stepped through the mud and touched Robin's hand. "Come back when you need to," she said. "You're always welcome here."

"Anderson disagrees."

Molly's smile was knowing and somehow sweet.

"Anderson's last child is dying," she said. "Forgive him any harsh words."

Robin bit her lip and shook free of the *desgastas's* grip. Molly coughed a small sound, but let her go.

The tents drooped low to the ground, soaked by the rain. The camp seemed to close around Robin's throat. She walked quickly, freed by the boots to hurry blindly through the mud. She heard voices in the distance and fled from the sound, flopping through the muck until she broke from the cluster of tents and made the city highway.

Once on the cracked pavement Robin turned away from the city and the *desgastas* camp. She worked her way along the highway, stopping here and there to consider the pavement, trying not to think of Anderson's face or Molly's easy smile. At last the rain began to ease up, and thin clouds blew away across the sky. The afternoon sun shone with a sluggish light. The pavement beneath Robin's feet, washed clean by the lingering storm, brightened.

She could smell the ocean again, and when she stepped off the highway onto soft sand her throat closed in relief. The sand was still wet from the rain and steamed gently beneath the sky. Robin pulled her feet free of the rubber boots, and stripped off her city silks. Quick and naked in the sun, she dashed across the beach and dove into the sea.

The water caressed the mud from her skin and the worry from her brow. She swam until the sun began to drop in the sky, until the wind began to pick up once again and darker clouds rode the horizon. She swam with the fish, and they seemed to share in her joy. Amongst all the quick, perfect schools she saw only a handful of creatures marred by disease.

When she was ready to leave the cradle of the sea, Robin caught three of the fish in her bare hands and took them with her from the water. She wanted fish for dinner, fresh fish gathered from the sea, snatched from the greedy waters. She would show Atlass how to prepare the meal in his sterile kitchen, how to fry the flesh and strip it from thin bones.

Leaving the fish to flop on the sand next to her boots, Robin dressed again and wandered down the beach in search of sea grass. She had an idea. She would show Atlass how to grind the weed and make it into the spice she loved.

She found the grass several meters down the beach, growing sparsely on the flat shore. She crouched in the sand by the plant and saw that it was dying. The long leaves were brown and dry, the stems covered with small yellow blisters. The grass grew in a small hollow close to the water, and as Robin watched, lazy waves rolled up the beach and flattened a few of the stalks.

She ran her hands over the stems, seeking, and the blisters were firm beneath the strength of her fingers. She pressed down harder with her thumbs, but the welts wouldn't break.

"You won't burst them. They're hard as stone."

Fingers still wrapped around a dirty stalk, Robin squinted up at Grizwald. The *desgastas* stood over her, his eyes merry. Robin didn't see the man's rusted cart anywhere.

"You've tried?" she asked. She wondered if the man spent his whole life wandering the sand.

He nodded and dropped to his knees on the sand. "When I first noticed the blisters on the grass."

"Is it all dying?" Robin looked out along the sand. This beach was flat, free of the rolling dunes she knew from Harold's shore. Every few yards she could see more of the brown grass sprouting on the shoreline.

"Not dying," Grizwald corrected, "just changing. Watch."

He yanked several of the weeds from the ground and laid them across the sand. His movements were practiced, as though he had already spent hours or even days studying the grass. He stroked the plant patiently, squeezing along the edges of the welts. Then he grunted and his fingers spasmed. The blister beneath his hand popped free of the stalk and rolled across the sand.

Robin caught the tiny bud before it found the sea. About the size of a pebble, it wasn't a blister after all, but maybe a seed. The thing was perfectly round, the clear skin unyielding. Robin held it on the palm of her hand and saw that beneath its skin the bud was filled with yellow fluid.

"What is it?"

"Don't know," Grizwald said, smiling at her disgust. "But look — here."

The loosened bud had left behind a cavity in the weed's stem. Grizwald used the edge of this thumbnail to widen the gap.

"Wet and green as spring," he said, and Robin saw that he was right. "The grass is healthy beneath the first layer."

"What does it mean?"

Grizwald shrugged and rose to his feet, brushing sand from his knees. A wide smile cracked his young face. Robin saw that he was missing several teeth.

"I don't know," he said, "but I don't eat the grass anymore. The taste has changed. It's foul."

Robin looked at the bud in her hand and sighed. She dropped the yellow sphere to the sand and rubbed her palm clean.

"Where's your cart?" she asked.

"Up the shore."

"Do you spend all your time waiting on the beach?"

His grin stretched. "Most of it."

"Why?"

"It brings *pesos*," Grizwald said. He shrugged narrow shoulders and started back along the beach. Robin followed. In the distance she could see the black stumps that were her boots and the silver shine of her dinner, motionless in the sand.

"I won't work in Carpenteria," the tattered man continued. "This seemed the next best thing."

Grizwald stopped before the boots. Robin's fish were nicely dead, and her mouth watered at the thought of the fresh meat. She stuck her feet into the boots and scooped up the fish. Wind blew wisps of hair across her mouth. She brushed the strands away.

"There are *desgastas* living in the city, now," she said. "Ten moved there from the camp."

"More than ten. I watch, I keep count. They move in behind those walls because they think there will be a cure any day now. They forget the mistakes of our great-grandparents, the mistakes that made us what we are." He passed a hand in the air before his unblemished face.

"Is there a cure?"

"Do I know?" Grizwald arched his shoulders, spread his hands, and laughed. "Ask me about the sea, ask me about the grass. You want to know about science, ask Jesse Grange."

"I will," Robin decided, thinking of Anderson's bitter eyes.

"Fine," Grizwald said. He threw his arms around Robin's shoulder, pushing her gently away from the sea. "And now you should run home, before the rain starts to fall again."

Robin followed his finger to the clouds in the sky and saw that once more they had gone black and cold.

On the way back to the city gates, Robin passed the *desgastas* camp. Rain had already begun to fall in big wet drops that hit the pavement and scattered. The camp was silent, the tents tightly secured, but Robin wasn't alone in the storm.

A *desgastas* child played at the edge of the camp. The little girl looked barely out of diapers. Her curly brown hair was

caked with dirt and her plump cheeks puffed in concentration. As Robin approached, the girl scooped up a handful of
mud and rubbed it across the edge of the highway. Painting,
Robin thought, remembering her own artistic mud baths.

"Hello," she said when the girl peered up at her boots.
"Shouldn't you be somewhere dry?"

The child laughed and held up a handful of dripping
muck. It was then Robin saw the sores running across the
little girl's forehead. One of the wide brown had swollen
nearly shut and the second was already beginning to tear
bloody mucus.

Eaten, Robin thought, and rocked back on her heels in
horror. This was something she had never seen before, this
death in a babe's eyes. The child was too young to be so finally ill. Anderson hadn't been exaggerating.

"Michelle!" A *desgastas* woman broke from the circle of
tents and flopped through the mud. She gathered the laughing child close and glared at Robin. The rage in the line of
her mouth was very clear. Robin immediately backed away.

The woman pulled her child against the sway of her
heavy skirts and began to shuffle back to the camp. The
child clung to her mother's hand, but she looked back once
at Robin and wiggled chubby fingers.

Speechless, Robin stood in the rain, clutching her fish.
Her dinner no longer appealed. The little party she had
planned seemed foolish. The Keeper's disease was alive,
even here, living on the edge of Jesse's mythical city. Yet
death had changed. Now it killed off entire families in one
quick swoop. And it ate even the young.

Shaken, Robin turned from the *desgastas* camp and went
in search of Jesse. The rain washed ash into her face as she
passed smoldering piles of garbage. Once she slipped on the
wet highway and dropped her dinner. She kept to her feet
and ran on, the fish bruised and forgotten, left behind in the
grip of the storm.

8

Jesse sat waiting for Robin when she finally climbed up the front steps of his house. He slouched in the foyer on one of the tiny ivory stools he kept about for guests and watched as she left dried mud scattered across the marble floor of his entrance hall. She shivered when he stood and she paused on the threshold. She could hear Isabella laughing in the kitchen, and she could smell the thick spices that usually announced Atlass's presence. She hoped the two were busy preparing dinner. She didn't want them to see Jesse's disappointment.

Jesse frowned at Molly's rubber boots, and reached out to pinch the dirty silk of her shirt. He wore one of the white cotton uniforms he used in the lab. As always, he looked freshly bathed and free of stains. He lived as an icon in his city, forever held above reproach. Robin wondered if he remembered scrubbing dishes in Harold's dry sink or scaling malformed fish in the kitchen of his brother's House.

"Where have you been?" he asked at last. Robin watched as he ran a hand over his skull and she was absurdly amused. He had cropped his hair again in the manner of scientists and politicians, but she thought he missed the drape and warmth of long hair.

"Outside," she answered his question with a shrug.

"Outside the city."

She nodded once. Jesse turned his back to her with a sigh. Robin sat on the stool he had vacated and began tugging off her boots.

"What were you doing outside?" he asked the wall, massaging the back of his neck. She saw that his hand was shaking.

"I went to see the camp," Robin said. "I wanted to see the people."

"Why?"

"They are *desgastas*," she said, immediately defensive. "They're my people. I guess I wanted to see if they were like me."

"Of course they're like you. Every single one of them. You cut your teeth on their dogma."

"So did you," Robin pointed out as she pulled her right boot free. Her bare foot was grimy, made brown by dried mud. She wiggled her toes and flakes of dirt fell to the marble floor.

"I did." Jesse turned around and Robin got a good look at his face. There were pouches beneath his eyes and his skin appeared gray in the light of the foyer. She searched for signs of Harold but couldn't find any resemblance at all.

"Why did you go?" she asked. "Why did you leave the House and the shore?"

A wry smile wrung his lips. "Three months. Four? You've never asked me that question. Why now?"

Robin shed her last boot and crossed her ankles, rubbing shin against shin. "I won't abandon my people."

"As I did?" Jesse arched a brow. "You're only a child."

"So were you."

"I was a grown man," Jesse said. "An adult. I knew what I wanted."

"Fame and *pesos*." Robin scratched a muddy wrist. "Harold said you hated being poor."

"I hated watching my family dying on that shore. I hated sitting by while the Keeper did nothing."

Robin shook her head. "You were never one of us. You never understood."

Jesse's green eyes flashed. "Harold's little echo. Do you have a thought in your head my brother didn't birth?"

Robin ground her teeth and looked at her hands. Splotches of mud blackened her fingernails, turning the pale ovals dark.

"The men and women in the camp think there's a cure," she said at last, when some of her rage had lessened.

"There is no cure."

"Grizwald said you might—"

"There is no cure," Jesse repeated, his words clipped. "Do you think I would hoard such a miracle? Do you think I would keep it from my brother? There is no cure. I thought I had one, long ago, with the Mark. Instead I sold this city a fancy way to separate the diseased from the lucky...." He waved a hand, as if dismissing his creation, dismissing the controversy. "Born *desgastas*, die *desgastas*, just as your Keeper said."

And that was all. Before Robin could speak another word, Jesse left her. He slipped away across the hallway as though afraid of Robin's expression. She heard Jesse greet Isabella, and laugh with his lover, and she knew that he would stay safely in the kitchen until she picked up her boots and left the foyer.

So she sat a while longer, just to be contrary, while she remembered the bags of weariness beneath Jesse's eyes and wondered.

The next morning Robin woke before the sun. She clambered over the side of her huge bed and pulled new silks from her closet. She dressed leisurely but kept an eye fixed out the running window on the dawn, determined to be away from the house before Jesse stirred. The plush carpet made her movements soundless and light as she crossed from the closet to the bathroom.

The third floor bathroom matched Robin's suite perfectly. Pale marble cupped a deep bathtub and swirled along the wall into a shelf and basin. The towels Jesse provided were as snowy as the tile floor, but early in her stay Robin had gone hunting for more colorful terry cloth. Now the linens hanging on hooks along the marble walls were fuzzy and bright.

The rubber boots stood upright on the bathroom sink, drying in the recycled air. Robin had washed them in the basin the night before, scrubbing the black rubber until the last of the mud ran down the pipes and disappeared. The boots shone beneath the bathroom lamps, Robin doubted they had ever been so clean before. She touched the pair and found that overnight the boots had stiffened as they dried.

When she bent over the basin she caught the reflection of her face in one of the many bathroom mirrors. For some reason, Jesse seemed to love mirrors. Reflective surfaces populated his home, from the shiny industrial appliances in the kitchen to the full-length mirrors in the bathrooms. Robin wasn't sure what Jesse saw when his reflection looked back at him from the walls. Her own face, blinking from the depths of a bathroom looking glass, was pale and stubborn. She had forgotten just how pointed her chin was, and how her pale hair could grow into a wild tussle if not trimmed appropriately.

Harold had kept a tiny pair of scissors in a cupboard in his House and had used them regularly to cut Robin's hair. The shearing of her locks had become a monthly ceremony, a renewal. She remembered how the Keeper had tossed the trimmings into the air, letting the ocean breeze take the bits of floss where it would.

Now Robin let the locks hang free in her face. The strands tickled her cheeks and brows, but she wasn't quite ready to go in search of scissors. She would let it grow a while longer, and when she finally found the courage to shorten her locks, she would make the shearing her own ceremony and take the clippings out of the city to the sea.

She washed her face, splashing water over the edge of the basin, and scrubbed the mud from beneath her fingernails. By the time she sat on the bathroom floor to tug on her boots the cuffs of her blouse were soaked, but she felt clean, fresh, and awake. The chill of the water had chased the last bit of sleepiness away.

Robin left her suite stealthily, trying to walk as quietly as possible. The carpet muffled her steps when she walked the third floor, but she hesitated once she reached the stairway. The marble steps were dull in the early morning light, but she knew they would echo with the clunk of her boots.

She inched her way down three floors, clutching the cold banister as she went, and had almost made it safely to the foyer when she saw Atlass. The big man watched her from the bottom of the stairwell, eyes narrowed, and his mouth hard beneath his broken nose. A robe of matte silk hung across his broad shoulders and dropped to his knees. Robin thought he looked forbidding until she saw the tiny silk slippers on his feet, and then she had to laugh.

"They're Jesse's," Atlass growled. "I couldn't find my own without turning on the light."

"Your heels are hanging way out the backs," Robin said. She allowed herself to clunk down the last two steps until she reached the foyer. "Are you sure you won't tear them?"

"A little early for class, isn't it?" he countered. "What are you doing up before the sun?"

"The sun's on its way up. And you know I don't attend the college anymore."

"I like to pretend," Atlass said. "It makes me feel better. I don't like to think of you running about this city with no supervision and too much time on your hands."

"I'm not a child."

He made a face and lowered the palm of one hand several feet until it rested on the crown of Robin's head. "You've got some growing to do before I can call you an adult. Where are you going?"

"Just for a walk."

"Inside the city walls, I hope?"

Robin nodded.

"Good," Atlass said. He tucked both hands back into the folds of his robe and turned toward the kitchen. "Be back for lunch and we'll have something to eat before I go to the shop."

Robin watched him shuffle across the marble in the undersized slippers. She opened her mouth, and then shut it again. Atlass stopped as though he had heard and looked back over his shoulder.

"Someone has to look after you," he said, answering the unasked question.

"Nobody bothered before," Robin retorted.

"No?" Atlass raised one eyebrow, a habit he must have picked up from his lover. "Who put that medallion around your pretty neck? Who kept you safe, as an infant, on that empty shore? Who kept you fed as a child, who kept you warm and safe? Why else would your Keeper have struggled to live so long, if not to look after you?

"Now it's Jesse's turn," Atlass went on. "But I'll carry the ball for a while, until he's ready."

"I don't need it," Robin said, irritated.

"You do," Atlass said, limping to the kitchen. "Be back by lunch time."

Robin gritted her teeth and glared at the big man's spine, but he ignored her. She waited until he disappeared into the kitchen, and then she turned and stomped as quietly as possible to the front door. The door scraped across marble when she pulled it open. She paused, looking back into the foyer, hoping she hadn't been heard. But the building remained quiet but for the slight rattle of pots and pans in the kitchen.

Robin lingered for a moment, listening to Atlass's comfortable noises. A spark of sudden humor eased the tension in her throat. She wondered, for just a moment, what it would have been like to grow up in Atlass's care, fed regularly and teased often. She lingered for a breath and then shut the front door and hurried away from the white building.

The President's palace grew from the very middle of Carpenteria, piercing the horizon until the spire was lost in the morning glare. At night, man-made light colored the very tip in oranges and purples. Robin was reminded that beauty faded beneath the harsh glare of the sun. The tower rose straight and white and proud. She approached the edifice cautiously until she neared the wall that looped around the palace spire.

This barrier seemed to be an exact replica of the circle locked around the city itself. Robin edged along the sidewalk until she could reach out and touch a curve of the wall. The wall felt cool beneath her fingers, and was perhaps half as tall as the original. Trailing her hand along its surface, Robin followed the swell around the tower until she found the palace gates.

And here again she discovered another replica, a smaller version of the city portcullis. Yet here no city guards waited and when Robin touched the latch she saw that it was only decoration and immovable. The palace gates, she realized, were not meant to open.

She leaned against the bars and peered in at the spire. Sunlight had begun to trace the length of spire. Robin couldn't find any windows in the smooth surface. The president, like his people, lived shuttered away from the world.

Grass grew between the portcullis and the palace in an extensive lawn that echoed the curve of the wall. Robin could smell damp on the vegetation, and in the distance she thought she could make out bright flowers and dwarf trees. Gardens?

Then she blinked and gripped the bars in her fists. People walked among the flowers and trees, a group of four. She could make out the flutter of their silks and the movements of their hands. Two women, she decided, noting the paint on their faces, and two men.

Uneasy, Robin looked away, and then back, and then away again. When she swiveled away from the palace for the third time, she saw that she wasn't alone on the sidewalk. A cityborn youth slouched behind her on the pavement. As she watched warily he stepped forward and peered over her shoulder.

"What do you see?" he asked.

"People," Robin said, staring now not at the lawn but at the young man. She recognized his face, she thought, and the deep blue dye in his short hair. A student, she remembered at last, and swallowed her annoyance.

"In the gardens?" the student asked. Apparently enthused, he brushed past Robin and pressed himself against the portcullis.

Robin hung back and let the youth look his fill. After a moment, he tore his gaze from the lawn and smiled at Robin.

"Sometimes he comes out, in the afternoons," the student explained, as though determined to make Robin feel his excitement. "He doesn't seem to notice us, but I'm sure he pays attention."

"Us?" Robin asked.

The young man pointed a slender finger away from the gates. Robin turned and saw a knot of students standing down the street, grouped closely together on the pavement. They held banners of silk over their heads, but Robin couldn't read the words painted on the fabric.

"What are they doing?"

"Protesting," he said. Light glittered off the dye in his hair. "In the name of the *desgastas*."

Robin crossed her arms and frowned across at the group of students.

"My name is Martin," the youth said. When Robin glanced back around he was eyeing the *tronera* at her neck. So he knew who she was. Maybe he remembered her face from the college, but even if he hadn't, he certainly knew her medallion.

"There is a cure, in there, you know," Martin said his expression now grown earnest. "They keep it in the palace so it won't get into the streets."

"*Who* keeps it?" Robin challenged. She supposed she seemed young and foolish in billowing silks and borrowed boots. She felt a long way from Harold's shore, a very long way from the life she understood.

"See?" Martin pushed himself against the portcullis again. "There — the two women in the garden with him. Do you see?"

"A man?" Robin asked. She stepped a careful distance away from her eager companion.

"President Harlan," Martin hissed, nudging after. "Jeff Harlan. He's the tall skinny one in the red silks. You can see the top of his head from here." The student reached out and grabbed Robin's arm. Before she could protest he yanked her close. "And see the two women next to him? In blue and in gold, there. Those are the Sayers sisters. Their family funds every lab in the city. Jesse Grange works for them. He developed his first Mark with their money. They made him the city hero. Some say he's their pot of gold, others say he's their puppet."

He glanced at Robin as if surprised to discover her silks in his hand. When he released her, she backed quickly away until the bars of the false portcullis dug into her ribs. She thought she should run, but she could not quite turn away from the youth's passion.

"The cure belongs to the Sayers family," Martin said. "They hired the men to do the research, they hired the men to produce it. And now they keep it locked away, because they don't want to give it out. And they use it to keep Harlan under their thumb. He's a good man, he helped to make this city what it is, but he's growing old now and leaning more and more on others." He bent along the bars, leaning over Robin until she could smell the meat on his breath. "The sisters won't give it out because they want the *desgastas* eaten into extinction. Why cure Bruster's when you might let the diseased die out instead? That's how the Sayers sisters think."

Robin studied the figures on the palace lawn. She couldn't make out distinct faces, but she saw the way one of the two vibrant women reached across to take the president's arm. And she saw the way Harlan folded his spine so that he could lift the woman's hand to his lips.

"Carpenteria belongs to the Sayers family," Martin said, looking out over the top of Robin's head. "If not in word, then in deed."

"What does that mean?" Robin turned from the lawn and scowled up at the student.

"I've seen it," Martin said. "And now it is time to do something. The *desgastas* don't belong out there, squatting in the mud. There's no reason to keep them exiled. Their cure exists! They can live amongst us."

Robin snorted. "The *desgastas* out there are self-exiled. They won't enter the city because they won't take the Mark. We distrust technology, Martin. Those people are out there in the mud because they won't let the Mark be put into their bodies. They remember our oldest stories, they stick to the old ways. Technology made us what we are, gave rise to Bruster's, and poisoned our land, so now we live away from it."

"You're here," Martin replied. He nodded at her *tronera*. "And there are others. They just need a little help, a little encouragement. They don't belong out there."

"And they won't pass through the city gates," Robin argued. "As long as the Mark is required."

"Not even for a cure?"

"Not even for a cure," Robin said, although in her heart she wasn't sure.

"All right," Martin lowered his voice. "And what if the Mark wasn't required? What then?"

"Don't talk foolishness." Robin was beginning to tire of the student's game. "Even I know the cityborn wouldn't allow such a thing."

"The cityborn won't have a say," Martin smiled. He lifted a hand to touch the gate and Robin saw that his nails were capped with gold. The flash of sunlight off the tips of his fingers made her shiver.

"What?" She scoffed to muffle her unease. "You'll sneak my people into the city, one at a time, in the dark of night?"

"Don't laugh," Martin warned. "It might be done. There are not so many of you that it is impossible."

But Robin did laugh. She couldn't help herself. And just so easily fear vanished beneath the youth's puffed self-importance.

"You are cityborn," she pointed out. "You wear the Mark. You have nothing to lose. Stop playing games."

She could smell his breath again, and his eyes above hers were manic. "It's not a game. I've seen."

"Seen what?" Robin laughed again.

"There *are* unMarked *desgastas* in the city," Martin murmured. "Under the city. UnMarked, unlicensed, *desgastas* kept in cages beneath Carpenteria."

"What are you talking about?" Her amusement fled.

"They've kept them there for years. Adults, children, it doesn't matter. They take them while they're still free of signs, and they lock them in tunnels beneath the city."

"I don't believe you."

"Believe it," Martin spat. "How do you think they developed their cure? They needed test subjects, didn't they? They needed them enough that they'd risk bringing unlicensed souls into their precious Carpenteria. Because if they were licensed, or Marked, then people would begin to wonder, where did those *desgastas* families go? And if any *Desgastas* go missing from the camp, who's to care but a few helpless souls? There's nothing the *desgastas* can do from outside the city walls, no one here will listen to their stories. It's a perfect setup. So the govs smuggle in one or two at a time, and they're still down there. They die down there."

"I don't believe you!" Robin said again, but this time her voice cracked.

"Then I'll show you," Martin promised. "If that's what it will take." And he took her arm, pulling her away from the palace walls.

Along past the city center Martin ducked into a side street, a white alleyway with no destination. The street ended a few feet away from its mouth where it fetched up against the back of a building. Martin stopped against the building, feeling along the smooth white wall. Robin waited, skeptical, until the student whooped under his breath.

"What?" Robin took a step along the pavement.

"Sometimes it's hard to find. It blends into the side of the wall. City magic. But I've found it."

"What?" Robin asked again.

Martin moved slightly, revealing a dark gap in the white wall. A hole, Robin saw, cut as a square into the building. Thick shadows gathered beyond the opening.

"Service tunnel," Martin explained. "Once you've found the grate, the rest is easy. Come on."

"Where does it go?"

"Down," Martin giggled. He rolled his eyes at Robin's expression. "This city was built upon another, you know. And that one over a first. There are tunnels beneath Carpenteria, tunnels and sub-basements and old cellars. Some new construction, too. The Sayers family built their labs beneath the palace."

"Is that where you're taking me?"

"No." He put a leg over the lip of the square hole. The lower half of his body sank into blackness. He held out a hand, beckoning. "There are finger- and footholds along the shaft. They're deep enough, but be careful."

Martin seemed to slip a little bit, his shoulders jerked, and then he began the climb into shadows. Robin linked her fingers together, and then tossed her head when she found her hands were shaking. Swallowing a breath of morning air, she squared her spine and approached the hole.

The sunlight painted only a few inches into the square. Robin could see the rough edges of the shaft and the handholds Martin had mentioned. Spaced evenly, the carved rungs dropped into the depths.

"Coming?" Martin's call echoed along the shaft.

Robin didn't reply. She swung her left leg over the edge of the hole, fumbling with the toes of her boot until she found purchase. After that it was easier. The handholds were sturdy and evenly spaced. As Robin's eyes adjusted the darkness eased until she could see down into the distance beneath her feet. The shaft fell twenty feet or so, and she thought she could make out a dirty floor at the end of the shaft.

Martin waited at the bottom. He grasped Robin's shoulders when her boots scuffed dusty concrete, and held her until she steadied.

"This way," he whispered. He gripped her wrist, pulling her on.

The dusty room was small, square as the service shaft. Long tubes of blue flashed along the ceiling, giving off a very small amount of light. Under the weak illumination Robin could make out metal shelves in one corner of the room and wooden barrels in another. The space appeared raw, as though cut from the earth and then shored up with concrete. There was no sign of the white city pavement.

"Along here," Martin said, still tugging. There were two doors in the farthest corner of the room. Martin chose the second.

Concrete disappeared and the walls were now packed earth. Robin could smell the wet in the soil. More blue tubes lined the ceiling. The bulbs appeared to grow out of the dirt itself. The light was still faint, and Robin felt somehow more secure if she kept one hand trailing along the soil walls. Dirt crumbled and fell beneath her fingers, but the walls held.

"Dug out years ago," Martin said. "Maybe decades. Can you imagine the machines they must have used?"

Robin couldn't. She walked at Martin's back and thought she could pick up the scent of sea salt beneath the rich taint of loam. She wondered if the old passageways could possibly extend as far as the seashore.

The tunnels twisted and doubled back. Once Robin thought Martin was leading her in circles. Three times the student turned into a new passage, or picked a second branch. The tunnels all looked and smelled the same. In one rough corridor the light tubes failed and they stumbled on in the dark, but eventually they walked again beneath bulbs that worked and Robin could see again.

When Martin stopped, Robin nearly knocked her chin on his back. His hand squeezed her wrist, and suddenly she knew he was afraid.

"Here," he said, the words jumbled on a breath. "In here. Go see."

"What about you?"

"I've seen it once," Martin said. Robin felt him shudder. "This is for you. Come around."

The tunnel ended at a closed door just beyond Martin's chin. The door was wooden and bound with straps of leather. The dirt walls seemed to slant around it. Robin touched the wood. The door cracked open.

"Go on," Martin urged. "I'll wait here."

Robin pushed the door and more light flooded the tunnel. Here illumination was stark and white, the kind of hard glow provided by city technology. Squinting her eyes against the brilliance, Robin stepped out of Martin's tunnel and through the door.

A cellar, she thought, *or an old storage room.* The walls were city material, but the floor was concrete and she could still smell the dirt of the tunnels. The old light tubes had been replaced by new panels of sterile white. The beams from the panels cut everything down to size and sculpted the dimensions of the room.

Robin picked out a table in the middle of the room, and a row of chairs against one wall. The table was city furniture, but the chairs were rusted metal. Another table, high and rectangular, lay in the shadows just to Robin's left.

One end of the old cellar had been restructured. Cages lined the back wall, cages of seamless white bars. The cages rose from floor to ceiling, breaking the back of the room into small cells.

Robin approached the bars slowly. Halfway across the room her knees began to buckle, and she stumbled, stirring up puffs of dust. She dropped to her knees on the concrete, spreading her palms on the floor, and stared into the first cage.

The *desgastas* in the cage glared back without recognition. Blisters obscured most of the young woman's face, and beneath a flop of long, dark, hair her eyes were dull. Robin crawled forward. The woman shifted slightly in her cage, revealing more blisters along the graceful curve of her throat.

Robin stopped, still on her knees, and gaped. The woman wore no *tronera*. Her eaten throat was free of jewelry. Had the cityborn taken her medallion, taken away her badge of faith? Robin crept forward again until she reached the bars of her cage. Only then did she understand.

The young woman wasn't *desgastas* after all, but cityborn. She wore the expensive silks of a Lady, and her long fingernails were still gilded with fading color. Her left palm lay open against her thigh, and just below the joint of her thumb Robin saw a faded Mark. The pattern was almost lost beneath the scars on her dark skin, but Robin could still see that the Mark itself had turned black.

Martin had been wrong. The diseased woman had never been born *desgastas*, Robin could feel the truth in her gut. She knew, without a doubt, that the people locked behind bars were all cityborn.

Robin wrapped her fingers around the bars of the cage and pulled herself upright. The cityborn Lady didn't move. Slowly, afraid of what she might find, Robin walked from cage to cage, staring in beyond the bars. She counted ten such prisons, some smaller than others. Each cage had a tenant, some cages had more than one. There were adults and children; in one prison a group of five children huddled together. Robin wondered if they were a family.

Each inmate showed signs of Bruster's. The stages varied, but the disease was there. And every thumb Robin could glimpse wore a blackened Mark.

All of the imprisoned were cityborn. There wasn't a *desgastas* among them.

Robin wandered back along the line of cages until she reached the first cell. The young woman's eyes had drooped shut. She appeared to be asleep. Robin could hear the Lady's lungs strain and whistle each time she took a breath. Bruster's had reached her organs.

"Lady?" Robin whispered through the bars. "Lady? Shall I free you?"

She heard a thin squeak from across the room, Martin protesting from his place in the tunnel. Robin ignored him. She wriggled a small hand between two of the bars.

"Lady?"

The young woman's eyes flashed open and she twitched as though slapped. Her head came up, eyes wide, the whites stained black. Her mouth opened, stretching horribly. Her teeth were rotted, but it was the ghastly oval of her mouth that made Robin cry aloud. The disease had somehow changed the cityborn, stretched her skin until her bones appeared malformed.

The Lady came to her feet with feral grace and lunged at the bars. Robin jerked her hand away just in time. The woman's arms were overlong, her fingers twisted into claws beneath her painted nails. Her hands came through the bars, and Robin had to jump back to avoid being caught by those eerie fingers. In the background, she thought she heard Martin shriek.

Robin backed away from the bars. Then she forced herself to stand and watch, to note the inhuman hunger in the woman's eyes, to witness the way the muscles in the Lady's face bunched and shivered beneath the scars of healed blisters. The woman threw up her head and screamed once, and then again. Robin saw now that behind the curtain of beautiful hair the woman's cheeks were too long and too prominent.

Then, abruptly, the life went out of the young woman and she collapsed into a boneless heap in one corner of her cell. As Robin stared, the Lady wrapped long arms around her knees and hid her face in her thighs. She muttered wordlessly to herself, and coughed, and when she subsided Robin could hear her lungs still bubbling.

"Robin!" Martin stuck his head around the door. His whisper hung on the air and then quavered. "They've heard. Someone's coming!"

"What do you mean?"

"They're coming along the tunnel. I can hear them. If we run now, we'll make it. Come on!"

But Robin had found the latch on the cell. It nestled between the bars, a tiny thing without a keyhole. She touched the bolt with a finger, wondering if the cell could be opened.

"Robin!"

She ignored his calls until too late. She fumbled with the latch, thinking she might somehow free the poor souls beyond the bars. Then the tunnel door swung wide and footsteps scraped against the concrete. Robin turned slowly, steady despite the pounding in her heart.

Jesse held Martin's forearm in his left hand, and a child's wrist in his right. Martin struggled. His eyes rolled in his head and his mouth worked soundlessly. Robin ignored the student and looked at the child.

A cityborn toddler, dressed in silks and slippers. He hung like a dead thing in Jesse's grip, but his eyes were wide and aware. Eyes that were blue against black, and still lovely, but Robin couldn't find a shred of sanity anywhere in their depths.

"Robin," Jesse breathed. The creatures in their cells muttered at the sound of his voice.

"Let me go!" Martin wailed. He scraped at Jesse's shoulders with his free hand.

Jesse relaxed his grip and the student fell free. Martin cowered for a moment on the concrete, and then he was up and running. He lurched across the cellar and into the mouth of the tunnel. Robin waited, listening to the muffled sound of Martin's desperate footfalls, until the tunnel was silent again.

"Is that one of them?" Robin asked, staring again at the toddler.

"One of whom?" Jesse asked. Robin thought he was trying to sound pleasant, but at the end of each word his teeth snapped audibly together.

"One of your experiments?"

"What are you talking about?"

"Is he normal, then?" She bent forward at the waist and held out a hand to the child. "He's not *desgastas*."

"Robin, wait—"

The child snuffled at her hand. He hissed between his teeth and then darted at her fingers. Jesse yanked the boy back, but not before Robin saw the strange seams along his jaw, and the lumps beneath his skin.

She drew away. Jesse held the boy close to his side. The Keeper's brother watched Robin carefully.

"He knows me," he explained after a moment. "He doesn't like strangers."

"He's inhuman. What have you done?"

"Nothing," Jesse said.

"They're infected. All of them. Is it Bruster's? What is it doing to them?"

His eyes narrowed to green slits, and Robin remembered his face waiting beyond the gates of Carpenteria. He had been so sure, then, that she would enter his city. What did he expect her to do now?

"Don't be afraid," he said gently, and reached out. Robin saw his hand coming, saw it about to close around her wrist, just as his other locked the child against his thigh. She jumped back and his fingers grasped only air.

"Robin."

The child whimpered and in the cages the cityborn shifted and moaned in answer. Jesse's chin came up. His gaze fastened on the second of the cages.

"I don't have time to explain. This child needs to go back to his mother."

"Into the cage?" Robin kept her eyes on Jesse's face as she edged slowly away. "Why do you keep them locked up?"

"They need the security." Jesse led the boy across the concrete floor, approaching the second prison. "They're safe here."

"Not from you," Robin said as Jesse's hand fell upon the latch.

Jesse paused. His head came around in surprise. The child twitched against his side and began to wail. Answering cries rattled the cages. They were the cries of animals, the cries of the damned.

Robin turned and ran.

"Robin!"

But she knew he wouldn't come after her. He wouldn't release the child just to chase her down. And the howls of the cityborn were too immediate.

She flew past the wooden door and down along the tunnel. She couldn't remember the way back to the surface, and she lost herself twice before she stumbled over Martin. The student sat hunched against a crumbling wall, head bowed. He looked up when she approached. Robin saw the horror on his face.

"It's just me," she said. "Take me back."

Silent and pale, he took her elbow and led her through the maze of tunnels. His fingers bit into her skin, but he didn't speak until they reached the service shaft.

"I didn't know. Dr. Grange!" He shuddered as Robin set her boot into the first handhold. "I didn't know."

"Who else?" Robin began to climb. The stretch of her muscles took her mind from the pain in her head. "You said he was their puppet."

"He developed the Mark," Martin protested. "He wouldn't—"

"He would," Robin interrupted. They climbed in silence until she reached city air.

It was afternoon above the ground, and the sun shone across white buildings, making Robin's eyes water.

"What will you do, now?" Martin asked, apparently bolstered by the sunlight. "Will you help us bring the *desgastas* in?"

"No," Robin said.

"But you have to. There was your proof. There is a cure. Your people need it! You have to convince them."

"No," Robin said again. She showed Martin her back and started down the alley. "I saw nothing of a cure. And the *desgastas* don't belong in a city such as this. Down there, in that cellar. That was our history. It's happening all over again."

"Where are you going?" Martin came after her, reaching. Robin dodged his hands easily.

"Away. Out of the city. To the camp."

"To live?"

Robin walked on.

"Fine," the student spat. "Go out there. Squat in the mud with your people. But you'll be back. The *desgastas* will come. You'll see. They want the cure. And when we show them what's been going on beneath the city, then they'll want more. They'll want revenge. You'll see."

Martin's cries quickly degenerated into whining. Robin tried to convince herself not to listen, but she thought she heard the ring of truth beneath his whimpering. The *desgastas* wanted to believe in a cure. Would hope be enough to bring them through the city gates? What if there was no Mark to keep them back? And what if they were told that lost *desgastas* were being tortured in the bowels of the city?

What if they believed the lie?

They would come for their own, Robin knew. The promise of a cure, the rumors of degradation, it would be enough to bring them through. And for what?

Terrified by the thoughts circling in her head, Robin began to run. She jogged on, through the city streets, past Jesse's home, past Atlass's cafe. She ran until she reached the city gates, until she passed her Mark beneath a guard's scanner and breached the portcullis.

Robin ran until the breath popped in her lungs, but in the end she arrived too late. The decision had already been made.

9

Two weeks after Robin disappeared from Jesse's home, the *desgastas* swept into the city from beyond the gates. They swarmed through the white streets, smashing windows and trampling many of the huge city ferns. The mob looted shops and overturned trash receptacles, leaving the spilled food and garbage to rot along the sidewalks. Isabella, who ventured out of the house only a day after the rush of violence, swore that they had dirtied or destroyed everything between the city gates and the palace. She returned home in tears, horrified by the new stink in the city. The *desgastas* had thrown garbage through the front door of her beloved university, and they had ripped the computer terminals from each cubicle.

"They just left the terminals lying there," the grocer's daughter stuttered. "They broke them because they could."

Jesse watched Isabella as she paced the room. He tried to feel anger. He wanted to be horrified by the careless contempt of the *desgastas*, but instead he kept thinking of Robin. He remembered the contempt on her face before she fled from him, before she had escaped his hidden cellar. The pretty silks Atlass had bought her hung forgotten in her suite. She hadn't even returned home before leaving the city.

And he didn't know whether she had gone to join the *desgastas* in their filthy camp, or whether she had found a way to return to Harold's shore. Either way, her absence worried Jesse.

Five afternoons later, Jesse stood on the porch of Atlass's ravaged restaurant and looked out across the soiled streets. He hoped that Robin had somehow made her way back to the House. She would be safer on that shore, beneath the gray sky. A week since the city gates had been breached and Carpenteria continued to suffer.

Jesse knew that the *desgastas* were living in the palace. He didn't know how Jeff Harlan fared. The palace was blocked off, the secret entrances Jesse had used so often closed for good. The students' doing, he supposed. The students had always known the tunnels in and around the old city. It hadn't occurred to Jesse to stop their exploration. Now he wished he had.

He didn't really know this new generation of college youngsters. He didn't know if they had helped the *desgastas* shatter windows and spread garbage. He was afraid they might have helped to murder the two young men who had tried in vain to close the gates. One of the guards had been brutally beaten, his bones broken before his throat was finally cut. Jesse had seen the body. The boy's battered face had made him sick.

He couldn't help but wonder how many similar murders had gone on behind the palace walls.

Most of his city hadn't decided what to think of the riot, but Jesse had heard many of the cityborn calling the *desgastas* rebels. Even if the city didn't understand the takeover, the people knew — in principle — who was behind it. He heard their whispered fears that the unMarked *desgastas* might contaminate Carpenteria. A few of the cityborn had even approached Jesse with their worries. They were afraid to drink city water, afraid to leave their homes now that their carefully guarded environment had been breached. Jesse should have known how to reassure the cityborn, but he couldn't dredge up the right words.

Footsteps crunched on the mucky sidewalk. Jesse glanced up, startled from his sluggish anxiety.

Atlass hopped from the street onto the porch. He shook black mud from his boots before stepping onto the newly scrubbed porch. Jesse eyed the big man's filthy boots and shook his head. The footwear that had been so unfashionable was now a necessity. Those few who wouldn't wear the rubbers now went barefoot through the garbage.

As if reading Jesse's thoughts, Atlass coughed and then smiled. "Lario Pete is making a mint selling these things out of the back of his shop. His register is overflowing with *pesos.*"

"Of course." Jesse turned away. He scowled into the empty shop. "Pete should be giving them away. Only cityborn merchants could spin gold from this mess."

Atlass shrugged and held out one of the two wooden brooms he carried. Wry amusement warmed his eyes. "I found these at the old antique shop down the way. They were the last. The shop mistress can't keep them on her shelves."

Jesse grabbed the broom and walked into the shop. Broken glass completely covered the hardwood floor. The shards glittered and danced even in the dim light. He found the blackest corner and bent over, sweeping slowly and methodically toward the outside light. Atlass stood in the doorway and watched. His face was expressionless, but Jesse could sense new worry in the big man's tense shoulders and sweating forehead.

"We're lucky none of the residential buildings have windows anymore," Atlass said after a moment. He crouched over his own broom and began sweeping glass to the center of the shop.

"Only vain shopkeepers stick to the tradition of glass." Jesse allowed his lover a smile. "Maybe now things will change."

"Never," Atlass snorted. "Not until they stop making the stuff."

Jesse chuckled sadly He kicked at a piece of blue glass that had stuck in the grain of the hardwood floor. Atlass growled and stood up. He rested his broom against a lopsided table before turning to face Jesse.

"They were asking at the antique shop whether they should dig out the old filters we ran before the Mark. And the breathing masks. Old Nancy Windlow is so afraid she's threatening to wash her husband and kids in bleach."

Jesse refused to look up. "A few unMarked *desgastas* living in the city won't make a difference one way or another. Tell your friends to stop holding their breath."

Atlass wasn't amused. "They're asking questions, Jesse. They're afraid."

"Of course they are," Jesse said. He plucked another shard from the wood and set it carefully on a table. "Tell them not to be."

"I try. They won't listen. They want to know what's happening in the palace. They want to know what's happened to the president."

Jesse looked up, saw the big man's unease, and smiled gently. "We'll find out soon enough."

"Isabella thinks there's been a misunderstanding. She thinks the students will straighten everything out in time."

"And what do you think?" Jesse asked softly.

Atlass shook his head. He returned to his broom, holding it between clenched hands. "I think you're right," he said, suddenly angry. "Those kids were behind the whole thing. They were bored, looking for a cause. They let the *desgastas* in—"

"And couldn't slow them down," Jesse said. "Their cause was too volatile. They made a mistake."

Atlass shook his head again, "Isabella doesn't want to see it."

"At least she isn't holed away in the palace," Jesse said. "She's unaware, for now. And she's safe."

"And Robin?" Atlass wondered.

"I don't know."

They swept for a moment in silence, bending every once in a while to pluck glass from the floor. Outside the shop winter began to drizzle. Where the wet touched the streets, garbage began to turn foul with mildew and rot.

"You may lose business," Jesse said, looking out at the dirtied pavement. "In fact, you probably will. People will be afraid to come out in this mess."

Atlass lifted one hand and shook his fingers at the torn coffee shop. "It might be better if things quiet down here for a while. I don't want to have to pay for new glass every other week."

Jesse laughed as he pulled a piece of colored glass from beneath his boot. He held the shard up to the failing light

and a rainbow fell from his hand to the floor. Atlass made
a startled noise, but Jesse ignored the big man's expression. He dropped the shard into a pile of broken glass.
Light rain misted through the shattered windows and
dripped into the mud. The water turned the trampled
streets into an ugly stew.

Jesse watched the drops fall for a moment longer.
Then, sickened by the sight of the filth, he went back to
his sweeping.

Later that evening Atlass bustled about Jesse's huge
kitchen while Jesse sat in the darkness of his study and
watched the city news channel as it scrolled down his terminal screen. Long ago, before the newsnet was much
more than entertainment for the rich, before the president
had equipped every household and apartment with a
smooth black screen, Jesse had tired of the glitz and glam-
our that made the nonstop broadcast such a hit. He had
modified his terminal and turned the video option off.
The pretty faces and the hi-tech graphics disappeared.
Instead, stark black and white words ran across his screen.
He couldn't do anything about the inane chatter that filled
the time between each news segment, but at least he
didn't have to watch the false smiles and cosmetic faces.

Atlass called Jesse's version of the news boring and
two dimensional. He had his own screen in the kitchen. A
bigger and more expensive version of Jesse's, Atlass's
screen would play the full-blown video and it was usually
on whenever the big man was home.

Isabella preferred Jesse's version. She told him that
many of her friends from the college were bored by the
colorful prattle and had adapted their terminals as well.

Jesse remembered his university days with fondness,
and he still found Isabella's eagerness amusing and fresh.
But he often wondered if she was as innocent as she
seemed. He began to think that she knew very well that
the damage to the city was the fault of the students, her
friends and classmates.

Sometimes he thought he caught a strange look in her
eye. He could not help but wonder if she might have had

a hand in the *desgastas's* freedom. But then he would re-member her grief at the violated college and change his mind. Still, Jesse sometimes feared that Harold had made a mistake in suggesting Isabella accompany Robin into Carpenteria.

He kept to his study, closed away from the fetid streets and alone with his thoughts. He watched the letters follow each other over the terminal and waited patiently. Through the newsnet he learned that Angie and Josie Sayers were being held in the palace, as were other high ranking govs and their families — husbands, wives, and children who had made their homes in the sumptuous spire so that they could be at Harlan's beck and call. Fifteen families, fifty cityborn in all. Jesse counted their names over and over again while he waited for news.

In the afternoons, in the hours between late lunch and sunset, when the streets were deserted of life, Jesse would leave his study and climb down into the bowels of the city. His labs were closed and locked, the shiny metal doors secured with a code he couldn't break. Again, he recognized the work of cityborn students. The *desgastas* had no such affinity where technology was concerned. Jesse spent many hours trying to convince the doors to open, yet the code held firm.

But Jesse had been a student once, himself. He knew the old tunnels as well as anyone. The labyrinths he had mapped as a young man remained fresh in his head. He got lost several times, but after two or three days of trying, Jesse made his way to the converted cellars.

The wooden door at the end of the old tunnel remained unlocked. The cellar itself looked untouched. The blue-haired boy knew of the room, and Robin certainly, but no one had come for Jesse's poor souls. He hoped that meant Robin had made her way from the city for good, but he didn't really know what to believe. Maybe it was simply that no one cared about his prisoners.

They waited for Jesse as if he had been away for months, rather than a handful of days. Their eyes were bright and feral, burning behind the bars of their cages. They muttered as he approached, whispering in their own nonsensical language, lost and inhuman.

They were in pain, Jesse knew. He saw it in their faces, in the set of their bones. One of the two youngest boys locked his stretched hands around the bars of his cell and howled until Jesse brought him the solace he needed.

Water. They sucked water down by the bucketfuls, as though they couldn't get enough. The old spigot in the corner of the cellar still worked, but it spat only a trickle, so Jesse spent most of his visit filling plastic buckets with the liquid. He carried the water from cell to cell, allowing the tortured cityborn to drink until they eased.

They wouldn't eat. The food he had left them on his last visit, and again before the *desgastas* had broken through the gates, lay untouched and rotting in each cell. Jesse fretted over their lack of appetite, but his prisoners appeared unharmed. They seemed content to subsist on endless mouthfuls of water. He began to think they no longer needed true nourishment.

Then he found the little girl, dead in the corner of the very last cell. She had been his first babe, handed to him just after she had reached her third month. Two years she had lived in his care, in his cellar, and she had been doing well. Before Jesse had journeyed to Harold's shore, before he left his children in Harlan's care, the girl had been lucid more often than not. Often, she had allowed Jesse to touch her. He liked to imagine she enjoyed the contact.

He had never given her a name, but in some secret part of his soul he called her Andy.

The little body lay curled in a small pile on the concrete floor of the cell. The cityborn Lady who had for a while been the child's surrogate mother seemed unaware of the death in her prison. The woman watched Jesse as he unlatched the cell and slid into her cage. Her eyes were clouded and glazed, distant. She slouched against the bars, nearly hidden in baggy silks, and sucked at the tips of her fingers. As Jesse passed, she whispered to herself, but the words were broken and nonsensical. Like most of the other cityborn prisoners taken by the disease, her mind had quickly broken and fled.

Jesse ignored the Lady and knelt by the babe. Stubble covered the child's head. Jesse stroked the soft fuzz. He had kept her skull shorn, intent on the changes and quakes beneath her cranium. Now the sight of her pale, misshapen skull brought tears to his eyes.

Jesse steeled himself and looked further, trying to find the cause of the child's death. Black fluid pooled beneath the body, but that in itself was not unusual. Jesse's lost souls coughed up gobs of the poison. They seemed to lose almost as much fluid as they sucked in. The volume of the black puddle was not unusual, not if the child had been sitting in one place for any length of time. Perhaps she had settled down, drifted off. Napped, and then died gently in her sleep. Perhaps her tortured body had simply given out.

Then Jesse's fingers found the dents on the child's chin, and around the base of her mouth. At first he couldn't believe it, but then he knew. Tooth marks. The child had been nibbled on while she lay on the cold ground. Here and there the flesh was torn. In one place the edge of her cheek had been gnawed down to the bone.

He glanced over his shoulder at the cityborn Lady, but the creature appeared asleep. Her horrible eyes were shut, her hands curled along her side. Her chest rose, and then stuttered, and then rose again. Jesse tried to think of her as she had been before her blisters peaked, before she lost her beauty, and her humanity.

He turned back to the babe and searched the whole of the little body thoroughly. Even so, it took him minutes to find the wound in the dim light.

Most of the child's left wrist had been torn away. Sharp teeth had snapped through artery and muscle, broken the warped bone. A killing wound, Jesse knew. Artery torn, the babe would have bled to death. But where was the blood? Except for smears of lung fluid, the little girl was dry and clean.

He searched the sleeve of her tunic, and found a spot of blood on the silken cuff, another near the shoulder. And that was all. The child must have bled copiously, but Jesse couldn't find any real evidence.

He looked again at the sleeping Lady, and suppressed a shudder. Jesse hoped she had killed the babe out of necessity, prodded by hunger because she could no longer stomach the meat he brought. He wanted to believe that her instincts had been pure, but he found he couldn't. She had torn the little wrist, nibbled briefly, and then let the child die. He wondered if the killing had been vicious. He wondered if the babe had been aware.

Jesse lifted the tiny body and carried it from the cell. The cityborn woman didn't look up when he stepped past her, nor did she open her eyes when he slid again through the cell door and secured the bars. Even so, he thought the Lady was aware, he thought she waited.

For the first time, as he set the dead child on a table in the corner of the room, Jesse trembled. He knew each of the twelve cityborn prisoners. He could feel the weight of their attention. They were lost, he understood, and mad, but for the first time he wondered if they retained enough humanity to realize their predicament and find him responsible.

He couldn't afford to worry. The cityborn here didn't have time for his fears. So he left his broken Andy alone on her table on the edge of the cellar and crossed to the old spigot, prepared to carry around the day's last dose of water.

Much later that same evening Jesse hid in his study, closeted away from the rain and alone with his thoughts. He watched the letters follow each other over the terminal and tried not to think of the dead child he had smuggled to the burning fields. The terminal scrolled endlessly, but Harlan's name hadn't shown up at all in the last three days. The silence made Jesse uneasy.

Somehow a city reporter had compiled a list of the *desgastas* holed up in the palace. Robin's name wasn't in the file, but Jesse wasn't reassured.

He touched a corner of the screen. The words running across the screen would be saved to his terminal. He would pick them apart at a later date. He didn't expect to find any real answers on the newsnet, but ingrained city habits kept him glued to the screen, searching for a miracle.

A sharp rap echoed along the marble walls, bouncing from the front of the house. Jesse looked up and away from the news, tilting his head in anticipation. The front door grated open. He half expected that it would be Robin, the prodigal returned home. Apparently Atlass hoped the same thing, because the humming in the kitchen stopped. Slippers scraped across the marble floor of the foyer. Jesse closed his eyes, listening to the soft sounds of the home he loved so well. Atlass stopped just outside the study. Jesse could sense his lover's warm presence through the door. The sudden rich smell of roast chicken, carried from the kitchen on the big man's hands, made Jesse's mouth water.

Atlass spoke and laughter answered. Jesse knew then that it wasn't Robin who had passed into his house. Robin rarely laughed. He had forgotten Isabella, out late at a seminar. Even terrified of the new city streets, the woman would not miss her schooling. He vaguely remembered telling her to be home before dark. He wondered that it had gotten late so quickly.

Opening his eyes, Jesse traced one finger across the smooth screen and listened. Closer now, nearly outside the door, Isabella laughed again. As always, the sound made Jesse smile.

"You're covered with chicken guts," the woman teased Atlass. "I could smell you from outside. Is dinner ready?"

"Almost." Atlass's voice was low. The man tended to be cautious when Jesse was in his study. "Did you have a good time?"

"Fair." Isabella fell suddenly sober. "We didn't talk much about anything but the *desgastas*."

"Ah," Atlass said. "I'm surprised there are enough young people left outside the palace walls to make up a seminar."

"More than enough," Isabella said. "We're not all so reactionary." She sounded briefly ashamed. "There are plenty of students who had nothing to do with the revolt."

"Only because they didn't have the courage to tromp along with your buddies and open the city gates," Atlass said. "In fact, I think I'm surprised you're still with us."

Jesse brought his finger to his mouth. He sucked on a knuckle, amused by the censure in his lover's voice. Atlass enjoyed Isabella's company, but the big man never hesitated to speak the truth as he saw it.

Outside his door, Isabella sounded surprised. "You think I belong there, in the palace. You think I should have helped open the gates, trash the city?"

"I didn't say that," Atlass huffed. "In fact, I'm not sure you weren't out there in the mud, that night. I don't care. Your choices are your own. If you choose violence, if you choose murder, so be it. Maybe you think the result is worth it."

"I would never choose murder," Isabella said, undaunted. "But I do think the *desgastas* deserve a chance at a normal life. A cityborn life."

Jesse frowned. He didn't like the fervent excitement in Isabella's voice, or the way her words thrummed. She had passion, he heard it even through the study door, and passion could be dangerous.

"They're saying that the govs have a cure. A real miracle," she said. "But the president is keeping it to himself."

"I wouldn't know the truth of the matter. And neither would you. You'd do better not to listen to rumors."

"If it's true, then the *desgastas* need a champion or two."

"But if it's not?" Atlass rumbled.

"*He'd* know, wouldn't he?" Isabella said after a moment. "Has he said anything?"

"No. And I haven't asked."

Isabella snorted. "I find that hard to believe. Underneath it all you're as curious as the rest of us. And just as worried."

"I'm only worried about him," Atlass said. "The rest of it can wait till later."

In his study Jesse was touched but cynical. He suspected that Atlass was trying to tell him something through the closed door. No doubt the big man was tired of watching Jesse fret.

"Where is he?" Isabella asked. "At the lab?"

"He hasn't been to the lab for weeks. Instead, he wanders the streets until nightfall." Atlass sounded disapproving and Jesse winced. "He's in the study reading the news and waiting for dinner."

"Oh," Isabella whispered, as if suddenly aware of the study door. "You'd better finish it, then. Can I help?"

Jesse listened as his family retreated to the kitchen, and then he turned back to his screen. The stream of words continued across the console, but Jesse looked beyond, startled by the reflection against the words. His face in the darkened glass stretched thin and sallow. He didn't remember his eyes being so wide. His hair was growing out again, but Atlass would shave it back to regulation length by the end of the week.

He sighed, rubbing at his eyes and longing for dinner. Maybe in the morning, after the sun rose, he'd go back to the cellar. Check on his cityborn and make sure they were still safely locked away from the turmoil above.

Jesse pulled his fingers from his eyebrows and was struck suddenly by letters on his screen. He sat up abruptly, leaning forward. There it was again, and again, and again. Finally the news had picked it up.

Jeff Harlan's name danced across the terminal in bold type. They were reporting news of the president at last.

For the second time in a day Jesse crossed out of Carpenteria to the burning fields.

The city burned in jewel tones beneath the dark of the sky. Only the President's Palace remained unlit, the pinnacle white and plain against the other colors. Jesse walked until he could see the rose glow of the city walls, until he could pick out the red flash of the portcullis, and then he had to stop and wait in line.

Other cityborn were leaving Carpenteria, traveling beyond the walls to see their president. For some it would be a first. Most cityborn Lords and Ladies were afraid to leave their city. They imagined the poisoned land outside Carpenteria was somehow catching. Jesse knew they weren't far from wrong. Now, curiosity urged the cityborn to bravery. Even the horrors they had heard about the land beyond wouldn't keep them back.

Each Lord and Lady wanted to see their beloved Jeff Harlan one last time. The man was a legend, and had in his youth been the heart of the city.

Jesse lingered in the line and thought about returning home. He had carried dead little Andy's body to the fields through the network of underground passageways. He could travel those tunnels again, later, and see the president without the crowds. He almost turned back.

But Harlan would lie in state for only a day. If all reports were true, the president's body was badly decomposed, and more than ready for burning. The president's physician, locked with the rest behind palace walls, had been allowed to issue a statement over the net. Harlan had been dead for several days, the physician wrote, and nothing could have been done to save him.

Two sentences. Jesse had read the message over and over, wondering who had closed the physician's mouth. The *desgastas*? Or cityborn students?

The line of mourners moved quickly. Jesse listened to the mutterings of the people around him. They believed their president had been murdered, Jesse realized. At first he thought it likely as well, but then he looked across the port-cullis at the cityborn returning from the other side of the walls, and he saw something different in their faces. Not rage, and not simple grief. The emotion Jesse glimpsed was something greater, something fierce. Fear, he thought, and horror.

He gave his hand to the guard at the gate, allowed the man to scan his Mark, and then he was through. The burning fields were past the abandoned *desgastas* camp, past the pile of smoking garbage. Jesse followed the crowd of cityborn until he found Harlan's body.

The president had been given his own pyre. The gaunt man lay stretched across his bed of logs, guarded by two men in military yellow. Jesse wondered briefly where the two men had come from, and who had arranged the President's body. Somehow, he had imagined that all the govs and military had been trapped in the palace with Harlan.

As Jesse edged through the crowd, he heard weeping. The president was beloved even in death. A soft-spoken man, he had managed to win the hearts of his people with his quick smile, his childish love of sweets, and the real affection he had shown each citizen in his city. President Harlan had loved the cityborn, and had done his best to make Carpenteria their haven.

Harlan had been Jesse's friend for many years, but Jesse could feel nothing of grief beneath the pounding of his own heart.

At last Jesse stood on the very edge of the crowd. If he rocked onto his toes, and tilted his chin, he could look directly into Harlan's face. What he saw made his stomach turn and his throat clench.

The president had been badly beaten. Bruises darkened his cheeks. Harlan's nose appeared shattered, and his skull broken in several places. He looked as though he had been through a war.

"The *desgastas*," a woman behind Jesse wailed. "The *desgastas* did this!"

Jesse ignored the woman's cries. Ducking from the crowd, he took four steps across the field and scrambled up Harlan's pyre. Cityborn gasped and cried out. The two men in yellow stepped forward, but Jesse held them still with one sharp word. He gripped the logs and pulled himself up along the small mountain of fuel until he could touch the president's face.

And there it hid, the blemish Jesse's eyes had picked out from among the scratches and bruises. A tiny bubble of fluid, the ulcer still bubbled below Harlan's ear, glistening on that one bit of unmarked skin. Jesse touched the sore. He had to be sure, he had to know.

The blister compressed beneath his finger, and thick fluid ran around Harlan's ear.

Bruster's.

Jesse clung to the pyre and searched Harlan with his eyes. Impossible to tell if there were more of the blisters. The corpse was badly marked in so many other ways, and the flesh was already beginning to decompose. Jesse couldn't tell if the blister had been the first, or the last of many. He couldn't tell if, beneath the shattered bones, Harlan's body had begun to change.

He searched out Harlan's left arm, then stretched up over the wooden pyre until he could examine the president's stiff palm. There, beneath the man's thumb, he found Harlan's Mark. The pattern had turned black beneath the skin.

Bruster's. In a man born clean. In a man who had never left Carpenteria in his life.

Jesse released the pyre and dropped to his hands and knees on the field. Cityborn hands reached out and helped him up. From all around, he could hear the sound of weeping. And from above, Harlan's dead eyes looked out over the walls of his city in mute accusation.

10

Early the next morning Jesse jammed the lock pad on the doors of the Sayers's underground warehouse and broke into his labs. The act was unthinkable, akin to murder. In Carpenteria, where cityborn remembered enough of the past to retain a strong fear of the unknown and unprocessed, privacy reigned supreme. Buildings were born without windows, walls were built to be unbreachable, and even city parks were designed with an eye towards inscrutability. Every door had a lock, and the people of Carpenteria treated the electronic pads with the outmost respect. Burglary was unthinkable, the act of a madman.

Even so, a lock that couldn't be bypassed could be broken.

The code that kept the underground laboratories closed was not impassable, but Jesse didn't have the time or the desire to fight that duel. Instead, fueled by a new urgency, he used a tiny mechanical pick to unscrew the number pad from the wall. The lock face fell easily into his hand, revealing a mass of clear wires. There were at least twenty of the strands, but Jesse had helped to build security in the city, and he knew how to take it down.

He yanked on the correct fiber, snapped it from the wall, and the lock jammed. The lights on the number pad flashed and then froze. Jesse set the pad on the ground and hurried to the metal doors. The panels grated against concrete, sticking, and Jesse strained against the handles. He didn't know how much time he would have. As soon as he'd jammed the lock, he knew an alarm had flared somewhere in the president's tower. In Harlan's time, the rare and unspeakable act of burglary would send the city police immediately in his direction.

Now, he didn't know what would happen. The alarm might go unnoticed, unreported. Or any police still in service could already be on their way.

Jesse was not a strong man, and the doors would only part sluggishly, and only slide so far. After a moment he lay still against one cold panel and trembled. He could see his distorted reflection on the metal surface. For ease he had dressed in the baggy linens of his lab uniform, and his gaunt reflection appeared lost in the material. He looked like a child, sweating and impotent.

Swearing under his breath, he attacked the doors again. The crack he'd managed to start widened by several more inches. At the last moment metal stuck on concrete and the doors refused to give at all. Jesse pressed his forehead against his fists, eyes closed, until the knots in his muscles relaxed. Then he went to examine the crack.

There was just enough space between the doors that a child might squeeze through. Jesse had been born as delicate as a girl, and over three decades later his bones were still small.

He blew out air until his chest went flat and his lungs began to protest. When he edged between the doors, linen caught on metal and tore. Jesse felt metal scrape his thighs. For a breath his skull stuck. Desperation hit and he squirmed, and at last he popped free.

The labs were black as night. Jesse waited until his lungs stopped rasping and he could hear past the thumping of his heart. Even after his body settled he waited, listening for company, but the room remained lifeless. He couldn't even pick out the usual thrum of his equipment.

"Lights," he said. The room responded.

Bulbs warmed and immediately Jesse could see the rows of shining metallic tables he so loved. The tables spread out in great armies before him, marching into the distance, dividing the warehouse into zones. When he'd first come to the city, scientists of every sort lived at the tables, stroking their machines, laboring to find answers. Later, Jesse had directed many of the same men. Now most of the tables sat bare. The huge room remained a monument, an unused reminder of lost hope.

Jesse's footsteps echoed as he walked down a length of table to his own station. He switched on his computers. At the familiar whir of machinery his heart eased. The light reflected from the screens washed his skin and torn uniform green. He touched the terminal, smearing his reflection, and waited for answers. He looked at the numbers released across the screen and inhaled in relief. Whoever had shut down the room and locked the doors had left his research intact.

Closing his eyes, Jesse clutched at the sharp edges of his table, waiting for the machine to finish gathering data. After am extended silence, the computer beeped a query. Jesse sighed. Then he opened his eyes, banished emotion, and went to work.

The deepest hours of the night he spent in his cellar, listening to the whistling breath of a dying child. The boy was not the youngest of Jesse's prisoners, but he was the newest inmate, and the disease had advanced very slowly through his small body. Although the child had lost most of his wits he had not yet become violent. Over the last few days the disease had begun to take its toll on the thin body, and when Jesse lifted the child onto the examination table, the boy wailed out his exhaustion.

"Hush," Jesse murmured. "I know the table's cold. It'll just be a moment." He looked into the swollen, tear-streaked face, and wished briefly that he had bothered to learn the boy's name.

The boy hiccupped. He coughed, expelling black liquid in a violent spray. Jesse sighed and cleaned the goop from the boy's face with the end of his sleeve. The child sniffled, brown eyes wide and lost. Jesse reached into the pocket of his lab coat and pulled out a packet of cookies stolen from Atlass's kitchen.

"They're sweet," he coaxed. He held up one biscuit, lifting the offering before the child's nose. The boy snuffled again and then snatched at the biscuit.

Taking advantage of the boy's distraction, Jesse quickly ran his hands over the child's skull, down his throat, under his armpits, and at last over bare knees, ankles, and toes.

The blisters on the boy's flesh had healed to scars, but the hair loss was just beginning. His irises were still clear, and the nodes in his throat and armpits were only slightly swollen, but lumps were already forming beneath the skin at the child's small joints and above his kneecaps.

Jesse glanced at his patient. The boy appeared more interested in tearing apart the sweet with his fingers than in eating. The cookie was almost down to crumbs. He passed the child a second biscuit, hoping to keep him distracted a while longer, and then bent over the boy's left knee. Jesse pushed gently into the joint until he was able to manipulate the fluid to build up around the kneecap. Then he reached into a pocket, fumbling around with one hand until he managed to free his depressor from the fabric of his coat. A glittering cylinder no longer than Jesse's index finger, the instrument was a hardier version of the syringes Jesse had worked with as a young man.

Holding the child's leg as still as possible, he set the depressor against the flesh of the boy's knee and squeezed the cylinder. The instrument popped. The child screamed. Jesse ducked the pummeling of small hands and held the depressor steady as long as possible.

The child's screams turned into a weary, hacking cough. Jesse straightened.

"Hush," he soothed. "We're all done. Hush." He slipped the depressor back into his pocket and stroked the boy's rough skull. "Do you want another cookie?"

But the child was beyond reach. He began to scream again and beat at the metal table with his hands and heels. Jesse sighed and stroked, and waited. An endless while later, the boy's cries turned to sobs, and then to broken wheezes. When the little body went limp and boneless, Jesse at last carried the boy back to his cell.

Jesse spent the next afternoon in his study, alone. He switched off the terminal and dimmed the lights. Restless and preoccupied, he wandered along the shelves that lined the study wall. He brushed fingers over ancient book bindings and old ROM cases, hunting. At last he chose a particularly tattered favorite. He carried the book to the one padded arm chair in the room and tried to squint through the gloom at the pages.

He couldn't read. His mind jumped around in circles, and the words blurred. He flipped a page and then flipped it back. He thought of leaving the book, returning to his desk, and reactivating the terminal. He didn't, but only because he was afraid of what he might find. So he paged back and forth through the novel, unable to be still.

When he'd rolled from bed in the early morning, Atlass had already been up and fretting. The big man had been reading messages from the newsnet, and the content had scared him. Intending to soothe his lover, Jesse had started his breakfast in front of the screen, scrolling through sentence after sentence. In the end, he had left the remainder of his meal untouched. He couldn't stomach the food.

Now, as he curled in his armchair, the frightening sentences danced before his eyes, imposing themselves across the print of his paper book. He squeezed the cover of the novel, trying to forget the whispers and the pleas for help.

Most of the messages had been posted overseas. Several were days old, the dated news on a net that ran faster than sound. There were horror stories from the Little Europes, from Asia, even from the small islands off the Balkan coast. From places that were supposed to be free of Bruster's, and clinically sterile. From metros that, forty years before, had been touted as havens, safe ports for the wealthy refugees who had fled Jesse's continent.

Maybe the privileged hadn't outrun their man-made plague after all.

Harold's *desgastas* had believed that the land remembered, that the poison would spread. Now Jesse was beginning to believe it had. Not even Harold, with his dour predictions and adhesion to the old traditions, not even he had imagined the disaster Jesse now envisioned as he huddled in his chair and tried to read his antique book.

Later, he heard the front door when Isabella came home for the night, and he started to life when she called a greeting. No answer was returned from the depths of the kitchen, so Jesse presumed that Atlass lingered upstairs somewhere, still worrying.

He heard footsteps up and down the hallway as the evening drifted away, but he recognized the tread and did not bother to break away from his thoughts or close the pages of his book. He rose once and crossed the room, stretching his spine and trying to ease knotted muscles, but he returned to his chair without opening or even approaching the study door.

He listened for a while to the harsh winter rain when it began pelting the walls outside.

The rap on the front door startled him, and Jesse's impatient heart quailed. He stood up and dropped the book onto the seat of the chair. He padded over carpet to the study door. The panel cracked open at his touch.

The hallway was empty. Jesse walked slowly, stepping carefully, and as he went he listened for sounds from upstairs. But he heard nothing, not even when the loud banging on the front door repeated

Jesse opened the door. Cold rain blew into the house. Usually Jesse liked the wet, but this new moisture was affecting the garbage on the streets. The smell made him gag. He pulled back, opening the door all the way, and looked into the night.

"Dr. Grange?"

"Yes?" Jesse said. He peered out at the storm until, between sheets of rain, he made out the shape of a man. A *desgastas* stood below the stoop. Trickles of water ran about his *tronera*, turning dull metal to shining silver.

"Will you come with me to the palace?"

"At this hour?" Jesse asked, although he wasn't surprised. He thought he knew why he had been summoned. His crime had been discovered, they must know of his presence in the Sayers's laboratories.

"Robin would like to speak with you, sir."

"Robin?" Jesse felt a thrill tickle his spine. Dread quickly followed, a sharper pain in his head. So she had thrown in with the rebel camp, and now she was as trapped as the rest.

"I'll come," Jesse said. "Just let me get my coat."

He ducked back into the study, stuck his head in a closet, and found his winter overcoat. He shrugged the floor-length canvas over his silks. He reached again into the closet, fumbling until he found his boots. Stripping off his slippers, he stepped into the rubbers and hurried back to the front door.

The *desgastas* had stepped in from the rain. He stood in the foyer, shaking water onto Jesse's marble floor. He glanced up when Jesse approached, and flashed a smile.

"Nice outfit, Gov."

"I'm a scientist, not a politician," Jesse snapped, irritated by the mirth on the man's mouth. "Are we ready?"

"Most important Lord in this city," the *desgastas* muttered, "and he dresses in a canvas raincoat." But he moved obediently into the storm. Jesse followed, pulling the door closed before trotting down the steps and into the street.

The rain and wind seemed to suck the light from city buildings, and Jesse soon felt lost. He frowned into the heavens, trying to find the palace spire, but the clouds were too thick, so he kept his eyes on the *desgastas* and his head bent against the chill. Coat and boots protected his body and feet, but the rain stuck Jesse's short hair to his head, and sliced at his bare hands. Each summer he forgot how nasty the cold seasons could be. Each year winter blew into the city with a vengeance, seeking to remind.

Cursing, Jesse hunched his shoulders and tried to keep up with his guide.

They reached the palace just as the storm blew itself out. The rain slowed to a trickle, and Jesse was able to make out the palace wall through the wind and night. The *desgastas* brushed his shoulder, demanding attention. Jesse nodded. They circled around to the back of the palace, and then stopped. Jesse rocked back on the heels of his boots and clicked his tongue, impatient. The *desgastas* didn't appear to notice.

The man ran gnarled hands over the wall, and then pulled a grate from the concealing white. More tunnels, Jesse knew, and followed the *desgastas* into the depths. He had to wait at the bottom of a ladder while the *desgastas* replaced his grate. Jesse took that moment to look around.

As a student he had longed to reach the deepest tunnels beneath the president's home, but had never found them. As Harlan's trusted friend, he had been introduced to one or two of the shortcuts beneath the city. He'd learned the way from the palace to the Sayers's labs. He knew the stretch of tunnels from the labs to his hidden cellar. As an adult Jesse had been too engrossed in his own work to wonder about the other secret ways that hollowed the ground beneath Carpenteria. He hadn't thought to investigate further.

Now, as he looked about, Jesse saw that the passage the *desgastas* had opened was more corridor than tunnel. Carpet ran the length of the floor. The walls were palace white, draped with colorful tapestries. Jesse guessed there were cameras hidden in the elaborate ceiling joints, and maybe other security measures as well. As an exploring student he would have been easily caught, and certainly punished.

"This way," the *desgastas* said. The man stumped down the corridor, grinding mud into the carpet. Jesse followed after. Fastidious, he wished his own boots weren't quite so filthy.

More twists and turns, more fancy tunnels, three staircases, and at last, a door.

"President's office," Jesse said, properly amazed. He had been to the office many times in the past, but never quite so effortlessly.

"Easy to find, if you know the shortcuts," the *desgastas* replied with a grin. "Go on in."

"Robin?" Jesse asked.

"Go in," the man said, smile still in place. He opened the heavy white door and waved Jesse through.

Jesse remembered the room. He'd always loved the neutral carpets, the bright wall hangings, and the heavy desk. Oak, he recalled, an antique. A massive chair crouched behind the desk, also an antique. Oak and leather, now the luxuries of the past.

Harlan had liked to greet Jesse from that chair. The president had loved to showcase his collection of priceless furniture. The man who waited for Jesse now ignored the chair and sat on the edge of the desk, as though comfortable against the unyielding wood.

"Jesse Grange," this second *desgastas* said. "Make yourself comfortable."

Jesse studied the man's face in silence. The man was large, taller even than Atlass, and old. Perhaps the oldest carrier Jesse had ever seen. Most men born with Bruster's in their blood didn't live into their fifth decade. Most were lucky if they reached forty.

"Do you remember me?"

Jesse turned his back on the desk. He understood by the light in the man's eyes that a game was being played. Jesse understood games, they were a cityborn way of life. And in Carpenteria, when games were played, Jesse made the rules.

Back still turned, Jesse shed his raincoat and hung it neatly over the carved cherry wood hat rack Harlan had treasured. He pulled off his muddy boots, one and then the other, and placed them deliberately on the very edge of the beautiful carpet. Then, barefoot and light as a child, he walked around the unyielding desk and sat in Harlan's leather chair, forcing the *desgastas* to shift position. Comfortably ensconced in the president's chair, Jesse brushed a hand through his hair, shaking away rain drops.

"I remember your stubborn mouth," he answered at last, flippantly. "I don't remember your name."

The *desgastas* flushed. Jesse felt a stab of satisfaction.

"Michael Anderson. You used to visit the camp, to pass out vitamins. You gave my wife a cream for the pain, when her face began to peel."

"A long time ago," Jesse said. "Five years at least. I don't remember how many *desgastas* I tried to ease. I recall your wife, she was very patient with me. Didn't complain when my clumsy fingers bruised her flesh. You had a family. Two girls, a boy?"

"Dead," Anderson replied, eyes cool.

"I'm sorry."

"You stopped coming out soon after my wife died. Did you give up on us?"

Jesse leaned forward in his chair. He stretched across the desk and chose a nugget of chocolate from Harlan's candy bowl. The bowl was pretty crystal, and the president had always kept it full.

"I gave up on the situation. There was nothing I could accomplish out there in the mud."

"Nothing but soothe our pain, keep us fed."

"There were Houses for that. Or even the city," Jesse said. He popped the piece of chocolate between his teeth.

Anderson rapped knuckles on the corner of the desk. "You know very well you and your Mark denied us the solace and wealth of this place."

"Not me," Jesse said. He licked chocolate from the tips of his fingers, neat as a cat. "You. Your decision not to take the microbe into your bodies. I grew up in a House. My brother was its Keeper. He was stubborn as the land, and I watched him pass down the old traditions, warping good minds as he went."

"The *desgastas* remember the past."

"And so do the cityborn. Why do you think we live in this sterile city? Why do you think the govs bought the Mark so happily? We haven't forgotten. We're doing our best to re-engineer what we lost."

"You've done nothing but make small pockets of land livable, and barely so. Your Mark might right a few recessive mutations, might clear up a contagious cancer or two, might weed out those whose lines are too damaged to breed. But what about the real problem? What about Bruster's?"

Jesse stared into Anderson's gritted teeth. "I've spent most of my life trying. Apparently miracles are hard to come by. Maybe I'm only allowed one a lifetime."

"You're a cold bastard."

"Where's Robin?" Jesse asked. "Is she really here? Or was your man just waggling a lure?"

"Robin's in the palace. I've decided you won't see her."

"Because I won't shed tears over your predicament?" Jesse arched both brows and tried to hide the clench of his fingers. "Forgive me if I'm cynical. You're in the city now. In fact, you're living in the President's Palace. In the very fat, I'd say."

"You talk fluff like a cityborn," Anderson growled.

"Perhaps because I *am*?" Jesse propped his chin on his hand. He peered up through his lashes. "I may have been born in the dirt, but I'm cityborn to the bone."

"You're dancing on a stage," Anderson retorted. "But the act won't work on me, Doctor. I remember you, those nights out and around our tents. You were hard as bone, quick with the tongue, you didn't talk around corners. You were never like the other govs. You meant business. And you still do."

Anderson pushed away from the desk. He walked around to face Jesse's chair. "A cityborn fop wouldn't have broken into the Sayers's labs, Doctor. But you, funny clothes and lovely eyes and all, did. You haven't changed. So if you want to see your ward, drop the act."

"Very well," Jesse said, voice immediately hard. "Tell me how Harlan died. Did you kill him? Or was he already dying when you broke down his door? How far advanced were his symptoms? Was he lucid?"

Anderson's head reared back. He took a pace away from Jesse's chair. Jesse climbed from the leather embrace and followed after.

"Are there others?" he guessed. When Anderson flinched, he sighed. "There are. How many?"

Anderson wouldn't look around. "Most of the govs. A few of the military. One or two children."

"All cityborn?"

"Every last one." Anderson locked his fists behind his back. "They think we brought it. They're panicking. We've had to lock most of the diseased men and women in the west wing. Those who are still healthy are afraid."

"And so are you."

Anderson swore, and swung around. "These people need a cure, Doctor. We're not monsters. We can't sit and watch them die."

"You'll have to. There is no cure."

Anderson's face contorted as though he struggled against anger. "Robin believes you have one. So do the students. So, now, do I."

"Why would I lie?"

"Because you're like all the other govs, Doctor. You want to see us dead. You want your city cleansed."

"*My* people are dying as quickly as your own." Jesse let his tone go cold. "And it's *my* city you've taken hostage in your clumsy way. Believe me, if I had a cure, I'd inject every one of you myself."

Anderson's cheeks went white. Jesse saw the rage, and understood the fear, but he wouldn't allow himself to show the man his sympathy.

"I have nothing to give you," he continued. "Except maybe some ease. Let me do what I can to make the sick more comfortable." It seemed a bleak offer, but it was all he had.

Anderson cursed again. His fists shot out, and clenched around Jesse's forearms. "They're changing, Doctor. Before they die, they—"

"I know," Jesse interrupted. "Let me help them."

The *Desgastas* stilled, and peered down into Jesse's eyes. Jesse met his gaze calmly, but it wasn't enough to reassure. Anderson flinched away, releasing Jesse so abruptly he tottered.

"I've seen your brand of help before," the *desgastas* said in a whisper. "And it lasts only until our deaths begin to bore you." He swung away. He his hand and waved Jesse's escort forward. "Take him back home."

The other *desgastas* stepped forward, but Jesse squared his shoulders. "What about Robin?"

Anderson sank into the president's leather chair. He folded his hands on the solid old desk. "I told you I've changed my mind. You won't see her. Not until you bring us your cure."

"At least tell me if she's well."

Anderson lifted his chin, and his mouth was bitter, "She's well, for now." He shifted his hands restlessly, folding and unfolding his fingers. "Stay away from the Sayers's labs."

Jesse felt his stomach boil, but he kept his face straight. "I need those machines."

Anderson's eyes were as sour as his mouth. "I admire your courage. But if you haven't found a miracle for us by now, I fear it's too late. Stay away from the labs. I don't have the manpower to patrol every inch of the palace labyrinth. And I don't have the patience. I don't want to find you've broken into those rooms again and somehow released a new horror into the world. I don't trust your motives, Doctor, and now I find I can no longer rely on your skills. So I tell you again, stay away from the labs."

Jesse resisted the urge to cry his despair aloud. Instead, he folded his hands and nodded once. The younger *desgastas* edged around the room, gently herding Jesse toward the door of the office. Jesse allowed himself to be moved, and only looked back once as he left Harlan's beloved room.

Anderson sat alone behind the president's desk, head bowed and fingers curled. He slouched as though at ease, but Jesse noted bone showing white through the skin of his knuckles.

As his escort led him back through the palace corridors, Jesse searched the faces of the few people they encountered. He saw the Sayers sisters, and one or two other cityborn he recognized, but he couldn't pick out Robin. If she truly lived among the *desgastas* in the palace, then she was well hidden.

Winter rain continued to turn the days bleak. Eventually Jesse began to notice a change in Carpenteria. The same cityborn who had seemed at first to ignore the *desgastas* in their palace now began to retreat into their homes. For more than a week Jesse's people had gone about their business as if nothing had happened. Despite the ever-present evidence of the riots, the cityborn had carried on. They had danced nightly despite filthy streets, shopped daily at their treasured stores, and spent the usual hours in coffee shops and restaurants that were now stained and broken.

After Harlan's death the crowds began to thin. More rain and wind turned the filth on the streets into a thin swamp. People stayed at home, afraid to battle the elements, afraid of the silence in their palace. The cityborn had loved their president. When Jesse looked out false windows onto deserted streets, he feared Harlan's death had broken his people's spirit.

Occasionally, when Jesse stopped to peer at the winter, he would find a form or two behind the sheeting rain. They stood poised on street corners, or lounged under the eaves of ghostly buildings. Students, he knew, recognizing the dye on their skin and in their hair. He didn't know their names, and their faces always changed.

He didn't know whether they were children who hadn't joined the riots, or children who had and now ventured out of their sumptuous lair to check on the city they had betrayed.

He suspected Isabella spent her share of hours patrolling the rotten streets. As the city seemed to sag and change beneath the weight of the *desgastas,* so did the grocer's daughter. A week and a half after the occupation, Isabella chopped her hair and rubbed blue color through her short locks. She studded her ears with bits of glass and smeared green around her expressive eyes. The makeup only served to make her face seem longer.

She spent only a small amount of time in Jesse's home. When at last one night he managed to catch her on her way into the evening, he was saddened by the wildness in her eyes. She seemed close to hysteria, and her frantic beliefs carried the scent of ravings.

"Death is here," she muttered, pinned beneath Jesse's skeptical frown. "The *desgastas* brought it."

"You let them in," Jesse replied. "What happened to your compassion?"

"They've killed us." She wouldn't look into Jesse's face as she squirmed slightly in place on the marble floor. "We made a mistake. We didn't know. And now most of us are dead."

The statement made Jesse balk. He reached for Isabella, wanting to see her face, wanting to know if she spoke the truth. Before he could catch her she was gone, away into the ferocious winter.

After that night Isabella rarely came home at all, and when she did, she locked herself away on the second floor. Jesse didn't know how she fared. Eventually, he stopped caring. His city had changed her. The slender rebel with the colored hair and flashing eyes seemed somehow other than the awkward woman whose company he had learned to enjoy on his brother's shore.

New faces appeared in the city. Jesse watched these strangers from behind the safety of his windows. He noted unusually pale skin and hair, and listened to strange accents. Travelers from overseas, he guessed. Pilgrims or refugees, he didn't care which. Either way, the alien faces made him uneasy.

With the influx of travelers came a new tension, and new violence. Scuffles broke out in the streets. Angry groups tangled day and night. Jesse thought his cityborn were stunned by the sheer number of refugees and strangers, and beginning to be afraid. He saw the threat of violence reflected on previously genteel faces.

Jesse continued to lurk behind the closed door of his study. He watched his people through false windows and tried to imagine how he might save them.

11

Barricaded behind the palace walls, most of the *desgastas* managed to ignore the harsh city winter. Robin herself drifted through days at a time before she remembered to pause in her duties and take a moment to turn on one of the false windows. Snow had come to Carpenteria in thick gray flakes that melted before they touched ground. The weather buried city streets until even the remnants of the riot were covered in dirty slush.

As she watched the snow drift across the palace lawns, Robin wondered if it stormed at the same time on Harold's shore. She knew from the Keeper's stories that such bitter cold was a rare and new thing. In centuries past the winters had been as bright and sunny as the summers. But Robin had grown up with the cold. As far back as she could remember the *desgastas* in Harold's House had dreaded the change in seasons, feared the killing freeze. The cold always sent one or two into the sea before it passed. The ill were often too weak to withstand the sapping winds.

In the winter cityborn Lords and Ladies wore long canvas coats over their silks. The coats were waterproofed and lined with synthetic fibers, fuzzy on the inside and dull beneath the rain. Anderson dug out a pile of such coats from somewhere in the depths of the palace. Robin was given one of her own but she rarely wore it. The coat felt too wide across her shoulders and hung past her ankles. It ended up in a crumpled pile in one corner of her new room.

Robin had been given her choice of rooms. The palace suites seemed endless, and the *desgastas* and students were very few. Some of the suites were still occupied by the govs and their families, but most of the cityborn had been moved to the west wing. Many of the president's Lords and Ladies had been sick when the *desgastas* swarmed into the palace. Now they were dying. Rooms opened up quickly. Most remained vacant. No one had the time or the desire to clean away the stink of death.

Robin picked one of the smaller suites. She liked the tiny room both because it was hidden away at the end of a winding corridor, and because it was full of color. She imagined the bright dreams she would have in the vibrant four-poster bed. But in the end she spent very little time in the room at all.

Desgastas and students had built a makeshift hospital in one of the larger ballrooms on the first floor of the palace. When Greta discovered ranks of cots in the military barracks, Anderson ordered the extras moved into the ballroom. Ailing cityborn found their way to the palace, fear and discrimination forgotten in the longing for comfort. They came in unending streams, following rumor, or perhaps welcomed by a *desgastas* hand. Robin never knew who started the migration, or how Anderson monitored the flow of cityborn bodies. She knew only that the crowd of needy never thinned. The flimsy white beds filled up quickly, until it became hard to find an empty cot. Then the sick were arranged on blankets on any free floor space. Eventually the hospital was expanded into a second, smaller, room as well.

The main hospital was Greta's territory, but the second room became Robin's responsibility. An old supply closet, it was half the size of Greta's ballroom, and very dark, but a spigot ran into a basin in one corner of the room, and the water that splashed free of the pipes was cold and sweet. Robin kept the spigot running because her patients thirsted constantly. She kept the false windows off, because the dying preferred the gloom. She learned to find her way in the semi-darkness, and memorized the paths from bed to spigot and back again.

Most of the time Robin preferred the shadows. She didn't want to see her patients' faces. She feared the changes she might find in their bodies, and the death she might see in their eyes. She remembered the monstrous cityborn locked away in Jesse's cellar, and as she fumbled her way through the dark room, she wondered which of her own wards would turn feral.

But they didn't. Every evening Molly brought food and fresh bandages. Then lights would have to be turned up and bodies searched for new blisters. The cityborn in Robin's closet were dying as Harold had died, eaten by Bruster's and betrayed by failing lungs. Robin often saw confusion or madness on the faces of the dying, but never the feral hunger she had encountered in Jesse's cellar.

Once she thought she saw the beginnings of something horrible. One pretty Lord lingered longer than usual, unwilling to die. He tossed endlessly on his cot, and refused every offering of food. His fingernails fell out and his hair came free in clumps until he was as bald as an infant. One evening, as she changed his bandages, Robin thought she saw tiny ripples moving beneath his skin. Fluid gathered beneath the flesh along his joints where it hardened into crippling lumps.

He died after three torturous days, and Robin never knew if she had merely imagined the changes in his body.

The dead piled up in great numbers, and for a while the bodies remained cloistered in one of the huge kitchen freezers. The students were afraid to touch anything related to Bruster's, and the *desgastas* were too busy trying to survive to bother with the cityborn dead. Eventually the freezers began to overflow, and at last Robin volunteered to cart the dead out of the city to the burning fields. Molly offered to help. Together they managed a gruesome train: cityborn dead in carts pulled by unwilling *desgastas* women.

The train went out every morning, the carts were always full, and yet the hospital cots never seemed to empty.

Before sunrise one morning, Molly joined the chain of carts at the mouth of the tunnels. She passed Robin a slim plastic mask.

"What is it?" Robin asked, pinching the rubber.

"Breathing mask," Molly explained. She mimicked pulling the apparatus over her head, and then grinned without humor. "They're giving them out now. They think Bruster's is in the air. They think it's passed along when we cough, or when we sneeze. So the cityborn will wear them to keep from breathing the disease *in*, and we will wear them to keep from breathing it *out*."

Several of the *desgastas* women laughed. Robin snorted. "Did Anderson agree to this?"

"His idea," Molly said. "He found them in an old storage room when he was trying to dig up more cots. They used to be afraid of airborne diseases all the time, before Jesse developed his Mark. Now they're just afraid of us."

Robin pulled the mask over her head and positioned the filter at her mouth. "This is crazy." The words echoed between her ears. She wasn't sure they had made it past the mask.

But Molly heard and smiled. "Crazy as a cityborn Lord. But smell!"

"What?"

"Take a breath."

Robin huffed doubtfully, and then blinked. The mask pinched her mouth, but the air she inhaled smelled clean. She couldn't taste the sickly reek of the dead they carted, or the sour smell of sweaty fear that seemed to permeate the *desgastas* women.

"Exactly," Molly said. She smiled at Robin's comical reaction and waved one hand at the dead piled in the carts. "Fresh as a breeze."

After that morning Robin wore the mask every time she journeyed through the tunnels. Not long after, she wore it in the hospital, as well.

Robin worked and slept in her closet, afraid to leave her patients. She learned their names and their sorrows, and she held their hands when life bubbled away. She didn't let them see her fear. She had learned from Harold how to be stoic. She forgot Carpenteria, she forgot Jesse, she forgot that the men and women dying on their cots were cityborn. It was as if she walked the shore again, as if she worked with Harold to give her Housemates' ease, and then give them to the sea.

When Anderson came for her, he had to wake her from a sound sleep at the foot of a dirty cot. The cityborn child who had died on the cot still clutched Robin's numb hand. She had to free her fingers from the dead grip before she could rise.

"Come with me," Anderson said. He took her arm and led her through the gloom.

She let him steer her through the maze of corridors. She couldn't find it in herself to wonder where he was taking her. The cityborn child had lingered into the night, and even Robin hadn't been able to quench her wild thirst. The child had cried as she died, and her howls had torn at Robin's heart. Now Robin was tired, her senses dulled. She wanted only to sleep.

Anderson didn't seem to notice her exhausted silence. He took her through corridors and down stairs and at last to the industrial kitchen in the depths of the palace. Robin had been there only once before, early on, in search of something the dying might stomach. The kitchen itself was huge. The floors were a dull black tile, and the walls were lined with stainless steel cabinets. Robin stood on the edge of the room and looked at the gleaming ovens. An endless bank of refrigerators hummed to her in chorus from one long wall. They reminded Robin of the larger freezer where the *desgastas* still kept the dead before they could be carried out of the city.

"Harlan ate well and often," Anderson said, dropping her hand. He went to one of the refrigerators and pulled it open.

"They're not still full?" Robin asked. She had been too busy to wonder where supper came from. Now such an abundance of food amazed her.

"What do you think we've been eating for the last week?" Anderson blinked at her. "His palace was full of hungry government families. Important govs who liked to throw parties. There's enough in here to feed us for a half a year."

Robin swallowed as he pulled bread and cheese from the mouth of the unit. She couldn't remember the last time she had paused to chew a real meal. Most of the food she saw in the hospital she passed on to the sick who would still eat.

Anderson set the food on the gleaming bright table that bisected the room and then went back for more. Robin stayed where she was. When Anderson finally came back, this time clutching a plastic container, he gave her an impatient look.

"You mustn't stop eating just because you can't save the world. I've watched you. You were skinny to begin with, but now you're nothing but ribs and bones. Fasting won't change anything." He reached under the table and pulled out two industrial stools. "Wash your hands and come eat." He pointed at a stool.

Robin dragged her boots across the tile to the nearest basin. She scrubbed her hands under a stream of hot water, and then dragged herself back to settle where Anderson pointed. The stool was so cold it stung her through the denim trousers she wore. Robin could smell the bread and cheese and her stomach rumbled. She hunched over the table and tried to find anger. The man didn't have the right to pull her away from sleep.

Anderson smiled and climbed onto the other stool. He pulled the lid off the plastic container and the scent of meat made Robin's mouth fill with saliva.

"What is it?" she asked.

"Ham. Ham sandwiches with cheese. Sound good?"

"Very," Robin admitted reluctantly.

"No mayonnaise," Anderson said, sounding disappointed. He began putting sandwiches together with easy competence.

Robin watched. His hands were callused and his face was lined, but his eyes could be kind. They were very gray, she thought. He was much bigger than Jesse. Much taller than she was. He wore a rounded *tronera* over his shirt, and for the first time she noticed that the disk was gold. He glanced up and saw her watching and grinned. He handed her a sandwich and she studied it.

"On the shore we tended to our dying and then ate when we could," she said, feeling the fresh bread spring beneath her fingers. "Compassion came before hunger."

Anderson had his mouth around a sandwich. He took a bite and chewed slowly, watching her over the bread. She thought that he was considering her. Then she thought maybe he was remembering her journey to his tent. She wondered if he understood that her brisk words over his dying son had been Harold's form of compassion, the only form she had ever understood.

Anderson swallowed and nodded his head at her sandwich. "There are too many dying, now. The rules have to change. Eat."

"Why does all this food sit here, when it should be up in the hospitals?"

Anderson shrugged. "How old are you? Thirteen? Fourteen? Old enough to use your eyes. Wise enough to understand. This food won't save your patients. Nothing will. But this food might sustain the living. For a while longer."

A *desgastas* sentiment and one Robin had almost voiced over his son's deathbed. Anderson would waste stew on a dying *desgastas* child, but he wouldn't feed the cityborn. She found she couldn't blame him.

She picked up the sandwich and lifted it to her nose. Her stomach grumbled again.

"Well?" Anderson asked when she paused.

"I didn't know you had noticed me—" She stopped.

"Lurking among my people? Did you think you could hide?" Anderson grunted. He took another bite of his sandwich and spoke around ham and cheese. "I noticed you the first day, even though Molly tried her best to hide you. She's more forgiving than I am. More open. I still say you don't belong."

"Because of the Mark?"

"There is that. You passed willingly through those gates. You gave up your shore for the forbidden. And now you want to save the cityborn. You wear the *tronera*, but maybe your heart is uncertain."

Robin bit into her sandwich. The meat tasted salty and wonderful. She closed her eyes and heard Anderson grunt again.

"At first, I wanted to throw you from the camp. But Molly convinced me otherwise. She said you had courage and heart. So I decided to pretend I didn't see you."

Robin opened her eyes. "Should I be grateful?"

"No. Maybe I'm trying to apologize. I've seen how you work in that hospital. You do have courage, and heart, and too much steel for a child your size. Maybe I can forgive the smear on your hand."

Robin almost smiled, and then she sighed. "I'm sorry about your Jason." Because, although it went against her training, she felt it had to be said.

The gray eyes frosted over but she couldn't regret her words. Anderson ate in silence, and Robin finished her sandwich. When she was done she wiped her hands on her jeans.

"And now you're living in the city. There's no Mark in your hand, no microbe in your body, but you're here. Keeper of a dying band behind forbidden walls." She licked ham and cheese from her thumb. "Is it worth it?"

"It will be. When we have our cure."

"And then what?"

"And then we leave this poisoned place. Move on. We'll take our camp somewhere far away, where we can forget death and learn to live off the land again. The way our ancestors did. The way we are meant to live. Once we have our cure."

"If it doesn't come too late," Robin said. She slid off her stool. Her patients waited for her, and there were dead to be collected.

"It has already come years too late," Anderson replied. He finished his sandwich in one bite, and then dropped from his own stool. Robin waited while he brushed crumbs from his fingers. They left the kitchen together.

Robin met Angie and Josie Sayers late one night, as she was passing from her closet to the main hospital in search of fresh blankets. She didn't recognize the sisters at first, and wondered only why two cityborn Ladies had found the courage to visit the hospital. She ignored their painted faces as she helped Greta fold a pile of clean blankets, but when she turned back to her closet she found the two women watching her.

They followed Robin to the very mouth of her closet. Then, in one elegant maneuver, they blocked her way.

"Robin Grange?" The taller of the two squinted. She wore her wavy blonde hair high off her neck. Dyes sparkled on her cheeks and lips, and her silks were too scant for winter. A rubbery mask hung around her neck, but she seemed in no hurry to pull it over her nose and mouth.

"I'm not a Grange," Robin said over the blankets loaded in her arms.

"You're Jesse's ward?" The second Lady looked pinched beneath her cosmetics.

"I'm *desgastas*," Robin corrected. "Are you ill? Do you need help?"

"We know what you are," the first responded after a moment. "And we don't need help. *We've* come to help *you*."

Robin's skepticism must have shone through, because the smaller sister laughed aloud. Her mirth broke free in a cackle, and rocked her on her feet.

"She looks like she's doing quite well without us, Josie."

Then Robin remembered. She clutched the blankets against her chest and tried to edge by. If Martin had spoken true, the women were beasts in their own right, and murderers. If Martin had spoken the truth and the Sayers sisters had kept their cure from the *desgastas*.

"If you let us go," Josie loomed over Robin. "If you let us free of this hell hole, we'll see you get your right."

"You'll not go free," Robin said. A flush of rage heated her brow, emotion hotter than she had felt since she had left Harold's shore. "Not until you give us our cure."

Angie smiled. The skin of her face pulled tight against her skull. "Our family is very rich, little Robin. You'd have a life you never imagined."

"I don't want your money!" Robin spat. Her voice stuck on a shrill note. Out of the corner of her eye she saw Molly rise from a patient and turn.

"Your money, too, Robin," Josie said gently. "Have mercy on your sisters. Let us go."

"What are you talking about?" Robin's ears rang. She didn't understand the feverish light in Angie's eyes.

"You're a cityborn child, little Robin," Josie said. "Didn't your Keeper tell you? Bred in deception and dumped in a village on the shore."

"Our mother," Angie hissed, "raped by a *desgastas* animal. He ruined her, broke her spirit and killed her body. And you were the sad result."

Robin dropped her blankets and lunged at the woman, but Molly pulled her short.

"Hush," the *desgastas* cautioned. "Pick up the blankets and go to your patients."

Robin couldn't move. Josie watched her with wide blue eyes. Angie wore a snarl across her painted mouth.

"Let us go," Josie whispered, "and we'll make you a part of our family, as you were meant to be. You'll be rich and respected. You'll not squat in the mud any longer."

At Robin's side Molly tensed. Angie began to chuckle. Moving stiffly, Robin bent her knees and gathered the scattered blankets back into her arms. Then she rose and turned on her heel, and strode into the gloom of her closet. Molly followed Robin, but the Sayers sisters stayed away from the stink of death.

Robin dropped the blankets onto a clean spot of floor and then made her way to the spigot. In the darkness, one of her patients began to choke and cough.

"The sisters are crazy. They always have been. Too many *pesos* fuddled their pretty heads long ago," Molly said. Her voice echoed strangely in the tiny room.

"Now I understand," Robin muttered. She ran her fists under the stream of cool water, and then splashed her burning face.

"What?" Molly asked.

"Now I understand," Robin said, "why the Sayers family hates *desgastas* so.

Molly didn't answer. Robin brushed water from her cheeks. She began to distribute the fresh blankets. Molly worked at her side, in silence, but Robin imagined she could hear strain in the other woman's breathing.

That night, Robin found sleep for the first time in her borrowed suite. She fell into the bed and dropped into sleep before she had time to admire the multi-colored canopy or the warm sheets. She slept restlessly, and dreamed of Harold and his shore. The Keeper followed her across the dunes, insistent in his pursuit, but Robin couldn't understand the words he spoke.

When she woke, her heart pounded frantically, and the sheets twisted around her like one long snake. She shrugged free of the coverlet and slid from the bed. It took her a moment to find the fake windows behind the opulent curtains. She had to search the walls, fumbling, until the grids buzzed to life.

Outside, snow blew in drifts. The city streets were deeply buried. The city itself appeared deserted. The suite was warm, overheated, but as Robin looked into the night, she clutched her arms across her chest and shivered.

She turned off the windows and crawled back into bed, but sleep wouldn't come. Instead her exhausted mind wove the Sayers sisters into every thought. At last she jumped to her feet again, and searched across the carpet until she collected her clothes. Boots and socks were harder to find in the dim room, but she kept the lights off. She was used to the dark of her closet, and was beginning to prefer it.

Dressed, Robin hurried back through the palace to the hospital. Even in the deep of night, the ballroom remained far from silent. The dying struggled to breathe, and the living struggled to stay calm. Robin spotted Greta bent over a struggling patient. Molly passed a jug of water to another. For the first time Robin noticed how worn their faces were. She wondered if her own was the same.

She passed quickly through the ranks of beds, intent on reaching her own ward. She had almost made it to the closet when her knees locked and she found herself rooted to the floor in shock. There, on the old cot at her feet, Angie Sayers raved.

Robin's knees gave out and she dropped slowly to the floor. Angie didn't seem aware. She tossed beneath blankets, plucking compulsively at the edge of her cot.

Robin sat hunched on the floor. Numb, she watched the Lady twist and mutter, until Greta crossed the room and knelt at her side.

"She came in with the moonrise," the *desgastas* said. "Didn't you know?"

"I left early," Robin whispered. "I thought I'd sleep in a real bed for one night."

"And a good thing, too," Greta squeezed Robin's shoulder. "You needn't try to nurse every patient."

"She's dying already."

"Looks it," the *desgastas* sounded matter of fact.

"She seemed well yesterday." But Robin remembered the woman's pinched face and frantic eyes.

"It happens," Greta said. She expelled a breath. "Will you watch her?"

"Move her to my closet," Robin said. She climbed slowly to her feet. "I'll find room somewhere."

Angie lasted two days, and then three, and then a fourth. And then Robin began to be afraid. The woman raved less, and even in the dim closet Robin could sense Angie's sudden stillness. The cityborn Lady lay on her cot, alive and aware, and feral. Robin could sense the change. Every evening, when Molly brought her lamp, Robin examined Angie for anything unusual, but found nothing. The woman's face had broken and scarred, and her lungs sounded wet, but her condition seemed to have stabilized.

Robin found herself avoiding Angie's cot. She let the woman go without water until she begged, and only changed Angie's blankets when Molly or Greta were around to help her. Angie seemed quiet, calm, and aware, but she didn't speak. Robin imagined she could feel the woman's eyes across her back, their weight a constant burden.

And then one afternoon, Angie's craving for water turned from husky pleas to wild howling. Robin remembered the screams of Jesse's prisoners, and knew. When she tried to give Angie water, the woman swallowed a bucketful. Then she snapped her teeth at Robin's fingers.

Robin sent Molly for Anderson and waited. When the older *desgastas* finally appeared, night had fallen. Anderson turned on the lights in the small closet. Robin's eyes were dazzled. Her patients whimpered and coughed. Angie began to scream.

"Look at her hands," Molly said.

Robin edged away, but Anderson bent quickly and snagged one trembling hand from the air. Angie screamed again. Then abruptly she fell silent. Her eyes gleamed beneath the city bulbs. Her fingers twitched in Anderson's.

"Like claws," Anderson muttered. "Harder than bone."

Robin was more interested in the cysts that seemed to ripple beneath the skin on the woman's arms, and the feral light in her eyes. Angie's hair hung in limp strands. When she tossed her head, long tangles fell from her skull in hanks and scattered on the floor.

"She's not the first," Anderson said at last, releasing Angie's fist. "It's just a mutation. She's dying like the rest."

Angie shifted suddenly on her cot and lashed out. Her fingers brushed Anderson's cheek, and left behind one long, deep cut. The *desgastas* cursed and slapped his palm over the wound. Molly gasped and backed away until she stood at Robin's side.

"She should be locked away," Robin said.

"Don't be foolish." Anderson wiped blood from his cheek. He frowned.

"She's mad," Robin said. She thought of Jesse and his cellar. "She needs to be contained."

"She's just delirious. Turn the lights back off."

"Lights," Robin ordered. She breathed a sigh of relief when the bulbs went out.

"Ask Jesse," she continued, and then stopped when Anderson made a sharp sound.

"What does Grange have to do with it?"

"Let it go, Robin," Molly interrupted before Robin could reply. "Go back to your rest. I'll look after the Lady."

Robin hesitated. She could just make out Anderson's form as he moved in the dim light. She shook her head at Molly, and waited patiently for her eyes to adjust again to the gloom.

But Anderson wouldn't let her stay.

"Go," he ordered. "Finish the night in your own bed. You're exhausted, imagining horrors, and you need the rest."

Robin started to protest. Anderson cut her off.

"Go," he said. "I'll stay for a while, and help Molly keep watch."

Robin let her feet drag, but she left. She found her way back through the palace to her suite, and into her vibrantly colored bed. There she lay back on the coverlet, fully dressed, waiting out the night. She wouldn't close her eyes, for Jesse's tortured creatures lurked like ghouls on the back of her eyelids.

In the morning, when she returned to her closet, Angie was gone. A new cityborn Lord lay in her cot. When Robin tracked Molly down, the *desgastas* seemed startled by Angie's disappearance.

"Anderson sat with her all night," Molly said. "I didn't see him leave. She must have died in the early hours."

Robin nodded agreement, but when she readied her train, she watched carefully while the *desgastas* loaded their carts, and couldn't find Angie's body among the dead. Just to be sure, she searched the freezers herself, walking between the walls and shivering convulsively, but the icy vaults were empty.

Robin stood for a long moment in the freezer, thinking, until Molly called her to join the train. The chill of the vault stuck to her bones all the way through the tunnels to the burning fields, and then back again. The cold found a bitter echo in her heart.

Late that night, Robin's feet took her down through the palace to Harlan's industrial kitchen. Her appetite had finally returned, and the still of the night soothed her nerves. For the moment she had managed to steal away from her ward and forget the dead, and at last her stomach wanted feeding. She needed a sandwich and solitude.

But the lights were on in the kitchen. Startled by the glow, Robin hesitated in the corridor, and almost turned back. Then she heard a whisper of melody, a soft voice singing an old tune. She recognized the *desgastas* accent. Still, she lingered, until her stomach growled viciously and forced her into the kitchen.

Molly looked up from her seat at the gleaming counter and grinned. The *desgastas* had tied her long hair back into a multitude of braids. She'd cleaned the filth of the hospital from her hands and clothes. She looked fresh, and relatively spotless, except for a streak of crumbs across her chin.

"Chocolate!" Molly pointed the tines of her fork at the piece of cake in front of her. "Can you imagine? Only the cityborn rich bake whole cakes of chocolate."

Robin slid around a giant refrigerator. "You seem to be enjoying yourself."

"Chocolate," Molly breathed again. "It's wonderful. I never imagined...." She broke off, smiling. "There are two or three cakes in that freezer there. Thaw yourself a piece."

"No, thank you."

Molly shrugged. "Your choice." She tasted a forkful of cake and sighed in bliss.

Robin swallowed her amusement, opened the nearest refrigerator, and rummaged around until she found a wedge of cheese and a bowl of strawberries. Most of the berries had gone bad. Robin picked through the bowl until she found three free of mold. She settled against the counter with her find.

She nibbled at her cheese, and watched Molly eat, amazed at how much of the cake the *desgastas* managed to smear across her face.

"You're making a mess," she said at last, unable to watch the disaster in silence.

"I'm having fun," Molly replied. "And don't scold. There's not much of it to be found anymore."

"Food?" Robin wondered, incredulous.

Molly wrinkled her nose. "Fun, you dolt. Stop standing there like a grump." She waved her hand at an empty stool. "Sit down. I'll find another fork, and you can help me finish."

"I don't want any."

"Shut up and sit down," Molly said without heat. She yanked open a drawer, plucked out a fork, and set it on the counter. "I'm trying to be nice. Come share."

Reluctantly, Robin clambered onto the stool. She picked up the fork. "You don't need to be nice."

Molly shrugged again. She licked chocolate from the tines of her fork. "You need some cheering up."

Robin frowned, suspicious. "Why?"

"I like to see you smile. You have a pretty smile."

Robin blushed. "That's stupid."

"Maybe," Molly grinned, unruffled. "Have some chocolate cake. And pass me a strawberry. We'll call it a trade."

Still scowling, Robin passed the *desgastas* a berry and then leaned over, scooping up cake with her fork. Molly finished the strawberry in two bites, and watched as Robin considered the dessert on her fork.

"Eat," Molly urged.

Robin licked a bit of chocolate from her fork. The taste exploded across her tongue. She shut her eyes in bliss.

"Good?" Molly whispered.

Robin opened her eyes and smiled.

"Want some more?" Molly asked, deadpan, and then snorted when Robin lunged across the counter and attacked the cake.

12

Five days later Robin learned, through Molly, that Anderson had sent for Jesse. They were working alone in the hospital, for Greta had gone in search of rest. Molly usually kept a cheery disposition as she tended the dying, but on this morning Robin noted unusual lines of strain around the young *desgastas's* mouth. Robin kept an eye on Molly as she tended her own patients, and so she was ready when Molly suddenly tossed a roll of bandages to the floor and attacked a bucket with the toe of her boot.

Molly's kick overturned the bucket. Water spread quickly over the ballroom floor. Robin jumped to her feet, gathered up an unused blanket, and began mopping up the liquid. Molly stood above the toppled bucket. She watched Robin for a long moment, and then suddenly she sighed and relaxed.

"I'm sorry," she said, brushing straggles of long hair from her damp cheeks.

"It's been a long morning," Robin said without emotion. "Would you like to take a break?"

Molly grabbed a second blanket and fell to her knees on the floor, scrubbing at the puddles Robin hadn't reached. They pushed their blankets across the floor, over the feet of the cots, and above and around them the dying wheezed.

"I won't leave you here alone," Molly said. She puffed as she mopped. "Maybe when Greta gets back."

"I'll be fine," Robin said. "I don't need you again until we're ready to load the evening train."

Out of the edge of her eye she saw Molly wince.

"I can't believe we're making two trips a day now," the *desgastas* whispered. "The fires burn endlessly, and the bodies keep coming."

Robin didn't reply. She dabbed a small puddle and at the same time reached up to soothe a whimpering cityborn Lord.

"I saw three *desgastas* in the last train," Molly said, her voice barely audible. "I just looked down into the cart and there they were. Three faces I knew. Gaza and Jose, and little Marta. I didn't even know they were ill. They weren't here in the hospital." She paused. "I think it's broken Greta."

The floor felt dry. Robin stood up, tossed her sodden blanket onto the pile of daily laundry, and then reached for the empty bucket.

"Greta is *desgastas*." She peered through the shadows at Molly. "She has lived with death all her life. She won't break."

In the gloom, Molly shook her head. "It's different. Marta was only six. We weren't meant to die this way. Even the *desgastas* live into adulthood. What it's doing to them," her hand fluttered, encompassing the ranks of beds, "it's started on us."

Robin shook her own head. The empty bucket clanked against her side as she carried it to the nearest spigot. Molly followed. The *desgastas* waited while Robin ran cool water from the spout. Then she took the bucket, effectively blocking Robin with her load.

"Some of the men are ready to run. To leave the palace, and the city. They say there is nothing here but death. I think I believe them."

Robin glanced down into the bucket. The still water looked black as ink. Then Molly's hand trembled and the water rippled. For just a moment, Robin remembered the same eerie ripple beneath Angie's skin.

"What about the cure?" she asked, still watching the bucket.

Molly shrugged and the water in bucket the rolled. "We've been here for weeks. Most of the students are dead along with their promises, burned to the bones on the field. Angie Sayers is dead, her sister has disappeared. The people in the city are afraid to leave their homes, and when they do, they wear masks. It's killing their own. If there is such a cure, wouldn't they have used it by now?"

Robin didn't know.

"This place is a tomb," Molly said. "Don't you think we should leave it?"

One of Robin's patients began to mumble. Her disjointed words echoed from the mouth of the closet. Robin started for her ward, but Molly swung the bucket, and again Robin had to stop.

"Anderson's sent for Dr. Grange," the *desgastas* said.

"Jesse?" Robin hesitated.

"You know him best. Will he help us?"

"If he has a cure," Robin said, "he will help us." But she couldn't forget the eyes of the cityborn locked away in Jesse's cellar. Immediately chilled, she wrapped her fingers around her elbows and fled past Molly to her closet.

Later that afternoon, after Molly had rested and Greta had returned, Robin left the hospital and dressed for the winter. She wore extra socks in her boots and wrapped her canvas coat until it was as snug as it was likely to get. The coat was still too large, so she pulled the silken belt from a pair of trousers and used the bit of fabric to tighten the canvas around her waist.

The *desgastas* always used the back tunnels out of the palace, but Robin decided to tromp across the icy lawn instead. The snow drifts were thigh high, making her glad of the extra socks. By the time she reached the front gate, she wished for mittens. On the shore, she'd had a pair made from denim. She wondered what sort of gloves were to be found in Carpenteria.

The portcullis in the palace walls had no latch. The gate was for decoration only. Five paces along the wall Robin found a second door. Martin had discovered it, before Bruster's had claimed him. Robin didn't think the door had ever been used. Not even the president had left his palace by the front gate. Govs, Robin guessed, preferred to do everything in secrecy.

She felt along the door with numb fingers until she discovered the latch, and then pushed. The door swung open easily, without a sound. Robin scrambled through more snow until she fell free of the palace walls. She closed the door again quickly, and then felt foolish. The streets were empty. No one had seen her slide through the hidden gate. She buried her naked fists in a fold of canvas and trudged carefully along the street. Wind stung her eyes, and she had to bend her head. The snow beneath her feet looked virgin, unmarked by other footprints. The drifts smelt faintly metallic, like the sea. Robin was glad the snowfall had let up for the moment.

As a child, she had once tried to swallow the frozen water. One mouthful of the flakes had left her tongue slick and greasy, and turned her stomach sour. She never tried to swallow snow again.

Robin didn't see another soul until she reached the city marketplace. There the streets were still deserted, but at least a few brave merchants had opened their doors for business. Robin wandered along the frosted windows, peering into one shop and then another, looking for mittens or a warm hat.

Halfway down the street she paused. Beyond a particularly large pile of snow, color glittered. Pink and orange and gold, all swirled together into a misty cloud. Intrigued, Robin stalked the color, slid over the snow, and found herself with her nose pressed against a frozen window.

Reflected fire spun and split in the ice crystals along the window, turning the flames into cloudy color. Inside the shop a little man worked the fire from a wand, waving the iron tool first this way and then that, sculpting glass. Even through the window the fire seemed to warm Robin's flesh. She blinked, and then ducked through the door into the shop.

A bell tinkled. The cityborn turned on his stool. The fire snuffed from his wand as though by magic. The glassblower's hair hung past his shoulders, dyed green to the tips, and he wore makeup across his brows like a woman. But his eyes were kind, and Robin thought he smiled behind the ugly mask he wore over his mouth and nose.

"Good afternoon," the glassblower said, words muffled. "Are you looking for something special?"

"Just looking," Robin said. She kept her hands balled in her coat, afraid that if she freed them she would accidentally smash the wonders displayed throughout the shop.

There were castles and creatures and portraits and tiny feathered hats. Mythical beasts and globes containing bits of synthetic snow glittered behind the counter. Flowers and exotic birds and imaginary worlds lit up plain wooden shelves. Each treasure was crafted of colored glass, each twinkling jewel beautiful. Robin stood in place and tilted her head, trying to absorb every sculpture at once.

"Take your time," the glassblower said, gracious as only a cityborn Lord could be. "If you need help, ask."

He flicked his wand back to life and returned to his sculpture. Robin watched the fire burn for a moment longer. Then she began to walk from shelf to shelf.

It took her a long time to see every glittering creation, but at last Robin found herself standing again before the front door. The glassblower snuffed his flame and looked over his shoulder.

"Nothing appeals?" he asked, managing to sound incredulous and amused at the same time.

"I don't have any *pesos*." This was not necessarily true. She supposed she still had access to Jesse's accounts, but she had too much pride to use his money.

The cityborn arched his shoulders in a shrug. He spread his hands, eyes wry over the hump of his mask. "Pick something anyway. Two somethings. One for yourself and one for a friend."

Robin stared at the little man in disbelief.

"You're the first customer I've had in days," the glassblower said. "And besides, what does it matter, a few *pesos*, in a world such as this? How do I even know if I'll see the next sunrise? Take a gift or two. Make me happy."

Robin hesitated still, afraid the cityborn would change his mind, but the glassblower only sat on his stool and waited, watching as if to see what she would choose.

So she circled the store once more, searching the glass wonders even more carefully. In the end she picked a tiny pink shell for herself, and a golden butterfly for Molly. The sculptures felt fragile between her fingers. She handed her finds over to the cityborn with relief.

"Good choices," he said with a wink. He wrapped the pieces of blown glass carefully in cloth. "Take them home quickly. My sculptures don't like the cold."

Robin nodded, speechless. The glassblower pushed the wrapped glass gently into a large silken wallet, and then passed the parcel back.

"Thank you," she mumbled, clutching the treasures to her chest.

"Thank *you*," the glassblower corrected, eyes twinkling. "And, child?"

"Yes?" Robin stiffened, suddenly wary. Perhaps the cityborn had tricked her somehow, after all. She should have known. Nothing in Carpenteria came free.

"Find yourself a mask," he said, voice very kind. "The air in this city isn't safe to breathe anymore."

Astonished, Robin shook her head. The cityborn swiveled away on his stool, and fired his wand. Robin lingered a moment longer in the warmth of the shop, reluctant to face the wind. At last she pushed slowly through the snow, afraid to stumble and jar her parcel. She looked back once. Just past the drift of snow she could see the cloud of colors gathering in the glassblower's window.

Molly loved her golden butterfly. Robin knew the *desgastas* had never before owned anything quite so beautiful. Molly set the glass sculpture on a makeshift shelf in the hospital, high above rolls of bandages and piles of blankets. In the afternoons, when the light in the ballroom seemed somehow less heavy, the butterfly sparkled.

Robin's own sculpture found a place in her palace bedroom. The pink of the shell contrasted strongly with the jewel tones in the room, and Robin loved the struggle of color. She spent extra minutes in the room, minutes she would ordinarily have spent with her patients, just so she might enjoy the beautiful piece of glass.

New faces filled the hospital, *desgastas* faces. Robin found men she knew from the labor crews in her closet. She helped them die as she had her Housemates, but the speed with which Bruster's ravaged their bodies frightened her. For the first time she realized that her lack of years no longer buffered death.

Late one cold afternoon, Robin found Greta hidden in a corner. The *desgastas* woman stood as if struck senseless, staring blankly across the shadows at a wall. For a moment Robin couldn't help herself, hooked by Greta's dazed expression, she turned to study the wall, expecting to find something horrific or miraculous. She saw nothing in the gloom except the usual crust and smear of fluids across plaster. In their struggle to save lives, the *desgastas* women had little time to spend on cleaning the walls and floor of the ballroom. They had grown used to the filth, and did their best to keep it from the dying.

"What is it?" Robin asked. She reached to touch the back of Greta's rough blouse. "What do you see?"

The older woman started and blinked. She looked away from the wall, summoning a wry smile, but Robin saw the tears in the corners of her eyes.

"What is it?"

Greta blew out a breath, and the smile set on her lips. "Anna," she said. "Anna and my husband. Both." The tears spilled over and ran across her cheeks. All at once, Robin understood.

"Where?" She took the other woman's hand, squeezing tightly, as she had crushed Andy's on the day Kris had collapsed. Robin knew how to temper comfort and strength. "Show me where."

The *desgastas* nodded. She wiped her free hand across her eyes. "I was just getting them water. I needed a bucket. But I—" She faltered, confused, and the tears began to leak again.

"Here," Robin said, "I have a bucket. Stay here while I fill it."

She hurried to a spigot before Greta could move. She filled her bucket to the lip with cold water, and then lugged it back. Greta still stood in place, staring at the walls. Robin touched her shoulder.

"Show me."

Greta swallowed. She took the bucket from Robin. Robin understood — the *desgastas* wanted the comfort of caring for her own family. So Robin followed empty handed as Greta wound through the rows of cots.

Her daughter lay beneath a pile of blankets, almost lost in the coverings. Anna's breath rasped. Robin thought the girl was unconscious. Greta's husband half sat and half lay across his cot, eyes fever bright. Dark fluid ran from his nose, but he was aware. He smiled reassuringly at Greta.

"I've brought you water," Greta said. She stroked sweat-soaked hair from her husband's brow.

"Anna's asleep," he said. His voice cracked painfully. Robin knew he longed for the water.

"Drink your fill," she said. "We'll bring another bucketful for your child. Right now, she needs her rest." She wondered if he knew the girl was nearly dead. And then she saw the way he smiled bravely up at his wife and guessed that he did.

"Tend your daughter," Robin told Greta. She took the bucket from the *desgastas's* reluctant grip and knelt on the floor alongside the cots. Greta's husband hefted the bucket in hands that quivered.

"Thank you," he said. "You're Robin?"

She nodded and helped to steady the bucket. "Drink it all," she said. "And maybe then you'll be ready for some soup."

"My name's Raphael," he answered. "And soup sounds wonderful."

Robin watched as Raphael clutched the bucket around its mouth and sucked down the water. His thirst seemed unending. Robin found herself unable to look away from the convulsions of his throat as he swallowed. She had never seen such a fierce need to drink in anyone on Harold's shore. She didn't know what it meant.

A long minute passed before Greta's husband drained the bucket and passed it back. Robin saw, from the way he licked moisture from his lips, that he needed more.

"I'll fill it again," she said. "And bring you some of the soup."

Raphael shook his head. "Anna first."

Robin started to argue, and then shut her mouth. She rose to her feet, carrying the bucket. She glanced over at Greta. The woman cradled her child, tears running unchecked.

"I'll be back soon. With water and a meal." Robin gave Raphael her promise before she started away through the cots. Greta had waited too long to come for help, perhaps because she was afraid to face the truth, and now the woman had brought her husband and daughter to the ward to die. Robin thought the child would be dead before she returned. She knew Greta would want time alone, with her husband, to mourn.

So she dawdled a bit, stopping here and there to check on a patient. She stuck her head into the closet and saw that Molly was tending her patients. Molly's eyes were hard, all laughter gone. She looked at Robin, and mouthed a question. Robin shook her head. There was nothing to be done that might save Greta's small family.

Robin left the closet and circled around the ballroom. She filled the bucket at a free spigot, found a clean cup for soup, and then continued back until she found Raphael's cot. Anna lay motionless beneath stained blankets. Raphael's cheeks were wet, but he smiled again as he accepted the water and food. Greta sat on the edge of her husband's cot, one hand kneading at his thigh. Only the constant movement of her fingers betrayed any emotion. They were *desgastas*. Their child was dead, their grieving quickly done. Now they were ready to move on.

Robin sat with them for a while, and then she left Greta the bucket and toured through the hospital, counting *desgastas* among cityborn. She counted twice, just to make sure the number was correct. When she finished the second round, she went in search of Anderson.

She knew he spent most of his time in the president's office, eating and even sleeping in the formal suite. She didn't know how to find the room itself. Eventually she crossed the path of a man in military yellow, and asked him for help. The man looked harried and exhausted. His skin was dark and lined, and without the soft sheen she had learned to expect in the pampered cityborn. But she didn't think he was *desgastas*, either. He wore the Mark on his left palm, and nothing around his throat.

The soldier guided her through corridors and between floors. She rode in a lift for the first time in her life. Her stomach almost rebelled when the floor began to rise. She was very glad to step again onto steady ground.

"Here," he said at last. He stopped before two large white doors. A pair of *desgastas* men guarded the portals. Robin recognized their faces and thought she knew their names.

She thanked the soldier and waited, watching as he marched down the carpeted hallway and disappeared around a corner. Then she looked at the guards.

"Is he in?"

One of the men nodded. He opened the door a crack, and pushed his head into the room. Robin couldn't hear what he said, but after a moment he opened the door all the way.

"Go in," he said, standing aside to let her pass.

The president's office was huge, too opulent for Robin's taste. Anderson sat in a deep chair behind a desk that seemed over large for the room. A bowl steamed beside his right elbow. Robin wondered if it was the same soup she served to the dying, nine floors below.

"Little Robin." He sounded tired. "What can I do for you?"

"Did you talk to Jesse?" She crossed the room and stood in front of the desk. She could smell his soup, and see that he had eaten very little.

Anderson's beautiful mouth twitched. "Do you have spies in the palace, then?"

"Molly told me."

"That girl is never ending trouble," he said, but he sounded amused. "I talked to your Doctor Grange. He wouldn't help us."

"Wouldn't, or couldn't?"

Anderson shrugged. "Does it matter? Maybe, in the end, there is no cure for us."

Robin felt her stomach turn to acid. She sank into one of the hard chairs before the desk, and clasped her hands in her lap. Suddenly, she felt very young.

"You're afraid," Anderson said, surprised. "Little Robin of the courage and heart. Brave Robin of the desolate shore. I didn't think you ever turned a hair."

Robin glared. "I'm not afraid to die."

"Really? Then what has made your knees as weak as my soup?"

"There are almost as many *desgastas* in the hospital as cityborn. I've just counted."

"Did you think we were immune?"

"I don't know." To her horror, Robin heard her voice rise. "I thought maybe this was different. Maybe it was—"

"What?" Anderson interrupted. "Some sort of punishment? The cityborn have been healthy for decades, they've ignored our need for almost as long, so now some higher power decides to smite them where they stand as punishment?" He laughed. "Is that what your Keeper taught you would happen?"

Robin hunched her shoulders. She stared at her hands. Anderson's laughter dried up. He lifted the bowl of soup. As he sucked hot liquid over the porcelain edge, he studied Robin thoughtfully.

"The students and many of the cityborn believe we brought this curse into the city ourselves, because we didn't take the Mark, because our bodies were genetically dirty. Many others think it's the result of some experiment gone awry, down in the Sayers's labs. Maybe Doctor Grange made a mistake somehow, in his zeal to save the world. Maybe he's poisoned us all. I don't know." He set his bowl down, propped his elbows on the table, and stared hard at Robin.

"Maybe," he said, "maybe the land has just finally given us up. The scientist, the govs, they thought they patched it up, prevented the worst with the Mark and their high city walls. It's happening overseas as well. Maybe the land has had enough. As good a theory as any, don't you think?"

Robin reached up and fumbled with her *tronera*. She thought of Harold, trying to make a living from the unforgiving shore. Life in the House had been hard, and sometimes deadly. But Harold had understood the days, the nights, the turns of the seasons, and the tempers of dune and sea and animal. They had suffered, but the land had never betrayed them.

"What do we do, now?" she asked at last.

Anderson's eyes narrowed. He ran the tips of his fingers over his mouth, as if carefully considering Robin's question.

"I think we die," he said, and Robin's fingers began to shake. "But not here, not in this city. We've never belonged inside these lifeless walls. And now there's violence lurking in those empty streets. People are afraid, and they blame us. We made a mistake, we were led to foolishness, and now it's too late. But we'll move on."

He pushed back his chair, climbed to his feet and walked around the desk until he stood at Robin's feet. She looked up into his face and saw sorrow and resignation. For a moment, she imagined she saw Harold's patient ghost looking through the other man's eyes.

He cocked his chin at the false windows on the lush office walls, and then glanced back at Robin. "As soon as the wind and snow eases up, I'm taking any *desgastas* who are still healthy enough to walk, and we will leave Carpenteria. We'll return to the camp, or move on, down to the beach. Maybe," and he shot Robin a quick look, "we'll press on to your House, to your Keeper's shore. And we'll die in peace, away from this city's false promises."

He was *desgastas*, and he was ready to die. At peace. It didn't matter that the disease they had grown up with had turned monster, and now played by different rules. *Desgastas* were raised to meet death, and Anderson stuck to his training. Robin swallowed. She tried to find the same resolve. Her stomach still churned, and her eyes watered, but her hands steadied.

"You'll help me," Anderson decided. "You know how to live off the land. And you've made friends in the camp."

"What about my ward? There are many who won't be able to leave their beds. They need me to—"

"They're dying," Anderson cut her off. "All but dead. Nothing we do will save them. You know that. It's the way of our life. Surely you haven't forgotten."

Robin looked up. She searched for bitterness, but his face and eyes were blank.

"I need your help, Robin. For now, champion the living, those of us who are still strong. Lead us to your shore. And there we will tend another ward, and there we will each of us die with some peace."

He even spoke like Harold. Resigned, yet also impassioned, and so very sure that his way was the right way. And maybe it was. Robin had been taught to trust in her Keeper. Harold was gone, and now Anderson looked after the *desgastas*. They were different people, yet very much the same.

"Will you help?"

She nodded, and found that she could stand again, although her knees wobbled. Anderson held her firm with one hand until she found her balance. Then he ran a finger along her cheek, up until he touched her hairline.

"Watch the weather," he said. "In a day or two, the snow will break again. Then we'll go. Be ready."

Robin nodded again. Her head felt heavy on her neck. She licked her lips and found her mouth very dry. Anderson helped her to the door. She straightened her spine as he pushed open the panel. By the time she faced the guards, she felt calm again. She stepped through the doors, head held high, eyes fixed forward. Anderson touched her cheek once more, and then disappeared back into the office. The guards shut the white doors behind him.

Robin went straight to her suite and wrapped her canvas coat around her silks. She paused before her pink shell, patting the glass once with the tip of her thumb, and dug up a smile. Then she left the room, almost running as she hurried through the palace. It took Robin eleven floors to reach the underground tunnels. She ran down the grand stairs, avoiding the lifts. Her breath rattled by the time she reached the first tunnel, but she didn't slow to a walk.

She chose the tunnels the train used every morning, and she ran through the earth without stumbling. She knew the way by heart. She might have run it with her eyes closed. She took every correct turn without hesitation. By the time she sprang out onto the burning fields, she had found a new burst of energy, and her lungs no longer labored.

She zigzagged away from the fields and their noxious pyres, and jogged until she found the broken highway. Snow speckled the pavement, and fell in whirlwinds from the sky but the heat and smoke from the fields kept drifts from piling. Robin ran on. She bypassed the abandoned *desgastas* camp and ran until she reached the sea.

On the sand the rain had gathered in gritty puddles. Robin kicked through the mud, scattering seaweed. She trudged across the beach until the ocean touched the toes of her boots. She stood on the edge of land and water, waiting until her breath slowed, and then she bent and scooped a handful of seawater from the waves. The liquid ran through her fingers, but she saved just enough. She brought the sea to her mouth, and sucked.

The inside of her mouth stung, but she swallowed anyway. The sea tasted salty and metallic, lukewarm. It tasted of death and rot and mutation. Whatever had tainted Harold's shore had moved on. Now it licked at the edge of Jesse's city.

She scooped up more of the ocean, staring into the tiny puddle in her palms. She imagined that if she looked hard enough, she could see the poison swimming in the water. But she saw only the murk of sand and salt. Briefly enraged, she tossed away her handful of ocean. The water fell to the sand in fat drops.

"Searching for answers?"

Robin wouldn't let herself jump. She turned angry eyes over her shoulder at the *desgastas* and his cart. She snarled.

Grizwald winked. "So bitter, for one so young."

"Why aren't you in the city?" Robin growled. "Why haven't you frozen to death?"

He laughed, and gestured at his cart. "I have resources. The wind doesn't blow me away, and the snow doesn't fall here. I need to make a living. *Pesos*."

Robin stared across the desolate beach. "What living? You're alone with the sea."

"I like the sea." Grizwald shrugged. "But I'm not alone. I make *pesos* daily. They keep coming."

Robin looked out at the tossing sea. "Who?"

Grizwald shrugged. He pulled his cart along the sand. Robin scuffed after him.

"I don't know who they are," he said. "Pale as yourself, child. European, I think. Not the children of migrants, or natives, like myself." He grinned, showing even teeth. "They come from across the sea, I suppose. In big boats. The boats don't stay, they just drop their passengers off. And I cart the luggage."

Robin snorted. Grizwald slid her a look from beneath lowered eyelids.

"They bring mountains of luggage," he said. "As though they plan to stay. And I make hills of *pesos*. Life is good."

"But short," Robin muttered. "If they've come to stay in Carpenteria, they've come to die."

Grizwald's gaze shifted from the sand. He stared at Robin gravely. "Then I'm sorry. They wear hope like armor. I think they're running from something, something that waits over the seas."

"They'll find no help here," Robin replied, the sour taste of the sea still stinging her tongue.

Grizwald walked on in silence. Then he stopped, settling his cart in the sand, and waved at Robin. "Let me show you something."

She dogged his steps across the beach and into a hollow near the sea. There he crouched above the shoreline, and pointed one sharp finger at a tangle of grass.

"Do you see?" he asked. When Robin blinked, he frowned. "Look closer."

She dropped to the sand at his side, hunching her shoulders against the wind, and stared at the grass. After a moment's hesitation, she allowed herself to see. She stifled a gasp.

The yellow welts had grown, and were now swollen to twice the size of an orange. Fruit, she realized. The grasses were growing fruit. Something new, something different, something changed. She reached to pluck one of the yellow spheres. Grizwald didn't move to stop her.

The fruit dropped easily into her palm, separated from the bent stalk of the grass. The skin of the fruit felt soft and solid. She hefted the sphere in her hand, and knew its weight. Curious, she lifted the thing to her mouth.

Grizwald made a sound and batted the fruit from her hand. It fell to the sand, but not before Robin had taken a nibble. The flesh sat on her tongue, for the moment sweet and tangy, but she couldn't ignore the horror on Grizwald's face, so she didn't swallow. She bent to spit the bite from her mouth, and as the flesh moved on her tongue, it began to dissolve.

Robin bent at the waist and retched, trying to spit the acid from her mouth. The liquid stuck to her tongue, burning like fire, and began to trickle down the back of her throat. Coughing, she clutched at her mouth and heaved.

Grizwald moved abruptly, scooping a fistful of damp sand from the ground and grabbing Robin's jaw. Cursing, he pried her mouth open, and dumped the sand between her lips. Robin's eyes began to stream.

"Rinse," Grizwald commanded. "With the sand. Rinse it around your mouth. Don't swallow."

Robin tried. The sand coated her mouth and tongue and throat, and seemed to stop the spread of the fiery liquid.

"Good," Grizwald said as Robin wept. "Now spit."

She bent again and hacked out the sand. It fell in clumps from her mouth and at last the agony began to ease. Still heaving, she sank to the beach and rubbed at her mouth.

"Poison," Grizwald said succinctly. "Do you always act before you think? Did I tell you to eat? Just look, I said. *Look*."

Robin couldn't answer. She sat in the sand with her chin in her hands. She wondered if her tongue would swell, closing off her throat. The skin on the roof of her mouth already felt as though it were peeling away in strips.

Grizwald sat cross-legged at her side and gently patted her back and shoulder blades.

"Rest and wait. It will ease."

Robin shot the man a watery look. To her surprise he blushed.

"I tried it once, too," he admitted. "Just once. Your mouth will feel like char for a day or two. At least you didn't swallow. I sucked down just a drop, and it nearly killed me."

He rose to his feet, brushed sand from his knees, and held out a hand. "I'm going to start supper. Come with me and sit by the fire. Until you feel you can speak again."

Robin grasped his hand and let him pull her upright. He set a small fire up the beach, using the cart as shelter from the wind, and began to fry his supper. Robin sat on the edge of the warmth and watched. Grizwald had two fish and three tiny crabs. The smell of blackened fish made her stomach growl, but her mouth hurt too much to eat. And when she leaned over one of the little crabs and saw the blisters beneath its shell, she knew that the catch off Jesse's shore would no longer taste as sweet as it once had.

She sat in Grizwald's company until the sun set. The rain began to fall again in earnest. She looked up into the night sky and guessed that the storm touched the city as well. She worried that the sleet would turn quickly to snow, and wondered if Anderson would get his chance to leave the city. Maybe the *desgastas* would simply have to brave the weather.

When the last of the light winked away, Grizwald tucked Robin's coat around her chin and sent her home. She walked slowly, deep in thought, mouth aching. She thought the damage wasn't permanent, but she wondered what sort of fruit grew at the water's edge and burned like the sun.

She took the tunnels back to the palace, and then climbed floor after floor to her room. Still in her coat, she collapsed on the bed. She fell asleep immediately.

When she woke, her mouth ached, but she could swallow with ease. She dressed quickly and dashed down five flights of stairs to the hospital.

There she found that Greta had joined her husband on his drooping cot. The older woman tossed in fever. Blisters bubbled along the backs of her hands. Robin's heart broke. She woke Greta, and allowed her a bucket of water, but when she went to touch Raphael, she found him dead.

Greta wouldn't let Robin remove the body, so she left them there together, the dead and the dying, sharing one cot in the ranks of many.

Robin wiped her eyes and went in search of Molly, only to find that both the young *desgastas* and her golden butterfly had vanished.

13

On a particularly cold morning, Atlass came home from his shop in a sweat. Jesse met his lover at the front door with a towel, ready to wipe the sleet from Atlass's hair. Jesse took one look at the big man's pinched brow and felt a wave of dizziness shake along his own bones.

"What is it?" He wrapped the towel along his lover's shoulders, and caught his breath when Atlass sagged against him. "Are you ill?"

"Just tired." But his teeth began to chatter as he said the words. When Jesse laid a hand across Atlass's cheek, he felt fire burning beneath the clammy skin.

"Come to bed," Jesse urged, determined not to let his terror show.

He had to help Atlass up the stairs and into bed. The big man fell across the coverlet in something close to a faint, and slept for a day and a night, while Jesse hovered near, waiting for the first blister to pop to the surface.

When Atlass woke on the second day, unblemished and cool again to the touch, Jesse was too exhausted, too shredded by fear to believe. But Atlass appeared healthy again. The big man rose from the bed, showered and broke his fast, and then hurried to check on his shop. Jesse was left alone with the remnants of horror.

He mustered his frantic energy and took it with him into the bowels of Carpenteria. He went first to his cellars, to his lost souls. He found them waiting, untouched by the winter. Three of the creatures refused to drink his offering of water, and he knew they were dying at last. He feared their cage mates would take advantage of their weakened state, so he moved the three listless cityborn into their own cage.

That left six of the changed creatures still alive, still determined to linger.

There was nothing Jesse could do to save the dying, so he left the six food he knew they wouldn't touch and retreated from the cellar.

Atlass's drawn face hovered on the backs of Jesse's eyelids. His feet led him through tunnel after tunnel until they found the Sayers's labs. The metal doors were still cracked open. The lock pad hung detached from the wall. Jesse slid through the crack, intent on his machines. Atlass's weakness had shattered his control. Jesse needed another brush against hope.

Before he could call for the lights, Jesse was hit from behind, bowled to the freezing concrete floor. He thought first of Anderson and of *desgastas* guards hidden in the blackness of the lab. Then Jesse heard the bubbling of tortured lungs and recognized the nonsensical murmurings of madness.

The creature came at him again, a darker patch in the blackness. Jesse felt teeth fasten at the base of his right ankle. Swallowing a cry, he kicked out, trying to free himself from the searing pain. The heel of his boot found flesh. The creature howled and released his leg.

Hunched over and in pain, Jesse ordered up the lights. The room flooded with shafts of white and silver. Jesse caught a flash of movement as the creature shuffled into the shadows beneath one of the long tables. He bent over his ankle and found it bleeding. The gash was nasty, the skin torn through the silk of his trousers.

He hobbled toward the crack in the doors, but the shadows shifted along the tables as the creature ducked from its hiding place. It knocked Jesse to the ground once again, tearing at the joint of his left shoulder with its claws. He tried to shake the thing free, but it clung, digging into his flesh with inhuman need.

As Jesse writhed beneath its foul weight, he caught a glimpse of the creature's face. A cityborn Lady. Beautiful, once. A gov. He knew her name, he knew her importance, and suddenly he understood her wild anger. He had come upon her unannounced, trespassed in her territory, cornered her in her lab.

Angie Sayers, the younger of the two sisters. The skin of her face was broken and almost unrecognizable, and Jesse could feel the welts beneath her skin as she brushed over his body.

He had seen her so recently, in the palace, and already she was changed. So very quickly she had become something other.

Somehow finding her name gave Jesse courage. He took a breath and thrashed beneath her clawed nails, arching until she was forced to let go. Then, before she could retreat again beneath the tables, he brought her down, wrapping his arms around her waist and throwing her frail body to the floor.

She froze beneath his grip, as though startled by his initiative. Her lungs rasped as she muttered softly to herself. Jesse moved before she could find her courage or her hunger. He broke her neck quickly, expertly, snapping the fragile bones in one quick motion.

He was small, but he knew how to kill, and Angie was already savaged by her disease. Her body sagged against him as Harold's had. Her lifeblood ebbed away in a trickle of sticky black liquid. Jesse waited until her lungs stopped completely. When she was quiet he spread her carefully across the floor.

It was only then he noticed the manacle around her crooked ankle. The creature was shackled, chained to the table she had hidden beneath. Jesse ran his fingers along the white links, heart pounding. He knew what the manacle meant. The poor woman had been set as a guard in her own lab.

She had been chained to wait for him, Jesse knew. Which meant they would know already of his trespass. They would be coming. If he ran, they would only track him back to his home, and maybe take Atlass or Isabella as well.

Swallowing anger, he stroked back Angie's sparse hair and settled cross-legged on the floor. His ankle throbbed and his shoulder bled nastily, but if he kept his eyes narrowed he could ignore the pain. He edged along the concrete until he could settle Angie's head in his lap. Then he waited, a second guard, chained in his own way to the empty room.

Jesse set the lights to dim, and shut his eyes against the tears that threatened to leak along his cheeks, and that was how Anderson found him, keeping a last vigil over Angie's tortured soul.

Anderson's guards took Jesse to the west wing of the palace and locked him in an empty suite. The room was dark, the walls draped with curtains. When he pushed the heavy fabric aside he found windows. Real windows, he thought, until he moved to slide open a sparkling pane and found technology instead. His fingers itched and burned when he broke the holographic field. The image wavered. False windows, and the technology was cheap. Jesse stuck his fingers in his mouth, soothing away the itch. He wished that he could feel cold air through panes that didn't exist.

He pressed his forehead against a drape of velvet curtain and remembered the real windows outside the city. He had cursed the air that blew through Harold's House because it had chilled him to the bone. Now he longed for its sting across his face. There were very few windows inside his city. He had never missed them before, and he hadn't really expected to find one in the palace. He was confused, upset. He felt foolish.

He pulled his fingers from his mouth and walked along the walls of his prison, yanking the rest of the curtains away from the false windows. He activated each wall, letting in the pale winter light. Jesse almost laughed. His prison had no bars. He felt naked, visible, but he left the windows on. He wasn't ready to go back to the heavy darkness, the closed mustiness that reminded him of death.

Slowly he explored the rest of the room. He had spent many nights as Harlan's guest in the palace. He knew the suites well. They were all built on the same pattern. His prison was smaller than most of the rooms he had seen, but it was still lush. Everything was silk and velvet, deep red or soft gold. A gilt mirror hung on one wall and a vanity crouched beneath. A large bed took up most of the remaining space. More red velvet draped an inviting mattress. Atlass would have found the space cloying.

As far as he could tell, the room had no bathroom.

Jesse climbed onto the center of the bed and crossed his legs. He looked out the windows and waited as evening edged its way across the snow-covered palace lawn. He considered the things he knew. Eventually he lay down across the velvet coverlet and closed his eyes and tried to forget. He fell asleep.

A sound outside the door broke apart a dream of Harold. Jesse tried to hold onto his brother but the fragments slipped away. He woke and lay still, listening to the murmurs outside in the hall. He recognized Michael Anderson's voice. Jesse sat up, brushed a hand across gritty eyes, and took a breath.

The door opened. Anderson slid through. Jesse watched as the man blinked in the light and then frowned at the windows. For some reason the repeating view of winter seemed to irritate him.

"You need them all on?"

Jesse shrugged and ran a hand over the rumpled coverlet. He lowered his eyes, trying to hide his concern. "The room was musty and dark."

"This from a man who usually lives like a rat in a hole."

Jesse heard the scorn in Anderson's voice. He tried to be amused. He peeked up through his eyelashes, studying the man's face. Anderson's cheeks were lined and weathered, the eyebrows bleached, but the man's mouth was humorous and beautiful. Jesse recognized deep sorrow in the man's eyes. He wondered why he hadn't noticed the emotion before. He wondered if the *desgastas* regretted Angie's fate.

"Darkness bothers you?" Anderson asked. "Now that your fancy city is dying?"

Jesse found himself amused. "Are you trying to scare me? Michael Anderson, I've seen greater horrors than you might imagine." He looked down at his hand on the bed and studied the way the white of his fingers blurred into the red of the velvet. Then he smiled. "Very little scares me anymore. If the end is coming, I've made my peace."

Anderson coughed. Jesse looked up quickly, wondering if the sound was mirth, but the eyes that glared at him were cold and angry. Anderson stared down at him for a moment longer. Then he turned and walked across the room. He leaned back against the vanity until the delicate furniture groaned.

"And you're not afraid to die?" Anderson shook his head. "Of course you're not. You'll have a clean death compared to the rest."

Jesse swallowed. He forced his shoulders to lift in a shrug. "You're going to kill me, then."

"You've committed murder, Doctor. I understand Angie Sayers was a very important person. A friend of yours, in fact. Somebody has to be punished for her death. Don't you think?"

The man was taunting him. It hurt. Jesse pressed his palms into the bed and let the velvet envelop his fingers. Then he shook his head.

"You set her up for death. You knew I would break back into the labs. All you had to do was chain the poor woman up and wait. She baited the trap. She deserved better."

"She was mad as a dog," Anderson said. "She probably never noticed when you snapped her neck."

Jesse lifted his chin and studied the Anderson's face. The man's expression was still and flat, but he thought the eyes were now wet with anger. Even from across the room their gaze made Jesse feel cold and hollow.

"Let me tell you, Dr. Grange, Angie Sayers isn't the only sacrifice I've had to make. My people are dying as quickly as your cityborn, because I foolishly let a smart-mouthed student convince me to cross over forbidden walls in hopes of a cure that, apparently, doesn't exist."

Guilt clawed at Jesse. Clawed and scratched until he had to look away from Anderson's face again.

"It's not your fault," he said to his hand on the bed. "The end was coming long before the first of the *desgastas* camped outside the walls of my city."

"And you've been trying to fight it off, all these years?" Anderson guessed. He crossed to the foot of the bed. His shoulders left a shadow across Jesse's fingers. "And you've failed. Have you been lying to your people, letting them think that behind your walls they were safe from contamination, safe from retribution?"

He reached down and laid his own blunt fingers over
Jesse's slender hand. "Maybe you lied because your president, or your govs, asked you to. Paid you to. And you've
done a good job, created a paradise. But now death has
finally come, and your people are wild with fear. Some
already imagine you've created this curse, by mistake, in
your labs. What would they do if they found out you've
been lying for how long, Doctor — years?"

Jesse flinched. He felt his stomach rise in rebellion. He
swallowed carefully, willing calm, willing emptiness. The
control didn't come but he found he could pretend. Under
Anderson's hand he could sit and be still and pretend.

"I think they'll hang you from the city walls. Strip your
skin, crack your bones, set your head on a pristine white
pole. There will be no honorable place on the burning
fields for you. You'll be left to rot beneath the winter sun.
A fitting punishment, don't you think?" Anderson
laughed as he paced back across the room. His shadow
slid along behind him. Jesse watched it with feigned interest.

"I don't blame you for Angie's death," Anderson said.
He ran his fingers across the vanity and then brought
them up to touch his lips. "You're right, I set you up.
Because I wanted you punished. When I realized, when I
finally believed that you were telling the truth, that you
had no cure, that you couldn't even save your own
people, then I began to wonder. And to think."

"And then," Anderson continued, "then I realized that
you brought this new plague upon my people. You and
your lies. You painted this city as an impenetrable fortress,
and your poor people believed it. Even the *desgastas*
believed it. We camped outside your walls, longing for the
safety beyond, believing that Carpenteria was a haven. If
not for your lies, we might have moved on, moved away
from this poisoned land."

"There is no safe haven, "Jesse said. He almost brought
himself to mean it. "There never was."

"More lies!" Anderson snarled. "And now it's too late
for me to find the truth. It's too late for us all. Your Mark
was a clever idea, Dr. Grange, and it might even have

saved a few lives. But it was never meant for something this big. It's a façade, a diversion, and it bought you a few years, a nice home, a life of ease. But now your time is up, the truth has come calling."

He touched the vanity one last time and then left the room. Jesse caught a glimpse of the guard in the hall before the door closed, before he was left alone with his windows. He slid from the bed and turned the screens off one by one and brought the darkness back.

They fed him much later. He ate at the vanity, leaning against the same corner Anderson had touched. He slipped pieces of hard cheese between his teeth and let his eyes adjust to the shadows. As he ate he noticed that the bottoms of the heavy curtains had frayed and were unraveling. Even Harlan's beloved palace was deteriorating beneath its beauty. After a moment, Jesse finished the cheese, turned down the lights, and went back to the bed and slept.

On what he thought was the fourth day they stopped feeding him, and on the sixth day he pulled the curtains back away from the windows but it was night and the room remained black. He sat up until dawn waiting for the sun to rise and when it did the light bounced across the snow and hurt his eyes. He narrowed his lids and sat patiently until he could see again through the glare.

On the eighth day Anderson came back and Jesse looked at the man's face and knew that his time was finally up.

But it wasn't.

"A handful of my people tried to escape this place, last night," Anderson said after he shut the door. He examined his prisoner. "They took the tunnels as far as the city center. Three men, two women, and a small child. We found them this morning, just inside the city gates, torn to pieces, trampled by a mob. Your people have gone mad with fear, Doctor. They won't let us leave."

Jesse had taken to sitting on the floor in the pale sunlight. He stayed on his haunches in the patch of glare and let Anderson face him from across the room. He saw that the beautiful mouth was made harsh by loss.

"Take the tunnels out," Jesse suggested. "Most of the cityborn don't even know they exist. They were a secret of the president, and of the govs. And the president and his govs are dead."

Anderson laughed. He collapsed back against the door and laughed and laughed until the sound that came from his throat turned dry and raspy. Jesse waited until the convulsion was finished and then rose to his feet. He walked across to the vanity. He was able to move without leaving the light. The windows shone at him from every angle.

One piece of dried cheese sat alone on the vanity. Jesse picked the wedge up and offered it to Anderson.

"Have you eaten?"

The *desgastas* stared down at Jesse, brows lowered. "I told them not to feed you."

"They haven't been," Jesse said, his hand still extended. "I learned long ago how to hoard. Eat."

Anderson reached out and took the cheese. He ran the wedge between his fingers. His mouth twisted. "It's as hard as a rock."

"It's days old," Jesse said. He paced back across the room and settled again on the floor. "It won't hurt you."

"It's your last," Anderson said, glancing at the vanity.

"I expect I won't need more. Why else have you come, if not to give me to the city and watch me hung across the portcullis? Drawn and quartered, trampled like your poor fugitives." Knowing that none of the fear he felt touched his face, Jesse stared at Anderson. "If you're so certain this city is death, why haven't you led your people away? You've made this palace your House. You're Keeper of the lost. Lead them away, now, before you lose even six more innocents."

Anderson's eyes blazed. He tossed the wedge of cheese to the floor. It bounced under the bed.

"So be it," Jesse said, unruffled. "But unless you put some meat back on your bones you'll have trouble dragging me from the room. You look awful, and I'm stronger than I seem."

"You smell," Anderson accused.

"No doubt," Jesse returned. "Me and the pot."

"The pot?" Weary curiosity changed the man's wan face.

Jesse gestured at the vase he had cloistered away in one corner of the room. "I made do. A shame to ruin such a lovely piece of art. Harlan must be spinning in his grave."

"What are you talking about?"

Jesse allowed his eyebrows to arch in surprise. Genuine confusion marked Anderson's mouth.

"No bathroom," he explained gently. "Wasn't that part of the plan?"

Disgust clouded the man's eyes, and then something that Jesse imagined might have been embarrassment.

"No. I didn't think...." He trailed off and rubbed a hand across his wind-burned face.

"No apology necessary," Jesse said. He felt a twist of pity in his throat. "I made do."

He rocked to his knees and edged under the bed until he found the piece of cheese. He stood up, crossed the room once more, and this time held the offering before Anderson's eyes.

"You need your energy," Jesse suggested. "One piece of dusty cheese won't help much, but heaven knows as soon as you leave this room you'll forget the needs of your body."

Anderson snatched the cheese from Jesse's hand and grabbed a savage bite. It took him a moment to chew and swallow, and then he sighed.

"I can't get the *desgastas* free," he said.

"And why not?" Jesse asked without moving. "Surely you haven't forgotten how easily you broke in. Break out again."

Anderson took another bite. He paused before answering. "Winter is harsh this year. Most of my people are already close to death. Where will we go? Not back to the camp. We've survived the snow seasons before, but not one like this, not with plague in our midst. How can I let my people die in this city? But how can I make them live outside its walls?"

"You can't," Jesse said. "Each of us will die before the season is over."

The rage came back. Anderson set the last of the cheese back on the vanity and stepped with precision out of Jesse's reach. He walked along a bank of windows. Jesse followed after.

"I'm tormenting you," Jesse sighed, "and I don't have the right." He stood in the sunlight, lowered his chin, and then lifted his hands, palms up. "I understand what you're saying. You want the *desgastas* to die away from the taint of technology in this city. My brother wanted the same of his wards. So, then take your people to my brother's shore, live in his empty House until the last of you rot. Harold's House is the closest, and it's warm enough, even in the winters."

"I've thought of it," Anderson admitted. He stopped at one of the windows and stared out at the lawn.

"And?" Jesse stopped a stride behind.

"How will we eat? How will we live?" Anderson said. "We are *desgastas*, but we know nothing of the land. Many of us were born outside your city walls, grew up in the shadow of your garbage. We scavenge. We eat only because the labor crews bring us *pesos* and food. We lost the old ways, dreaming of a cure, living for your promises."

Jesse said nothing. His attention wavered. He gazed out across the president's lawn, and watched the snow drift along manicured gardens.

"Take Robin. She knows the old ways. My brother filled her with his tradition, with his wisdom. She'll keep you alive on the shore, until the last of you dies."

"I've thought of it," Anderson repeated. "It won't work."

"Why not? Your alternative seems little better."

Anderson watched Jesse, eyes inscrutable. But there was something in the set of his shoulders, in the twitch of his mouth. Jesse's spine suddenly stiffened.

"What is it?"

Anderson only shook his head.

"What game are you playing?" Jesse crossed the room in a bound and grabbed the *desgastas* by his silken collar. In an instant Anderson was furious. He shoved Jesse away, and crossed his arms over his chest.

"I don't trust you."

Jesse wanted to laugh. "Of course not. In your eyes, I'm the bringer of plague. But this is something different. This is something new, the lines on your brow. What are you trying to hide?" A thought occurred. He smothered an unlooked for pang of sorrow. "Are you ill?"

Anderson growled. "Four days without food. No bathroom. I hoped for a broken man and I get sweetness and light."

"Are you ill?" Jesse asked again, sure of the answer.

Anderson's eyes flashed. "Not me. Not me. Your child, little Robin."

Jesse flinched as though stung. His heart cracked and his lungs began to strain, but he wouldn't let the fear show. He blinked his eyes, forced the tears away. Anderson huffed, as if annoyed. Then he grasped Jesse's shoulder, squeezing with one callused hand.

Jesse jerked away. "Is that why you wouldn't let me see her? Is she dead?"

Anderson didn't answer. Jesse felt the grave eyes studying him. Their weight was heavy, searching, but at last Anderson sighed and moved away. He found a spot brighter than others and settled his arm along the wall. Jesse watched him carefully. Anderson waited in the glare from the windows. Then he shrugged.

"Not dead," Anderson said. "The blisters started four days ago."

"Four days?" Jesse's heart lurched. He peered through the light and up at Anderson.

"She's doing well. Well enough. I've moved her from the hospital, set her up in her own suite. She doesn't deserve to die on a cot surrounded by cityborn." Anderson smiled but it was a twist of rage. "She's a brave child. I'm giving her the ease I can, but it's too late. She can't lead my *desgastas* to her Keeper's shore. She won't last two more days."

Jesse felt his hands tremble. He folded them in his lap. But Anderson saw and laughed.

"Now at last I have said something that's scared you," he leaned forward.

Jesse bit his lip. "Let me see her."

"No." The denial pained Jesse. He closed his eyes against it.

"You can't help her, Dr. Grange." The voice was low and harsh against Jesse's ear. "You killed her. You'll see her when I'm ready. If at all."

"She may not last much longer. I need—"

"What?"

"Nothing," Jesse muttered. "Nothing." He bit the inside of his mouth, trying to ignore the fluttering of his innards.

"Good," Anderson said.

Jesse waited but there was nothing more. Footsteps along the floor, the slam of the door, and then silence. He knew he was alone but he didn't bother to open his eyes. He kept his thoughts in the darkness and let his mind work.

They started feeding him again and twice a day the guard led him down the hall to a communal bathroom. The bathroom was huge and lovely, squeaky clean and empty. Once it would have been packed with visitors and residents, now Jesse was the only one to use it. The guards let him shower in the mornings and somehow provided him with a razor to shave the stubble from his face.

No clean clothes and his meals consisted solely of bread, fruit, cheese, and water, but he felt more human with the grime and the smell cleaned away. He began to look forward to his trips down the hall. His guard was always mute but he could study the changing faces and try to guess how many new dead were being burned outside his city.

He wondered about Isabella and worried that she was still alive. He hoped that Atlass was keeping her safe. When he thought of his lover he turned his face to the windows and stared until his eyes watered and he could think of nothing but the endless lawn.

There were certain things he wouldn't allow himself to think of at all. Robin, dying alone. His lost cityborn, imprisoned in their cellar, forgotten and untended. And his future execution, the image of his own blood steaming in dirty snow.

He shut off that part of his mind and slept well, and was surprised at how rested he felt.

Another endless week passed before Michael Anderson came back. Jesse had expected the man. He'd had days to prepare. This time he knew that Robin was dead, and that his own time was up. He thought briefly of Atlass. Then he schooled his panic away.

The man who came through the door was clenched and thin. His hands trembled and his eyes were ugly, sunken holes. Jesse stood against the windows, waiting. He wasn't sure Anderson was sane.

"Aren't you going to offer me some cheese?" The voice was worn and desperate but Jesse relaxed. He heard the sanity beneath the despair.

"I'm sorry," Jesse gestured at the vanity. "I've eaten it all. I've become accustomed to regular meals again." He nodded to the bed. "Why don't you sit down before you fall down?"

Anderson grimaced but he crossed the floor and dropped heavily onto the bed. Jesse waited until Anderson settled and then opened the suite door. He smiled at the startled young guard.

"Get this man some food, something nourishing. A lot of it."

The guard glanced over Jesse's shoulder at Anderson. He must have seen something surprising because he grinned before he turned and ran down the hallway.

"Don't think about it," Anderson spoke from the sunlight. "I'd break your skull before you were halfway down the hall."

Jesse shut the door. He turned around. "I wasn't going to run. I was just admiring the young man's energy. You don't see much of it anymore."

"Energy?" Anderson snorted. "You look like you've got some."

Jesse laughed aloud. To his own surprise the mirth felt real and sweet. "I'm afraid I'm enjoying my stay."

Anderson stiffened and Jesse's laughter fled.

"I'm not trying to make you angry," he said. "But it's become a relief."

Anderson looked at him.

"To let go," Jesse explained. "Not to wonder any longer, not to worry. For years I've raced death, and now I find I can't stop it. I'm ready."

Anderson's eyes narrowed and he made a sound that was half grunt and half sigh. He opened his mouth but a knock on the door stopped his words. Jesse turned away to answer it.

The food steamed and there was a lot of it. Jesse nodded at the guard. The young man smiled. Jesse closed the door and carried the platter to Anderson.

"Eat," he said, setting the platter on the bed.

"Eat, eat," Anderson mimicked. "Is that all you can say?"

Jesse selected a roll from the platter. He took a bite. The bread was warm and smeared with butter. Jesse chewed slowly, savoring the taste. Anderson hesitated but when Jesse reached for a second piece of bread the *desgastas* began to eat as well.

"The guard likes you," he said through a mouthful of apple. "They all like you."

"Close up I'm not quite the tyrant they expect," Jesse said. He picked two hard-boiled eggs from the platter and found a spot on the floor across the room. He began to peel the first egg, carefully separating shell from rubbery flesh.

"You look harmless enough," Anderson admitted. "But I know better."

"Mmm," Jesse allowed, attention on his egg. "Have you come at last to throw me to the mob?"

"Robin doesn't wake. But I can still get fluids down her throat."

Jesse almost dropped his egg. "She's alive?"

"Most of the sores have dried up into scar tissue. Her hair is growing back in."

Jesse couldn't move. He clutched his egg and tried to inhale.

"But she weighs nothing. And when she breathes her lungs bubble." Anderson chose another piece of fruit.

Jesse took a an absent bite of his egg. He blinked at Anderson. Anderson looked back, questions in his eyes. Jesse wanted to reach out and soothe. Instead he chewed a moment longer and then swallowed.

"How many days has it been? Since the first blister?"

"Two weeks, almost. And she's improving, I'm sure of it."

Jesse rolled a chunk of egg between his thumb and forefinger. He shook his head. "This plague has made you forget your roots. She's simply dying. In the old manner. You remember the stages. It's working on her insides."

"You can't know that," Anderson scowled. "She's been different from the others. This is different."

"It's the same. It's always been the same. She's just taking longer to die."

"You bastard," Anderson whispered. "I don't know why I bother to come here. You don't deserve to know."

"It's not for me." Jesse studied his second egg. "It's for you. You're lonely and frightened and you still think I can somehow save you."

He expected Anderson to protest but the room was silent. Surprised, he glanced up. The other man was crying. Great wet tears ran down his seamed cheeks. Jesse looked away, unwilling to witness the emotion. He cracked his second egg on the floor and began to peel it with his thumb.

"You want me to tell you that she'll be all right. That you'll be all right. I can't. I thought you were resigned, Michael. What happened to your faith?"

Anderson jumped from the bed. He grabbed Jesse by the shoulder. Startled and in pain Jesse dropped the egg. It bounced on the floor and left a patch of slime in the sunlight.

"Do you have it?" Anderson hissed. He shook Jesse once and then again. "Has it started on you?"

"No," Jesse said. The man's fear surprised him.

Anderson crouched in front of Jesse and glared. He smelled of bread and meat, and the salt of tears.

"It doesn't matter if you were born free of it. It doesn't matter." He sucked at the air, his hands clenched. "I'll kill you first. Your time is almost up."

"No doubt." Jesse edged along the floor until he was free of Anderson's hands. He picked up his egg and pulled away the broken shell. "I'm not sure why you're keeping me around."

Anderson paced back to the bed and ate another roll. Then he stretched out across the coverlet and closed his eyes.

"I want you to take her back."

"What?" The words were soft. Briefly, Jesse wasn't sure of what he'd heard.

"To the shore," Anderson said. "She wants to go back. She wants to die in her Keeper's House. Before she went under she asked and asked...."

Jesse stared at the bed. He said nothing.

"Maybe I've waited too long. I didn't want to let her go. I needed her here. But I want her to die at ease. And she doesn't have any time left."

Jesse felt a quiver of excitement, scenting freedom, but he kept his voice steady. "Why don't you take her?"

"I've told you. I have to stay here and help our people die."

"They'll die just as thoroughly without you."

Anderson twitched an angry hand but didn't open his eyes. "You were right. I'm the Keeper here. The *desgastas* trust me, despite my mistakes. They need me to help them keep their faith."

"And do you have enough faith to ease their way?"

"No," Anderson said. "When I close my eyes to pray I see the blistered face of my son."

Jesse wiped greasy fingers on his shirt. "Let her die here. It will be easier on both of you. She won't know."

"No," Anderson said. "I promised her. I promised her that she could die in Harold's House." His fingers moved on the velvet. "I'm her Keeper, I won't let her down. And neither will you. You'll see her there safely."

"I thought you wanted me to stay," Jesse said. "So you could bleed me in the city's honor."

"You'll come back." Anderson rolled his head in Jesse's direction. "Then I'll kill you."

Jesse laughed. "You think I'll give her to the sea and then come trotting right back so you can gut me? I'm not such a fool. There's nothing for me in this city but death."

"Really?" Anderson's eyes gleamed. "You leave your family so easily."

"They don't need me. They'll adapt."

"Will you?"

"Of course."

"I think you're lying." The mouth that Jesse so admired gaped with malice. "You're not so different than I am. I don't think you can leave them to die without you."

"They're perfectly healthy."

"For now," Anderson said. "But even if they stay that way while you're gone, somebody has to be punished for Angie's murder."

Jesse stiffened. "You wouldn't execute an innocent person."

"I might." Anderson's angry smile burned across the room. "Your lover is a big man, Doctor. Surely he could have easily broken Angie's neck with his little finger. Josie Sayers wants blood before she dies. Your cityborn want someone punished for their pain. They want you, but Atlass might do in your stead."

Jesse bit the inside of his lip until he tasted blood. He swallowed against the lump in his throat.

"We know who really killed Angie, Doctor. But it's only you and me. And you're the one I want to see die." He shifted his head on the coverlet and closed his eyes once more. "I know you'll protect your family. I know you'll die for them. You'll come back after Robin is laid to rest, and you'll scream when I tear you to pieces. But you'll die willingly to save your lover. Am I right?"

Jesse shuddered and went cold. Somehow he was on his feet, eggshells crunching beneath him. The world faded to black and red and it spun around his head. He launched himself from the sunlight and clawed at Anderson's throat. Anderson was larger, and had been waiting, but he was weakened by grief and ill use. Jesse managed to bring his fist down across the man's mouth and blood burst into the light. Anderson yelled and Jesse groped for his windpipe. He squeezed and squeezed, listening to Anderson wheeze, knowing how easily he could kill the man who kept him imprisoned.

And then Jesse fell flat on his back on the floor, the breath knocked out of him. The young guard stood over him, fists raised. Jesse gasped for air. The guard kicked him in the ribs, again and again. Jesse tried to roll away and the booted foot connected with the back of his head. Stunned, he lay still, staring up at the ceiling and trying to find air.

"Enough!" he heard Anderson say. "Leave us alone."

The guard tramped out of the room. Jesse winced at the sound of his heavy boots. The bedsprings shifted and Anderson stood over him. The *desgastas* wiped blood from his mouth. Drops of red fell across Jesse's forehead.

"I won't hurt Atlass, Dr. Grange," his voice sounded hoarse and bruised. "If you give Robin the peace she needs and then come back to me. Is that understood?"

Jesse refused to answer. He stared at nothing and thought of murder. Anderson hissed and lashed out with his foot. Jesse gasped and then laughed brokenly.

"Not so different from your lackey."

Anderson struck him again. This time Jesse couldn't laugh.

"I'll ask you once more," Anderson said. "Do you understand?"

"Yes," Jesse coughed. "Yes."

"Good. I'll come for you at sunrise."

14

His guard came before the sun saw the horizon. Footsteps in the hallway woke Jesse from a deep sleep and when he opened his eyes the windows were still dark. He lifted his chin from velvet and thought that if he squinted he could just make out the drip of blue moonlight. But when he sat up he saw that he had imagined it. The moon had already disappeared, though morning was still far away. He stretched and sighed and waited as the guard lingered outside his door.

His ribs hurt. He suspected they would be purpling with bruises. He rubbed his left arm and the twinge of pain made him angry. Swearing under his breath he limped across the floor and pulled open the door.

The young guard gaped at him, astonished.

"Well?" Jesse snarled. "What are you waiting for?"

The boy's mouth opened and closed. Jesse felt abruptly ashamed.

"Afraid, were you? Don't worry. I'll forgive you the broken ribs. You were only doing your job."

The guard took a step backwards. In the dim light Jesse glimpsed the denim bag swinging on the boy's arm.

"What's in the bag?"

The guard quivered. Jesse sighed and took pity.

"They're not really broken," he said patiently, "just sore. And I may look like I want to eat you, but I won't. It's early, I'm tired, and you're behaving like an idiot. What's in the bag?"

The boy blinked. He straightened, and then shoved the denim at Jesse.

"Clothes," he managed. "You're supposed to dress before I take you to Anderson."

"Fair enough," Jesse said. "Mind if I use the bathroom? I'd like to freshen up before my ordeal." He showed his teeth.

The boy nodded and Jesse started down the hallway. Then he stopped and turned back.

"What's your name, child?"

"Quinn." It was a mumble.

"All right, Quinn," Jesse said. "Sit tight, I'll be out in a minute."

In the bathroom Jesse ordered the lights to their brightest setting and rummaged through the bag. In the sack he found brand new jeans and clean underwear and boots that looked like leather but felt like synthetic fiber. Underneath the boots, a deep blue flannel shirt and a black cable knit sweater of thick wool were crumpled together in a ball. Jesse used the sink and a hand towel to wash. Then he layered the clothes carefully over his swollen ribs.

He peered into the mirror and practiced looking calm. His hair had darkened from the weeks indoors. It fell into his eyes and around his ears. Somehow, during his confinement, parts of Jesse had eased. His skin was pale and smooth, the lines around his eyes and mouth had disappeared. He looked eighteen, he looked lovely; Atlass would have eaten him alive.

The thought made him laugh and the face in the mirror sparked with joy. What did it mean, he wondered as he looked into his glowing reflection, that he thrived while his city died? He was very much afraid that it meant madness.

He locked the thought away with a shrug and another smile. He left his soiled clothes on the bathroom sink and slung the denim bag over his shoulder. The guard lingered on the bright hallway carpet, looking uneasy. Jesse took a moment to admire the boy's earnest stance and then cocked a finger.

"I'm ready," said. "Shall we go?"

The boy named Quinn pressed his lips together, nodded, and then started down the corridor. Jesse followed in his new boots. He tried to smother his eager smile.

Anderson waited in the president's office. He looked
Jesse up and down and then passed a hand over his eyes.

"You're ready," he said. "You look as though you belong on the shore."

"You've been there?"

"No. Robin's told me."

"She must have painted a pretty picture," Jesse smiled.
"We wore rags on the shore, not shiny boots and expensive
sweaters."

Quinn made an embarrassed sound. Anderson's lips
twisted in annoyance.

"Not that I'm ungrateful," Jesse continued. "My old
clothes were beginning to smell like a sewer."

"Enough." Anderson rubbed a hand over his mouth.
He pushed his chair away from the president's desk and
stood up. "*Are* you ready?"

Jesse nodded. Anderson marched around the desk and
preceded Quinn through the door. Jesse followed more
slowly.

"Why yes, thank you, Michael, I slept well." He pitched
his voice so it echoed up and down the long hallway. "My
ribs are a little sore this morning, but it's nothing to worry
about."

Anderson ignored his taunt, but this time the sound
Quinn made was a definite snort of mirth.

Robin's room must have once been the mirror image of
Jesse's prison. The bed still wore the same velvet coverlet.
Someone had stripped away the heavy curtains and carried off most of the furniture. The bed itself had been
moved into the center of the room. A small stand by the
headboard held a vase full of flowers. The blooms were
purple and looked fresh. Jesse crossed the room and
pressed a bud to his nose with one finger. It smelled of
rain. He closed his eyes and then opened them, and forced
himself to look from the flowers to the bed.

Robin slept in a boneless sprawl, curled on her side, one
thin hand flung out across the coverlet. Her cheeks were
puffy with scars and her eyelids black with bruises. Her
lips were white and cracked. Jesse ran a hand across the
patchy stubble on her skull.

"She won't wake," Anderson said. "I've given her something to kill the pain. She sleeps most of the time now, anyway. But I didn't want her to wake on the road."

"Are you ready to let us go?" Jesse looked at the other man and thought again how heartbreak made the proud face beautiful, how much Anderson had lost and how easy he would be to love.

"For now." Anderson refused to meet Jesse's eyes. "There's a cart waiting outside one of the tunnels beneath the palace. Quinn will take you there. The cart is small, so you'll have to walk. But it runs well and it should keep Robin safe and warm until you reach the sea."

"And then?"

"There will be a small boat waiting. The cart won't fit aboard. Wrap her in the blankets. Keep her warm. There will be extra food and water as well, and what medical supplies I could spare. The rest is up to you."

"You're not seeing us off?"

"My place is here," Anderson said. "Quinn will carry her as far as the tunnel."

Jesse shook his head, "Let me take her."

Anderson moved as though he wanted to object but at Jesse's look he held his tongue. Robin seemed terribly light in Jesse's arms. The blankets dragged at her thin bones. He pressed her forehead into his shoulder and ran a thumb along the lobe of her ear. The skin there was still smooth and warm, untouched by her disease.

"Fine," he said, resting his chin on Robin's prickly scalp. He peered up at Anderson. "We're ready."

Anderson nodded once. "Quinn."

The boy opened the door. Anderson set a shaking hand on a corner of the empty bed. Jesse stood still, watching until Anderson's shoulders steadied. He waited while the man's harsh breathing quieted, waited until the room was silent.

"Keep your faith, Michael," Jesse said, trying to be gentle.

"Just make her comfortable," Anderson said without looking around. "And then come back. I'll be waiting."

Jesse smothered a sigh. He flashed an encouraging grin at Quinn. The guard returned a slow smile. Jesse walked past him and led the way from the stale bedchamber.

Time passed slowly as they made their way through the palace. The halls seemed to wind and repeat, doubling back along each other. The floor beneath Jesse's feet was one endless carpet. Never changing and never ending. But Robin was light in Jesse's arms and Quinn walked the corridors without hesitation. Jesse tried to speak to the boy once or twice but Quinn seemed too wrapped in fear or sorrow to respond.

They met no one as they walked. Jesse chased away his own unease by counting his footsteps and watching Robin's eyelids flicker as she slept. Occasionally he wondered what she was dreaming. An hour passed and they reached the belly of the palace. Quinn turned right, into what Jesse thought was a shadow on the wall, but it was a door, a carved hole that lead into a new species of hall. Here the floor was carved of stone, the walls hung with old and faded tapestries. The air smelled of mold.

Robin shifted in Jesse's arms, as though disturbed by the new thickness in the air. Jesse bent to whisper words of comfort into her ear and she settled. He studied the pulse that beat in her throat and then looked up at Quinn.

"Almost there?"

"We are there," Quinn said. He led Jesse around a dusty corner.

The guard touched another door in the wall and produced a key. Jesse watched as the boy fumbled in the gloom. After a moment the lock clicked open. Quinn pushed the door free and cool air blew in, dispersing the dust. The air tasted of the early morning, and it smelled of smoke. Jesse carried Robin through the door and at last they were outside the palace, outside the city walls. Jesse hadn't known they had come so far.

The cold sun lit the sky a bright pink, but smoke dulled the color and stung Jesse's eyes. Quinn coughed once, and then again, and then spat into the ashy snow.

"There," he said, nodding his head. "There are extra blankets in the back."

Jesse looked where the boy's chin pointed. The cart was small, just as Anderson had warned. And it was old, as rusted as Grizwald's. But except for a thin layer of ash, the vehicle was clean, and it had a steering pad instead of a push handle. The controls chirped when Jesse bent over the pad. He spoke a word and the cart hummed to life. Jesse found just enough room to bundle Robin into the back. He arranged her carefully, tucking the extra blanket around her shoulders. He placed his denim bag under her head, hoping it would protect her skull from further bruising. Then he spread one more blanket across the lip of the vehicle, shielding Robin's face from the snow and wind.

Jesse turned to Quinn and found the boy standing in the shadow of the doorway. The guard lifted a hand. He pulled a flask from beneath his blouse and held it out. Curious, Jesse accepted the offering.

"Water," Quinn said as Jesse examined the small plastic bottle. "The wind dries your throat."

"Thank you," Jesse said, surprised and gratified.

The boy looked ashamed. "It was for me. But—"

"Thank you," Jesse said again. He reached out and squeezed the boy's shoulder. "Tell Anderson Robin is resting well."

Quinn nodded and then dipped back into the wall. The door closed behind the boy. Jesse stood alone with Robin and the gritty morning. He secured Quinn's flask under the waistband of his jeans, then tilted his head and scanned the horizon until he found the road in the distance. Swallowing hard, he began to walk towards the stretch of cracked concrete. The old cart, true to its programming, hummed along at Jesse's shoulder. The blanket over Robin's head sagged already under a thin layer of ash and snow.

The highway spread ahead under the ice, no longer the pristine white Jesse remembered. He set himself on it anyway, walking slowly so as not to slip. The cold mush sucked at his boots. In the distance the fires burned. Jesse set his back to his city and began to slog through the muck.

Slowly the light in the sky changed. Jesse ignored the passage of time. He forgot his destination and concentrated only on staying upright in the wind. Once he looked up and the sky was purple. He found himself shivering. He stopped often, trying to chafe warmth back into his finger and into Robin's flesh.

Occasionally he had to stop and sip water from Quinn's flask. Jesse drank very little, just enough to wash the ash from his lips and clear his throat. Each time he stopped, after he sloshed the liquid through his mouth, he stilled the cart and parted the blankets to tip some of the water down Robin's throat. She swallowed without waking. Her face was flushed even in the cold, beaded with sweat, but she looked comfortable and Jesse knew she was oblivious.

He left the smoke behind and the winter weather seemed to ease. He thought that he could smell the sea. He looked up and the sky was black. He couldn't find the stars. His legs were stiff, well used, awake. Beneath his boots the snow had turned patchy and at last melted away until he could see the broken pavement of the road. Sand and shells lay scattered over the stone, mixed in the slush.

Jesse sang then, a song Harold had once loved. He sang a poem to the sea, a song of the old ships that wavered now at the bottom of the ocean, a song of warmth. He tilted his chin, and looked to the heavens, imagining that he could place the stars in the sky himself.

At last the road ended. Jesse stepped onto shifting sand. He could hear the ocean. He turned his head and he could see the breakers over his shoulder, over the cart. The waves rolled in the darkness, glistened silver along their edges. He squinted until he could pick out the boat Anderson had promised. Farther along the sand a torch burned yellow, sparking in the night. A figure held the torch high, watching, waiting. Jesse stilled the cart with a word and walked across the sand.

Atlass dropped the torch and sank until he sat cross-legged on the dunes. Jesse stood over him, looking down at eyes that were wide and bright. He could see himself reflected in the dark irises, steady and straight and burning with something like joy.

"You're alive," Atlass whispered. His tears began to overflow. "You're beautiful."

"I am lost," Jesse said. He stretched down to brush the wet from his lover's cheek. "But by now so are we all."

They spent the rest of the day a stone's throw from the sea. Jesse carried Robin from the cart and bundled her safely in one corner of Atlass's tent. She shifted in the blankets but did not wake. Jesse settled on his knees next to her shoulder while Atlass squatted in the sand at her feet.

"She looks awful."

"She's near death," Jesse admitted. He looked at his lover. "She wanted to go home to die. Anderson picked me as her escort."

"Why you?"

"I'm not sure. Maybe she asked for me. Maybe Anderson was afraid to have me in the city. Does it matter?"

Atlass shook his head. The shade of the tent stretched across the big man's face.

"You knew I was coming," Jesse said. "How?"

"Isabella," Atlass answered. "There's someone in the palace. I don't know who, someone she talks to. She knew Robin was dying. She knew Anderson wanted to send her back to the House."

"Anderson? Were you waiting here for Anderson?"

"He wouldn't see me." Atlass's voice broke. "I thought maybe I could convince him—"

"To let me go?" Jesse swallowed a laugh. "You'd what, beat him with a spoon until he cried mercy?"

"I went to talk to him," Atlass continued as if he hadn't heard. "In the palace. But he wouldn't see me. And then, four nights ago, Isabella sent word. She said he'd be ordering you out, and that he wanted me as hostage against your behavior. So I ran."

"You've been living out here for five days?"

"I'm not helpless," Atlass snapped.

"I know," Jesse said. "I'm sorry." He sifted his fingers through the sand. "But now you see I'm safe. I'm well. Will you go back to the city?"

"No."

"I would feel better if—"

"No," Atlass said. He held firm, his eyes steady. "I was desperate to free you. I didn't know what to do, what to say. And now you're here. I'm going with you."

"What about the café? What about Isabella? You'll be safe in the city. Anderson promised me, before I left."

"Safe in his jail?" Atlass scoffed. "No place is safe. Bruster's is everywhere. I belong with you. For as long as we have."

Jesse threw back his chin and laughed. "Always so romantic. You never change."

"You're wrong," Atlass said.

Jesse swallowed his grin. He reached across to touch Atlass's knee. "I know."

"I missed you," Atlass whispered.

"I know that, too," Jesse said. He smiled.

They slept deeply but Jesse woke again before the dawn, and slipped from the tent to walk the beach. The worries he had kept so tightly reined struggled free. He sat in the sand, hands to his head, and counted his mistakes. He had thought death would find him in his city, and now instead it would take him on Harold's shore. He only hoped he didn't live to see Atlass blister.

When the wind began to numb his nose and moth, Jesse rose to his feet and continued along the beach. Several strides later, in a hollow along the sea, he found Grizwald.

The *desgastas* lay dead, face down on the beach, and the gulls had long been picking at his corpse. His body rotted in a tangle of sea grass, one hand extended along the sand toward his abandoned pushcart. Jesse crouched over the body. The stench made his eyes water, but he forced himself to reach down and turn the man over.

The body rolled easily, leaving bits of flesh in the wet sand. Jesse swallowed. He considered what was left of the man's face. Grizwald had lost his hair and most of his eyelashes. His brows were mere slashes of purple flesh. His mouth hung open, gaping and smeared with sand. Jesse couldn't see any teeth, only a swollen tongue.

The *desgastas's* hands were ridged and scarred, his fingernails gone. The rest of his flesh looked torn by decay, but

Jesse couldn't tell whether it was decomposition or Bruster's that had turned the dead man to rot.

Jesse crouched over Grizwald until the sun pinked the sky, then he rose and went to wake Atlass.

Jesse didn't mention the dead *desgastas*. They ate a meager breakfast in silence, and then carried Robin from the tent and laid her in the bottom of the boat. She woke once when Atlass tried to give her lukewarm water from Quinn's flask. She swallowed reflexively as the liquid trickled over her tongue, but her eyes were heavy and unaware. She drifted away again before Atlass could give her more than three swallows.

"Is it a drug that makes her sleep so?" Anderson asked, his face flat with worry.

"No," Jesse said. "She's simply dying. Let her be."

Anderson closed his eyes and bowed his head over the girl's thin form. Jesse turned to meet the wind as he sent the boat across the sea.

This journey was colder than Jesse's previous. The fog hung low over the waves and the boat rattled in protest. The sun disappeared and Atlass began to shiver. Jesse guided the boat without hesitation. The sun dimmed in the gloom. The sea darkened to gray. But Jesse knew the way in his bones and he was not worried.

He looked back once to find Atlass asleep. The big man lay stretched beside the still bundle that was Robin. Atlass's mouth was set even in sleep. He'd grown, Jesse knew. He thought Atlass was becoming steadier, rooting himself in life, leaving his vague and bumbling optimism behind. Jesse sighed and moved away from the controls of the boat to stroke a hand along his lover's calf. Atlass didn't even twitch.

A long while later the sun broke through the fog. Jesse blinked moisture from his stinging eyes and smiled. Welcoming the warmth, he sang softly under his breath. The rattle of the boat seemed to soothe to a gentle purr.

His singing woke Atlass so that when the shore finally appeared, a smudged line against the clouds, the big man was awake to see it. He drew in a breath as they approached the breakers and inched along the boat to peer over Jesse's shoulder.

"Is that it?" he breathed.

"Yes," Jesse said. "There it is. My brother's House, still standing."

The building looked unchanged, Jesse noted as he eased the boat to a rocking stop. The gables still loomed, dominating the lonely shore. The House waited as it had the last time he had come across the sea. Only this time he knew there would be no welcome of any kind.

Still whispering lines of song under his breath, Jesse set the electronic anchor. He began to strip the clothes from his body. The fog clung to his skin and sent goosebumps across his bare flesh. When he reached for the metal buttons on his jeans Atlass started and pulled his eyes from the shore.

"What are you doing?" he asked, brow wrinkled.

"Going in," Jesse explained. "Someone has to guide the boat. I don't remember where all the reefs are. We'll have to go slow."

Jesse expected confused mumblings and protests, but Atlass only took a breath and nodded.

"Safe, is it?"

"Safe enough." Jesse smiled. He dropped his jeans at Robin's feet. Naked in the fog, bent to show Atlass the controls.

"We'll leave the anchor in the water," he said, shivering. "It'll give the boat some drag, so you don't run me down. Press this," he thumbed a switch and the boat leaped in the water, "to send it forward. Just a little bit at a time."

Atlass nodded, mouth hard.

"Don't worry." Jesse lifted a hand and pressed it against Atlass's sweater. He thought he could feel the big man's heart beneath his palm.

"Just look where you're going," Atlass said. "Don't run us onto a reef. I can't swim."

Jesse grinned. He moved to lean over the side of the boat. The water swirled black beneath the fog. He thought he could see the fish swimming beneath the surface, and he made a face.

"Here we go," he said, sending a smile over his shoulder at Atlass. He took a breath, closed his eyes, and arced neatly into the water.

Jesse cut through the oily heat. Keeping his eyes shut, he struggled back to the surface. Even in the winter the water steamed. He came up against the boat, nearly knocking his head on the bow, and opened his eyes. The sudden shock of cold air made them burn.

"How is it?" Atlass bent over the side of the boat.

"Warm," Jesse pushed wet hair from his face. "Hot."

"Then why are you shaking?"

"It's disgusting. I'll never get used to it," Jesse said. He bared his teeth. "Let's get this over with."

He swam to the prow of the boat and began a careful paddle through the thick water. The spiny fish flocked near his waist until he had to wave them away with his feet and hands. Atlass nudged the boat forward slowly so that it rode Jesse's wake.

They worked without speaking and stopped often. Jesse watched the reefs carefully, swimming ahead of the boat when he was uncertain. More than once he wished that Robin was awake and aware to guide them. Once, his foot brushed against something beneath the waves. He ducked his head into the water and squinted past the fish. He'd found Kris's boat. He remembered that Harold and Robin had sunk the dinghy to make a home for the creatures that managed to live in the heated water.

Jesse's left foot snagged on a sharp splinter in the hull. The foot throbbed. Blood pinked the dark sea. Excited, the fish swarmed closer and Jesse had to thresh his hands in the water to keep them away. He looked back at Atlass and saw his lover's face through the mist, white and frightened. Jesse lifted a hand to indicate the man-made reef and then swam on.

By the time they reached the shore the sun had once again been snuffed out by the fog. Jesse swam at the back of the boat, pushing until the bottom of the craft ground against the sand. The boat shuddered and then stuck and began to tip slowly on the sand. Atlass jumped from the bow and into the waves. He gasped as the steaming water brushed against his shins. Jesse would have laughed at the big man's expression if he hadn't been so exhausted. "All right?" he asked. He floundered through the waves and onto the sand.

Atlass nodded and took a breath. "Robin?"

"Wrap her up and bring her inside," Jesse said and started across the shore to the House.

"What about the boat?" Atlass called.

"I'll get it," Jesse said. "I'll do something with it, later. Right now let's get Robin inside and get her warm."

The fog bit into his bare shoulders. The warm sand made his scraped foot itch. He limped under the eaves of the House and onto the porch. The screen door hung from one hinge. Jesse pushed the screen aside and leaned against the solid planks of the panel behind it. The front door swung open and sand blew from the porch and into the House. Jesse stood staring into the shadows beyond the door, shivering as the wind dried the water from his skin.

Atlass thumped up the steps behind Jesse, Robin cradled in his long arms.

"Jesse," he said, calm, "you'll catch your death."

"Right," Jesse said. He set his shoulders and walked into the darkness, one hand stretched before his face. "Stay there. I'll find some light. There should be a candle in the kitchen."

There were indeed candles in the kitchen, along with Harold's treasured supply of matches. Jesse bumped his shins several times and smashed his nose once before he found them. He lit two of the candles and carried them back to the front hall.

"You're bleeding," Atlass said, a smile curling one corner of his mouth.

"Cupboard," Jesse muttered, rubbing his forearm across his nose and smearing blood on his upper lip. The candles flickered. Atlass stepped into the hall. The front door slammed shut behind him.

"Where now?" he prompted.

"Upstairs," Jesse decided. "In Harold's room."

The stairs creaked, but they were still solid. They were also covered with a layer of sand, just as Jesse had imagined. Everything felt gritty, even the floor of Harold's room. The unboarded window had cracked further beneath the weight of the winter storms. Sand had blown through the tiny seams, and mold had set in as well. Jesse set one candle in the sconce on the wall. He carried the second with him when he went to examine his brother's bed.

"Damp, but not yet rotted," he said, unrolling the futon in the candlelight. "It'll have to do. Put her here."

Atlass glanced around the room. Jesse could see him taking in the emptiness, the bed and the one old armchair, the pile of books in one corner. Certainly the books had been touched by mold, Jesse thought. He watched as Atlass bent and settled Robin on the futon. Atlass arranged the girl with care, making sure the blankets wrapped her away from the damp. He ran a large hand over her scalp, touched her chin with one thick finger, and then met Jesse's eyes over the bed.

"She should be clean and warm. We need to keep the wet out of this room. And sweep up the sand. I hate to think how many windows have broken in this place."

Jesse smiled at the echo of his old Atlass. "There should be blankets in one of the rooms down the hall. And nails in the cupboard in the kitchen." He touched his swelling nose, annoyed, and then picked up his candle from the floor.

"Give Robin some more of the water and then nail one of the blankets over the window. That will have to do till tomorrow. I'll walk into town in the morning and see what I can find."

Atlass nodded, but he didn't look away from Jesse's face. "Where are you going?"

"I'm going to set the nets so we'll have some breakfast. And I need to do something with Anderson's boat."

Atlass smiled.

"What?" Jesse asked, amused.

"Nothing," Atlass replied, but his eyes gleamed in the soft warmth of the candles.

"Good," Jesse said, grinning fiercely. "Take care of my girl. I'll be back."

The nets were on their usual hooks just inside the front door. Jesse examined the knotted ropes with his fingers and found that they were still strong. He untangled them with the old ease and then blew out his candle and went back out onto the sand. He threw the nets into the waves and anchored them to the shore, hoping the fish would cooperate and provide dinner. Then he went to look at the boat.

It was made to be light and easy to handle, but still Jesse had to struggle to drag the hull across the sand and onto the blocks behind the House. By the time the boat was safely settled he was panting and sweating even in the cold. He tried to find the sun but the fog had grown thick. Jesse thought the afternoon was fading. His stomach had started to call for dinner. He squatted on his heels in the sand and tried to get his breath back.

Jesse remembered the last time he had hunkered in the same sand, crouched before another boat. He remembered Robin's light step and eager questions, and he remembered Harold's defiance.

This time it was Atlass who interrupted his silence. The big man came around the side of the House with a bundle in his hands.

"Need help? I found some clothes in one of the closets."

Jesse looked at the black sweater in Atlass's hands. "My brother's," he said with a smile. "Harold liked dark colors." The jeans were black as well, and probably too long, but Jesse knew they would almost fit if he rolled them up and cinched the waist.

"Put them on the boat," Jesse said. "I'd better wash off, first."

Atlass looked down at Jesse's sandy haunches and both eyebrows lifted. "What have you been doing, wrestling with the crabs?"

Jesse laughed as he climbed to his feet. "The water's cooling down. I'll be just a minute."

The water was indeed cooling. The waves felt less oily against his flesh. Jesse ducked under the swells again and again, rinsing the grit from his skin and hair. His limbs were pale beneath the water, white as the belly of a fish. Beautiful, Atlass had said. And Jesse agreed.

When Jesse emerged from the sea Atlass waited beneath the eaves of the House. Harold's clothes were in a neat pile on one of the drier steps and Atlass clutched a clean cloth. A strip of blanket, Jesse thought. He reached for it, but Atlass shook his head.

"Let me."

The blanket was rough but warm. Jesse puffed his breath in enjoyment as Atlass scoured the water from his skin.

"Robin?" he asked, allowing his eyes to droop shut.

"Sleeping," Atlass said. He reached around and over Jesse's shoulders and wrapped the home-made towel firmly under Jesse's chin. "She took some more water."

"Good," Jesse said. He pulled the cloth from around his shoulders, then bent over the steps and grabbed the sweater. Overhead, the fog had swirled away, revealing thick clouds. "Looks like rain."

"Jesse?" Atlass said, and something new in his voice made Jesse pause and look around.

Atlass stood at one side of the stairs, straight and tall, his hands cupped loosely at his sides. His face was still but his eyes were wet and shining.

"I'm sorry," the big man said. "I should have come for you. Every minute I imagined what he might have been doing to you. There were rumors floating around, they said you were dead, that he'd shot you through the heart, or slit your throat across, or skinned you alive in the depths of the palace...." Atlass gulped a breath and shuddered.

Jesse pulled the sweater over his head, glad of the warmth of the wool. He stepped into Harold's jeans, and then reached for his lover's hand. He squeezed the trembling fingers, and then perched on the steps, pulling Atlass down until the other man sat at his side on the cold wooden slats.

"It worked for the best. You would have only walked into trouble. Anderson had the palace locked tight. And I," Jesse held slim fingers up to the moonlight, "I still have my skin. It worked for the best," he repeated more gently.

"I would have found a way. I *should* have found a way. I told myself I waited because Isabella told me to, she promised me you were unhurt. But I waited because I didn't have the courage. I know it." Atlass rubbed at his bent nose. "And you know it."

"It doesn't matter," Jesse said. But when he looked into Atlass's eyes he wondered. There was some emotion there he didn't understand, something greater than sorrow and deeper than guilt, an emotion closer to desperation.

"You're here now," Jesse said. Ignoring the uneasy flutter in his stomach, he looked away from Atlass's solemn gaze and out to sea. "And that's all that matters."

"Is it?" Atlass pulled his fingers from Jesse's grip and set them instead on Jesse's knee, gripping tightly.

"Yes," Jesse answered, making it a promise. And then, because he didn't like the worry throbbing at the back of his skull, he smiled and pointed a thumb over the waves. "There. See it?"

"What?"

"The rain. See it coming? Like a wash of indigo between moon and water. Soon we'll be able to hear it. You've never heard a storm move across the ocean, Atlass. It's wonderful. Listen."

Atlass didn't release Jesse's knee. The big man moved restlessly on the steps. The wood groaned in protest.

"Shhh!" Jesse rolled his eyes at Atlass's uneasiness. "Listen!"

He threw an arm around his lover's shoulders, holding the other man steady, waiting for calm to come again. Atlass muttered and then stilled. Jesse set his temple against Atlass's own.

They huddled together on the steps, sharing warmth and comfort, until the rain came across the water on great gusts of angry wind. The storm pounded across the sand in a staccato burst, and at last chased them back into Harold's House.

15

Jesse and Atlass spent the night in Harold's room, sleeping entwined on the floor next to the futon. Jesse woke to cold sunlight. Morning fell across his face in slants and warmed his cheeks. He sat up, stretching and wincing as his muscles twinged in protest. Beneath the coverlet they had stolen from Kris's room, Jesse could see that his skin had paled during his stay in the palace, and was now closer to ivory than the brown he was used to. The large bruise over his ribs had turned black and yellow, a reminder of Anderson's threats. His smashed nose still throbbed and the scrape on his foot itched fiercely, but his head was full of freedom and he smiled.

The sun cut through the makeshift curtains. Jesse rose to his feet and pushed back the blanket. Outside the air looked bright and clear. The fog had fled and the ocean gleamed under a blue sky. The breeze remained bitter and on the horizon clouds threatened, but for the moment at least the morning was perfect.

He let the curtain drop and paused to take inventory of his loved ones. Atlass slept on his side on the sandy floor. Sometime in the night he had pulled a second coverlet around the length of his nakedness. Dark hair fell across his broad forehead. Jesse thought that there were more lines around his eyes. But in sleep he looked eased and that made Jesse's heart light.

He walked carefully around Atlass's head and knelt alongside the futon. Robin sweated in her sleep. Her eyes shivered beneath translucent lids. He set his hand against her brow. To Jesse's surprise she shuddered and woke. Her lids parted to slits, the corners of her eyes gummy with mucus, but Jesse thought she was aware. Eager, he leaned forward. Her eyes searched, wandering around the room, and then found his face.

"Jesse?" Her voice was stronger than he had expected and made his chest tighten.

He stroked his hand along her face, down from her forehead until he cupped her chin. "It's all right," he soothed. "You're home. We've come home."

Her gaze wandered again, taking in the walls, and she looked as though she were trying to rise. The tendons in her neck stood out, but her head remained on the pillow, limp and lost.

"The House?" she whispered. Jesse nodded.

"Atlass and I came on one of the city boats," he explained, talking so that she wouldn't have to. "Your friend Anderson asked me to bring you safely here. And so we did."

"To die," Robin whispered.

Jesse glanced away. He felt her chin quiver beneath his palm and he looked back, concerned. She tried to smile. The light in her eyes made Jesse think of Harold, before the end.

"S'alright. Doesn't hurt so much. Stop," she said, voice thready and surprised. "Don't cry. Stop."

Grief ran in warm tracks down Jesse's cheeks. He wiped it away.

"I'll stop if you have some water. Liquids are good for you." He found the flask and held it up. "Yes?"

She smiled again so Jesse wet his fingertips and gently brushed the water over her dry lips. When he saw that she remembered how to swallow he tilted the flask and let Robin suck greedily at it until the liquid disappeared.

"I'll get you more," Jesse said. "I'll go to the well as soon as you sleep."

"I keep dreaming," she said after a moment. Her voice dipped. Her lids began to droop shut. "Strange dreams."

He stroked her chin again and kept his voice soft. "Don't worry, Robin. You're safe here. Don't be afraid."

She was almost gone, but she refused to look away. She frowned at him, glazed and curious.

"Jesse?"

"Yes, child?"

"You look different."

"Naked." He laughed quietly, teasing her. "Stark and bloody naked."

"Not that." Her eyes lowered and then shut. "Clear. Bright. Like glass. I can see through you."

"It's only me," he said. He reached down to squeeze her hand. But she was already asleep, consumed by her body's need to conserve life. He held her hand for a long while, until a movement at the foot of the bed made him look up. Atlass waited in the sunlight, the coverlet wound around his waist.

"She's asleep," Jesse said before Atlass could panic. "We're almost out of water. I need to go into town and see what I can find to keep us fed."

He pressed Robin's hand and then stood up. He searched around the room until he found his brother's clothes. He brushed the sand from the jeans and pulled them on. He rolled the cuffs several times and then looked around for the sweater.

Atlass scooped it from the floor and passed it to him.

"What happened to your side?"

"My ribs," Jesse said as he pulled the sweater over his head. It fit him well and he was surprised.

"Are they broken?"

"Just bruised, I think."

Atlass lifted a brow, but reserved judgment. He paused a moment, and then bent forward and laid a finger across Jesse's nose. The touch was a caress. The big man's eyes were soft.

"Nose looks better," he said. "I think the swelling's going down."

"Good." Jesse stepped away and sat down on the floor. He pulled on his boots. "They won't laugh at me when I go begging for groceries. I'll check the nets on the way back, maybe we'll have fish for breakfast."

"And for lunch and dinner, no doubt," Atlass said.

"No doubt." Jesse laughed. He bounced to his feet. His ribs pained him only a little and his foot not at all. "I'll be back."

"Good," Atlass said. "While you're gone I'll see what I can do about repairing this House of yours."

As Jesse ran down the stairs he was amused to think that the House had indeed become his own. Harold would have been horrified.

The shore was noisy. Groups of seabirds picked at the dead fish that littered the sand. Jesse jogged through the flocks. The sound of his laughter scared the birds away. He hurried along the waterline and then up the sandy path that led to town. Only as he reached the crest of the dune and started down the other side did he realize that he had forgotten a bucket for the water.

He almost turned back, but his spirit was light and he went on in the hopes that grocer Barnes would lend him a bucket for the day. He passed the hospital and its old generator. The building sat quietly as always. Jesse's form ghosted past, reflected in the cracked windows. He turned the last corner and stepped into town.

The streets were quiet. Sand blew along the road and into empty buildings. Weeds grew from the sidewalk. Trash rotted in the gutters. From the shadow of one building a small silver cat watched him with green eyes. At the center of the town the well sat alone and unwatched.

Jesse slowed to a walk. The cat moved from the shade and followed. The shops were untended. Most of the windows were cracked. Jesse's heart bounced in his throat and he began to run. The old plank still shaded the well. Jesse yanked the cover away and then let out a sigh of relief. The water looked clear and sweet. Swallowing his panic, he went in search of a bucket.

The grocer's shop was vacant. The front room smelled of garbage and greens rotted in wooden bins. The back room was empty, as well. Jesse couldn't see any sign of Isabella's father. An old bucket sat in one dark corner. Jesse took the bucket and then scrounged through bins until he found four flannel blankets and two denim shirts. He left a coin on the counter and went out for the water.

The cat waited for him at the well, blinking wide blue eyes. Jesse thought the poor thing looked emaciated and hungry. The cat mewed when he lowered the bucket and cried again when he winched it back up.

He stuck his hand in the bucket and let the cat lick the water from his fingers. The animal nuzzled his thumb and began to purr. After a long moment in the indecision, Jesse picked the cat up and took it with him from the town.

"Where did they all go?" Atlass wondered as he slid fish into Harold's old frying pan. The silver cat sat on the kitchen table, tail wrapped neatly around its paws. It watched the pan with sharp eyes.

"I don't know." Jesse sat down on one of the long benches. He folded his arms on the table and rested his chin on his fists, stretching his neck so he could watch Atlass.

"Dead?" Atlass suggested, very calm. He scraped at the frying fish with a metal spatula. The cat chuffed.

"Maybe," Jesse said. "But I didn't smell death. It was just empty. Everything left as though they had gone home for the evening and planned to come back again in the morning as usual. But the buildings were slumping and the food was rotting. The bell in the tower looked like it was ready to fall at any moment."

Atlass raised a brow and transferred the fish from the skillet to a cracked plate. He set it on the table in front of Jesse.

"Fork?" Jesse suggested.

"They're covered with sand at the moment. Use your fingers."

Jesse shrugged and began to pull apart the fish. The cat edged closer, waiting. Jesse pulled some flesh away from tiny bones and set the bit of fish on the table. The cat jumped on the fish as though afraid the meal would vanish, and then settled down and began to dine.

"Poor thing," Atlass said. "How long since it last ate, I wonder."

"It's all skin and bones," Jesse said around a mouthful of his own fish. "Probably been living off the birds. As we may have to."

Atlass blinked in surprise. Jesse shrugged one shoulder. "It's how it used to be. There's a rookery on one of the dunes by the old freeway. Robin showed it to me. She and Harold used to get their eggs from there, and so will we. There's always the fish. Maybe there's a pig or a chicken running around in the village. I'll go back and look, later."

"Bothered you that much?" Atlass asked. He reached across the table and pulled a hunk of fish from the plate. He munched slowly, then made a face. "Tastes like metal."

"You'll get used to it," Jesse said. He tossed some more fish at the cat and smiled when the animal began to purr.

"I can go back into town and look around," Atlass offered, "if it upsets you."

Jesse shook his head. "I had no friends there. Except maybe Isabella's father." He licked at oily fingers and sighed at the contentment of a full stomach. "I just need to think about what to do. Later."

Atlass took the empty plate. He set the crockery carefully into the sink. "Go up and see Robin. Then I'm going to put you to work."

"Already?" Jesse teased. "What about my nap?"

Atlass pulled a face and waved a hand. Laughing, Jesse ran up the stairs to check on his ward.

Before the clouds rolled in again, Jesse and Atlass made two brooms out of driftwood and rushes and swept the House clean. The work took most of the afternoon and by the time they were finished Jesse's back ached. When they set the brooms aside, he left Atlass puttering in the kitchen and went to look for dinner. He plucked more fish from his nets and then sat on the porch with the cat and watched the winter blow in. He knew he should be feeling the cold, but the cat climbed into his lap and warmth hummed in his veins.

He had almost fallen asleep when the screen banged. Atlass stood over him.

"Come in before you freeze."

"It's nice out here. How's Robin?"

"I boiled the bones and skin from your lunch," Atlass said. "She took the broth." Jesse saw that he was pleased. "She asked for you but you were out among the nets. I told her you were playing with the fish. She's asleep again."

"I'll go up and see her in a minute."

Atlass sat down on the steps and rested his long hands
on his knees. "How much time do you think she has?"

"I don't know," Jesse said. He changed the subject. "I'd
forgotten how quiet it is here. I think I liked living here
once. I might like living here again."

"If we can fix the windows."

"The blankets will have to do. Don't worry. Once we
get all the sand out it'll stay out. I think."

Atlass laughed. Jesse glanced over, curious.

Atlass shrugged. "It's different here. I feel like we're
waiting for something. But I'm not afraid."

Jesse stroked the mottled fur of the cat on his lap.
"Neither am I." He could almost believe his own lie. The
fears were snapped tightly away in the back of his mind.
Sometimes he forgot to hear them rattling.

Atlass shifted closer. His breath ruffled Jesse's hair. It
smelled to Jesse of herbs and fish. Jesse looked up into the
dark eyes and sighed.

"Do you want to talk about it?"

Atlass glanced away. "About what?"

"Atlass."

"Not yet," Atlass said quickly. "Not yet."

"You can ask, Atlass. I'll tell you true."

"I don't need to ask. I know. I know you."

Jesse stood up, dumping the cat gently into his lover's
lap. "All right. I'm going to go sit with Robin."

"Take her some more broth." Atlass buried his chin in
the cat's coat. Jesse waited but Atlass refused to look up.

Jesse lingered a minute. Then he nodded and went
into the House.

He woke in the middle of the night to Atlass's whispers. The big man's lips burned across Jesse's body. Atlass
clung and shook in his desire. Jesse imagined he could
feel the moonlight silver their skin as they twinned on the
floor. He opened his arms in welcome, gathering Atlass
close. And when he felt tears on his lover's face at the end,
Jesse said nothing.

When Jesse arose he tried to spoon more of Atlass's thin broth into Robin. She wouldn't take it. She roused only briefly from sleep, and even then she wanted only the water. He passed her one of Harold's old tin cups, steadying it with his own hands while she drank. He refilled it again and again until the bucket of well water was drained.

Once she had swallowed the last drop Robin drifted away again. Jesse balanced the cup beside the futon. He sat quietly for a long while, legs crossed at the ankles and elbows resting on his knees and watched Harold's legacy sleep.

The last of her hair had finally loosened and come out in handfuls. Scars ridged her bald head, and made the skull itself appear misshapen. Mucus ran from her eyes and nose almost continuously, thick and black. Jesse had seen the same fluids in some *desgastas*, before they died, and in his changed cityborn, after they decided to live.

Robin was born *desgastas*, she would let the disease take her, she would die. Or so Jesse prayed.

He cupped his chin in his hands and shut his eyes, listening to the falter of Robin's lungs. He remembered Harold's suffering, and his brother's refusal to die. He had seen the madness in Harold's eyes at the very end. His brother's ravings had been so similar to the cries of Jesse's lost souls.

So he had imagined the worst and killed his brother before he could see his fears turn to truth. He didn't regret Harold's death. In Jesse's mind, the Keeper's passing was merciful.

But if he saw the same feral light in Robin's eyes, or heard real madness in her delirium...

Jesse shivered and bit down hard on his tongue. He wouldn't think of it. Harold's murder had been necessary. Robin's might be impossible.

The next morning Robin's skin burned and she wouldn't wake for broth or even water. Jesse sat on his knees at her side, cold despite the weight of Harold's sweater and oversized jeans. He soothed her patiently. He wiped her with a damp cloth, but she continued to heat. Her skin flushed dry and red. It peeled away in sheets beneath his cloth. Her fever refused to break. The bubbling in her lungs became a rattle in her throat. Black frothed at her lips. Jesse cleaned the fluid away with a second rag.

His heart began to calm, his thoughts ran bittersweet. Surely, her body already welcomed death.

Atlass paced the room, unable to be still.

"There's nothing we can do to ease her?" he asked for the third time.

"We can't help her die. She needs to do it on her own."

Atlass flinched and worried at his lip. Jesse grumbled. He rose to his feet and handed his lover the rags. "Keep her cool and clean. Do the best you can."

"Where are you going?"

"She needs more water, whether she'll take it or not. Maybe I can find another bucket in the village. One has become a hassle."

"Fill the flask. Take one of those tin pots from the kitchen."

"I have only two hands," Jesse sighed. "I need another bucket. I'll try the old hospital, or maybe the church. There must to a graveyard of buckets somewhere. Certainly they wouldn't have taken the things with them. Wherever they went."

He tried to make it a joke, but Atlass didn't smile. He stared down at Robin.

"What if she goes while you're out?"

"You can handle it," Jesse said.

"I can," Atlass said. "Can you?"

Jesse didn't answer. He bent to kiss Robin's cheek and to wipe more fluid from her lips.

"Jesse," Atlass grabbed his arm.

"I can't stay," Jesse said, and was astounded to hear his voice break. "I have to go. I need to get away, just for a little while. Don't you understand?"

"I do," Atlass said after a moment. Jesse saw that he did. "When will you be back?"

"In time to make dinner," Jesse smiled. "Just stay with her. Please?"

"I will," Atlass said calmly. "Come back. Bring us water."

Jesse dipped his chin in a nod. He brushed his fingers across Robin's brow a last time and then left the room without looking back.

Wind ruffled the deserted beach. Despite his promise to Atlass, Jesse walked away from the House and away from the town. Harold's jeans flapped around his ankles. He had to stop twice to roll them. The stink of dead fish assaulted his nostrils. He looked out along their corpses and saw that there were more of the bloated bodies than he remembered from the past. He stepped among them, stopping to peer at crooked mouths and disfigured eyes. Skin had already rotted from the bone on many of the corpses. Jesse thought he saw sores between the scales.

More than the unnatural sea was killing them off, Jesse realized. They were suffering in other ways, tainted. And so, what happened to the creatures that ate of their meat?

"And so the world ends," Jesse told the fog.

He gathered driftwood from the sand as he walked, bundling the broken branches over his shoulder. He passed the rookery where the seagulls sat huddled against the cold, feathers puffed and eyes half shut against the wind. He whistled at them, flapping one hand, but the birds refused to be moved. Jesse moved on, intending to pull grass from the dunes for Atlass's supper.

When he walked up the hill of sand and under the broken back of the freeway overpass he saw that he was not alone on the beach. Someone had put up a tent of boiled canvas. The fabric rattled in the wind, wet and flimsy. Jesse doubted the overpass gave it any shelter at all. Then he saw the wooden easel toppled in the sand and he dropped his firewood.

"Front," he called. "Richard Front!"

He heard no reply. Jesse ran up the dune. He stopped outside the tent, afraid for a moment of what he might find. Then he took a breath and pulled aside the dangling flap. The tent was empty. It smelled clean and salty, and of seaweed. A small cot sagged on the sandy floor, crafted from the same canvas as the tent. A blackened kettle stood in one corner next to a pill bottle. Across from the canvas cot a wooden bucket lay half buried in an exposed patch of sand.

A second, plastic version rocked gently in the breeze blowing through the canvas. Jesse ducked inside the tent and made a beeline for the buckets.

The first held tubes of paint. Jesse picked one up. The tube lay chill in his hand, and smooth. Smears of green paint ringed the lid. Jesse took the tube with him when he stepped back out into the fog. He craned his neck, searching. The weather had turned the sand hard, but he could look back down the shore and see his footprints. His were the only marks he could see in the sand. He looked up at the overpass, remembering that Robin had climbed it. But he saw no way up the concrete legs.

He had a sudden image of Grizwald, lying cold and dead and alone on a similar beach.

"Richard Front!" he shouted into the wind, turning on his heels.

He heard a sound. At first Jesse didn't understand. Then he looked out to sea and saw the figure splashing through the waves. Rigid, Jesse stood on the sand and clutched the tube of paint.

Richard Front wore a rubber suit. The suit bared his arms and legs but covered his torso well enough. Seams creased the rubber and in places the material looked pitted. Jesse wondered if the heat of the water had softened it.

The doctor climbed up the dune and stood over Jesse, dripping warm water. His expression was wary. He shook his head and more water fell free of his tangled hair.

"The Keeper's famous brother," he said. "Why have you left your city?"

Jesse gripped the paint, unable to find the words.

"I hope you've come back to die," Richard Front said. He walked past Jesse to his tent. "There's nothing else here for you."

Jesse scrambled after him. "Harold's last ward is ill. I've brought her home."

The young doctor shrugged and disappeared into the tent. Jesse stood outside the canvas flap, squeezing the tube of paint in his palm. Muffled grunts echoed from inside the tent and he heard the sticky sound of warm rubber stripped from skin. When Front stepped back through the flap he wore a torn brown bathrobe and stained leather sandals. He sat on a piece of driftwood and pulled a glass jar from a pocket in the robe.

"So she can die like the rest of us." The doctor dipped three fingers into the jar and began rubbing yellow cream onto his bare legs. Jesse wrinkled his nose at the smell. "Eucalyptus," Front explained. "Some enterprising boy brought a case of cream from a village down south. Promised the smell would keep away the germs." At Jesse's expression he gave a bitter laugh. "Probably bunk. But who's to say? Certainly no more silly than anything else I've seen. We all do what we can. I've heard stories of a town in the mountains where they sacrifice a boy child every four weeks to keep the demon away. I've not yet turned quite so bloodthirsty. Instead I bathe twice a day and rub putrid cream on my chest."

"Is that what it's become now?" Jesse wondered as he stood over Front. He thought he saw the glint of fear in the other man's eyes. "A demon?"

The doctor shrugged. "It's become something more than it was. It sucks up the living daily. Who knows? A virus, a mutation, a plague. The final apocalypse?" His narrowed eyes fastened on Jesse's face. "I know one thing: if it's Bruster's, it's changed. Become airborne, likely."

Jesse frowned up at the overpass, refusing to listen, and Front snorted. "I'm a doctor. I know a transmittable disease when I see one. Eighty years ago, maybe, we would have been able to save ourselves. But now?" He shifted on his log and his gaze quickened. "What I want to know is, how long has this been going on? How long have you idiots in your city been trying to hide the end of the world? You must have known. How long?"

Jesse shook his head. Front hissed through his teeth. "Won't you even defend yourself, O revered Dr. Grange, savior of our continent?"

Jesse kept silent. At last Front bowed his head. "I think perhaps you are as unnatural as the disease, doctor. You look healthy enough."

Front curled his legs back under his robe. He held up his jar. "Cream?" When Jesse ignored the jar he shrugged and stuck it back into a pocket.

"Are they all dead?" Jesse asked.

"The village?" Front arched his brows. "Most of us. My wife. The mayor. All the children. Burned behind the church. The rest went on, down the shore. They hoped to make the safety of your city."

"The grocer?"

Front nodded and Jesse felt a pang.

"How many went on?"

"Five healthy, two blistered. Each of them came into this world free of disease." He paused. "Will they find what they need?"

Jesse lowered his brows. Front sighed. "I didn't think so. But who was I to tell them otherwise?"

"Why are you still here?"

"I'm not sure." Front dug his sandals into the dune. "Why should I run?" he shrugged. "I thought maybe I'd follow the freeway. My father used to tell me there were riches at the other end."

"Like the rainbow."

Front twitched, and then laughed, "Like the rainbow. But I've decided I should see what I can before I die."

"You won't get very far in a bathrobe."

Front shot Jesse a cynical smile. "I've got a pair of trousers in the tent somewhere."

"What will you eat? You'll starve. Or certainly die of thirst."

"Does it matter?"

"Yes," Jesse said. He lobbed the tube of paint from his hand. It fell to the sand between Front's feet. "Come back with me. To my brother's House."

"So you can burn me when I die?" The fear behind Front's eyes became a visible thing.

"Or you can give me to the sea," Jesse said, a challenge.

Front picked up the tube of paint. He rubbed the plastic between his thumb and forefinger. "The only human company I could ever stand for long was my wife's."

"There are plenty of empty rooms. You can lock yourself in at night and run away to the dunes to paint during the day. We won't bother you, but we'll feed you. You look as though you need it."

"Thank you," Front was sarcastic. He looked around at the overpass, considering. "Who is 'we'?"

"My ward. My lover. Myself."

Front grunted. "Three doomed souls. And I'll make a fourth."

"The House is large. And fairly warm. The snow will come, sooner or later. It always does."

Front shuddered and glared at his rustling tent. "Unfair. But probably true." He stretched and then stood up. "A day more and I would have been gone, safely on my way to see what lives along that stretch of road. You have impeccable timing, Grange." He paused, surprised, and looked past Jesse's left shoulder.

"Is that your cat?"

Jesse turned. He watched as the creature made its way across the sands, a purpling fish gripped in feline jaws. The cat trotted the last few steps, pounced on Jesse's booted feet, and then dropped the fish with a growl. Jesse looked at the misshapen tail fin next to his ankle. He grimaced.

"Here," he said. He picked up the cat and handed the animal to a startled Front. "We'll feed you both something fresh when we get home."

Front stared at the cat and then began to laugh. The sound was light and unexpected. Jesse grinned in response.

"Just how many wards do you have?" Front accused.

"Only the one. Strays are another matter."

Front chuckled again and then sighed. He hoisted the cat over one shoulder, stroking its bristling fur. He nodded to Jesse.

"Take us home and get us fed, then."

Jesse carried the easel and Front's two buckets, the first weighted down by tubes of paint. Richard Front carried the cat. They walked slowly back along the shore, Jesse watching the House as it appeared through the clouds and the young doctor looking out at the waves.

"I came out to gather water for Robin," Jesse said when he was able to see the steps and the front porch of the House. "I thought maybe I'd find extra buckets in the village."

"You were going the wrong way," Front pointed out, expression wry.

"But I found my buckets, after all," Jesse said. He hefted his load. "And if I had gone back to town—"

"There's nothing left but the ghosts."

"And the well," Jesse said after a moment of silence. "One thing you never forget, growing up in that House — how important the water is."

Front stopped suddenly before the House.

"Assuming it's clean," he said, "How do you know Bruster's isn't living in that well, breeding in the water?"

As Jesse stared, Front's voice went up, suddenly high with grief.

"Maybe it was the well that killed them all?" He clenched his hands around the cat. The animal struggled until Front dropped it.

Jesse shook his head. He propped the easel against the porch and set his buckets on the bottom step. The cat ran up the steps. It pawed at the screen door, begging to be let in. Jesse climbed onto the porch and opened the door. The creature darted into the warm shadows. Then Jesse turned back and looked down at Front.

"The disease doesn't live long outside the body, Doctor," Jesse said. "In this new form it's very fragile. The human body is just the right temperature. Too much cold, too much heat, it dies. It's been transmittable for almost a year, now. We think. And you're right. It's airborne. But only under certain conditions. We thought."

Richard Front stood pale and still before the porch.

"So keep taking your hot baths," Jesse said. "Who knows, they may save your life. There's always the hope. But get rid of that awful cream. It's foul."

He let the screen door bang on his heels. Consciously, he allowed his mind to rush ahead to more pleasant worries. The nets would have to be checked again, and more water drawn from the well. He'd have to go back out for eggs, and grass, and the driftwood he'd forgotten in his surprise.

But first he would see Robin.

16

Robin's fever rose in the hours after midnight. Atlass swabbed her down while Jesse and Richard Front carried buckets of cool water from the village well. Atlass suggested ice to bring down the girl's temperature. Front mocked the big man's innocence.

"Ice is a city luxury. Next you'll be asking for a good steak."

Cold, fresh water from the depths of the ground was the best Jesse could do. Even unconscious, Robin cried for a drink. Atlass managed to spoon huge quantities of well water down her throat.

Front said little to Jesse as they hurried back and forth over the dunes. The moon shone high above the horizon, and the night sky was clear. Thin winter light illuminated the empty village. Broken windows glittered. Dust coated the church tower and the bell hung from a single frayed cable. Jesse stopped beneath the tower and looked up at the bell before he passed. He thought he saw frost on the brass. He knew he glimpsed cracks along its lip.

Front walked through the village at an easy pace, seemingly calm. But on the way out again the bucket shook in his hand, sloshing water. Jesse supposed the man faced his own private ghosts on the empty streets. Jesse saw nothing in the night but their footprints in the sand. He thought he could walk the path from the House to the well and back again in his sleep.

Sometimes the silver cat accompanied them into the village. The animal seemed unalarmed by the empty buildings. The cat hunted the shadows, and twice in the night it flushed out little rodents. The cat dropped the mice at Jesse's feet as he filled his bucket. Front gave the cat the praise it deserved, stroking a hand over the silver fur, but Jesse spent his time examining the hapless rodents. The mice looked frail and thin. One of the two had lost most of its fur.

The cat wouldn't eat its catch, so Jesse left the little bodies lying in the street.

As the sun climbed in the sky Robin's fevered skin began to dry and crack. Her eyelids peeled. The skin around her scars broke and bled. Front dug his cream out of a pocket and Atlass smoothed it over Robin's face in the hopes that the oil would ease the fissures in her skin. The smell of eucalyptus and grease thickened in the room. Jesse tied the blanket back from the window, hoping a breeze would clear the room. When he turned from the rush of clean air he saw that Robin had begun to convulse.

Jesse's heart jumped to his throat. For a moment he stood back in his little cellar, watching in horror as his latest cityborn orphan drummed heels and spine against the concrete floor.

He forced himself to move, reaching for her arms, intending to hold her safe and still, but Atlass brushed him aside.

"Out," the big man ordered.

Jesse shook his head and picked up a rag. He dipped the bit of cloth into a bucket and then rubbed it over Robin's face, mopping up blood and sweat. The cloth left a trail of wet over Robin's cheeks and smeared Front's cream across her skin. Instead of sticking to Jesse's rag, the blood mixed with the cream, turning Robin's face a gory pink.

Jesse heard himself groan. Atlass grabbed him by the shoulder and plucked the rag from his hand.

"Leave be. I'll clean her up once she stills," Atlass said as Robin shook on the futon. Front knelt at the girl's head, trying to hold her snapping jaws still.

"It's the damned cream," Jesse argued, although he knew it was not. A rage he barely understood clenched his fists and locked his jaw. "Get it off her!"

"No," Atlass said. "She's been doing this off and on all night. I've been handling it. Out. We need more water. Get a bucket and go."

Robin's teeth gnashed. Jesse gripped his lover's hand, pleading, but Atlass held firm. He pushed Jesse out into the hallway, set an empty bucket at his feet, and shut the door. As Jesse stood in the empty hallway, fear began to throb behind his nose. He thought he could hear Robin's heels drumming behind the closed door. The sound frightened Jesse. He knew it as the sound of madness. His stomach lurched and he ran from the House, leaving the bucket behind.

Once on the sand he calmed, but he couldn't face the village. So he walked until he stood before Front's abandoned tent. Sand had blown through the loose flap and a lonely seagull ran along the outside edge of one canvas wall, looking for food or warmth. The gull was a puff of mottled feathers in the warm shadows, and Jesse stood watching the bird for a long while.

At last the gull moved, lifting its beak to the sky. The bird thrashed away in a swoop of awkward wings. Jesse stepped past the tent and under the highway. He ran his hand over one concrete pillar and then walked on to the next. A half-buried lump of broken concrete jutted from a mound of dry sand and he sat on it. The concrete felt cold through his brother's jeans. As Jesse sat still and waited for the chill to leave his bones, a second bird fluttered around Front's tent. Jesse watched the gull, imagining he could count each of the bird's feathers. At the edge of the sand the tide began to come in.

The blood beat behind Jesse's nose. He squeezed his lids shut, pressing back tears.

When he opened his eyes again the sea had reached the very edge of the broken overpass and Atlass stood in front of the tent.

"Come back to the House," he said. "Her fever's broken."

Jesse pinched the bridge of his nose and peered at Atlass. The big man looked very tired. Lines of dried sweat or tears marked Atlass's face and his shoulders slumped. Jesse wondered if he felt the chill of the wind.

"Your young doctor says she might make it another day," Atlass continued. "He swears he has never seen the like."

"He's not 'my' young doctor," Jesse said in a sigh, still massaging his nose. "I think he doesn't like me much at all."

"Come have supper," Atlass urged. He showed Jesse a brave smile.

Jesse didn't shift from his perch. "When will you stop protecting me, Atlass?"

Atlass waited in the sand, wind ruffling his hair, and said nothing.

"Or are you protecting yourself?" Jesse wondered. "Are you afraid that if you don't keep me under your wing I'll fly free and you'll have to see me as I am?"

"I know you," Atlass said, unshaken.

Jesse jerked to his feet and balanced on the chunk of the freeway. He spread his arms wide and leered across at his lover.

"Not so very different from the boy I was when I first seduced you?" He made a show of examining one white hand, and then pushed up the sleeves of his sweater to bare pale arms. "Perhaps even prettier? You certainly can't seem to keep your eyes off me. Or perhaps it's that you're afraid of me, now. Is that it? Do I frighten you? After so many years together, do you see in me a stranger?" The last words rang against the overpass. Atlass's face froze.

Jesse twitched his shoulders and the sleeves fell back into place. He let his scowl soften. He willed Atlass to understand. "But I've changed. I've committed murder once, here on this shore. Over and over again in Carpenteria, I watched them die. All in the name of science." He crouched so that he rocked on his heels on the jab of concrete. "But now I fear I'll have to do it again. And suddenly it's not so easy. Suddenly I'm questioning the past."

Atlass took a step across the sand. Jesse hissed a warning through his teeth.

"Jesse." Atlass stopped. He held out his hands. "Come down."

Jesse rocked on his heels on the concrete. He bent and wrapped his arms around his ankles, resting his buzzing head on his knees. When he shut his eyes he saw again his lost souls, trapped behind cold bars in the depths of his city, waiting. He swallowed hard and tried not to be sick.

"I told you once, a long time ago, that I was mad," Jesse said. He narrowed his eyes against the pain. "Why didn't you believe me?"

He heard Atlass's boots slide in the sand. A shadow blocked the pale sun but Jesse wouldn't look up.

"She's getting better," Atlass said. "Her fever has dropped. She's not one of your subjects, Jesse. She's not gone feral. She's improving."

Jesse almost laughed. The cold or sorrow made his nose run. He wiped one hand across his upper lip, and kept his eyes tightly closed.

"This is how it begins, Atlass. Too many times I've seen it happen. They look to improve. Their hair starts to grow back, the scars stop bleeding. The families think maybe the disease has finally gone. But you can still hear it in their lungs. And see the change in their eyes.

"And their loved ones, spouses, children, parents. You see the hope on those faces, the expectation of miracles. But it's no miracle. It's something awful. I know. I've seen. I've been called to houses, seen the healing bodies, and wished for their deaths. Prayed that whatever lurks underneath the scars will give up, give out. It never does."

Alone behind his eyelids, Jesse inched his fingers down his bare feet until he felt the scratch of broken concrete. He rubbed the rock, buffing the tips of his fingers until the nerves went numb.

"I've had fifty-two, all told. Not really very many, I know. Most have been lucky, and died soon after infection. But there are tales of many, many more overseas. For a while, the govs sent these creatures to me so I might save them. Then, later, when he had finally seen that there was nothing that might save those already changed, Harlan kept bringing me more of the poor souls. So I might use them to save us."

Jesse slitted his lids and peeked across at Atlass. The big man waited in the sand, unmoving, unspeaking. So Jesse squeezed away the light again and clutched his rock and continued.

"Fifty-two, all told, over three years. All of them cityborn. Not a true *desgastas* among the changed. Harlan called them monsters. Often, I thought of them as my children. No different from the other, healthy cityborn I worked to save. It was the first real inkling that we hadn't stilled the *Sacramento* tragedy, after all.

"They're not monsters, not really. But they have no..." he hesitated, searching, "...humanity. No loves, no hates, no passions. They exist because they are still alive, and their lungs still labor. Sometimes, I would look into their eyes and see nothing. Nothing at all. Other times, a hunger, an animal longing. But, after the first few months of change, they wouldn't eat anything I brought them. Water, huge quantities of water. But nothing else. They'd thin down, become nothing but marbled skin and brittle bones and big, wild eyes.

"Eventually, they'd go mad with hunger. Attack their cell mates. Take one or two bites, give up. Sometimes, nibble on themselves."

Jesse opened his eyes and looked up. Atlass's face had gone white, and he had bitten through one corner of his lower lip.

"When they were down to bone, and maddened so that they threw themselves upon the bars of their cells, or tossed themselves over and over again to the floor, then I'd kill them. Snap their necks. Easy enough, in practice. But after the first fifteen, I understood that I had been too gentle. I began to take risks. What did they have to look forward to? Harlan believed only the healthy still mattered. And after a time, I knew he was right.

"I tried everything I could think of to come up with a cure. Not for the *desgastas*, as people believed, but for this new horror. I put my remaining thirty-seven mad children through every test, every workup, every idea I could think of. I tried each wild plan that came to me in the night. Nothing worked. Very few lived long enough that I needed to snap their necks, send them on. Most died horribly, by my hand, in the name of a cure."

Jesse rested his jaw on his knees. He stared across at the sea. "In the end, I had only nine left. Harlan might have brought me more. New cases were popping up every day, but I refused. I turned the coward. I saw this new horror in every corner, on every face I loved. I imagined I saw it in my brother's ravings, and so I killed him, before I could even be sure. I might imagine I see it in you, in your weary face, in the slack of your shoulders. It had me running scared. It still does."

"But where did it come from?" Atlass whispered. Jesse glanced out of the corner of his eye and saw that the big man still waited, rooted on the dune. Only the long fingers of his hands trembled.

"I don't know." A gull skimmed the waves, plunged, and then lifted into the sky again. "Harlan truly believed it was Bruster's, mutated in the *desgastas* over the years and breathed over our city. It could be possible. There are a few fugitive *desgastas* overseas, and probably the genetic pattern in families that hadn't yet been diagnosed when the first exodus began.

"The *desgastas* Anderson believes it is a punishment from the land. And the land is changing, the poison still spreading. I see it every day."

Jesse's feet were chill on his perch. He hunched over his knees, squeezing his arms around his thighs. "*Desgastas*, who have been gently quarantined in Houses, watched by Keepers, or in the city, Marked as a caution, these *desgastas* still manage to mingle with the healthy. Quarantine was never really possible, I suppose. Who is to say that some cross of *desgastas* and cityborn didn't birth a new mutation?

"For that matter, who is to say I didn't bring this about with my own Mark? A microbe, meant to correct genetic malfunction, meant to root out and label the *desgastas* mutation? I might have fallen into the same trap George Bruster first set. Snared by hope, ruined by haste. How can I say the *desgastas* haven't been right in their lust to avoid city technology?"

"No," Atlass said, steady. "You worked on the Mark for a decade. You were sure of it."

"As sure as Bruster was of his bacteria," Jesse returned. "We all take a gamble. And, suddenly, it seems there are no answers. The only thing I can be sure of is this: Bruster's and this new form have the same genetic root. Everything traces back to the *Sacramento*. Everything always will. When that cruiser went down, it spoke our death. We've been running from it long enough. Now we've lost our lead."

Atlass moved at last. Mouth set, he crossed the dune and laid his hand along the crown of Jesse's head.

"Come home and eat."

"No," Jesse made a low sound. "I won't." He coughed and rubbed a hand over his eyes. "I can't face it. Not again. Not in Robin."

"She's well," Atlass insisted. He bent at the waist and helped Jesse from his seat. "I can feel it. Maybe fear has made you blind. So," he continued with a small smile, "you must trust me. Take a chance, for me. Come and see her. Play the game a little while longer."

Jesse tried a laugh, but it caught in his throat. "I can't."

"You can." Atlass waited, implacable. He stretched out his hand. Jesse winced. Winter blew across the dune and under the highway, but Atlass's bulk shielded Jesse from the bitter sting.

"Come home and eat," Atlass said. Jesse wiped his eyes and took the proffered hand.

Robin woke briefly in the night. She took water, but wouldn't speak. Atlass seemed unafraid as he stroked her brow, but Jesse trembled as he watched. He knew, from experience, how cunning this new disease could be.

But the next afternoon Robin was still free of the fever. She was aware, and in pain, but she managed to sip at Atlass's broth. The silver cat curled on the futon at her feet while Jesse sat in Harold's chair and watched Robin eat. She didn't speak but her eyes tracked Atlass about the room and when Front passed into the room she shifted as though uneasy.

"Don't you worry," Atlass soothed. "This man's a doctor and a friend."

Jesse scoffed. Front ignored him. Atlass rubbed Robin's brow with his long fingers until she slept. The lump in Jesse's stomach seemed to thicken. He found he couldn't

eat. When Atlass forced food on his lover, the food only
came up again.

"Nerves," Atlass said, and at last he let Jesse be.

The next day Atlass propped Robin against a mound of
blankets and pillows. She sat upright while she swallowed
his stew. Richard Front walked the room from wall to wall,
wild with joy. The man couldn't seem to take his eyes from
Robin's monstrous face.

"Her fever's gone," he cried later, standing nearby as
Jesse fished the sea. "Have you ever seen it before?"

"No," Jesse admitted.

"What does it mean? Has she beaten it?"

"Unlikely."

"But not impossible! Do you understand what this could
mean? If she only," the man stuttered, lost for a moment in
dreams, "if she only strengthens. Her blood might be used
as a vaccine. It would be simple to draw out the antibodies.
Simple—"

"And dangerous." Jesse plucked a fish from his net and
turned a cold eye on the young doctor. "You're getting
ahead of yourself. Don't let hope trip you up. She has a last
bit of strength before death, and that's all it is. She'll re-
lapse."

And Jesse waited, night after night, for his words to
come true. He sat in the moonlight beside Harold's futon
and watched the Keeper's last ward sleep. She seemed to
dream easy, twitching little in her sleep. But she still didn't
speak, and when she woke, he couldn't meet her eyes long
enough to search out sanity.

"She's healing," Atlass said, six days later. He lay barefoot in the sand and watched as Jesse collected water for the
dishes. "I can feel it."

"You're a mystic now?" Jesse quizzed. He pulled the
bucket through the steaming water and yanked it back onto
the sand. "Or you have a degree in medicine?"

"You don't want to believe."

"It's too soon, and too unlikely. I've had hope before. I've
always lost it."

"But she's living. Right in front of our eyes, she's thriving."

"If she thrives, then it's because she's no longer human. Forgive me if I don't share your joy. I can't find it within myself to break another neck or drown another loved one."

"You're wrong," Atlass insisted. "This is something wonderful." His mouth was thin and hard.

Jesse set his bucket on the sand and looked out over the water. He pressed his arms against his sides. The damp air made his lips tingle. He could feel the rain coming again. Soon Harold's shore would be pitted with mud and puddles of grit.

Atlass traced his fingers through the sand. "Front won't leave her alone. He's waiting for her to speak as though life depends on it. He's waiting for you to do your magic, save the world once again."

"I'm sure he is. He doesn't want to die any more than you do. That man fears death. I can see it in his face."

Atlass lowered his eyes, "Are you so eager to die?"

"Better death than the terrors I've seen."

"And I'm afraid," Jesse added as he lugged the bucket up the beach and away from Atlass's pained face, "that the greater horrors are still to come."

They sat together while night closed in and watched Robin as she slept. Atlass folded in Harold's chair and Jesse curled at his feet. The big man ran his nails over Jesse's head and brushed the sand from his hair.

"What will she do, if it doesn't take her?" Atlass wondered.

"What do you mean?"

"How will people accept her?"

Jesse closed his eyes. Even behind his lids he could see Robin's seamed face and scarred hands. She would never be easy to look upon. Restructured skin stretched her mouth. The puffiness around her eyes would ease, maybe. But her hair sprouted in only in patches and her skull appeared melted, lopsided. She would never be the pixie again.

"If it doesn't take her," Jesse echoed.

"What will she do?"

"I don't know. But I don't think you need to worry about it," Jesse said. He let his head rest against the back against of Atlass's knee. He fell asleep pressed against the chair and when he woke he had a crick in his neck.

The moon hung above the clouds and the wind blew sand and sleet through the broken window. Jesse staggered to his feet and fastened the blanket against the cold. Atlass snored in Harold's chair. Robin slept in a ball, her fingers folded beneath her chin.

Jesse shed his sweater and settled on the futon. He edged Robin's head onto his thigh and gripped one of her twisted hands in his own. She slept on and her breath was warm against his ribs. Harold's *tronera* glittered and reflected moonlight across her scalp. Jesse hummed under his breath and waited with Robin until the sun rose, trying to keep her warm.

Richard Front set up his easel in a corner of Harold's room and spent his days painting. Atlass learned to move around the doctor. Jesse ignored Front completely. When Robin woke she watched the doctor with blank eyes, and didn't appear to object to the smell of the oils or the sound of brush on canvas.

Atlass found a pig and several chickens in the village. Jesse helped him slaughter the pig and smoke the meat. Together they built a driftwood pen for the birds. Despite heavy rain, the chickens seemed to flourish in the enclosure, and the hens soon began laying. The eggs were fresh and the pork wonderful. Atlass put on flesh and regained some color. Even Jesse managed to keep most of his meals down.

Jesse haunted the shore during the day. Nerves sent him to walking, or to long swims among the fish. After sunset, the water was just warm enough to make bathing beneath rainfall enjoyable. He lured Atlass out under the clouds on such evenings and taught the big man to love the nights.

Eventually Robin left Harold's room. At first Atlass kept her to the porch, wrapped against the clouds, where he could watch her always. Then he grew brave and helped her along the sand. Jesse watched from a distance. The girl walked obediently at Atlass's side, stiff in her new body, mute but apparently lucid.

"She watches the birds." Atlass reported. "And she steps around the fish. She's aware, Jesse, and she's growing stronger."

"Then why won't she speak?"

The big man shrugged, eyes eloquent. "She eats. She takes the broth as easily as water, and sometimes fish steak."

"They all ate in the beginning," Jesse said, refusing to hope. "Wait and see."

Jesse spent a cold week lurking under the freeway. He wanted to learn its secrets. The sleet soaked his skin and turned the sand in his hair to mud but he found what he was searching for. The handholds were shallow, visible only to fingertips. Jesse stripped off his boots and used his bare toes to find purchase. The skin ripped from his fingers and blood ran in a bracelet around his wrist, but the cold numbed his fingers and he found his way up the pillar and onto the overpass.

The highway fell out into the air, broken where it met the sea. In the opposite direction asphalt stretched east, away from the shore. The concrete shivered and shifted in the wet and Jesse had to squint to steady it. Glass and metal sparkled in the thin light. The trash cut at Jesse's feet but in his excitement he didn't notice. The pounding in his heart sent him along the freeway and toward the mountains.

He walked carefully, stopping now and then to examine some bit of rubbish along the asphalt. He found a length of rope, covered with mud. He gathered the line up, looping it over his shoulder. In the gutter he stumbled upon bits of rubber, and then a whole tire, no doubt much like the one Robin had found as a child. A smashed watch gleamed on the asphalt. Farther away an old couch sagged, made black by the rain. Jesse put the watch in his pocket and sat on the couch while he waited for the sun to set.

Light fell away over the sea, buffered by clouds. A flash of green dropped into the depths, momentarily illuminating the shore. Jesse sat until near dark and then he worked his way back along the freeway to the beach. The climb down the pillar was harder than the stretch up. Jesse dropped most of the way, falling on his hands and knees in the sand. The landing jarred his teeth and started a pulse of pain in his head.

He groped in the dark for his boots and brought them up with clumps of wet beach. He carried the boots under one arm, brushing the rubber as he went. His feet were numb and the tips of his fingers were beginning to sting. He licked at his nails and tasted old blood on his tongue.

Robin and Atlass waited for him in the shadow of the House. Jesse could not see their faces in the night but he could smell the eucalyptus ointment Atlass still rubbed into Robin's damaged skin.

"We've waited with supper," Atlass said, when Jesse drew close. "Front's reheating the chicken."

"Chicken! Glorious chicken!" Jesse drawled. He threw his lover a smirk. "If I'd known we'd escaped fish for the night I'd have been back sooner."

"Where've you been?" Atlass returned the smile, but his eyes drooped and the curl of his lips was weary.

"Hunting," Jesse said. He tossed his rope onto the porch. Robin bent slowly and picked it up, running the coils through her fingers.

"Come eat," Atlass said before Jesse could speak. He cocked his head, shooting Jesse a look, a warning without words.

Jesse nodded very slightly. He pretended he didn't see Robin exploring his find. "In a moment. Let me wash my feet. I think I've got glass between my toes."

He hobbled down the beach and splashed into the water. The salt bit at his feet and he gasped and then thrust his hands beneath the waves. When he stood up Robin crouched at his side. Jesse flapped his hands in the air, trying to ease the stinging. He peered cautiously at Harold's ward.

"Where's Atlass?"

Robin still held the rope, wound about her wrists and coiled between her palms. The gloom of the night hid any expression on her face. Standing thigh deep in the waves,

Jesse craned his neck until he found his lover, a shadow waiting on the beach. Relieved, he schooled his mouth and cocked a brow at Robin.

She wore jeans and a turtleneck and both were too big for her. Old clothes, clothes that might have fit before her body had betrayed her. Her hair had grown out a bit, if unevenly. She seemed unaware of her appearance but occasionally he caught her fingering the seams in her face.

"The rope's from the freeway. Your freeway, do you remember? Harold said you climbed it, once, long ago. Quite a climb." Jesse displayed torn fingertips. "I don't know how you managed."

He hoped she smiled but he wasn't sure. The waves washed up around his knees and wet trousers dragged at his thighs.

"Are you cold?" he tried, after a moment of silence. "Maybe you should go back to Atlass. He'll feed you. Chicken sounds almost delicious, don't you think?"

Robin didn't stir. Jesse remembered the solemn faces of Harlan's monsters, the blank stare, before the hunger set in and the madness began. He swallowed away revulsion. Robin turned her face toward him. Jesse imagined he could feel the weight of her gaze. Hands shaking, he dipped into his pocket and dug out the watch.

"An old timepiece," he explained. "A few repairs and I might get it to keep the hours again."

Robin's hands came up, pale as silver beneath broken moonlight. Her flesh felt cold and hard as her fingers brushed his palm. She took the watch carefully, picking it up by the frayed band. The hair at the back of Jesse's neck rose.

Robin held the watch to the sky a moment longer and then ran her thumb over the shattered face.

"You can keep it if you want," Jesse offered. "I'll fasten it around your wrist. Won't run for now, but it's interesting to look at."

Her fist closed around the watch. She gathered the time-piece close, at the same time tangling the fingers of her free hand in Jesse's rope.

Jesse couldn't find any more words. He waited a while longer in the ocean, allowing the waves to break across his legs. He could feel Atlass waiting on the sand, and at last he swallowed a sigh and turned to take Robin's hand. She wouldn't give up the watch or the end of her rope, so he had to move around her small body and take her elbow. She followed quietly as he tugged her from the sea. Atlass met them on the front porch, blankets in hand.

Jesse couldn't stomach dinner. He ducked out early from the kitchen, ignoring Atlass's pained frown. He climbed the stairs and wandered the House until his feet found their way to Kris's room. Head aching, Jesse fell upon the cold bed and stared blindly out the window.

He was afraid. Robin's broken form, living and moving inside his brother's House, frightened him. The hope that bit at his heels made his stomach flop. And the horror made it twist again.

Jesse fell asleep, sprawled on his side, and dreamed of Kris. He woke to the taste of bile in his mouth and to pain in his hands. Robin sat on the edge of Kris's bed, arms extended over the old blankets, her hands around his own. The tension in her fists squeezed his palms, and made the torn ends of his fingers throb.

"Don't cry," she said, as she had once before. Jesse's stomach roiled. Gasping, he sat up. He threw his legs over the side of the bed and clutched at his middle, trying to keep the acid in his throat from rising.

A single candle guttered in a sconce on the wall. Robin released his hands and reached to bring the light close. She stretched slowly, delicately, but the candle stayed steady in her hand as she brought it to his face.

The light did awful things to her cheeks and hands. The flame brought the scars and lumps into focus. But Jesse sought her eyes, and what he saw there brought his stomach back under control.

"You carried me back from the city," she said. "I don't remember."

Her voice scratched. The sound was husky, the tone deeper than a child's should be. Her lungs still bubbled, but only faintly.

"I remember searching for Molly. Her butterfly was gone, so I knew she had run from the city. She told me she would, but I didn't believe her. I remember being angry that she left without saying good-bye.

"I don't remember anything more. Not until you led me from the sea. And Atlass fed me chicken. Too much chicken."

Jesse almost smiled. The candlelight turned Robin's quizzical expression fierce, but not feral. He watched the light splinter across her cheekbones and remembered Anderson's tale of the six frightened *desgastas*. Six refugees, dead in the snow, because the city wouldn't let them free.

"Atlass likes to see you eat," Jesse said, "because it reminds him you're alive." He edged forward until he managed to shield the light of the candle with one hand, softening its glow. "Your Molly is dead, my dear. The *desgastas* who ran from the palace couldn't make it out alive."

Robin's expression didn't change. Jesse reached to touch her nose, to stroke her chin, but she flinched away. Shifting on her knees, she set the candle on the floor and dug under her sweater. Jesse waited.

She pulled the broken watch from her clothes, and set it on the floor between the candle and Jesse's feet. Jesse didn't understand.

"Fix it," Robin said.

"All right." Jesse lifted a brow, confused. "I just need—"

"Tonight," Harold's ward said. Jesse looked across her face, and found it fearsome.

"All right," he said again. He palmed the watch and slid from the bed.

Robin huddled in the light of the candle, waiting. Jesse felt a prickle of fear tease his spine once again.

Richard Front's paintings were of Robin. He dashed off one canvas after another and stacked them inside the House. The paintings cluttered Harold's room and marched in lines down hallways. The smell of paint over-whelmed the scent of the ocean. Jesse thought he could taste turpentine in his food. He knew he dreamed of colors when he slept.

"The man's possessed," he said as he helped Atlass stack canvases away from the kitchen.

"Robin's his salvation. He thinks he will live because she does. She's his miracle, he worships her. Other people will too."

"Other people?"

"People in the city. People across the seas. Even the *desgastas*. What will they do, when they've found out she's beaten the death?"

"And you plan to tell these people, tease them with a miracle? Like Isabella's friends teased the *desgastas* with the promise of a cure for Bruster's?"

"Jesse." Atlass set a painting against the wall. Sweat put a sheen on his cheeks. "This is the real thing."

"So you say. So Front says. I say we need time yet, time to see."

"We don't have time, Jesse."

Jesse paused over a painting. He glanced up at his lover's wan face. Somewhere in the back of Jesse's mind, fear nibbled. He pushed the pang away.

"Hush, Atlass," Jesse stepped across the room and grabbed Atlass's hand, forcing the big man to be still. "Don't let Front use you."

The big man's fingers clenched, and then he let out a breath. "I wasn't so afraid of it until I thought we had hope."

"I know. But you have to listen to *my* truth. Our world is ending. It doesn't matter if Robin has found a miracle. There are too many people infected. It's too late to stop it."

"Jesse."

"It'll be all right, love. We'll live as we can, as long as we can."

Atlass jerked. His hand shivered against Jesse's palm.

"I'm sorry." Jesse released the shaking fingers. He tucked his own fists up under his armpits.

"No. But you're ready to let go and I'm not."

Jesse cocked his hip against the kitchen sink and gazed out at the winter.

"Front says you might use her blood — to save the rest. He says you'd know how to do it." Atlass frowned across the kitchen table. "And you would know, wouldn't you? Three years, you've been trying. And Robin's your answer."

"Three years. Fifty-two lives lost. More. More every day. I'm sorry, Atlass. I just can't believe."

"Why not?" Atlass brought his knuckles down on the kitchen table, thumping the wood and startling Jesse.

Jesse shifted his hip on the counter and wrapped his arms around his ribs. "I'm sorry."

Atlass took a breath, and then let it out. He pulled his hands carefully from the table top. He crossed the room and pressed his chin against Jesse's scalp.

"It doesn't matter."

"Are you sure?"

"I'm sure," Atlass said, and gathered Jesse close. Jesse leaned in the circle of his arms and watched the ocean creep up onto the beach. Against his spine, he could feel the fitful pounding of Atlass's heart.

17

Two of Atlass's hens died overnight. Jesse climbed into the pen and fished out their frozen bodies while the other chickens ran in circles about his feet. He watched the birds squabble, and saw that their eyes were clear. Their feathers gleamed in the sunlight. Jesse thought they looked healthy, but still he was cautious. So he collected every egg from the sand and rolled them in the hem of his sweater.

He carried the dead hens and the eggs around the corner of the House where he coaxed a fire from driftwood. The eggs broke when he dropped them into the flames. The dead hens burned easily. He watched their feathers singe and curl while he poked the fire with a stick. The underlying scent of cooked meat made his stomach growl and he was ashamed.

Jesse sat for a while in the sand. He waited for the fire to burn itself out. His feet itched. He rubbed his left ankle, and finally pulled off his boot, pinching between his toes until he found tiny shards of highway glass. He tossed the pieces into the fire. The screen door rattled and chickens screeched. Richard Front ran across the porch and onto the sand. The young doctor hurried away along the beach, head down and hands folded against the cold. If he saw Jesse, he gave no sign.

Jesse shoved his foot back into his boot. He scuffed out the fire and left bones to smoke among dying embers. He ran his hand over his scalp, thinking. His hair had grown again, almost beyond his ears. He was glad of the length because it kept his scalp from the cold.

At last he left the shade of the House and followed Front's footsteps over the dunes. The tide was running high. The water kissed the heels of his boots. Jesse kept his eyes on the sand as he walked.

The fish were dying in greater numbers. Their bodies steamed on the beach. Jesse walked among the corpses and poked at their diseased flesh with his boot. Scales fell apart under the pressure, and the bodies stank of rot. Farther along the shore he found gulls among the fish. The small bodies were covered with blisters and bare of feathers. Jesse squatted in the sand and studied their dirty beaks. He counted twelve of the birds, and couldn't help but feel regret. He gathered more wood from the sand, and built a second pyre for the gulls.

Front found him there on the shore, bent over sand and driftwood, tending flames.

"You can't burn every dead thing on this shore," Front said. "You'll run out of wood long before the last fish floats from the sea."

Jesse tossed a crooked branch onto the pyre. The smoke made his eyes water. He sneezed.

"I don't like to see them rot."

Front muttered under his breath as he folded into the sand at Jesse's side. Jesse lowered his chin and peered into the fire. He didn't like Front's new energy, or the manic delight the doctor displayed day and night.

"Robin's gone swimming," Front said. "Just past the breakers. Do you see her?"

Jesse bit down on his surprise and frowned out across the water. He saw nothing but the whitecaps and fog.

"There," Front said. He pointed at the distance and then smiled, although Jesse still didn't see. "She's taken to the water like a pro. Been out there all morning. I imagine the water might do her muscles good."

"She swam like a fish, before." Jesse snapped a thumb-sized twig in half. He balanced the tinder carefully at the edge of his little pyre.

"Before," Front snorted. "Before is past, Grange. Look." He thrust out a fist and uncurled his fingers. Flames sparkled on a metal cylinder as it rolled from his palm to the sand.

"Depressor," Front said. "An older version, I know. But it works. I walked back to the village this morning, to my house, and dug this up. I used to keep it around for emergencies. Who knew when I'd need to draw blood, or give a kid his boosters?"

Jesse scowled at the instrument. Front brushed the cylinder with a knuckle, rolling it across the sand until it bumped against Jesse's knee.

"Take it. Use it."

"I won't." Jesse scooped up sand and began to smother the fire. White smoke wreathed in the cold air.

"I know how to draw the blood. But I can't do the rest." Front leaned across the sand. He set a hand on Jesse's boot. "I'll come back with you, to the city, to your labs. I'll assist in any way you need. But you're the only one who might finish it successfully. Atlass says you've been trying for years. And here's your chance."

"Atlass says!" Jesse felt fury strain his brow. "You two have been sifting through my mistakes?"

Jesse kicked a last wave of sand over the fire and then pushed to his feet. Front rose with him. The young doctor snatched the depressor from the beach and grabbed at Jesse's wrist. His fingers bruised. Jesse tried to pull away, but Front's grip only tightened. His eyes blazed.

"Atlass is afraid," Front hissed. "And you are blind. You see your own pretty face reflected back at you every day, but you don't see the rest of us. We're dying, Grange. When's the last time you've seen past your own patrician nose? When's the last time you've taken a really good look at your lover, Doctor?" He brought the depressor up and pressed the cylinder against Jesse's throat, as though the instrument had sharp edges. Jesse didn't move.

"I feel it beginning in my blood. But Atlass is so far gone I can hear it in his lungs. How can you be such a fool?" He gave Jesse's wrist a vicious twist, yanking at bones and twisting tendons.

"Take this." He slapped the depressor against Jesse's palm. "And use it. But use it soon, because your lover is only one step away from becoming another body to burn."

Front released Jesse's hand and took a step away, around the smoking fire. Jesse dropped the cylinder and sprang after. He snatched at the young doctor's arm, fueled by rage, and brought Front down easily into the sand. Front cried out as he fell. Jesse settled on the larger man's chest, one forearm across Front's throat, one hand tangled in Front's long hair.

"I've fifty-four murders to my name. My soul is already overbalanced. The death of one puling coward won't make a difference."

Jesse heard his own words echo between his ears, and felt distantly amazed at his frigid calm. His heart constricted in his chest, and broke. For an instant the pain was unbearable. He gagged. But he wouldn't loosen his grip on Front, and after a moment the agony eased away. Jesse felt nothing.

He set all his weight on his forearm, and watched Front struggle to breathe. Still he felt nothing.

"You should have come to me as soon as you realized Atlass was ill, Richard. You've done yourself no favor."

Front wheezed, unable to speak. The younger man's face purpled. Jesse thought about letting him smother, and then he envisioned dragging the doctor's face through the embers of the fire. His fingers twisted in Front's hair.

He forced himself to let go. He sat up, removing his fist and forearm. Front clutched at his own throat, and tears wet his cheeks. He gulped at air and wept.

Jesse climbed carefully from Front's chest. He straightened and walked across the sand until he found the depressor. He plucked the instrument up, tucked it in the waist of his trousers, and looked out at the ocean. He could see Robin now, a tiny figure bobbing among the waves, some meters in the distance. She swam toward the shore. Jesse moved to meet her.

Wet sand crunched as Front sat up. "Where are you going? What are you going to do?"

Jesse kept walking.

Front's voice sounded as gritty as Jesse's boots upon the dune. "Damn it, Grange. Answer me!"

Jesse watched the ocean, and Robin. Front's cries swirled behind him on the wind, but Jesse didn't hear.

Robin came to shore quickly, and reached the sand before Jesse could intersect her path. He kept on, over the dunes, until he found her. She crouched naked beneath the shelter of the overpass, dripping in the cold, huddled in the sand. Robin wore his watch around her right wrist. She clutched something smooth and yellow in her hand.

She looked up at the sound of his boots, startled, and shifted in the sand. Jesse walked until he stood at her feet.

"Where are your clothes?"

She shook her head, but didn't answer. A part of Jesse wondered if it hurt her to speak. He didn't care. He couldn't feel anything except the winter around his heart. He noted that the watch on her wrist had stopped again, and that the object in her hand was a fruit of some sort, bright as the sun, and chewed around the rind.

He grabbed his sweater at the hem and stripped it over his shoulders.

"Put this on." He wanted her horrific body covered.

Robin complied, moving slowly, as though each lumpy joint pained her. The sweater had been large on Jesse, and it hung to Robin's knees. She looked up at him. He saw the moment her eyes found the shiny instrument at his waist. He caught the flash of suspicion in her eyes and knew, at last, that she was as lucid as he.

He couldn't join her on the dune. The same nervous energy that had kept his stomach churning now propelled him over the sand. He paced back and forth at her feet. She watched him, and he frowned back. After he had crossed her shadow three times, Robin moved. She lifted the fruit in her hand to her mouth, and took a bite. Jesse paused to watch juice dribble over her chin.

"What is that? What are you eating?"

"It's good," she spoke at last. Her voice sounded no better than it had by candlelight.

"What is it? Where did you get it?"

She took another bite. Jesse watched as she considered her answer. He recognized the distrust in the set of her spine, the same distrust she had shown when he had first come to the shore.

She eyed him, and then swallowed. "It grows on the shore. It's the fruit of the sea grass."

"The grass has never born fruit."

"It does now," Robin said.

Jesse held out his hand for the fruit. Robin shook her head and clutched the rind to her chest.

"You wouldn't like it."

"Why not?"

She shook her head again. Then she shrugged. But she wouldn't pass him the yellow fruit.

"I'm glad you're feeling better," Jesse said.

She tilted her chin up, and pale light fell across her grotesque face. The scars allowed very little expression, but Jesse remembered the set of her lips, the display of anger.

"What's wrong?"

"Are you going to take me back?" She was as sullen as she had been when Harold was alive. The regression surprised him. He felt a pinch of disappointment. He pushed the emotion away.

"No. You're not going back."

Robin ducked her head and nibbled at her fruit.

"Robin. I need your help."

She chewed carefully. She wouldn't look at him.

"People are dying, Robin. And with your help I might be able to save them."

"Richard told me."

Silently, Jesse cursed the man. "Has he been bothering you?"

"No. He was interesting, at first."

"And what did he tell you?"

Robin flashed him a look of disapproval. He remembered, vividly, the day in Kris's room, with Sam Brier's book. She had never enjoyed being treated like a child.

"He thinks you might separate antibodies from my blood. Use them to save the dying."

"I believe he might be right. I've been trying for a long time. I've never had a chance like you. Someone who has survived, someone who came through the change intact."

"Is that why you kept them? In case you needed their blood?"

His poor lost souls, closed away in their cellar. He'd forgotten that she had seen.

"They didn't come through intact. The disease took their minds. I couldn't help them. They couldn't help me."

Robin munched around the curve of her fruit. Jesse could see that the yellow sphere hid a seed. The seed was black, and looked as big as his thumb. Robin ate carefully around it.

"Who would you save?" she asked. "The same people who killed Molly? The same people who kept the *desgastas* outside their gates? The same people who wouldn't supply the Houses with fresh food or water?"

"Anyone who is left. Anderson. Richard. Atlass. The *desgastas* struggling in the palace. Myself." He watched her face, saw her eyes shutter. "There are so few. Don't they deserve a chance?"

"Maybe it won't work."

"I think it will."

"Then you've changed your mind. Richard thought you wouldn't do it. He thought he'd have to do it himself.

Jesse dug his heels into the sand. "You agreed?"

Robin wiped juice from her chin. "I hadn't decided. He's from the village. Why did you change your mind?"

"Atlass is dying."

From beneath heavy lids he saw Robin still.

"You didn't notice?" he said. "Then I'm not the only blind fool in the House."

She dropped her fruit to the dune and struggled to her feet, lost in his sweater. She reached for his hand, but it was Jesse's turn to flinch away. Her hostility had vanished. He glimpsed a wholly adult sorrow in her blue eyes.

"So, you see, whether I've changed my mind or not, whether I believe or not, I have to try. One last time."

"Jesse."

"And it might work, this time. You've survived it. You're sane, as far as I can tell. I think it might have something to do with your parentage. Cityborn mother, *Desgastas* father."

He stopped himself, and then saw from the quiver on her

lips that she already knew. "Something in the genes, in the combination. Although you couldn't be the only child with such parents. Impossible. But maybe, in your case, something went right, something clicked."

"Jesse." Her hand came up again. And again Jesse took one step away, dodging her comfort.

"I'm rambling, I know." He balled his fists, shoved them in his armpits, kept himself from shaking. "I need your blood, Robin. I need this chance. Not for myself. Not for Anderson, or Front, or even your poor *desgastas*. For Atlass. You'll give me your blood."

"All right."

"Or I'll take it from you."

"Jesse! All right, I said." She thumped a bare foot on the dune, wavering between the petulance of a child and the exasperation of a woman. The disease had matured her. Harold might have been proud.

She held up her left wrist. A coil of scars ran across her arm and across her palm, almost obliterating the black Mark beneath her thumb.

"Take it!" she said, and then hesitated. "Will it hurt?"

"Only a little," Jesse said. He pulled the depressor from his trousers and reached for her hand.

He left Robin beneath the freeway and scuffed slowly away along the dunes. The depressor felt warm against his belly; he imagined it was the heat of Robin's blood. Jesse cupped the instrument with one hand, afraid to lose his treasure. Rain began to mist from the sky. The drops stung his cheeks.

Atlass waited on the front porch, beneath the eaves of Harold's House.

"You've been gone a long time," he said.

Jesse brushed past the big man and into the House. He stalked through the kitchen and up the stairs to the second floor. Harold's room was empty. He slammed the old door behind him and tossed himself across the futon.

He had to wait a long time before Atlass found the courage to come after him.

The big man cracked open the door and squeezed through. Jesse kept his eyes shut. He struggled to keep the rage from his face. He sought the ice around his heart and tried to bring it up. He heard Atlass thump across the floor, and was glad when his lover bypassed the futon.

"Front's gone back to the village. He said you nearly choked the life from him. He said he's afraid to stay in the House."

"Good," Jesse said.

"He said he told you."

Jesse wrapped his thumb and forefinger around the depressor. He heard Atlass shuffle on the floorboards.

"About me," the big man continued. "He said he told you about me."

"The man talks too much," Jesse said, coldly, "and you talk too little. Apparently."

"Apparently," Atlass echoed. "Jesse, I'm sorry. I couldn't tell you."

"Then it's true. How long?"

"Since just before we left the city."

"A very long time to still be alive," Jesse said, determined to be heartless. Rage was too close to the surface. "Show me. Where is it that I didn't see it, didn't feel it? I know your body like my own." He opened his eyes, propped himself on his elbows, and waited.

"Just one. Between my toes." Atlass shed his boot. He touched a shaking finger to his left foot. "Just the one."

"Like Robin." Jesse crossed his ankles. "Maybe you'll survive it after all."

"I don't think so." The trembling spread quickly, from Atlass's hands to his shoulders. He shuddered in place. Jesse had to look away. "I don't feel well. And I'm not sure I'd want to live, not like Robin, not in a ruined body. I'm not sure I could stand to live as... a monster."

"Grow up, Love. Sometimes living is the harder choice. Sometimes, you don't have a choice."

At the endearment, Atlass let his breath out in a rumble. He crossed the floor, squatted beside the futon, and sought Jesse's eyes. His own glistened.

"I'm sorry, Jesse. I should have told you. I shouldn't have gone on pretending. But I was alone in our home when I found that blister between my toes, alone in the city. And all I could think of was that I had to get to you. I had to be with you. And then, when I had you again..." He set a large hand on the futon, beside Jesse's, almost brushing him. "I couldn't let you go. And I couldn't tell you the truth. I shouldn't have gone on, I shouldn't have let you make love to me. I should have kept away. I've probably infected you ten times over. I know you're furious. You should be."

Jesse snatched his hand away from Atlass. He bounded to his feet.

"You're right. I'm furious, Atlass. And not because you've shared your diseased carcass with my own. I'm not afraid of dying. I'm afraid of living, without you. You should have told me. You should have given me a chance to shore up my heart, to say good-bye."

"There's still time." Atlass moved around the futon, but Jesse dodged his lover's touch as he had Robin's.

"No," Jesse said, "there's not. Death has finally come for you. I can hear it bubbling in your lungs. It will have you in days. It's too late."

"No! Jesse!" Atlass grabbed the edge of Jesse's sweater. Jesse jerked away. "Where are you going?"

"To the village, to gather water. Enough to keep you soothed when the thirst comes. And to the sea, to gather fish. Enough to keep Robin and Front fed while I'm gone. If they're to be your nurses, they'll need full bellies, don't you think?" He tried to be flippant, but his words sounded of mockery, or sarcasm. "I'm going to the city, love. I've got Robin's blood, just as you've begged. And I'll deliver your precious miracle. If you can hang on a day or two longer."

"Jesse." Atlass bent to Jesse's level, his expression fierce. "I love you."

In the doorway, Jesse held up a hand. "I don't want to hear it. Get yourself on the futon and rest. I'll send Robin up later. She'll keep you company."

"Will you come and say good-bye, before you go?"

"No," Jesse said.

"Jesse!"

"We'll fight it out when I get back, Atlass. So keep your-self alive."

Atlass made a broken sound, but Jesse refused to hear it. He left the room in a bound of fury, and took the stairs two at a time. He knew Atlass followed, but he refused to look back. And when he stepped out of the House onto the shore, the frigid winter numbed away the sharpest edges of his sorrow.

18

Jesse spent the night outside the House. He waited on the shelter of the porch, cross-legged on the worn floorboards, wrapped in an old blanket. The night was clear, the clouds shredding, the puddles at the edge of the sand melting into the sea. Still Jesse's breath fogged on the air. He kept the blanket wrapped to the edge of his chin, tent-like, trying to ward off the cold as he waited for the moon to rise. His lips chapped in the dry air, and his nose began to run, but he sat unmoving, listening to the roar of the ocean.

Before the moon topped the stars Front crossed the dunes and passed beneath the eaves of the House. Jesse watched narrowly as the man clunked up the steps from the sand and onto the porch. Front was dressed for travel, in heavy boots, worn trousers, and a frayed sweatshirt. The young doctor wore a bright orange scarf around his throat and ears. The knitted scarf looked soft, fuzzy, and well loved.

"Trying to freeze away regrets?" Front asked as he bumped up the last step.

Jesse didn't like the man's smirk. He rubbed his cheek against Harold's old blanket and said nothing. Front leaned back against the porch railing. He tilted his face to the sky as though counting stars.

"I thought you'd be on your way, by now. You don't have much time to waste. I thought I'd have to catch up to you."

"Catch up?"

"I'm coming with you," Front said, still eyeing the stars.

"I don't need you."

"You don't need anyone," Front agreed sarcastically, "but I'm coming anyway."

"To keep an eye on me."

"I don't want to die. And I don't trust my salvation in your hands. Where is it?"

Underneath the blanket, beneath Jesse's sweater, the depressor felt like a brand against his skin. His hands itched to stroke it, to take it out and check the vial, to make sure the blood remained inside. Jesse didn't move. He met Front's accusation without blinking, and flashed a bitter smile.

"Come with me, then. I don't care. Just don't get in my way." He bunched his shoulders beneath the wool, and brought the blanket up until it sheltered his nose. "I leave at sunrise."

"Why are you waiting? Why are you lazing here, as time slips away?"

"I'm thinking," Jesse said. "Let me be. If you're so desperate, go on without me. I'm sure *I'll* catch up with you. Before you hit the gates, at least. Of course, we only have one boat." He continued in his best cityborn drawl, "I don't like to get my feet wet. You'll have to swim. No? Then we'll go together, after all."

Even in the night, Jesse could see the flush on Front's cheeks.

"Give me the blood," the young doctor said. He held out an imperious hand.

"No." Jesse wiped his dripping nose. Despite his resolve, he sighed. "Go inside, Richard. Warm up. Get some sleep. I'll wake you when the sun rises."

"I'll wait." Front walked across the porch. He found a place against the House, and curled his body out of the cold. "Here."

"Suit yourself." Jesse shut his eyes. He listened to the mesh of sand and water. The cold crackled in his hair. Night air moved sluggishly through his lungs, and bit at his tongue when he inhaled.

Robin came off the beach as the moon began to fade. Jesse had thought her safely asleep in the House. She padded across the porch, barefoot, as though the winter couldn't touch her. She wore faded denim from throat to ankle, so Jesse knew she hadn't been in the sea, but she

smelled of salt and the slight sheen of moisture on her skull
made him think she had been very near the water.

Robin stopped before the screen door, considered Front,
and then glanced at Jesse. Jesse felt the weight of her gaze,
but didn't lift his head. He stared instead at the skin of her
bare toes, unable to look away. The arch of her foot looked
swollen, lumpy as dough, but he thought that if he had the
courage to reach out and touch, her feet would feel cold and
hard as marble.

Jesse looked more closely, squinting over the edge of his
blanket, and frowned. And then he did reach out, scraping
the edge of Robin's foot with his thumbnail. The nail came
away covered with white powder.

Robin stood rigid in front of the door while he touched
her flesh, but as soon as he pulled his thumb away and
brought the powdery nail to his tongue, she dropped into a
squat at his feet.

"White tide?" Jesse licked his nail clean and arched his
brows.

She blinked once, and then nodded. He saw for the first
time that she carried a sack over her shoulders. It was the
same denim bag he had borrowed from grocer Barnes. The
bag appeared heavy and bumpy, as misshapen as Robin's
own body.

"What's in the bag?"

"Fruit." Robin spread the mouth of the bag, and Jesse
caught a glimpse of yellow.

"Have you been gathering those all night?" Somehow he
didn't like to think of her alone on the beach. He knew she
had grown sturdy, and that she spent her days between
sand and sky. But sometimes he feared the sea would rise
up and snatch her away, give her back the death she had
cheated.

Robin shrugged. She closed the bag and rose from her
crouch, but not before Jesse recognized the faint smile on
her broken mouth. She reached for the screen door, but
Front spoke up, and she paused.

"What did you mean, a white tide?"

Jesse swallowed a snort. He expected Robin to ignore the
village doctor and go into the House, but she still lingered,

as though waiting for Jesse to answer. He wouldn't. He cleaned the tip of his nose again on his blanket and stared out at the brightening sky, studiously ignoring Front.

"What's a white tide?" Front persisted, looking first to Jesse and then to Robin.

Jesse thought he heard the girl sigh, but she answered with more patience than she had ever shown Isabella.

"It comes every midwinter." She bumped her bag against the screen door. The metal groaned. "White flecks on the sea. The white washes ashore and dries, coating everything in powder. Andy used to collect the powder, and use it on her skin. She said it smoothed her calluses."

Jesse remembered Harold's wife walking the winter shore with a bucket and a trowel. Once or twice he had followed her, adding handfuls of white powder to the weight in her bucket.

Front scowled, confused. Jesse rolled his eyes at the shore. His dislike for the village doctor was easy, palatable. Much more palatable than thinking of Atlass, than examining the fear that constantly clutched his throat.

"The white tide is evidence of Bruster's mistake," Jesse explained to Front, speaking precisely as though to a child. "During the coldest cycle of winter more than half of the bacteria die. The white powder is simply corpses of the lost."

"The cold kills it?" Amazed, Front peered through the growing dawn at the sea.

"George never understood why. But it was probably the doom of his miracle. If not for the numbers lost each winter, Bruster's bacteria might have kept pace with the poison in the sea." Jesse cracked stiff knuckles beneath his blanket. "There'll be a white tide on the city shore, now. The taint has spread so far, at last. And the cold is fierce in the north."

"And does the powder work on skin?" Front wondered aloud.

Jesse swallowed a sarcastic reply. Tucking his blanket more securely over his shoulders, he staggered upright, stomping his feet as pinpricks of blood returned to his toes. Keeping his back to Front, Jesse shot Robin a wry smile.

"Come inside, my dear. We need to go over Atlass's care and feeding."

He reached over Robin's shoulder and pushed open the screen door. Front made a move as if to rise, but Jesse shook the edge of his blanket in warning.

"Stay where you are, Richard. Watch for the sun. I'll be out and ready before the stars disappear."

Front muttered, but stayed put. Jesse edged into the House and waited as Robin slipped after. She walked past him to the kitchen, lugging her bag of fruit. The scent from the bag was tangy, and Jesse had a sudden flash of Isabella's laughing face the day she brought him her father's apples.

"What is it with the fruit, child?" Dragging the ends of his blanket, Jesse followed her into the kitchen.

She set the bag on the scuffed table. "It's good."

"You said that before. But—" He reached into the bag and curled his lips at the expected slap of her hand. "You won't let me touch them. Why?"

Robin calmly pulled the denim from his grasp and tied the mouth of the bag shut. Then, moving carefully, as though afraid to bump a limb against anything sharp, she settled on the edge of one bench.

"What about Atlass?" she asked.

He knew she had changed the subject on purpose. He considered forcing the issue. But he didn't have the time to stand in his dead brother's kitchen, arguing over food.

"Take care of him," he said simply. "Keep him alive."

She set her scarred hands on the planks of the table and looked into Jesse's face.

"I ran a ward in Anderson's hospital," she said. "I know how to ease his suffering. And I know how to give his body to the sea. I don't know how to keep him alive. I think it can't be done."

Jesse felt his fingers twist in the blanket. He forced his hands to relax. He forced gibbering fear into silence. He reached for the ice around his heart.

"You're still alive, are you not? Don't give me excuses, Robin. I need your promise. Keep him comfortable, keep him alive."

Robin dropped her chin until it touched the chain of her *tronera*. Her bent hands clasped together, a grotesque mockery of contemplation.

"I've spoken to Atlass," she said. Her eyes gleamed in the light of the kitchen window. The sun had almost shone its face. The stars were fading. "He doesn't want to live as I am."

"Feed him broth," Jesse said as though he hadn't heard. "And water, a lot of water. I've filled as many buckets as I can find. You'll need it all. When his temperature goes up, the water will help bring it down. It worked — the water — on you. You'll need more buckets than I could fill. Maybe I should leave Front to help—"

"No," Robin interrupted. "Take Richard with you."

"I need your promise, child."

"I've given you my blood, Jesse." She watched him in silence for a moment. Then she shook her head. "Say your good-byes. You might be sorry if you don't."

His own words, echoed from the past. The same warning he had issued Robin on Harold's last night. Jesse's stomach churned and his vision dimmed. He saw flashes of rage behind his eyelids. He clutched at his blanket, afraid to let go, afraid he might murder Harold's ward.

She hadn't changed. She remained sullen, cruel, and too clever.

But when he opened his eyes he saw he was wrong. She hadn't been torturing him, punishing him, poking at him with an echo of his own words. Concern brightened her eyes, and perhaps empathy.

He didn't want to see her concern. He yanked the blanket from around his shoulders, and tossed it across the table.

"Take it with you," she suggested as he turned to go. "The sea is ice before the sun rises."

"Atlass needs it more than I," Jesse replied. "See that you use it." He left the room and the House in a controlled walk, as though he couldn't feel his lover in every creak of the building, in every whisper of draft.

Front helped Jesse carry the boat from its block to the sea. The bottom of the craft dragged a bit on the shore, collecting white powder. The white flakes lined Jesse's boots and stuck to the cuffs of his trousers. He scraped his thumb across the rubber, scooping more of the stuff onto his nail, touching it to his tongue. It tasted of metal, of blood, and of failure.

Once the bow of the boat met the waves, Jesse began to strip. Front watched, incredulous, shivering beneath sweatshirt and scarf.

"Get in," Jesse snapped. "The sun is up. What are you waiting for?"

"You'll freeze to death."

"There are reefs in this water." Jesse spat each word into the dawn. He longed to smack each syllable across the doctor's face. "If I don't guide you through, the boat will tear. And sink." He folded his clothes and set them in the belly of the craft. The depressor went into the bottom of his left boot, and the boots were placed carefully on top of his clothes.

"Guide *me* through?"

Naked in the dawn, Jesse waded into the water and pointed to the control panel. "This switch, here. Thumb it and the boat will move forward. Don't run me over." As he glared at Front, he remembered explaining the same process to Atlass. In a sudden fit of violence, he longed to toss Front into the sea, to hold him down until the sea stole his breath.

"What is it?" the village doctor asked.

"It should be you," Jesse said, before he could stop himself. "Not Atlass — you."

"Because I spoke the bad news?" Front mocked. He brushed past Jesse, splashing through waves and climbing at last into the boat. "I don't think so, Grange."

Standing hip deep in the sea, glowering across at Front, Jesse suddenly realized he couldn't feel his feet. The water had numbed his toes. The sun would warm it quickly, but even the changed sea felt the chill of winter.

Jesse took a breath. He ran sloppily through the waves and dived into the water. The oily wet closed over his head, bringing goose bumps to his skin. He welcomed the cold, and swam on through a school of sluggish fish. The water carried the thrum of the boat's engines as Front motored after.

The sun worked quickly, and by the time Jesse had led the boat safely through the shallows, the water had warmed to almost comfortable. Jesse pulled himself from the ocean. He lurched over the side of the boat, shaking water from his hair. He looked once toward the shore, and then turned his back on the House.

He crab walked past Front until he could stand at the controls. Front wrinkled his nose when he saw the white powder clinging to Jesse's skin.

"Aren't you going to wipe that off? Get dressed?"

"Shut up, Richard," Jesse said, and thumbed the controls.

They walked the highway side by side, Jesse cupping Robin's blood to his ribs and Richard Front wrapped to the eyes in his scarf. Drifts of snow rose to their ankles. Jesse's boots stuck in the ice. Walking became something that jarred them to their bones.

Jesse didn't speak as they fumbled through the snow. Front muttered to himself, but the words were unintelligible.

The drifts were pristine, untouched by traffic. Jesse didn't know if at last the boats had stopped their pilgrimages from overseas, or if it had simply snowed overnight. He hoped for the latter. The seas had been empty during their own approach, but it was too much to hope the desperation overseas had passed. And he couldn't consider the more grisly alternative. Certainly the horror hadn't yet wiped out complete continents.

Certainly it hadn't.

Front spotted the city gates first. Jesse nearly ran the man over. Front stood, planted in a snow drift, and stared. Reluctantly, Jesse lifted his own face to the cold.

"It's incredible," Front breathed.

Jesse buried his fingers in his armpits and frowned. The city gleamed in the snow, a jewel set in a white background. The pastels of the towers were evident even in the daylight, the wintry sky faded against the gleam.

"It's beautiful," Front said.

"Unnatural." Jesse wiggled his fingers against his sleeves, thinking. He could see the spire of the palace blazing above it all.

"What is it?"

"The lights are for the celebration of night. They shouldn't be lit during the day. It's unnatural."

"I don't know why. I've never seen anything so lovely."

Jesse crunched on through the snow. Front stumbled in his wake. Clouds gathered overhead, turning the sky to black. By the time they reached the city gates the portcullis burned as brightly as it had in the deepest night.

There were no guards. Jesse approached the portcullis uneasily. The silence bothered him. Uncertainty made the back of his neck tingle. Jesse nudged the portcullis, and found it unlocked.

"It's open. Impossible."

"Obviously not." Front pressed against Jesse's spine. "What are you waiting for? Go on."

But Jesse hesitated in the rose colored light, waiting. Nothing happened, nothing moved. He turned up his left palm, studying the Mark beneath his thumb.

"Go!" Front thrust at Jesse's shoulders.

Jesse rocked in his boots. He looked over his shoulder at his companion and frowned. "Maybe we should use the underground entrance."

"What underground entrance?"

"There are tunnels." Jesse gestured in the direction of the burning fields, and realized that the air was free of ash. The fires were out. The fields were thick with snow, the drifts rose to man height along the walls.

"We'd have to dig," he realized. "I'm not sure exactly where the tunnel comes out."

"We don't have time." Front pushed at Jesse again. "What are you afraid of?"

"This is wrong."

"Go!"

Jesse went through the portcullis unhindered, his Mark untested. Front followed, slipping a little on ice. It was Jesse's turn to stop as he saw what lay at his feet in the snow.

"Turn around." He gripped Front's forearm. "Turn around. We're going out."

"What?"

Jesse set his boots in the snow, and yanked the bigger man after. But not before Front got a glimpse of the snow beyond the gates. The doctor choked.

"Who are they?"

"The guards," Jesse replied. He led Front back through the portcullis.

"But..." Front trailed off, and then swallowed. "Did they kill each other?"

Jesse glanced again under his elbow at the splatter of deeper red in the rosy light. "It looks that way. Come on — we dig."

Afternoon passed into evening before they found the tunnel and managed to dig the entrance free. Front worked diligently, scooping snow while Jesse scrabbled at the wall with his fingers. Briefly, as they worked beneath the fading sun, Jesse felt grateful for the other man's aid.

Ice covered the tunnel door and Jesse had to knock the frozen layers free. It took him another long while to find the hidden lever, and by the time the tunnel door slid open, the sun had set. Above their heads the city shone, a swirl of color. The tunnel was darker than Jesse remembered.

"Are you sure about this?" Front muttered.

"No," Jesse said. He stepped into the tunnel, slipping and sliding on the icy lip, and didn't wait to see if Front came after.

Front followed. He shut the door behind them with a groan and a curse. Together they waited while their eyes adjusted to the dim light.

"At least it's warm," Front said.

Jesse agreed, but didn't bother to answer. Once he could see past the toes of his boots, he started into the depths of the city.

He remembered the dirt floors and walls. He remembered the twists and turns in the labyrinth. Still, he had to

concentrate. He ignored Front's questions and counted his
own footsteps. Several times he stopped, listening, and
heard nothing.

When the mud floors turned to concrete he felt both relief and fear. He knew by the cant of the tunnels that they
were almost underneath the palace. The light was brighter,
the city bulbs stronger where they burned in the tunnel ceil-
ings. Jesse paused again and strained to hear past the
thump of his heart.

"You're trembling," Front whispered. "Why are you so
afraid?"

Jesse didn't reply. He set one hand on Front's collarbone,
and pressed the other across the doctor's mouth. Front
jerked away, but kept quiet. After a moment, Jesse crept on.

One last turn and he found the Sayers's labs. The huge
doors were split open, just as Jesse had left them on his last
visit. Through the crack he could see that the lights were on.
He though he could smell Angie's death in the recycled air.

Jesse puffed out a breath and slid between the doors.
Front struggled, but Anderson's guards had left the doors
just wide enough, and the bigger man pushed his way into
the warehouse. When he saw Angie's body, he hissed.

"Don't worry," Jesse said, and shot Front a cynical grin.
"This one I killed. Come on."

Holding his breath, Jesse bypassed Angie's decaying
corpse and stepped lightly over her chain. He paced down
the endless tables until he reached his own machines. The
terminal still glowed, and the screen responded to his touch.
Jesse smiled.

"Sit down," he ordered Front. "And watch the door. This
will take a while."

Front sat against a leg of the table. Jesse pulled the depressor from inside his boot and held it up to the light. The
metal cylinder still felt abnormally warm against his fingers, although he knew the heat was only that of his own
body.

He turned the depressor in his hand, gripping it between
his thumb and forefinger. A quick twist and the end of the
instrument popped off. A glass vial slid from the metal

cylinder into Jesse's waiting palm. Robin's blood sloshed in the glass tube, more purple than red.

"Ready, Richard?" Jesse didn't take his eyes from the vial.

"Yes," Front said, swallowing audibly.

Jesse slipped the vial into the first of his machines. The terminal clicked quietly. Almost immediately a cascade of symbols fell across the several screens. Jesse felt his heart stop and then start again. Perhaps he had not entirely abandoned hope.

Jesse lost himself in his work, lost himself in the numbers and patterns. He forgot the blood, forgot the living serum. Instead he played with equations and probabilities. The machines hummed beneath his fingers, augmenting each skill. Jesse had always been better with machines than people, better with numbers than the heart.

He surfaced only when Front shifted minutely on the floor.

"What is it?" Jesse asked, frowning at his screens.

"I thought I heard something."

Jesse glanced down at the other man. "Did you or didn't you?"

"I don't know."

Jesse held his breath and listened. Seconds ticked away. He heard nothing but the rush of air in the tunnels. He looked for a moment at Angie's purpled face and wondered if her ghost haunted the labyrinth. Then his machines called him back.

When he emerged again, Front's hand was locked about his wrist.

"Is it almost finished?" the young doctor breathed. "I heard something in the tunnels."

Jesse surprised himself by a flash of mirth. "Some*one*, Richard," he murmured. "There are no gargoyles beneath my city. Anyone chasing us is as human as you and I. As Robin."

Front wasn't amused. He ground Jesse's bones beneath his fingers and stared hard at Angie's corpse. "Damn you, you've got me dancing on pins and needles. Why do you think someone is chasing us?"

Jesse shrugged elaborately. "Intuition. The guards are down, the city is alight. It's wrong. And I'm not the most beloved soul in Carpenteria. Not anymore."

Front's grip loosened. "I heard something."

"Fine. Keep listening."

But the next time, Jesse heard it too. A flash of sound, a whisper of footsteps, and echo of voices along the passageway. He sighed and straightened, shutting down his machines as he did so.

Front gripped the edge of the table. "Did you get it?"

"Six vials." Jesse set the glass tubes one by one onto the table.

Front reached out, fingers hovering in the air. "Is it enough?"

"For now." Jesse stripped off his sweater. He set the six vials on the wool and gathered the sweater into a bundle. "If it works."

"Give it to me," Front reached for the bundled sweater.

"I think not." Jesse clutched the sweater to his gut and moved along the tables. He stepped again over Angie and peeked through the crack between the doors. "All clear, I think. Come on, Richard, how will we save you from death if we're captured by gargoyles?"

They hurried through the tunnels, trying to keep quiet in their heavy boots. Front began to pant. Jesse thought the man gasped in terror. He tried to be amused and failed. His own lungs were beginning to falter.

And they weren't alone in the tunnels. Jesse was sure of it. He heard soft cries now and then, bouncing from wall to wall, and once, the call of laughter. He reached around, grabbed Front by the cuff of his sweatshirt, and broke into a run.

"This way."

"Where are we going?"

"To the surface. They've got the tunnels blocked."

"They?" Front cried on an exhale. "They who?" He didn't seem to expect an answer.

Jesse dashed on, winding through the tunnels until he found dirt beneath his feet. He yanked Front forward and grunted in relief when they wheeled into a dead end.

"Up!" he said. He jerked a thumb at the handholds in the concrete. "You first, Richard. There's a grate at the top."

Front scaled the wall with ease, skimming the handholds from floor to ceiling. Jesse took a good bite of his sweater, and struggled up after Front, the bundle clutched between his teeth. The doctor paused at the last handhold. He thumped one fist against the ceiling.

"I don't see a grate. Where is it?"

Jesse barked an order around wool, and Front felt frantically over the ceiling. The doctor's boots scraped the top of Jesse's head. A hidden draft made Jesse shiver. Still, Front searched.

Jesse thought he heard a whisper of laughter on the draft. Balancing his weight on the tips of his boots and the fingers of one hand, he hung in place and pulled the sweater from his mouth.

"Left!" he hissed. "To your left. There's a lever. Pull!" He swayed and had to clutch the bundle in his jaws again, steadying himself with both hands.

Front found the lever. He groaned in desperation or triumph and pushed. The grate popped free. Front squirmed through the black square. Jesse squinted briefly and then scrambled after. He fell through the hole, and into snow, rolling to protect his bundle.

Jesse lay still in the drift, gasping air through the wool between his teeth. He could smell smoke again on the wind. He pulled the bundle from his mouth and slowly rolled onto his haunches.

"Shut the grate."

Front obeyed. The village doctor dripped sweat onto the snow. His arms trembled as he pressed the grate into place. The square disappeared, blending into the white wall of a building.

"Where are we?"

"An alley, not far from the gates. Ready?"

Front nodded and Jesse stood up. He checked his sweater, making sure it was still tied securely, and then started through the snow. Drifts clogged the alley. Jesse found himself pushing through piles of snow as high as his thighs.

Once they reached the streets the snow dropped away
into puddles of slush. Jesse paused, frowning at charred
façades. Front stood at his side, silent.

Every building had been burned from the inside out,
gutted at ground level. Marble faces were black with grit
and wreathed in smoke. The fires had gone out, but the
heat of the embers kept the snow at bay. And still the colored floodlights gleamed. Above the second or third
floors the buildings were beautiful, bright garnets in the
night. Only the ground floors gaped, decimated, as
though hit by a low-lying firestorm.

Jesse gripped his bundle and slipped along the streets.
The wind whistled through gaping holes in buildings and
store fronts. He listened for voices, but heard only the wail
of the winter. Around one corner, a fire still burned, flick-
ering flames at the edge of a park. Jesse stamped at the
heat. Front didn't move to help. Jesse kicked over burning
ferns until his boots grow hot, and then he gave up and
walked on.

Soon after they came upon the first corpses. Piles of
bodies sprawled frozen against ice or rotting in slush.
Jesse didn't recognize faces, but he picked out cityborn
silks, and the glass jewelry Isabella's students favored.
Once he thought he saw the dull gleam of a brass *tronera*
around a dead throat.

The corpses thickened until Jesse was forced to walk
across the dead. The stench shook him, and the crack of
bones beneath his feet sent him quivering as though from
a palsy. Three times, Front stopped and was sick. Jesse
waited patiently, unwilling to add to the man's torment.
His own stomach rolled like the sea.

"Is it the whole of Carpenteria?" Front wondered.

Jesse looked out over the streets of his city, trying to
count the endless dead, and then trying not to. "Perhaps.
Perhaps more." There were too many alien corpses alongside the familiar. Here and there Jesse spotted a froth of
ivory hair or the gleam of blue in a dead eye. Pilgrims
from overseas, lost and buried in a strange city.

Jesse stumbled over a slick of flesh and ice, and nearly
went down. His knee hit the frozen sidewalk with a crack.

Jesse swore at the pain. When he steadied himself and his bundle, he saw that Front had gone down at his side.

"Richard," he said, gentle despite his loathing, "get up. We're almost out."

Front lay still. Jesse blinked the sting of snow from his eyes, and stared at the splash of red across the other man's brow. Blood, he thought, and reached out to touch the thick liquid.

He fell before his hand found Richard's brow. The snap across the back of his neck sounded like his knee across ice, and then he went down, ears ringing, into the drift of snow with the rest of Carpenteria's corpses.

Jesse woke to whirling skies and bruising hands, jeering taunts and the glitter of glass in ears and brows and lips. Students, Jesse realized as they thrashed through the snow, dragging him at their heels. He sought eyes and faces, but found only feral laughter. He couldn't see Front anywhere. And then a particularly vicious hand sent him back into darkness.

He woke a second time, on the floor in the president's office. His head felt shattered to sharp pieces, and he thought he might be sick. He reached for his bundled sweater and found it gone.

"Hold him down. I don't want him up and struggling."

He knew the voice, recognised village accent. Isabella. He cracked his lids, trying to see past the spinning in his head. He made out the president's desk, and the brilliant tapestries on the wall. He couldn't find the grocer's daughter until she moved, obscuring desk and tapestries. At first, Jesse didn't recognize her face. Then she shifted again, and her eyes came into focus. They were bright and aware, free of madness. Above her brows, her long forehead was burned, as if by the summer sun. She held a makeshift mask over her mouth and nose, a square of purple silk, and her fingers looked very brown against the fabric. Studs of glass glinted in her brows, and ribbons twined around the tinted tufts of her hair.

"Jesse," she said, behind the square of purple. "How are you feeling?"

He opened his mouth to answer, but the taste of blood across his tongue made him gag.

"Keep him down," Isabella cried. "Don't let him up. Don't breath his air."

He didn't understand. "My sweater—"

"Are you cold, Jesse?" Isabella demanded. "Are you ill? Has it gotten you at last?"

Jesse tried to move, and bring Isabella's blurring face back into focus, but hands held him down, against the carpet. The pressure across his chest became too much and he lost consciousness again.

The third time Jesse woke, he was locked behind familiar bars, imprisoned in his own cellar.

19

Jesse lay on his back on the hard floor of the cellar and waited for his head to clear. He could taste blood in his mouth. He thought that he had bitten through his tongue. The back of his neck stung, and his eyes refused to focus.

Even prone and beaten he knew the room. The whir of the fans in the ceiling had been part of his life for years, and some nights he still dreamed the feel of stale air across his cheeks. He knew the gentle *ping* the old metal cages made when the floor shifted, unsettled by nearly ceaseless tremors in the depths of the earth.

He listened to the rattle of the shifting cages and missed the sounds of his prisoners. Jesse knew without opening his eyes that the changed cityborn were gone.

Several heartbeats later he rose to his knees, and then unsteadily to his feet. His bare torso was bruised and blood-stained, pummeled by students and scraped by the snow. He shivered, wrapped his arms around his stomach, and stumbled to the door of his cage.

The cage hadn't been cleaned, and his boots stuck to the floor. He knew the smell, remembered the reek of human feces and the thick black fluid his lost souls expelled in quantities. His nose didn't pick up the taint of death, or rotted flesh, but even so he was afraid to venture into the dark recesses of the cell. He didn't want to find the abandoned corpses of any of his children.

So he set his face against the bars of the cage door and tried to see into the rest of the cellar. He made out the metal table, crooked in the center of the room. And he could hear the drip of the spigot in the wall, another familiar sound.

Forehead pressed against the bars, he craned his neck this way and that, trying to see into the other cells. It was hard to tell in the gloom, but he thought the cages were empty. Once he caught a flutter of movement, but it was only his own shadow flitting across a far wall.

They were gone. In his heart he knew it. He only wondered if they had managed to escape on their own, or if they had died, thirsting for water in his prison. He thought of the corpses above, in the snow, and wondered if his changed cityborn had been among them. He hadn't seen even one face he knew. Death and disease and cold had marred the dead beyond recognition.

His tongue hurt, and the sharp taste of blood made his mouth thick. He spat into the corner of the cage. He coughed, and spat again. Beneath the dim city bulbs his blood looked black as lung fluid. The sight of the stain made his chest itch in sympathy, and he hacked once more.

"Grange? Are you finally awake, then?"

Jesse froze, hands clenched around the bars of his cell. Fingers still locked around metal, he swallowed blood and turned on his heel. He knew the voice, although the words were slurred. Yet for a moment the panic he kept locked in the back of his head broke free and ran rampant, blurring his thoughts. The black fathoms in the back of the cage terrified. He didn't want to move from the cell door and the freedom he imagined lay beyond.

"Grange?" Richard Front called. "You can't shake the bars free, I've tried already. Will you come here? I need your help."

The man's imperious tone knocked some of Jesse's pride back into place. He shook his head and plucked his knotted fingers from the cell door. Folding his hands behind his back, he paced the length of the cage and passed into the shadows.

It took a moment for his eyes to adjust and his nose to clear. The stains on the floor grew thicker as Jesse moved from the front of the cell. He could see splashes of black on the one solid wall at the back of the cage. A trail of dried fluid reached almost to the ceiling. The violence of the pattern looked like murder, a deliberate shedding of blood. The smell, sickly sweet and cloying, repelled.

Jesse took his gaze from the wall and found Front. The other man crouched in one dark corner, his back set against the solid wall, one hand clenched around a length of bar. His eyes were swollen, as though he had been crying, and his hair rose from his scalp in matted tangles. His hand on the cell shook against the metal cage.

"All right?" Jesse asked, feeling an unwelcome tug of empathy.

"Dandy," Front snarled, and then sighed. "Come help with him, will you? I've covered him up, but I don't know what else to do."

Baffled, Jesse peered beyond Front's spread legs. He scowled and took a step forward across sticky concrete, trying to see. When his eyes finally focused, his chin came up in surprise.

Front laughed at his expression, the bark of mirth made harsh by the small cell. "You're surprised. Do you know him?"

"Michael Anderson." Ignoring the revolted leap of his stomach, Jesse crouched on the filthy floor. He ran his hands over Anderson's limp body.

"He's close to death," Front said. "What did he do that they locked him down here, alone?"

"I don't know." Jesse's eyes still didn't want to work, but his fingers told him much. He felt the scars of advanced Bruster's on Anderson's face, and the seams of ruined skin along the man's neck. He found a pulse, but the bump of life was rapid and very faint.

"He was the leader of the *desgastas* exiles," Jesse explained as his fingers searched across Anderson's throat. "He took the city by force, because the students said he would find a cure for his people."

"And now he's dying in a hole."

Jesse didn't answer. He bent closer to the ground and squeezed Anderson's shoulders. "Michael? Michael, wake up."

Front laughed again. "Even you can't wake the dead, Grange."

"If I can wake him, maybe I can manage—" Jesse stopped abruptly, his fingers frozen against Anderson's chest. He knew the curl of rough fabric beneath his hands, and recognized the scratch of wool. "My sweater."

"His own shirt was torn through. I thought I should keep him warm. I couldn't get the sweater on him, but I've wrapped him as well as I could."

Jesse rocked back on his heels and stared at Front. "I thought they had taken it. When I woke, it was gone."

Front tossed his ruffled head. "You dropped it in the snow. I was aware enough to grab it."

"And they didn't take it from you?" Jesse couldn't believe it.

"They didn't want to get any closer to me then they had to. They were afraid of me, Grange. And afraid of you."

"Maybe they have good reason." Jesse hooded his eyes. He watched Front carefully from beneath his lids. "The vials?"

"I have them. All six. They're intact."

"Where?"

"Here," Front said without moving. He licked his lips, and the wet glittered in the shadows.

Jesse folded his hands in his lap and sat for a long moment. His head ached, threatening violence. He watched Front, and wondered if he would have to kill the man after all. One more death. Perhaps it would be a mercy.

But he could hear the rattle of Anderson's breath just beyond his own knees. The *desgastas* hadn't passed beyond help, not yet.

"Give me a vial," Jesse said at last. He straightened his shoulders and beckoned.

"What?" Front straightened as well, scandalized.

"Just one," Jesse urged.

"What for?"

"What do you think?" Jesse snapped back, his patience wearing thin. "This man's not dead yet."

"It's a waste!" Front protested.

"It's a trial," Jesse corrected. "How else will we know? Were you going to be the first to volunteer? I don't think so. You're too afraid of your own death to reach for courage." Blood soured his mouth and he spat again, this time in Front's general direction. "You were going to wait, let me try it on Atlass, see if it would work. See if it would kill. Well, the plans have changed. We're stuck in a cage, we don't have many options." He curled his fist, let it hang in the air before Front's nose. "Give me one vial."

The village doctor curled into the himself. Jesse could hear the hiss of his breath.

"Come on, Richard," Jesse injected all the sarcasm he could into the other man's name. "How else will you know?"

Denim scratched as Front moved against the concrete. He let go of their cage and reached around his ribs. Jesse caught the flash of glass and kept his expression neutral.

"Just the one," Front said. He passed Jesse a glass tube.

"We don't know how much it will take."

"Just the one!"

Jesse plucked the vial from Front's hand. Tucking the tube carefully between his knees, he touched Anderson's brow. The *desgastas's* skin felt clammy. Jesse could smell rot on the man's breath.

"Michael."

"He won't wake," Front said. "And what does it matter?"

Jesse shot Front an icy glare. Carefully, he pulled the vial from between his knees and set it on the sticky floor. In the gloom the serum looked as black as the fluid spattered on the wall. Gaze fixed on the vial, Jesse stood up and reached into his left boot.

"What are you doing?" Front hissed.

Jesse arched a brow. "He can't swallow the stuff. It needs to be injected." He grunted as he pulled Front's battered depressor from the depths of his boot. "I couldn't leave it behind. And I hoped they wouldn't search too carefully."

"You were right," Front said, distracted by the instrument in Jesse's hand. "How did you know? What are they afraid of?"

"Disease and madness," Jesse said. "The ruination of my city."

Front opened his mouth, and then shut it. Jesse turned from the doctor and crouched again on the concrete, this time by Anderson's head. The *desgastas* lay motionless, unshaken by dreams or raving. Jesse knew the man's death was very close. He pursed his lips and studied Anderson's slack face. Then he brushed his sweater from the *desgastas's* chest and reached for Anderson's left arm.

Jesse spread the limp arm across his lap. He could feel the rope of scars and the droop of muscle even through his trousers. He picked the vial of serum from the floor, and shoved the glass tube quickly into the depressor.

"Are you sure you need all of it?"

"I have no idea." Jesse set the mouth of the instrument against Anderson's bare forearm. "Luck, Michael," he whispered, and squeezed the cylinder.

The depressor popped. Anderson's breath faltered, and then caught again. Jesse could hear the bubbling in the *desgastas's* lungs. He moved from beneath Anderson's arm, and wrapped the man in the sweater again. Then he shoved the depressor back into his boot. Resigned, he sat on the floor and shifted Anderson's head to his knee.

"Now we wait," Jesse said, ignoring Front's nervous stare. He tilted his head back against the wall, and shut his eyes.

He didn't sleep, but he kept his eyes closed, and he managed to drift away from the pains in his heart and body. He didn't think of Atlass, or Robin, or even the serum in Michael Anderson's blood. He thought of Isabella. Over and over again he saw her burnt face, and the square of purple silk across her mouth. He wondered when she would come. Certainly she wouldn't leave him in the cellar to die.

Jesse wondered how she had unearthed his secret, and what she had thought of his lost souls. He wondered if she knew her father was dead, her village deserted.

Anderson stirred a long while later. Jesse knew the passage of time only by the stiffening of his own muscles. He sat up slowly, tendons pulling at the back of his legs, and opened his eyes.

The *desgastas* met his gaze. Jesse felt a twist of sorrow. Anderson's eyes were fogged, delirious or mad. The older man licked his lips, and the dry flesh cracked and bled.

"I'm sorry, Michael." Jesse touched the man's chin, wiping away blood. "I have no water."

Jesse expected Anderson to rave and howl, or snap at his fingers. He waited, cautious, his palm on Anderson's chest. Shaken by a deep tremor, the *desgastas* clenched his teeth and shuddered. And when his body finally stilled, Anderson's eyes had cleared. He coughed, and Jesse saw the black fluid run from his mouth. Jesse reached to clean it away, but Anderson stopped him with a look.

"Doctor Grange. You've come back." His voice grated, deeper even than Robin's croak. "Fool to the end."

"And you still have your wits about you," Jesse replied, gentle despite his cynicism. "Stubborn the death. Maybe you'll beat this thing yet."

"No." Anderson wheezed. He twitched and then stilled again. "I'll die before it breaks me. There are so many who didn't, so many mad, and violent... Hungry. We had to kill so many."

"Not your fault," Jesse tried to soothe him, but Anderson shut his eyes and drifted away.

Jesse cradled the *desgastas's* head on his lap. He did his best to clean fluid from the seamed face. He looked for Front, and found the man curled on the floor, apparently asleep. Jesse considered searching the doctor for the remaining vials of serum, but Anderson's head was heavy on his legs, and he couldn't find the energy to move. He rested his chin on his chest and listened to the suck of the ceiling fans.

"The students were stronger." Jesse didn't know when he became aware that Anderson stirred. The rough voice swirled in his dreams and brought him slowly awake.

"They knew the city, they knew the underground. They wouldn't let us leave. Maybe they were stronger in their conviction. Or maybe it was their terror that beat us back."

"How many are left?"

"Nine." To Jesse's surprise, Anderson laughed. The sound was a bitter gurgle. It stuck in the man's throat, choking. "Nine young men and women to our fifteen. They took us anyway, burned us out. Locked us away.

They're afraid of us. Too terrified to kill us, too frightened to let us live. So they've locked us away until we starve. Or until we're eaten to bones."

Jesse thought Anderson's voice sounded stronger, but his body still shook in Jesse's arms.

"I meant, in the city," he said. "How many are left in the city?"

"Your city is a grave, Doctor," Anderson rasped. He turned his face to the wall. "There are none but us left alive."

Jesse's hands quivered. He waited until his fingers stilled before he soothed Anderson back to sleep.

Voices in the air woke Jesse and sent Front bolt upright. Anderson didn't wake. For a moment, Jesse thought the *desgastas* was dead. But the man's lungs still gasped at air, and his chest still rose with his breath.

Murmurs bounced across the cellar, reflected from wall to wall. Jesse, who knew the acoustics of the room, didn't bother to shift, but Front had already reached the door of the cage. He shook the bars, and then cringed at the rattle of metal.

"They're in the tunnels," Jesse said. "Calm down."

"But they're coming this way."

"So they are. I hope you don't think they've come to let us out."

Front pressed his cheek against the cage door. Jesse thought he could scent the man's fear.

"Richard," he said, "what have you done with my vials?"

"They're safe."

"Not if you go throwing yourself around in a panic. Sit down and wait it out."

To his slight bemusement, Front nodded. Jesse watched the village doctor as he paced back across concrete. Then he freed himself of Anderson's weight.

"It's your turn to tend our friend," Jesse said. "Sit with him and keep quiet."

"And what will you do?"

"Greet our jailers."

Jesse walked as far as the door. He didn't touch the bars. He stood in the flicker of city bulbs and waited for Isabella.

She stepped from the tunnels into the cellar as though unsure, but her stride lengthened when she glimpsed his face. Two men dogged her footsteps, slight boys with buzzed heads and bruised faces. All three of the students wore swathes of fabric tied across their mouths. Jesse wondered what had happened to the city filters.

Isabella stopped three feet from Jesse's cage. She had dyed her hair a new color, a ripe purple to match the silk at her lips. Dye of the same color smeared her eyes. The artifice made Jesse mourn.

"You've changed, my dear," he said, saddened.

But the set of her brow held conviction, and he thought he saw a flash of cold wisdom in her eyes.

"How are you, Jesse?" she asked, watching him carefully.

"Thirsty," he said, thinking of Anderson. "Cold." He brushed fingers across his bare torso. "And hungry."

"Your eyes are clear, your face unblemished. Are you ill?"

"No."

A flash of emotion rippled her mouth beneath the silk, and somehow Jesse knew it was regret.

"It doesn't touch you, does it, Jesse? Why are you blessed? What have you done but perpetuate Bruster's mistakes?"

"So I'm no longer a hero, Isabella?" He faced her scowl. "It has Atlass."

"Then it will have you, soon." This time he couldn't read the turn of her mouth beneath her mask. "And your companion?"

"Don't you recognize our good Doctor Front?"

"How is he?"

"Thirsty," Jesse repeated. "Cold. Hungry."

"There is no food to be had," Isabella said. "The land has turned against us at last. Fruit rots before it ripens. Animals are born dead. And the grain—" She shuddered. "The grain is sour, poison. There is nothing to eat but the dregs in the palace refrigerators and the scraps in abandoned homes. There's nothing to share."

"Water, then."

"The city pumps still work," Isabella allowed. She hesitated, and then nodded to one of the young men. He crossed a room, filled Jesse's old bucket at the spigot, and brought back the water and a dipper.

"Set it outside the cage," the grocer's daughter said. She looked at Jesse. "I'm not opening the door. You can dip through the bars."

"This isn't enough," Jesse argued, gesturing at the bucket.

"It will do."

Jesse controlled an urge to snatch at the dipper. He ran a palm over his chest, winced at the scrapes and bruises.

"How is Anderson?"

Jesse considered Isabella through his lashes. "Nearly dead. Where are the rest of the *desgastas*?"

"Still alive," Isabella said. "Quarantined in the palace."

"And why are we here?"

"This is where we come to die."

Jesse didn't understand, but he didn't press.

"Richard." Isabella lifted her head. She frowned into the depths of the cage. "How is my father?"

Bars rattled as Front shifted, but the doctor didn't answer.

"Dead," Jesse said. "Our Richard is the last."

Isabella's long face fell. Jesse passed a hand through the bars, intending to comfort, but the grocer's daughter backed away.

"Why are you still here, Isabella?" he asked.

She shook her head. "I'll have someone bring you more water. Tomorrow."

"Why have you locked us up?"

"And if Anderson is dead," she continued, turning her back on the cage, "we'll remove the body."

Jesse watched her cross the cellar, watched as she climbed into the tunnel, watched until her companions disappeared as well. Then he sighed and scratched at the back of his neck.

She came again, alone, many hours later. Jesse thought it was night above ground, but he wasn't sure. His battered body had lost track of time.

Isabella sat on the floor outside the cage, next to the bucket and dipper. She pulled her knees under her chin, and although she wore denim instead of skirts, and had now shorn her long hair, Jesse was reminded of the girl he had known on the shore.

He rested against the cage door, as close to freedom as she would allow.

"How did he die?"

"It took them all," Jesse replied. "Wiped the village out. Four or five tried to run. Front says they were too far gone. I found him alone, living on the shore."

"Was it clean? Or did they... turn?"

"They died quickly," Jesse said. "I'm sure of it. I saw nothing that might indicate survivors of any kind. Nothing of madness."

"So many survived it here," Isabella whispered. "But they weren't whole. We had to kill them all. All that we could find. Your city is huge."

"Anderson said it was hard."

Her eyes flicked to the back of the cell. She listened for a moment to the *desgastas's* labored breathing.

"We didn't betray them, Jesse. We worked with them as long as we could. Until we were sure."

"That they were the carriers, the catalyst? I think you're mistaken, my dear."

"Do you *know* it?"

"No." Jesse pulled his knees against his chest, unconsciously mirroring Isabella's pose.

"We don't mean to be cruel," she said. She sounded as though she meant it. "We don't kill unless we have to." Jesse thought of Harold, of Angie. Of his fifty-two tortured children. "We keep them warm and clean in the palace. Until they show signs."

"And then you lock them away, here?" Jesse understood, at last.

"There are so few of us, now. There is no need for murder, for pyres. We can let them die on their own. This place is perfect for death, for secrets."

Jesse knew the truth of that. "Them?" he pursued. He wondered if she meant only the *desgastas*.

She didn't. "The ill. The diseased, once they show the signs. I can't watch them, wait to see if they die, or if they go mad. How can I?"

"How many students are left?"

"Five," Isabella said on a whisper. "Two, I think, will be joining you soon."

"And the *desgastas*?"

"They are a stronger people. They still have nine."

"And no one else, in the city?"

"I don't know. Sometimes there are shadows, and sounds. I think many escaped, made it up over the walls or through the gates. And I think some might live on, in the darkest buildings...." She shrugged. "There are rumors of violence in the night."

Jesse chewed a finger, thinking. "Tell me again about the food."

Isabella lifted her face to his, and chuckled. Not the full-blown laugh he remembered, but still beautiful. "Do you yet think to save the world? You're too late."

"Tell me."

"What more is there to say? The food is bad. The animals are poison. The water will go, too, I think. When the pumps fail."

"The pumps are strong. You have time."

"Then we will starve," Isabella said. "If we don't blister first."

"The grain?"

"Is poison. Burns the throat like acid. Bruster's re-engineered land has given way. Another failure, another lie."

"My land, too," Jesse said. Isabella rolled her shoulders.

"Tell me, why did you burn out the city?"

"There were too many dead," Isabella answered. "Fire cleanses."

Jesse looked up, a sharp glance, and caught a shard of hysteria in her eyes. She controlled it quickly.

Jesse nibbled his thumbnail, and thought of another question. Front beat him to it.

"Let us go, Isabella."

Jesse hadn't heard the man approach. He started, and swallowed a nasty word.

Isabella touched one hand to the cage door, the closest she had come to contact. "I can't, Richard. I'm sorry."

"We're not ill."

"You're safer here," Isabella said. Jesse heard the absolute in her tone.

"We're not ill!" Front protested. "The blisters haven't come out. There's still time—" He choked off, as Jesse's hand came down across his calf, a slap and a warning.

If Isabella saw the blow, she gave no sign.

"I'm sorry." She brushed a hand across her mask. "I'll fill your bucket again."

"You should have told her," Front protested once the grocer's daughter had returned to the tunnels. "We can save her. She'll let us go."

"How do you know?"

"Barter with her. One vial for our freedom."

"Another vial, Richard?" Jesse asked wryly. "Be sure to save some for yourself." He narrowed his eyes. "Tell her about the serum and she'll send her friends in, take all five of the vials from beneath your shirt. If she believes you."

Front brought an arm against his ribs. "Isabella Barnes?"

"Grocer Barnes's sweet daughter. I know. The same young woman who has helped to slaughter my city and lock us away in a filthy cell. Think on it, Richard. And try not to be an idiot."

Jesse stalked back across the cage. He dropped to Anderson's side. He pillowed the man's head again on his lap and leaned back, waiting. He shut his eyes, but he was too cold to sleep, and somehow afraid that, if he drifted off, Anderson would let go of life and slip away. Jesse couldn't let that happen. He needed the serum to work. He needed the miracle.

For the first time in long hours, he broke a vow and thought of Atlass. An ache started in his throat. He held tight to Anderson until he could swallow again.

Jesse kept his arms around the *desgastas's* shoulders, even after control returned. He couldn't make himself let go and he didn't until, just before Jesse fell over the edge into unwelcome sleep, Anderson's body began to convulse and his lungs began to froth.

20

Front carried the dipper from the bucket. Jesse tried to spill the water down Anderson's throat, but the *desgastas* wouldn't drink. Anderson's eyes rolled rapidly beneath closed lids, and his mouth gaped as he struggled for air. Black fluid ran in rivers over his lips and from his nose, down his chin and across his throat. Jesse tried to wipe it away, but the noxious liquid kept flowing, and eventually he gave up and concentrated instead on the man's shaking limbs.

"What is it?" Front backed away from the writhing body until the cage bars pressed into his spine.

Jesse wrapped one arm around Anderson's torso and the other over the man's skull. "I assume you've seen this death before, Richard," he said, cold as the band of ice around his heart. "Or did you run and hide when Bruster's took your village, *Doctor*?"

Front didn't move from the edge of their prison. "Not like this. It wasn't so violent. So..." He faltered, and then gestured at the flowing black stains across Anderson's mouth and chin. "It wasn't like that. What's happening?"

"Some of them end this way." Jesse pulled his sweater from Anderson's chest. The wool was wet and warm with the *desgastas's* fluid. "Sometimes their lungs give out."

"He's dying," Front said, words heavy and dull beneath the sound of Anderson's wheezing. "The serum didn't work."

"Apparently not." Jesse snatched at Anderson's mouth, trying to keep the snapping jaws from severing his tongue or slack lips. "Get me more water."

"We'll need it," Front protested. "What if they don't come back? We need to save what we have left."

"Bring me more water!" Jesse's shout rattled the bars. Anderson's body bounced in his lap. Jesse took a gulp of fetid air, trying to find calm. He looked across the cell, challenging Front's rebellious gaze.

"Bring me water," he repeated, more quietly. "And keep bringing me a filled dipper until I tell you that you may stop."

Still Front hesitated. Jesse saw the man's eyes shift and slide sideways. He imagined he could read Front's thoughts.

"Look at me, Richard." Jesse spoke gently despite the fury burning the back of his throat. "Do you see the murder in my eyes? I've warned you before. The only thing keeping me from your throat is the dying man on my legs. Now — bring me water."

Front studied Jesse's face, as though searching for truth. Then he looked at Anderson. The black stain had crept across his chest. It dripped over Jesse's trousers. A trickle of liquid had already touched the concrete floor.

"Front," Jesse cautioned, but the doctor was already moving to the door of their cell.

Front kept the water coming, one dipperful at a time. His hands shook, and he spilled drops of water as he crossed from the bucket to Jesse and back again. Jesse used each dipperful to sluice fluid from Anderson's mouth and neck. Sometimes he dribbled water past the *desgastas's* gnashing lips. He didn't think the man swallowed.

The convulsions seemed to last for hours. The cell stank of sweet fluid and pungent urine. Anderson's bowels had let go while his body arced. The floor about the *desgastas* glistened, and a spreading puddle of filth encircled his body. The black muck streaked Jesse's face and shoulders, and dripped in runnels along his bare arms.

Just as Jesse thought Anderson's bones would snap beneath the force of the convulsions, his body went limp. Jesse gasped, and slumped at Anderson's side. He wiped fluid from his own mouth, and blinked stinging moisture from his eyes. When he had the strength to move again, he turned a scowl in Front's direction.

Front stood at the door of their cage, shaking, the dipper hanging awkwardly in his grasp.

"The bucket's nearly empty," he said after a moment, some emotion making his voice rough. "I can't scoop the last drops out."

"It doesn't matter," Jesse answered. "He's dead."

"But he's not," Front whispered. "Look at his eyes."

Jesse frowned. He brushed more fluid from his face. He peered down at the body on his lap, and nearly cried aloud in horror.

Michael Anderson's eyes bulged, the lids stretched back from his irises. The eyes themselves seemed to bounce in their sockets, rolling in his skull, as though the convulsions that had left his body still rocked behind Anderson's nose. More black fluid began to run, in tiny streams, from the corners of his eyes, welling up behind the eyelids.

"Bring me the last of the water."

"I can't get it!"

"Then bring me what's left in your dipper."

There were only a few drops, a few sparkling remnants clinging to the metal spoon. Jesse shook the drops free, trying to clean Anderson's eyes, but the fluid rose too quickly, and soon his sockets were filmed with black.

Front knelt at Jesse's side, his mouth working silently, chewing air. "Look at his hands," he groaned.

Jesse looked, and blanched. The skin along Anderson's fingers seemed to be drying up, flaking away. As Robin's had, he remembered. But somehow this peeling of flesh was different, more thorough and more violent. The old scars dried up and then shriveled, bursting away from the skin, leaving craters. Jesse thought he could see smooth pink in the lopsided holes.

He realized, suddenly, that he could no longer hear the wet struggle of Anderson's lungs. He stared into the *desgastas's* face, looking for death, but the man's eyes still quivered beneath black muck. Jesse put his palm against Anderson's nose and mouth, searching for breath. He could feel nothing beneath the steady explosion of liquid.

"He's still alive," Front repeated. "Look at his chest."

Jesse looked, but couldn't discern any real movement of ribs. The writhing skin kept the body shaking, but beneath the tremors Anderson seemed as limp as a corpse.

Bits of scarred skin fell to the floor, absorbed black liquid, and then broke apart in the thick puddle. The sweet smell grew and the air in the cage became damp and heavy.

Richard Front gagged. "I think you should move away."

"Why?" Jesse asked, bitterly amused, although his own stomach rose to the back of his throat.

"This isn't death. This is something worse."

"Worse than death, Richard? And I thought you feared nothing more."

"I'd move away," Front cautioned. "Don't let it touch you."

Jesse looked up, past the fluid-matted hair that hung over his brows, through black gunk that coated his cheeks and eyelids, and laughed. Front shuddered at the sound. He stood up and backed away. Jesse cradled Anderson.

It seemed to last forever, to stretch on for days. Jesse feared Isabella would return in the middle of the struggle, or even worse, that she would send one or two of her cohorts. Then he feared that the pains in his body weren't phantom, and that days had passed, and that Isabella would never return at all. And then Jesse stopped thinking, stopped worrying, and simply witnessed.

Front slept, slumped in a heap against the cage door. He spat a scream when Jesse thumped his shoulder. Jesse's hand left a black smear across Front's sweatshirt. The other man stared at the streak in disgust.

"Is he finally dead?"

"Alive. Asleep." Jesse smiled. Anderson's fluid had dried to a mask across his cheeks and forehead. Jesse felt the mask crackle as his lips curled.

Front clutched metal bars. He pulled himself upright. "It worked? The serum worked? He's alive?"

"As Robin," Jesse said. "See for yourself."

Front lunged away, disappearing into the gloom at the back of their cell. Jesse leaned against the cage door. He gazed wearily at his old bucket. Half an inch of water still lined the bottom, but he knew Front was right. The bucket sat out of reach and there was no possible way to ladle up the water without tipping the container.

He sighed, and ran a dry tongue around drier teeth. He lifted one arm before his face, and saw that it was black from forearm to fingers. Sighing again, Jesse rubbed the back of his hand with a nail. He watched dried fluid flake away.

Jesse heard Front's faltering steps as the man returned. He kept scratching, too tired to face the explosion. Front didn't speak, but Jesse heard the catch in the other man's breath, and grinned at the empty cellar.

"Ready to go next, Richard?" he asked over his shoulder. "One vial ought to do it, maybe less. I suspect we gave the poor man too much in our panic."

Front gulped at the thick air. "Is he cured?"

Jesse shrugged, still staring across his cellar. "He's breathing normally, sleeping normally. His fever is down. Just like Robin."

"But... he's *not* normal."

"Just like Robin," Jesse agreed, "changed. Did you expect otherwise?"

Front muttered something inaudible. And then, "Is he sane? Lucid?"

"We'll have to wait and see. I think so." Jesse turned around. "I believe you have your miracle."

"No," Front said. Jesse saw that tears wet his cheeks. "Not like that."

"I don't understand," Jesse said, honestly confused by the man's stupidity. "What sort of illusion did you hold? You watched Robin find life again. What did you expect?"

"Not that." Front waved a shaking hand to the back of the cell. "*That* is not my miracle. Not... that."

Atlass had said much the same thing.

"Anderson might disagree."

"But you don't know, do you? How do you know, what he thinks, until he wakes?"

"I know," Jesse said. He set his back to Front, and rested again against the cage door, bone weary.

"Will you choose *that*, when your time comes, Grange?
You're the prettiest of us all. And you live by your looks,
and your charm. Don't think I don't see it. When the time
comes, will you give it all away to cheat death?"

"Of course."

"I thought the same thing. The choice seemed so easy.
Until it came upon me." Front grabbed Jesse's shoulders
and wrenched him around. "Look!"

Front turned his head, bent his neck, and exposed his
throat. He pinched two fingers across flesh until the blister
above his collarbone oozed.

"Your time has run out," Jesse said, unruffled. But he
was glad of the winter he kept around his heart. He didn't
want to feel sympathy for Richard Front.

Front's eyes blazed, his teeth showed in a snarl. "Clean
away all that black, and you might find your time has run
out, as well."

"I might." Jesse squirmed away.

"Where are you going?"

"To get some rest. I can't succor your soul, Richard. If
you decide to take the serum, if you need someone to hold
your hand, I'll do it. Wake me up. But not before then."

Jesse meant to go to sleep immediately, but the itch of
dried fluid on his skin made him pity Anderson. So he
spent several minutes struggling to move the much larger
man from the drying slick of flesh and body fluid. Front
didn't offer to help.

He managed, but just barely. He feared to scrape
Anderson's new flesh across the filthy floor, so he moved
the *desgastas* in inches, shuffling across concrete. He carried
Anderson as far from the back of the cage as possible, into
the brighter light at the cell door, and then gently spread
him across the concrete. Jesse regretted the loss of his
sweater in the chill of cellar. He wondered if Anderson felt
the cold.

He lay down on the cage floor next to Anderson, but still
he couldn't sleep. Exhaustion cramped his muscles, and his
head still throbbed. Jesse longed for a break, but he couldn't

let himself go. He propped himself on one elbow and watched Anderson.

The new skin was already losing its rosy color, becoming pale and cold. The change of color, on a man who had been as dark as the skin of a city tree, unsettled Jesse. What remained of Anderson's hair had bleached out, gone white. And the disease had sculpted his face, set the old lines as though in stone, frozen the rest.

Like Robin, Anderson resembled a corpse more than a living creature. Jesse thought that if he touched the new skin, he would find it cold and unyielding. But unlike Robin, most of the Anderson's bumps and scars had sloughed away. Where Robin was a taper, half melted by her fever, Anderson was death, caught and frozen into life before it could slip away.

Monstrosity, Jesse thought, and wondered what he had wrought with Robin's blood.

He found himself gazing at Anderson's fingers. He noted the lack of nails and wondered if broken claws would grow in to replace the old half moons. Anderson's chest rose on a breath, and Jesse watched the dull gleam of the *tronera* around the man's throat. The medallion was painted black with fluid, painfully dark against white flesh.

Jesse's head nodded, wobbling to his chest and then up again, but still he couldn't sleep.

And so he was aware, if not clear headed, when footsteps echoed in the cellar, pulled from the tunnels by the draft of the fans. He unfolded himself, stepped lightly over the sleeping *desgastas*, and waited at the mouth of their cage. Front watched from the shadows, stare glittering, but made no move to rise.

Isabella emerged alone from the tunnels. She stepped heavily across the cellar. Her cropped head was still purple, but the dye had faded, and she hadn't reapplied color to her face. She came without her mask, and her lips were pressed bloodless.

Isabella walked straight to the bars, bypassing the bucket and looking into the cage, but she didn't seem to notice the stains across Jesse's skin until he stuck a hand through the bars and touched her cheek.

She blanched. "What happened to you?"

"Anderson."

She glanced at the *desgastas*, lying so still on the floor, white as a corpse in the shadows. "He's dead at last?"

"No."

Isabella considered the quantity of gunk in Jesse's hair. "He should be."

"Where is your mask?"

"Useless. I gave it up."

"I see."

He traced his finger down her cheek, over her left shoulder and across until he gripped her wrist. Then he turned her palm to the air, studying the Mark below her thumb. The pattern was black beneath her skin. She was not born *desgastas*, but the infection was in her blood at last.

She considered her Mark, and then his face. Her eyes were liquid and steady, unafraid.

"Your friends?" Jesse asked.

"Infected, all. And getting drunk on the last of Harlan's liquor."

"Have you come to let us free, then?"

"I can't." She dropped her gaze from his face, and stared hard at the hand he still held.

"Why not?" He hadn't the time, but he dug up patience and held it.

"You're carriers. We're all carriers. I can't let you leave the city."

"What about your friends?"

"Locked in the west wing. With the *desgastas*. They won't leave the city."

Jesse raised both eyebrows. Dried black muck fluttered as dust before his eyes. "They went willingly?"

Isabella's neck stiffened. "They know it's right. They're ready to die."

"For a cause." Jesse shook his head. "The young are always ready to die for a cause. And you've always been earnest, Isabella. But do you really think a quarantine will help, now? It's overseas, Isabella. You must have seen the faces, the pilgrims streaming by the dozens through the gates. They were coming as I left, even before. From *overseas.* It's spread so far. You must see that it's too late for quarantine. Years too late."

"I can't help it," the grocer's daughter said. Her brow crumpled. "It can't all be for nothing."

Jesse exhaled. "Sit down."

Isabella glanced up, face blank. He dropped her hand and gestured at the bucket. "Sit on that."

It took her a moment to understand. Then she overturned the bucket, using it as a stool. The plastic bottom sagged beneath her weight, but the bucket held. Jesse sank to his knees in his cage and watched her through the bars.

"Robin's alive, Isabella."

She frowned, not understanding.

"She was blistered from head to toe," Jesse continued, "near death. Hours from the end. She begged to be taken back to the shore. Anderson agreed, and I carried her from the city. Through the tunnels," he said, answering the question in her eyes. "Only Anderson and one guard knew.

"She survived the change, Isabella. Survived. Sane. Lucid. It didn't turn her like it did so many others, it didn't take her mind, or make her a slave to thirst or nightmares."

Isabella sat on the edge of the bucket. Her wrists hung lax across the knees of her trousers. She listened to Jesse, rapt and yet somehow distant, as though he spoke a fairy tale.

"Robin's living on the shore. She's happy, and she's growing healthier every day. She's not pretty," he said, knowing Front listened. "But she's alive. Her body produced the antibodies needed to beat it back."

The bucket squeaked. Isabella fisted her hands, but her mouth had relaxed. She was a natural student, a scholar. She had been fascinated with his background, his legend, and she had learned his past. The grocer's daughter knew what he'd found.

"I've built a serum. It looks like a cure. When you chased us down, I was trying to get it from the city to the shore. To Atlass.

"I need to leave the city now, Isabella. Today. I need to get to Atlass before it's too late."

"It may already be," Front said from his lair.

"No." Jesse didn't look away from Isabella. "But I need to go now."

Isabella startled as though from sleep. Her hand came up to her cheek.

"The cure," she whispered.

"It isn't gentle." Jesse moved aside. "Look at Anderson."

Isabella frowned through the bars. She flinched away from the form stretched across the floor. Then she steeled herself, swallowed, and looked again.

"He filled with fluid. Bloated and peeled, and burst apart," Jesse said. "But he's alive."

"But how do you know he's sane? Has he come to?"

"Not yet. But I know."

She rocked on the bucket, thinking, and a flash of wildness disfigured her face. The strange emotion on her familiar face made Jesse cold. He had to remember that she had changed too.

"How much of it do you have?"

"Five vials. Five doses."

"Five?" She was incredulous. "So little?"

"The program has been replicated. I can build more anytime."

"Then I will let you free," Isabella decided. "Let you into the labs. You will build more."

"No," Jesse returned, jaw hard. "I need to leave the city. I need to get to Atlass."

"You don't have a choice."

"There are always choices. You will let me go, let me save Atlass. Once I have, I'll return and build you as much of the serum as needed. But not until I know Atlass will live."

"We need it now!" She sprang off the bucket and shook the cage.

Jesse leaned against the door and let the bars rattle his bones. "I'll leave you three of the vials, to spread among *desgastas* and students."

"Only three?"

"The *desgastas* are strong. Most will survive until I return. Your friends will need the serum before Anderson's people do."

"There will still be deaths. And I can save only three?"

"I won't be gone long. We may be able to save them all."

"But you're willing to take the risk, to sacrifice the innocent." She wouldn't believe it.

Jesse sighed. He dropped to his knees, crouching down against the bars until he could look up into her face. "I've never been a good man, Isabella. Harlan raised me to godhead, set me on Bruster's empty pedestal. And I enjoyed it. The *pesos*, the respect, the opportunities, I enjoyed every bit of it."

"I am not a good man, but I am loyal. Loyal to my brother, loyal to my family. And I will sacrifice any number of innocent to save the ones I love." He wrapped his fingers on the bars, below the clench of her own. "I don't have your heart. And I'm not afraid of death. Your friends, Anderson's *desgastas*, any survivors outside this city, they can all die. You can't threaten me with their lives. And I won't build your serum unless you let me save my family."

Isabella's face had turned to stone and her knuckles were bone around the bars. "Jesse." She turned his name to a plea.

"I'm stubborn, Isabella," he cautioned, "and I'm hard. I won't listen to your arguments."

She swallowed her protests and turned away. He watched her shoulders rise, watched her cross her arms in self-defense and anger.

"It's Atlass, Isabella," he said. "Let me go."

She paced around the cellar, stroked her hand over the metal table, flicked her fingers beneath the drip of the spigot. In the depths of the cage Front muttered and Anderson sighed in his sleep. When she returned to Jesse's prison, she wore the face of a stranger.

"We will wait until the *desgastas* wakes. If he is lucid, if he is well, then I will let you go. You need one vial for Atlass. You have five. Give me four to save those I can."

"The fourth is for Richard," Jesse said, implacable. "He has already blistered."

She wavered. She meshed her hands.

"I won't argue," Jesse said again. "I'm taking the good doctor with me. I don't trust him here, on his own, running wild in my city. Besides, I've promised our Richard his miracle."

"All right. The three doses. And you will return. When?"

"Four days."

"Four days," she allowed. Then she nodded, but her face didn't soften. "If the *desgastas* wakes sound of mind and body."

"Thank you." He inclined his head, and kept the relief he felt from his mouth.

But Isabella only shook her head and sat again on the bucket, refusing the touch of his hand. So Jesse left the bars and went back to Anderson to wait.

The *desgastas* woke sound of mind, blinking in the dim light as though it hurt his eyes.

"Hello, Michael." Jesse touched the man's brow and found it cool. "How do you feel?"

"Thin," Anderson's voice scratched unpleasantly. "Very thin."

"It's to be expected," Jesse answered, wry. "It took Robin several days to recover any of her strength."

"Recover?" Anderson tried to sit up. Jesse watched tendons strain, but the man's fingers barely moved.

"You've been given your cure," Jesse said. "It will take its toll. For a while. And then you'll be strong again."

Anderson's eyes, so brown in his pale face, were somber. "The others?"

"You'll have to convince them to live until I get back. We have a shortage of the miracle, at the moment." Jesse tilted his head and watched Isabella. She didn't move from her seat on the bucket, but he saw the attention in her posture. "When I return, we'll remedy the situation. Just keep them alive a little while longer, Michael."

Anderson nodded. He sank back against concrete. Three breaths later, the *desgastas* was asleep again. Jesse looked at Isabella. The grocer's daughter stared back, expressionless.

Jesse and Richard Front left the palace before sunset, well wrapped against the cold in borrowed garments. Front had given up his cache of serum, and Jesse carried two vials in a padded wallet at his belt. They walked quickly, aware of the eerie silence over snowbound sidewalks, and afraid of the dead buried beneath the drifts. Jesse remembered his last journey through Carpenteria. The horror he'd felt as he had trod on the icy flesh lingered.

But Isabella felt that the tunnels on the edges of the city were unsafe. She believed rogue cityborn haunted the underground labyrinth and made their homes beneath the ground, in the tunnels closest to the city wall and freedom. Jesse didn't know if Isabella was simply being hysterical, but he didn't want to risk the treasure at his belt.

So he took the route above ground. Front trailed in his footsteps, complaining at each slip and stumble. Jesse ignored the other man's swearing and thought only of reaching the shore.

They made it through the city center without incident, but as they approached the gate in the wall, Jesse's neck began to prickle. He paused, ankle deep in a snowdrift, and listened to the wind.

"What is it?" Front worried aloud. "Do you hear something?"

"Nothing but the wind," Jesse said, and walked on.

But he stopped again, three paces later, eyes dazzled by a flash of light across the snow. Front cursed, and pressed a forearm against his own eyes. Jesse blinked. He squinted along the black faces of burned out buildings, searching.

Still he heard nothing, but another glitter caught his attention. Light, shining on the snow, reflected off metal.

"Run," he said, and grabbed at Front's arm.

"What?"

"Run!" The order came out a snarl, and Jesse stumbled through the snow, making directly for the gates. He could see the portcullis in the distance where it rose against the gray snow.

Front stuck to Jesse's heels, swearing again. The village doctor moaned as they tripped over the dead guards in the shadow of the wall. The smell of rotted flesh made Jesse swallow convulsively.

Then they were through, safely past the portcullis and outside the city. Just beyond the curve of the wall, Jesse paused to look back.

And they looked at him, bright eyes from the ruins of the blackened buildings. They watched from the shelter of trampled parks. One or two were brave enough to stand tall in the snow, cityborn Lords in rags and denim, and pale faces in the outrageous fashions that were so popular overseas. The men were armed, with shards of glass and bits of sharp metal.

The thin figures watched Jesse, feral, waiting. Jesse hesitated only briefly, and then turned his back on the city.

"Come on," he said. He started down the highway.

"But—"

"They won't follow. Forget them. Come." He took large strides, trying to move quickly, determined not to run.

Front broke into a trot, and hurried along at Jesse's side. They were alone on the road. No creature followed.

Night fell. Rain swirled on the air, obscuring the horizon. They lost the highway in the fury of the storm, but it didn't matter. Jesse knew the way to the sea, and he walked with a purpose. He thought only of Atlass.

Front hung on until they reached Grizwald's beach, and then the village doctor erupted in blisters. His skin heated, and his lungs began to slop, and he was forced to make his choice. He grabbed at life, but it took him a long time to reach for it.

Jesse huddled in the shelter of their boat, listening to the other man's cries. Fear for Atlass bit at Jesse's heels, and he nearly broke his promise and left Front alone on the beach. But when Front finally made his decision and asked for the serum, Jesse administered the dose with a steady hand, and he held the doctor's hand as Front screamed himself unconscious.

Alone on the sand, curled against the side of the boat and away from the winter, Jesse listened to the skirl of the angry wind and kept guard while Front changed.

21

Jesse lurched from the sea, naked and cold, and found Robin waiting on Harold's porch. He waited at the edge of the water, searching the girl's face, trying to pick her expression from the shadows the House threw. Low waves wet his ankles, seawater warmed by the winter sun. A lone fish nibbled at his flesh, but still he didn't move.

In the end Robin took the step for him. She moved from beneath the eaves of the House and leaned out over the porch rail. Sunlight kissed her brow, highlighting the new growth of hair over her skull. The light scraped her malformed face, streaking up along her cheeks until it glistened in the corners of her eyes.

So Jesse knew. But he couldn't believe. He turned back to the ocean, and grasped the stern of the boat he had pulled through the shallows. Richard Front lay in the bottom of the craft, senseless despite the clutch of the breakers and the rock of the boat.

Jesse dragged the craft from the sea, beaching it as best he could. The water still snatched, and the boat still quivered, but it would stay safe, stuck on the wet sand, until Jesse was ready to return it to the blocks behind the House.

He hoisted Front upright. The village doctor swayed on his feet and murmured sleepily. Jesse picked the doctor up, cradling the limp body in his arms. Front felt very light against Jesse's shoulder. The man's breath tickled Jesse's neck.

Jesse crossed the beach very slowly, his eyes fastened on Robin's. She leaned over the edge of the rail, away from the gloom of the House, as though she enjoyed the cool sunlight upon her skin. The glisten of tears had disappeared, if tears they had been, and her eyes were dry and clear.

He stopped in the sand, below the porch, and looked up at her face. "I've brought you a ward, child."

"I'm no Keeper."

The flash of annoyance across her mouth eased him, but not enough. "Someone has to look after our Richard until he regains his composure."

She peered down at Front's lolling body, and the disgust in her eyes barely hidden. "Not you?"

"No."

She sighed. "I'm tired of ministering the ill."

Jesse stood in the sand and waited. The wind off the beach dried the water from his skin, and left behind goose bumps. Robin's foot tapped on the porch, not quite a stamp of anger.

Then she shrugged. "You're cold. Come inside."

He climbed onto the porch, carrying Front, and passed through the ancient screen door. Someone had scrubbed most of the rust away, and the metal gleamed dully. The door opened silently, squeak oiled away, and then Robin let it slam shut.

The House had been swept free of sand and the entryway no longer stank of mildew. Years of wax had been cleaned from the wall sconces, and fresh candles shone without smoking.

"I raided the village for supplies," Robin said when Jesse shot her a bemused look. "And Atlass helped me repair a few things."

"Was I away so long?"

"Long enough," she replied, surprisingly gentle.

They passed through the kitchen on the way to the stairway, and Jesse paused again. The battered table had been repainted a violent red. The planks shone despite pits in the old wood. The same paint had been applied to the cupboards and along the beams in the ceiling.

"It was the only color we could find," Robin said defensively. "We had to make brushes from bundles of grass."

"It brightens the room," Jesse returned, deadpan. Robin grunted.

Still holding Front, Jesse edged past the table and toed open one cupboard, and then another. The shelves were stuffed with village treasures. Matches and candles, thread, and an array of knives and eating utensils cluttered the counter. One or two strips of dried meat and a crumbling loaf of bread waited on a battered clay platter.

"This is all the food you could find?"

Robin cocked her head. "I saved the bread and meat for you. The fish in the sea will only turn your stomach. There are a few chickens left, but they're not for slaughter."

Jesse opened his mouth and then shut it again. "And what do you eat?"

"Fruit." Robin cocked a bent finger at the sink. Yellow spheres gleamed in the light from the one window. The fruit was piled high a chipped bowl, the bowl itself set carefully in the kitchen basin. "Richard will eat it as well."

"Richard needs a bed." Jesse said, taking one last look around the new kitchen. The room smelled musky, of the earth, and Jesse thought it was the perfume of Robin's fruit.

They climbed the stairs side by side. The walls of the House creaked in the winter morning, but Jesse knew from the press of empty space that he and Robin and Front were the only living creatures in the building. A lump formed in his throat. He swallowed it away.

Jesse paused at the top of the steps. "Kris's room?"

"I sleep there, now." Robin shook her head. "Harold's is clean."

The room was neat and pristine, the worn floor smooth and clean beneath his sandy feet. Cracks still marred the window, but Jesse's makeshift blanket had been taken down and real curtains, denim curtains, had been installed instead. A clean blue blanket shrouded Harold's sagging armchair, and another had been spread across the futon. Two new sconces had been added to the wall above the bed. Robin lighted the candles as Jesse rolled Front onto the futon. The silver cat lay curled at the foot of the mattress. The animal stretched uneasily when Jesse disturbed its rest.

Front trembled and muttered, and then curled into a ball. Jesse bundled the blanket about the man's thin shoulders. Candlelight hollowed out Front's cheeks and scored his brow.

"He'll need water when he wakes."

Robin stood beneath a glowing sconce and studied Front. "The fruit will give him the nourishment he needs."

"Will it?" Jesse couldn't keep the bitterness from his tone. "And what of me?"

"There are clean clothes at the foot of the bed," Robin said.

Jesse narrowed his eyes at the neatly folded pile. Flannel, denim, and a pair of boots. He recognized the shirt and the boots as Atlass's. They would be too big, but he took the shirt and trousers anyway. The boots he left in their place.

"How long ago?" Robin asked, flicking a finger at Front.

"Three nights," Jesse said, and walked from the room.

He bathed for a long while in the sea. He counted fewer corpses on the shore and wondered. He didn't see any fish at all in the water beyond the breakers. He wondered if the schools had moved on, farther north, maybe to the shore along Carpenteria, maybe past. Or perhaps, after decades of suffering, the creatures had finally died out.

The sun beat against the back of his neck, and by the time he stepped back onto the sand, afternoon had come and steam rose from the sea. He dressed at the side of the beached boat, rolling up sleeves and pant legs. Even so, the trousers drooped around his waist, and the shirttails fell nearly to his knees.

He walked around the boat and found Robin sitting in the sand, waiting.

"The sun feels good," he said, noting the way she held her cheeks to the sky.

"The white tide passed two days ago," she answered. "The worst of this winter season is over."

Jesse looked doubtfully at the drip of wet on the roof of the House, but said nothing.

"When did you give him to the sea?" he asked, after a long moment beneath the sun.

The girl's shoulders arched in her sweater, and she gave him a sharp look. "You are very calm."

"I grew up in this House," he replied, as if it were all the answer needed. "I grew up with *desgastas*. I grew up with death, as you did."

Robin touched the medallion around her throat and searched his face. Harold's *tronera* was warm against Jesse's own skin, but his heart was still cold, and he was able to keep his eyes and mouth empty of emotion.

"Come with me," Robin said at last. She rose awkwardly to her feet. "There's something I want to show you."

She led him around the corner of Harold's House, across the sand to where the dunes rolled away toward the village. There, in squares along the well-traveled path, a garden grew. Robin stopped on the path, in the very center of the plot, and let Jesse look his fill.

A small stake fence encircled the garden, separating cultivation from the wildness of the shore. Larger stakes popped up here and there from the flourish of green, giving the weaker plants backbone. Jesse saw sea grass, brown and heavy with yellow fruit, and something else of white and red berries. Thick vegetation, velvety as moss, grew on pieces of asphalt and chunks of concrete, apparently transplanted from beneath the overpass. The green was vibrant, and apparently unaffected by the cold or rain.

Jesse heard the cackle of poultry, and found the chickens — a rooster and three hens — caged at the edge of the garden.

"I'm not sure if the chickens will adapt." Robin tilted her head and watched the flutter of wings in the cage. "I've been feeding them bits of moss and fruit everyday. The fruit killed two, but the rest seem all right."

Jesse touched a shooting white stalk and thumbed thick purple berries. "What is this?"

"Don't you recognize it?" The girl reached around. She squeezed a rubbery stem. "A seaweed. It used to wash up in tangles and gobs. The stems were orange, and covered with pods. I used to pop them." She shrugged. "One day several weeks ago an albino version washed up. Several, actually. Some of them took root along the dunes and grew these berries. Atlass helped me transplant them."

"Can you eat it?"

"The berries are salty, good in stew. And the ends of the shoots are very tender."

Jesse plucked a berry. He rolled it between his fingers. "And if I swallowed one?"

"I don't know," Robin said. "Atlass tried one. Before he blistered. It made him sick. He couldn't keep it down."

"And the moss?" Jesse asked. He tossed the berry to the sand.

"Grew along the sides of an old bucket. I'm not sure what good it is, but it grows well on the rocks. Look at the chickens."

He walked the path through the garden, careful not to step on vegetation. The chickens were caged rather than fenced in. The pen was crafted of more wooden stakes, and the birds stuck their heads through the gaps in the wood. They squawked at Jesse.

"Look at their feet," Robin said from her place on the dune. "And the skin above their eyes."

Jesse squatted among the plants and examined the chickens. At once he spotted the scars and the wrinkles in unusually pale skin.

"They survived whatever disease killed off the others. And these four will take the fruit. They like the moss," Robin said as Jesse sat and considered. "They're not exactly healthy, but they've started laying again. What does it mean?"

"I don't know," Jesse said.

"Aren't you curious?"

"No." Jesse straightened, brushing sand and moss from his trousers.

Robin waited while he returned to her side. Then she turned her face to the sky. "So, did it work?"

"You saw Front."

"And on the others?"

"Anderson is alive, and was growing stronger when I left. I built six vials of the serum. One we used on Anderson, and I left three with Isabella. Two, I brought with me."

"You used one on Richard," Robin guessed. "Where is the other?"

"In the boat. I'll take it back with me, to the city."

"You won't keep it for yourself?"

"I don't need it."

The girl hesitated. "When will you go?"

"I told Isabella four days."

Robin snorted. "Isabella is running your city, now?"

"My city is dead. She is... baby-sitting... the remains."

Robin laughed. She touched Jesse with skeletal fingers. "Are you hungry?"

"No."

"Come and eat anyway," she said, and she smiled as she had before Harold's death.

After a supper of dried meat and old bread, Jesse sat in Harold's armchair, the cat curled in his lap, and watched Robin feed Richard Front her fruit. The young doctor chewed slices of yellow rind eagerly, but he still refused to speak. Jesse remembered Robin's own long silence, but then he recalled Anderson's need to communicate and decided that Front was merely sulking.

"He won't want any mirrors in this House," Jesse said scornfully, as Robin slipped a chunk of fruit between Front's lips.

"He'll get used to it," Robin said.

"I don't think so. I've learned our Richard has a weak spine. The serum should have finished him."

"But it didn't."

"Not for lack of trying," Jesse shuddered at the memory. He dangled his legs over one arm of Harold's chair. "Three days, and he screamed all the way through. I should have left him to die."

"You wouldn't have come in time," Robin said, catching at Jesse's unspoken thought.

"When?" Jesse asked, afraid of the answer.

"He left the House five days ago."

"Left?" Jesse sat bolt upright, spilling the cat. He gripped the back of the chair with white fingers. "What do you mean?"

Robin set the bowl of fruit on the floor and regarded Jesse with serious blue eyes.

"He's not in the sea, Jesse. It broke him, but it didn't kill him."

Jesse's fears howled in the back of his head. He tried to ignore them. "So you did." He didn't allow it to be a question.

Robin looked at Jesse, and then stared at the walls. He knew she was seeing Harold's drowned body twitching on the kitchen floor.

"I couldn't," she said, still staring at nothing.

Jesse rose from Harold's chair. Rage cracked away the winter around his heart at last.

"Why not?"

She blinked and turned, and the heat of her anger almost matched his. "I loved him too."

"Then how could you let him live on?" The accusation rose high in Jesse's throat, and then broke.

"I thought maybe he would come around. I thought I could keep him, for you."

Jesse laughed. The bitter sound made Front stir and mutter. "After what you experienced in the palace? After the creatures you saw in my cellar?"

"I couldn't do it!" Robin yelled. She picked up the bowl of fruit, and threw it at Jesse's head.

The bowl missed by inches. It hit the wall, shattering. Yellow rinds scattered across the floor, and bounced beside the futon.

"I couldn't do it," Robin repeated, and frowned down at a wedge of yellow.

"And the first thing your Keeper taught you was mercy," Jesse spat out, intending to wound. "All your temper, all your pride, all your childish preaching, and in the end the truth comes out. You are no *desgastas*. Even Isabella had more courage."

He crossed the room on coiled muscles, and then found that he had to pause in the door.

"Where did he go?" he demanded, cold again.

"Over the dunes," Robin answered, her own voice thick with rage. "East, toward the village. But he was mad, Jesse. Mad and violent." She faltered. "And I looked, later. I looked but I couldn't find him."

Jesse left the room without answering. He did not bother to look back.

He spent the night walking the dunes and haunting the village, and the next day, and the next. He drew water from the village well but ate nothing. He found no sign of Atlass, no evidence of any living creatures other than the monsters in his brother's House. Eventually his body gave out, and he fell into the dunes, so far from the House that in the distance the building looked no bigger than his thumb.

He lay in the sand for a long time, dazed. The protection around his heart and head had failed at last. Memories and sorrow and loss made him shake and moan. He longed to die.

But as he rolled beneath the sky, he glimpsed a patch of yellow. Jesse blinked until he focused, and then blessed the sea grass and its alien fruit. He crawled across the sand and lay in the tangle of vegetation, surrounded by thriving yellow orbs.

The first bite blistered his tongue. The acid ran down his throat, burning like fire. He felt the drip bite into his stomach and nearly cried out. The second bite wouldn't stay down. He retched the yellow pulp back up, and the pain of regurgitated poison was even greater. Tears ran down his face in runnels, and mucus dripped from his nose and into his mouth.

He took a third bite and his mouth went numb, his throat soothed to a distant ache. Jesse waited long enough to see that mouthful would stay down and then lifted the sphere again.

Robin knocked the rind from his hand. The fruit thumped to the sand and rolled out of reach. Jesse opened his mouth on a howl, but the sound that passed through his burnt mouth was more of a gargle.

"Now who is the coward?" Harold's last ward asked. She sunk to the sand cradled Jesse's head on her lap.

She tried to get him to stand, but he wouldn't rise, and she was too small and awkward to carry him back to the House. So she sat at his head and listened to his whimpers as he lay in the sand and waited to die.

He slept, instead, a restless sleep, fraught with dreams of Atlass, and nightmares of frozen corpses beneath the jeweled towers of his city. He woke to screams, and thought in annoyance of Richard Front. But the screams were his own, garbled and thick. He couldn't feel his tongue, or his lips, but his stomach boiled. He turned on his side in the sand, and clutched at his middle, and Robin supported his head while he gagged.

The pain in his stomach eased some and he dozed off, only to wake three more times and spew yellow poison to the sand. Robin held him steady each time, and when he woke a fourth time, it was night and cold, and Robin held a tin cup to his mouth.

"Drink," she ordered. "Carefully."

Jesse struggled. His mouth was still numb, and the water trickled ineffectively from between his slack lips. In the end, Robin had to tilt his head back and pour the water into his mouth. Jesse's body took control then, and he swallowed mindlessly.

He wondered how she had managed to magic cup and water from the dry dunes, but he couldn't speak to ask. She bent beneath the moon and considered his face.

"Are you ready to go back?"

He shook his head and lay down in the sand. Robin sighed. Jesse covered his head so he couldn't see her, but her shadow still fell through the moonlight and across his brow.

"He spoke a lot before madness took him," she said after a while. Jesse opened his eyes again, he couldn't help himself, but she had turned her head and he couldn't see her face.

"He feared what he would become in the end." She held up her ruined hands, and the moonlight made them wax before Jesse's eyes. "But not as afraid as he once had been. He helped me clean the House and design the garden. He saw the changes in the plants. I think he liked to imagine the land was adapting, and that we were adapting too, changing. The fruit fascinated him. He was never so foolish as to eat half a rind."

She hesitated, blew out impatient air. "I might have killed him that way, I suppose. I didn't think of it. Only you would think of it." She touched Jesse's cheek, fingers bone cold. "I didn't think of murder, or mercy, or even of Harold. I thought he would come out of it, like I did. And then it was too late.

"You're right, I should have known better," she sounded defensive again, and still so young. "I'd seen it before, many times. One night he simply woke up and knocked me down, and tried to tear out my throat. But there was still water left and it distracted him. He swallowed it down, and then went out across the dunes. Maybe looking for more."

The sand hissed as she straightened. "I'm sorry, Jesse. But it's over now. We haven't given him to the sea, but he's dead in all ways that matter, and you've used up more than enough time in mourning." She sounded all Harold, stern and pragmatic. "Come home with me, now."

And because she did sound like Harold, and because he was tired and sick, and because somewhere inside he was still the boy who had trod the shore before Jesse Grange became a city icon, he let her take him back to the House.

Two more days passed before Jesse could swallow anything but water, and even then bread and meat scraped painfully at his ruined mouth and throat. He could speak, but only in a hoarse whisper, and the words hurt him. He spent long hours in Harold's room, listening to the drip of candle wax, or in the garden, watching the plants grow and the chickens thrive, and thinking of Atlass. He often imagined he felt his lover in the precise design of the garden, or in the bright red paint of the kitchen.

Richard Front recovered before Jesse did, and soon the young doctor began to flourish, nourished by the yellow fruit. He spoke little, and watched his companions carefully. He took to dogging Jesse's steps, and late in their seventh evening on the shore, Front cornered Jesse in Robin's garden.

"You'll take me back with you," Front said.

Jesse regarded Front narrowly from his perch on a moss-covered slab of concrete. The cat circled about Jesse's ankles and rubbed the wedge of its head along concrete edges.

"Oh, I know how you feel about me," Front continued. He picked a handful of berries from a white branch and shook the little spheres on his palm. "Our Richard," he fluted, mimicking Jesse's sarcastic drawl perfectly. "Richard, the ineffectual doctor. Richard, the puling coward." He snorted. "Even Robin has learned to hide most of her disgust."

He walked along the path until he stood before Jesse's seat. "I don't need your respect," he said, yellow eyes flashing in a white face. "I don't even want it. What are you to me but a pompous ass who has made one mistake after another, and in the end, lost everything?"

Front's gaze settled on Jesse's clenched fist. He smiled. "Hit me, if you like. You're fast, but this body is stronger than it was."

"What do you want?" Jesse's broken voice scraped aloud.

Front shrugged. A late winter breeze blew through the garden and stirred the wisps of Front's remaining hair.

"I'll go with you, Grange," he said. "Or I'll follow on my own. But, as you said once before, it's a long swim. And I don't like to get my feet wet," he mocked.

"Why?" Jesse asked.

"Because you need me," Front replied. "Because *they* need me. You've already left them too long. And because I know what you're thinking. You want to rebuild that city. You look at me, and at Robin, and at the fruit growing in this garden, and at the chickens fighting in that pen, and you see another chance. And I think you're right. And, this time, I want to be in on the glory."

Jesse dragged his nails along the mossy concrete. "Food isn't growing in the city."

"This food will," Front said. He waved a hand at the garden. "You know it, and I know it. There are no more *desgastas*, no more cityborn, there is only *us*." He spread fingers across his chest. "And what we bring with us."

Jesse scraped his fingernails again along his mossy perch. "I'm too tired to try it again."

"Bullshit," Richard Front said, very gently. "Bull shit." He looked at Jesse and laughed. "I can see the gleam in your eyes, Grange. You can't stop thinking about it, can you? You've probably already figured out a way to get this," and he gestured around the garden again, "and your serum overseas."

"If there is anybody left to save. If not..." Jesse shook his head. "Anderson will bring his *desgastas* back to the shore. We can't rebuild a city on the backs of a few students."

Front shrugged. "There are people alive. I know it. We saw it. And besides, I told you, there is no more distinction between *'desgastas'* and *'cityborn.'* Only us."

"Only you," Jesse whispered. He considered Front's wide, yellow eyes and corpse-like grin.

"We leave tomorrow morning," Front said. "You've kept Isabella waiting past her deadline. She'll be furious."

"And what about Robin?"

"Robin?" Front shook his head, bemused. "Can't you see? That girl is happy here alone, in her Keeper's House."

Richard Front left Jesse alone in the garden. Jesse perched on his piece of concrete in the darkness and listened to the rustle of the vegetation and the scratching of the chickens. When the moon rose, Robin joined him.

"Richard says you're leaving in the morning."

"Our Richard," Jesse murmured, "has big plans."

"What will you do?"

"Go with him," Jesse replied. His ruined throat made the words rough as gravel. "I promised Isabella."

"Will you be able to save them all, do you think?"

"If there are any left to save," Jesse said. "Then, yes."

Robin drifted through the garden. She stroked the sea grass and Jesse could smell the musk of her fruit. "While he was still lucid," Robin said, "he called me *salvedora*."

"Savior," Jesse translated. Like *'desgastas,'* the word had its roots in the old migrant pidgin, and Atlass's choice of endearment almost made Jesse smile.

"Will you go overseas?" the girl asked, after a stretch of moonlit silence.

"It would be interesting," Jesse suddenly found he could smile after all. "They fled our continent so long ago. What will they think, now, if we come to save them?"

"I wonder what it's like."

"Rich." Jesse studied the moon. "They took all the real riches with them when they left us on our own." He glanced at Robin. "If I go, would you like to come?"

"No. I belong here."

"In Harold's House. Front believes there will be no *desgastas* anymore. You don't need to stay."

"I belong here," she repeated.

He sighed and touched her cheek. "I won't be coming back. I can't. I see him in every change of light."

"I know."

Jesse almost laughed at her courage. Or maybe the courage was his own. He reached over his head, drew Harold's medallion from around his neck, and passed it to Robin. Moonlight glittered on the links of the chain.

"Keep it for me."

"Are you sure?"

"I don't want to remember."

"I'll remember for you," she said.

And the self-importance in her tone did make him laugh. He touched her cheek again and ruffled her struggling hair.

"If you need me," he said, "come and find me. Or send someone. I expect most of Anderson's people will want to live here, on the shore."

"Maybe," Robin mused. "But why, if there is no longer a need for such a place?"

"Because it's beautiful, child," Jesse replied. He looked across the garden. He reached out, and pulled the girl close, and leaned back against her strength.

They sat together until the sun rose behind Harold's looming gray House and the warm dawn touched Atlass's garden.

Our titles are available at major book stores
and local independent resellers who support
Science Fiction and Fantasy readers like you.

EDGE Science Fiction
and Fantasy Publishing

Tesseract Books

Dragon Moon Press

www.edgewebsite.com
www.dragonmoonpress.com

Our titles are available at major book stores and local independent resellers who support Science Fiction and Fantasy readers like you.

Alien Deception by Tony Ruggiero -(tp) - ISBN-13: 978-1-896944-34-0
Alien Revelation by Tony Ruggiero (tp) - ISBN-13: 978-1-896944-34-8
Alphanauts by J. Brian Clarke (tp) - ISBN-13: 978-1-894063-14-2
Apparition Trail, The by Lisa Smedman (tp) - ISBN-13: 978-1-894063-22-7
As Fate Decrees by Denysé Bridger (tp) - ISBN-13: 978-1-894063-41-8

Billibub Baddings and The Case of the Singing Sword by Tee Morris (tp)
  - ISBN-13: 978-1-896944-18-0
Black Chalice, The by Marie Jakober (hb) - ISBN-13: 978-1-894063-00-5
Blue Apes by Phyllis Gotlieb (pb) - ISBN-13: 978-1-895836-13-4
Blue Apes by Phyllis Gotlieb (hb) - ISBN-13: 978-1-895836-14-1

Chalice of Life, The by Anne Webb (tp) - ISBN-13: 978-1-896944-33-3
Chasing The Bard by Philippa Ballantine (tp) - ISBN-13: 978-1-896944-08-1
Children of Atwar, The by Heather Spears (pb) - ISBN-13: 978-0-88878-335-6
Claus Effect by David Nickle & Karl Schroeder, The (pb) - ISBN-13: 978-1-895836-34-9
Claus Effect by David Nickle & Karl Schroeder, The (hb) - ISBN-13: 978-1-895836-35-6
Complete Guide to Writing Fantasy, The - Volume 1: Alchemy with Words
  - edited by Darin Park and Tom Dullemond (tp)
  - ISBN-13: 978-1-896944-09-8
Complete Guide to Writing Fantasy, The - Volume 2: Opus Magus
  - edited by Tee Morris and Valerie Griswold-Ford (tp)
  - ISBN-13: 978-1-896944-15-9
Complete Guide to Writing Fantasy, The - Volume 3: The Author's Grimoire
  - edited by Valerie Griswold-Ford & Lai Zhao (tp)
  - ISBN-13: 978-1-896944-38-8
Complete Guide to Writing Science Fiction, The - Volume 1: First Contact
  - edited by Dave A. Law & Darin Park (tp)
  - ISBN-13: 978-1-896944-39-5
Courtesan Prince, The by Lynda Williams (tp) - ISBN-13: 978-1-894063-28-9

Dark Earth Dreams by Candas Dorsey & Roger Deegan (comes with a CD)
  - ISBN-13: 978-1-895836-05-9
Darkling Band, The by Jason Henderson (tp) - ISBN-13: 978-1-896944-36-4
Darkness of the God by Amber Hayward (tp) - ISBN-13: 978-1-894063-44-9
Darwin's Paradox by Nina Munteanu (tp) - ISBN-13: 978-1-896944-68-5
Daughter of Dragons by Kathleen Nelson - (tp) - ISBN-13: 978-1-896944-00-5
Distant Signals by Andrew Weiner (tp) - ISBN-13: 978-0-88878-284-7
Dominion by J. Y. T. Kennedy (tp) - ISBN-13: 978-1-896944-28-9
Dragon Reborn, The by Kathleen H. Nelson - (tp) - ISBN-13: 978-1-896944-05-0
Dragon's Fire, Wizard's Flame by Michael R. Mennenga (tp)
  - ISBN-13: 978-1-896944-13-5
Dreams of an Unseen Planet by Teresa Plowright (tp) - ISBN-13: 978-0-88878-282-3
Dreams of the Sea by Élisabeth Vonarburg (tp) - ISBN-13: 978-1-895836-96-7
Dreams of the Sea by Élisabeth Vonarburg (hb) - ISBN-13: 978-1-895836-98-1

Eclipse by K. A. Bedford (tp) - ISBN-13: 978-1-894063-30-2
Even The Stones by Marie Jakober (tp) - ISBN-13: 978-1-894063-18-0

Fires of the Kindred by Robin Skelton (tp) - ISBN-13: 978-0-88878-271-7
Forbidden Cargo by Rebecca Rowe (tp) - ISBN-13: 978-1-894063-16-6

Game of Perfection, A by Élisabeth Vonarburg (tp)
   - ISBN-13: 978-1-894063-32-6
Green Music by Ursula Pflug (tp) - ISBN-13: 978-1-895836-75-2
Green Music by Ursula Pflug (hb) - ISBN-13: 978-1-895836-77-6
Gryphon Highlord, The by Connie Ward (tp) - ISBN-13: 978-1-896944-38-8

Healer, The by Amber Hayward (tp) - ISBN-13: 978-1-895836-89-9
Healer, The by Amber Hayward (hb) - ISBN-13: 978-1-895836-91-2
Human Thing, The by Kathleen H. Nelson - (hb) - ISBN-13: 978-1-896944-03-6
Hydrogen Steel by K. A. Bedford (tp) - ISBN-13: 978-1-894063-20-3

i-ROBOT Poetry by Jason Christie (tp) - ISBN-13: 978-1-894063-24-1

Jackal Bird by Michael Barley (pb) - ISBN-13: 978-1-895836-07-3
Jackal Bird by Michael Barley (hb) - ISBN-13: 978-1-895836-11-0

Keaen by Till Noever (tp) - ISBN-13: 978-1-894063-08-1
Keeper's Child by Leslie Davis (tp) - ISBN-13: 978-1-894063-01-2

Land/Space edited by Candas Jane Dorsey and Judy McCrosky (tp)
   - ISBN-13: 978-1-895836-90-5
Land/Space edited by Candas Jane Dorsey and Judy McCrosky (hb)
   - ISBN-13: 978-1-895836-92-9
Legacy of Morevi by Tee Morris (tp) - ISBN-13: 978-1-896944-29-6
Legends of the Serai by J.C. Hall - (tp) - ISBN-13: 978-1-896944-04-3
Longevity Thesis by Jennifer Tahn (tp) - ISBN-13: 978-1-896944-37-1
Lyskarion: The Song of the Wind by J.A. Cullum (tp)
   - ISBN-13: 978-1-894063-02-9

Machine Sex and other stories by Candas Jane Dorsey (tp)
   - ISBN-13: 978-0-88878-278-6
Maërlande Chronicles, The by Élisabeth Vonarburg (pb)
   - ISBN-13: 978-0-88878-294-6
Magister's Mask, The by Deby Fredericks (tp) - ISBN-13: 978-1-896944-16-6
Moonfall by Heather Spears (pb) - ISBN-13: 978-0-88878-306-6
Morevi: The Chronicles of Rafe and Askana by Lisa Lee & Tee Morris
   - (tp) - ISBN-13: 978-1-896944-07-4

Not Your Father's Horseman by Valorie Griswold-Ford (tp)
   - ISBN-13: 978-1-896944-27-2

On Spec: The First Five Years edited by On Spec (pb)
   - ISBN-13: 978-1-895836-08-0
On Spec: The First Five Years edited by On Spec (hb)
   - ISBN-13: 978-1-895836-12-7

Operation Immortal Servitude by Tony Ruggerio (tp)
  - ISBN-13: 978-1-896944-56-2
Orbital Burn by K. A. Bedford (tp) - ISBN-13: 978-1-894063-10-4
Orbital Burn by K. A. Bedford (hb) - ISBN-13: 978-1-894063-12-8

Pallahaxi Tide by Michael Coney (pb) - ISBN-13: 978-0-88878-293-9
Passion Play by Sean Stewart (pb) - ISBN-13: 978-0-88878-314-1
Plague Saint by Rita Donovan, The (tp) - ISBN-13: 978-1-895836-28-8
Plague Saint by Rita Donovan, The (hb) - ISBN-13: 978-1-895836-29-5

Reluctant Voyagers by Élisabeth Vonarburg (pb) - ISBN-13: 978-1-895836-09-7
Reluctant Voyagers by Élisabeth Vonarburg (hb) - ISBN-13: 978-1-895836-15-8
Resisting Adonis by Timothy J. Anderson (tp) - ISBN-13: 978-1-895836-84-4
Resisting Adonis by Timothy J. Anderson (hb) - ISBN-13: 978-1-895836-83-7
Righteous Anger by Lynda Williams (tp) - ISBN-13: 897-1-894063-38-8

Shadebinder's Oath by Jeanette Cottrell - (tp) - ISBN-13: 978-1-896944-31-9
Silent City, The by Élisabeth Vonarburg (tp) - ISBN-13: 978-1-894063-07-4
Slow Engines of Time, The by Élisabeth Vonarburg (tp) - ISBN-13: 978-1-895836-30-1
Slow Engines of Time, The by Élisabeth Vonarburg (hb) - ISBN-13: 978-1-895836-31-8
Small Magics by Erik Buchanan (tp) - ISBN-13: 978-1-896944-38-8
Sojourn by Jana Oliver - (pb) - ISBN-13: 978-1-896944-30-2
Stealing Magic by Tanya Huff (tp) - ISBN-13: 978-1-894063-34-0
Strange Attractors by Tom Henighan (pb) - ISBN-13: 978-0-88878-312-7

Taming, The by Heather Spears (pb) - ISBN-13: 978-1-895836-23-3
Taming, The by Heather Spears (hb) - ISBN-13: 978-1-895836-24-0
Teacher's Guide to Dragon's Fire, Wizard's Flame by Unwin & Mennenga - (pb)
  - ISBN-13: 978-1-896944-19-7
Ten Monkeys, Ten Minutes by Peter Watts (tp) - ISBN-13: 978-1-895836-74-5
Ten Monkeys, Ten Minutes by Peter Watts (hb) - ISBN-13: 978-1-895836-76-9
Tesseracts 1 edited by Judith Merril (pb) - ISBN-13: 978-0-88878-279-3
Tesseracts 2 edited by Phyllis Gotlieb & Douglas Barbour (pb)
  - ISBN-13: 978-0-88878-270-0
Tesseracts 3 edited by Candas Jane Dorsey & Gerry Truscott (pb)
  - ISBN-13: 978-0-88878-290-8
Tesseracts 4 edited by Lorna Toolis & Michael Skeet (pb)
  - ISBN-13: 978-0-88878-322-6
Tesseracts 5 edited by Robert Runté & Yves Maynard (pb)
  - ISBN-13: 978-1-895836-25-7
Tesseracts 5 edited by Robert Runté & Yves Maynard (hb)
  - ISBN-13: 978-1-895836-26-4
Tesseracts 6 edited by Robert J. Sawyer & Carolyn Clink (pb)
  - ISBN-13: 978-1-895836-32-5
Tesseracts 6 edited by Robert J. Sawyer & Carolyn Clink (hb)
  - ISBN-13: 978-1-895836-33-2
Tesseracts 7 edited by Paula Johanson & Jean-Louis Trudel (tp)
  - ISBN-13: 978-1-895836-58-5
Tesseracts 7 edited by Paula Johanson & Jean-Louis Trudel (hb)
  - ISBN-13: 978-1-895836-59-2

Tesseracts 8 edited by John Clute & Candas Jane Dorsey (tp)
 - ISBN-13: 978-1-895836-61-5
Tesseracts 8 edited by John Clute & Candas Jane Dorsey (hb)
 - ISBN-13: 978-1-895836-62-2
Tesseracts Nine edited by Nalo Hopkinson and Geoff Ryman (tp)
 - ISBN-13: 978-1-894063-26-5
Tesseracts Ten edited by Robert Charles Wilson and Edo van Belkom (tp)
 - ISBN-13: 978-1-894063-36-4
Tesseracts Eleven edited by Cory Doctorow and Holly Phillips (tp)
 - ISBN-13: 978-1-894063-03-6
Tesseracts Q edited by Élisabeth Vonarburg & Jane Brierley (pb)
 - ISBN-13: 978-1-895836-21-9
Tesseracts Q edited by Élisabeth Vonarburg & Jane Brierley (hb)
 - ISBN-13: 978-1-895836-22-6
Throne Price by Lynda Williams and Alison Sinclair (tp)
 - ISBN-13: 978-1-894063-06-7
Too Many Princes by Deby Fredricks (tp) - ISBN-13: 978-1-896944-36-4
Twilight of the Fifth Sun by David Sakmyster - (tp)
 - ISBN-13: 978-1-896944-01-02

Virtual Evil by Jana Oliver (tp) - ISBN-13: 978-1-896944-76-0

Leslie Davis

Leslie Davis lives in Washington State with three cats, two imps, and a lawyer. When she is not busy remodeling her old home or planting hydrangea, she spends time at the local yoga studio tying herself into knots. Sundays find her at home trolling the internet for the latest news on Battlestar Galactica and Fridays are spent hard at work on her latest novel.

She blogs regularly and will always answer a polite email.